LOVE UNBIDDEN . . . PASSION UNDENIED

Cléo extended the pole to him, and with it helped drag the pirogue to the bank. Together they pulled the heavy canoe out of the water, then collapsed side by side in the grasses under the blazing sun.

Evan turned at last to look at the girl. She might as well have been naked, he thought with a cold rage. The thin fabric of her skimpy garment clung to her body like an extra skin.

Evan rolled toward her. His hand curved around one breast, and as he felt its warmth through the wet cotton, his arousal was instant and unbearable. He kissed her fiercely, while his hand kneaded her soft flesh.

A gull's wild laughter just above them startled him and he raised his head. Cléo lay beneath him on the crushed reeds, looking up at him with wide, startled eyes.

Deliberately he lowered his head and took her ripe, fruity lips.

OTHER NOVELS BY VIRGINIA NIELSEN:

Love's Sorcery
Yankee Lover
The Marriage Contract
A Faraway Love
Traitor for Love

La Sauvage

Virginia Nielsen

A DELL BOOK

Published by
Dell Publishing
a division of
The Bantam Doubleday Dell
Publishing Group, Inc.
666 Fifth Avenue
New York, New York 10103

The Cajuns speak a French derived from that spoken by immigrants of nearly three hundred years ago, and today that patois is not consistent with contemporary French; indeed, the French would have difficulty understanding it. The author has tried to be authentic in her use of Cajun words and spellings.

ISBN: 0-440-20190-X

Printed in the United States of America

Published simultaneously in Canada

November 1988

10 9 8 7 6 5 4 3 2 1

KRI

To J.R.M., always a loving partner

ACKNOWLEDGMENTS

I wish to express appreciation for the gracious help given me by the following people of Houma, Louisiana: Louis Blum, Donna and Thomas Cobb, Pauline Lyons, Margaret Shaffer, James Sothern, and especially Frances St. Martin Dansereau; and to Sherwin Guidry and the Courteaux family of Montegut, Louisiana.

—The Author

Part One

Coco

Chapter One

Terrebonne Parish, Louisiana. 1838.

He wakened to the startled squawking of the mocking-bird in the tree beside the window. His bed was lit by moonlight filtering hazily through the gauze mosquito barre. He listened, but the night outside the shuttered long windows was still.

Then the child screamed again. *"Mama, mama!"*

Beside him in the big poster bed, Evan Crowley's wife moaned, and he laid a hand on her hip to quiet her. "I'll go this time, Lizzie."

Elizabeth pushed his hand away. "She's calling for me." They had had little sleep since it happened, and they were irritable with each other.

Evan lay back and watched her part the gauze curtain and slip through it. Stripes of moonlight stealing through the shutters fell on her pale, flowing hair as she made her way to the door of the nursery.

Then he heard the hoarse bark from the bayou, a hundred yards away from the house but unmistakably the roar of the bull alligator the slaves had named Ol' Debbil. Nanette must have heard him in her sleep.

He tried to go back to sleep, but murmurs reached him from the next room:

"I'se here, ma'am." It was the reproachful voice of Nanette's young nurse.

"Go back to bed, Sula." Lizzie's voice revealed her weary exasperation. "Don't cry, lovey, Mama's here."

"He was coming to get me," Nanette was sobbing. "Mama, he was going to eat me!"

Evan visualized the shudder he could hear in Lizzie's voice. "You were having a bad dream, dear. I'm here and Sula's here, and your papa's in the next room. Nothing can hurt you."

"Will Luke come back?"

"No, sugar, Luke won't come back."

"Ol' Debbil ate him!" Nanette wailed.

"Did you really see that?" Lizzie's carefully controlled voice asked.

"He pulled Luke under the water and ate him. Sula said—"

"Forget what Sula said!" Lizzie was suddenly sharp.

Evan closed his eyes and tried not to listen, remembering the terrifyingly gory stories his own nurse had delighted in telling him. The change in his adored child filled him with a helpless pain.

The unfortunate incident had cast a pall over the plantation on Bayou Black, and transformed his sunny indulged daughter into a trembling ghost of a child. Luke was the son of the cook, a family slave who had come with them from Virginia. He had been a lively, adventurous boy, a favorite of the other children who had run shrieking to the house, throwing the servants into hysterics. Three-year-old Nanette, who had seen everything, had not allowed her parents a full night's sleep since it happened, waking with screaming nightmares even from her naps.

There was silence in the nursery now. Elizabeth crept back to their bed, trembling, and whispered, "Evan, you've got to do something."

Evan Crowley was as upset as his wife was, but he disliked any unpleasantness and there had been quite enough of it already. He would have liked to forget the whole distressing incident and return to his normal routine, riding through his thriving sugarcane fields by day and gambling in the balmy evenings with the Creole brothers Poitevin, who were their only neighbors within twenty-five miles.

"What would you have me do, Lizzie?" he asked, with the impatience born of sleepless nights. "Flog the girl?"

"Flog *Sula*?"

Evan winced at the shrill note in her voice. The slaves had set traps, using a hen, a muskrat, and finally a young goat. His overseer had stalked the bayou with a musket, hoping for a shot at the reptile.

Lizzie knew all that, but she hissed, "Sula's little more than a child herself. Besides, she did drag Nanette away from the spot immediately. I'd flog her myself if she hadn't! No, Evan, you must get rid of the alligators."

"God knows I've tried," he said wearily.

"Yes, and what have you accomplished? A potentially valuable slave was lost—"

She was right. A healthy African boy Luke's age was worth five hundred dollars.

"—and the entire plantation is in mourning. And you

talk about flogging poor Sula for something she couldn't prevent?"

"Lizzie—"

"Oh, I know you didn't mean it, but, darling, you must *do something*!"

One of the things Evan, a quiet young man until his temper was aroused, had found attractive about Elizabeth Race was her vivacious conversation. The English girl with the wild rose complexion who had come visiting her relatives in Virginia was never at a loss for words. After five years of marriage to her he sometimes wondered why he had found that so desirable. He had heard enough talk in the past two days about that terrible scene on the bank of the bayou to last his lifetime. Now he wanted his rest.

"Quite right," he answered her, and turned over and went to sleep.

Two nights later, after he had spoken the simple funeral service for the slaves assembled under the oak tree at the bayou's edge, a ceremony he hoped would lay the incident to rest, they heard the old bull roar again, and Nanette woke screaming and sobbing for the fifth night in a row.

It was more than Evan could bear, and when Elizabeth asked passionately, "Evan, what are you going to *do*?" he told her, "Find a hunter who can kill the brute."

The next morning he ordered a valise packed with a change of clothes and the one-horse carriage hitched up —the one Lizzie used when she called on the neighboring Creole women for a morning *café noir*. With Rafe, the little stable boy, riding the mare, he set off toward Bayou Terrebonne and Montrose, the plantation of an American friend, where he spent the night.

Over a dinner served by white-coated black servants and presided over by his pretty South Carolina–born wife, Bill Hammond advised, "Go to the trader near the end of the bayou road. All manner of trappers and fishermen bring their catch there to be sold."

"I know M'sieu' Weill," Evan said.

"There's a tavern the trappers frequent kept by a Cajun called Jacques-le-grand—Big Jack. He can direct you to one of the swamp hunters who can clear out that nest of gators for you. But it's a rough place. Watch your step."

Leaving his change of clothes and promising to be back before the dinner hour, Evan set off in the morning.

It was early spring and the day was fair when he left Montrose. The mare moved briskly, encouraged by Rafe's light willow switch. The road ran beside the bayou, a stream of still water edged with a tangle of willows and briars and scrub oak overgrown with vines. Farther from the bank an occasional oak tree, festooned with streamers of moss, threw shadows across the road. Evan leaned back against the hard-cushioned seat and let his thoughts wander as he was carried along.

The sun would be hot today and he had the fair, easily burned skin that often goes with pale brown hair, but a finely woven straw hat shaded the eyes that the pretty Creole wife of his neighbor, Gaspard Poitevin, had whispered one evening were "blue like my sapphires."

This morning he had dressed, as he did every morning on his plantation, in a coat tailored of coarse Irish linen over white cottonade breeches, which were laundered for him daily. He had no concern about the success of his errand. His ingratiating manner and air of naturally expecting the best usually brought him what he wanted. In all his thirty-three years he had never known anything but the ease of wealth, but he considered himself a pioneer in the wilderness of this new state of Louisiana.

When he and Elizabeth were married, he had taken his bride and an inheritance from his grandmother to New Orleans. While Elizabeth, who was pregnant, remained in the luxurious home of friends in the city, he traveled with his slaves to deep Lafourche *Intérieur*, where he found rich bayou land on which to cultivate sugarcane. There he pitched a tent to live in while he supervised the cutting of cypress logs from the swamp that bordered his *arpents* and the setting up of a small sawmill. Eventually a suitable house was ready for Elizabeth, and the slaves were put to planting sugarcane and building a mill while he went to fetch her and his enchanting little daughter by steamboat.

Already the three-cornered "sweet grass" was bringing him fabulous wealth, which Evan considered no more than his due. His life was that of a successful planter, pleasant and deeply satisfying—or it had been until the incident on Bayou Black had bloodied its calm waters.

Rafe was taking him along the Terrebonne, one of the bayous his neighbors called "dead water" because it no longer received water from the river except at flood time. Scarlet dragonflies darted above the black water, which seemed to have no current but actually, Evan knew, changed direction with the tides. It meandered southeasterly to the region of lakes and marshes that lay between the farms and plantations and the Gulf. According to his neighbors, the marsh was populated by privateers and smugglers of slaves, as well as by trappers and fishermen.

With his heels Rafe guided the mare around a donkey cart filled with the crisp moss which would no doubt be used to stuff mattresses by the grizzled Cajun who cried cheerfully, *"Bonjour, m'sieu'!"* as they passed. The buggy's wheels grated over the sprinkling of oyster shells that a local farmer had spread to keep the muddy bank passable in the rains.

There were no plantations here, just the weathered houses of the 'Cadians, built high off the ground on the narrow strip of solid land along the bayou. Steep roofs overhung front porches wide enough to live on, and in the rear, one glimpsed kitchen gardens and some pastured stock. Beyond the gardens the land sloped back to the swamp.

The road ended beside a fish market and fur-trader's establishment. There was a dock beside the shed where some small fishing skiffs were tied up. To the right was the tavern Hammond had mentioned, built of unpainted cypress weathered to silvery gray. Behind it stood a cypress grove, knee deep in water. Through the deep shade, shafts of light fell on floating leaves and the reddish "knees" of submerged cypress roots.

"Stop here."

Rafe slid off the mare and held her while Evan stepped down from the buggy. He entered the tavern and found himself in an unpainted room, empty except for a few rough tables on which chairs were overturned. A huge man with his trousers rolled up above enormous bare feet was sluicing the floor with a bucket of water.

"Bonjour," the man said affably, dumping the last of the water from his bucket, and asked in French, "What does *m'sieu'* desire?"

Evan stepped quickly aside to avoid wetting his well-polished boots. *"Bonjour."* His education had included genteel French, which was far removed from the 'Cadian patois spoken in the bayous, but it enabled him to communicate. "I was told you could direct me to an experienced hunter."

"One finds many trappers in the swamps," said the tavern keeper. His flat black eyes were wary. "What kind of game, *m'sieu*?"

"I want the alligators cleared out of the bayou near my house on Bayou Black. There's an old bull there who snatched one of my slave children the other day."

"Ahn!" exclaimed the Cajun feelingly.

"I want him killed, and if possible the whole nest cleaned out."

"But some will always remain, *n'est-ce pas*?" The big Cajun considered him for a silent moment and Evan felt a flash of irritation. He did not expect subservience. The Cajuns were never obsequious, no matter how poor. But what riled Evan was that although he had lived on Bayou Black for almost four years, he still encountered suspicion in these interrelated descendants of the displaced fishermen and farmers from Nova Scotia who had settled here several generations ago.

The big man apparently made up his mind that it would not hurt him to be helpful. "Maybe I know the one you want. The old pirate called Navarre, that one has experience with alligators."

"A pirate?"

"So one hears. One hears that Lafitte chase' him out from his band. He live in the marsh now many years. A dangerous man, that one."

Evan regarded the tavern keeper doubtfully. "How will I find him?"

The Cajun laughed. "You'll never fin' him, *m'sieu*. You'll lose yourself if you try. He's the best, but he drinks much whiskey, and sends his fish and skins to market with his daughter." He studied Evan for another moment. "There are others who come here to sell their catch. I will take you myself to the market and we'll make inquiries."

"Merci," said Evan. "Will you pour a whiskey for me and one for yourself?"

"Merci, m'sieu'." He set down a chair for Evan, went to his counter, and returned with two glasses of whiskey. Putting one before Evan, he stuck out a huge hand. "Me, I'm Jacques Menard. They call me Jacques-le-grand, because there's a Ti-Jacques on the bayou."

"Crowley." Evan threw a gold coin on the table.

Jacques's eyes widened. He lifted his glass to Evan. "How will I know this man's daughter?"

"You'll know her," the tavern keeper said, wiping his sleeve across his mouth. "There's no other like her on the bayou. Men call her *'la sauvage.'* " He tossed off the rest of his drink and said, "Have another whiskey, my frien', then we go see if she is there now."

Outside, Evan indicated his buggy and asked that his young groom be fed. They crossed the road together and walked past several boats unloading fish.

"There's Navarre's daughter, that one! In the pirogue," Jacques said. "Her name is Coco."

Evan looked at the young woman shoveling shrimp from her canoe, a burnt-out cypress log, into a large basket woven of reeds, and sucked in his breath. She was indeed *une sauvage,* he thought, tall for a woman, with a fall of long black hair obscuring her face. The single garment she wore reached only halfway to her ankles, with a long rent exposing one thigh of a pale coppery hue. She was quite young, he judged, but her body blazed with a ripe femininity that brought the blood rushing to his face.

She hoisted her filled basket to her shoulder and walked, barefoot and erect, into the fish market. When she came back, Jacques called to ask her if her father would hire himself as an alligator hunter to M'sieu' Crowley.

She was already back in her pirogue, the long pole in her hands. She glanced at Evan and her almond-shaped eyes appraised him. She shrugged. "I don' speak for *mon père.*"

"Ask him to meet me here tomorrow," Evan called in French.

"He won't come."

Evan's temper began to simmer. He was not going back to Lizzie and Nanette without someone who could restore happiness to the plantation. He held up a gold coin. "Then I will go to him! Will you take me?"

Jacques protested, "It's a long way, *m'sieu',* and the sun, he is hot."

Evan scarcely heard him. He was staring at the girl, who stared back at him out of her strange unreadable eyes. Then Coco raised her long paddle and deliberately scraped aside a scarlet crayfish lying in the bottom of the pirogue in a half inch of water. There was a subtle challenge in the gesture.

Feeling a curious excitement, Evan responded by stepping into the pirogue. To his dismay it began rolling.

"Take care, *m'sieu'*!" Coco cried.

He would have stepped back on the dock, if he could have done so without overturning the pirogue. Instead, he squatted abruptly, grabbing the crossboard that was his seat, and the girl pushed away from the dock. Evan sat still, aware that his impulse had surprised the big Cajun as much as himself, and already regretting it. The girl remained standing, using the long oar now as a pole and now as a paddle, from first one side of the boat then the other, with a superb balance that he was not able to match.

Evan was a proud man, proud of his English colonist heritage, which he considered superior to that of his Creole neighbors, most of whom were descended from transplanted Acadians—although he was amusedly aware that in their pride of race and ancestry, they considered him the outlander. Certainly they would consider themselves superior to this daughter of a lawless swamp-dweller. Yet she had managed to make him feel inept.

They moved silently along a waterway that curved and twisted through the jungle of foliage along its bank, and the landing where Jacques stood staring after them was soon out of sight.

All signs of habitation soon disappeared. Gradually the horizon flattened until it became a world of water and alligator grass and reeds and thick-leaved marsh plants, with no landmarks except a blue line that might mark a distant cypress swamp. Evan was reminded uncomfortably of stories he'd been told about men lost in the crisscrossing bayous and waterways connecting lagoons and immense sea marshes fringing the Gulf coast, stories his Creole neighbors tossed back and forth over their whiskeys. The *prairie tremblante,* they called it. The trembling prairie. It was the place, they agreed, where a man could lose himself, ahn? They talked of pirates and smugglers.

But sometimes it happened to a man who didn't want to lose himself, sometimes to *un homme* who had practically grown up in the swamps. Every now and then one heard of a local fisherman who failed to find his way home, who paddled mile after weary mile through lakes and connecting waterways that looked each exactly like the one before, paddled until exhaustion overtook him and he could paddle no more.

"I hope you won't lose me," Evan said tentatively to the girl.

A little smile curved her lips. "Place yourself in my hands, *m'sieu'.*"

She spoke with superb self-confidence. He realized that he was placing a great deal of trust in the girl standing erect in the pirogue—no mean feat because it required the skill in balance of a tightrope walker.

He recalled the tavern keeper's odd wariness and suddenly a possible reason for it exploded in his mind. *What kind of game?* Had the big Cajun imagined that he was looking for an assassin?

Good God! The thought was a jolt and it made Evan look more closely at this stunning daughter of the "old pirate."

Sitting, his lowered gaze fell naturally on her brown feet. The toes were long and shapely, the instep arched high. The play of tiny muscles as she shifted her balance with the drag of the pole fascinated him. He allowed his gaze to move from her bare feet up her magnificent legs, so indecently exposed by the rent in her short shift. It was a garment that left little to be imagined. The soft mounds of her breasts were not large but exquisitely shaped.

But it was when his gaze reached her face that Evan's breath caught, and he felt an astonishing and unwelcome arousal. Until this moment Lizzie and their daughter, Nanette, with their peaches-and-cream skin and blue-gray eyes and classic short-upper-lip beauty, had represented his ideal of beauty. What he was looking at now was as different from their fresh English charm as night from day.

Examined with newly opened eyes, Coco's face had a languorous, erotic beauty. Her cheekbones were high and strong like an Indian's, her nose was that of a proud princess, her dark eyes had a mysterious Asian slant with surprising intelligence and a hint of mischief, and her lips were as full as ripe fruit. He stared, astonished and profoundly disturbed.

The look she returned, traveling from his black boots up his immaculate clothing to the elegance of his straw hat, made the air seem to vibrate between them. It was a look such as Evan Crowley had never encountered from a woman, a look both bold and innocent, one that combined a frank admiration and naive curiosity with a hint of a smile which he recognized, startled, as patronizing.

Adding to his growing discomfort was the knowledge that he was completely dependent on this girl for his return to civilization. The bayou twisted and turned and he had lost count of the times it split itself to encircle an island or disappeared into a lagoon. It was a spiderweb of waterways, this Louisiana gulf coast, a paradise for the pirates and smugglers who had made it their own territory under three governments. For all he knew the girl could be taking him in circles. And she knew that he was dependent on her. Evan saw the glint of amusement in her strange eyes and began to burn with a slow anger.

The *yanqui* was uncomfortable in her pirogue, Coco thought. His fair face was already flushed with the heat, and he slapped at the mosquitoes and gnats that hovered around his head as they moved through the quiet water. He was also frightened, which amused her.

But *mon dieu,* how blue were his eyes! It gave her pleasure to look at them and at the high gloss of his black boots, as shiny as a wet tern just up from a dive. And the whiteness of his clothing! Like the egrets that descended on the marsh in a white cloud to feed when the sun came up! How long did he think that would last in the swamps?

But, oh, what a beautiful man he was! When she had first seen him, standing beside the saloon keeper on the dock, her swift glance had taken in each detail of his appearance, from his unusually fair coloring and the pleasing arrangement of his features to the elegance of his dress, and she had been blinded by his perfection. Her heart had gone out to him, as it did to all beauty, with a yearning hunger.

He was obviously an important man in his world, Coco thought, observing more closely each detail of his apparel, including the gold ring on his finger. But he was not at home in the swamp, which was her world, a place of endless variety and beauty. She had not missed his spasm of distrust when the landing disappeared behind them.

"You don't like the mosquitoes," she observed in a friendly tone.

"Do you?" he asked irritably.

"They don't bite me."

Gulls had followed them from the landing and a half dozen were still with them, flying above her head with their cries that sounded like human laughter.

"How much farther?" he asked.

She laughed. "We've jus' begun, *m'sieu'.*"

She had not reached seventeen years without knowing that she was attractive to men, and she watched for signs that this very special man also found her attractive. She noticed that he avoided looking directly at her, yet could not keep his gaze from resting on her bare legs, and she was aware of his disapproval. Did he think she could pole her pirogue through the swamps to check her traps in long skirts?

A splash sounded ahead of them. She turned her head quickly. "A terrapin," she told him. "Look! There where the reeds are broken! See him?"

Evan searched the marsh where she pointed and finally saw the ugly reptilian head poking up among the salt grasses with its flat suspicious eyes on them.

"There are many like him in the marsh. He makes fine soup."

A delicacy to the Creoles, Evan knew, but they ate many creatures that he would not put on his table.

A white egret swooped over the pirogue and Coco lifted her head with a grace that matched the bird's flight to watch it glide down to disappear in the grasses. "He can walk there," she said, "but a man will fall through. That looks like oyster grass."

"Is the water deep?" Evan asked.

"No. But a man can drown in shallow water if he cannot find the surface, no? And the mud, it is deep, deep! A man could sink in it."

Evan shuddered, and slapped at a mosquito buzzing around his face. He was overheated and wished for a drink of cool water but guessed that the muddy stream through which she poled was already brackish.

Moments later she lifted her pole and pointed, and he saw a hazy blue above the marsh and blobs that could be distant oaks or even palmetto-thatched shanties on stilts rising above the grasses.

"Isle de Navarre," she said.

"Is that where we're headed?"

"Oui, m'sieu'." She did not try to hide her amusement at his relief.

As they approached it, the land on which the shanties stood seemed to rise above them until it stood some three or four feet higher than the surrounding marsh. Under a rude shelter made of upright poles and roofed with dried palmetto lay a cow and her calf and several pigs. Beyond the shelter some weathered buildings, also on stilts, came into view.

"You live there?" he asked, shocked.

"Oui." Her beautiful eyes, proud and mysterious, mocked him.

"Is there any land there at all?"

"See the trees? They are oaks. Oaks can't grow where there is no soil. It's a *chênière, m'sieu'*— an island where *les chênes* grow."

"Good God!" He had heard his neighbors talk about the *chênières*, those islands in the marsh. But this one looked to be no larger than his smallest canefield. "What do you do there?"

"I sleep there. All day I am in the marsh, setting my traps and my shrimp baskets in season. But it is there that I skin my mink and cure the hides for fur."

He looked at her strong, slender fingers. *"You* skin the animals?"

"Mais oui." She was laughing at him again. "The swamp gives me my living, *m'sieu'.*"

"But your father—"

"He traps some too," she said laconically.

And he smuggles, Evan thought, hearing again, *"A dangerous man, m'sieu'."*

"With my mother's people it was always the woman's work to cure the furs." Coco saw the expression on his face. "The swamp is my home, *m'sieu',"* she said gently, "and I fin' it beautiful. See!" she commanded him, sweeping an arm around her with glowing eyes.

Evan followed her gaze with only a glimmer of understanding. It was a strange and desolate world that he saw, empty of everything but tall grasses and myriads of birds and the secretive, sliding creatures who lived in water and mud.

He looked at the girl, standing with her legs spread for balance, her ripe young body silhouetted against the lonely sky, while the gulls wheeled above her head, uttering their mocking laughter. Behind her was a monotonous wasteland of salt grasses, silvery green and tan, bending flatter in the wind off the Gulf than his rich rippling cane.

Gradually, as he looked, he became aware of patterns of movement and design against a background of waters that ranged in color from pewter to bronze. Solitary white egrets studded the marsh like jewels. Above the lonely shimmering landscape hung the same cerulean sky and the same puffy white clouds that scudded over the plantation at Bayou Black.

"Don't you fin' it beautiful?" she asked.

"Yes," he said, but now his eyes were on her. He was dizzied by her beauty in this, her own setting, a world so alien to him that he resented it.

They had made a turn, and he saw that the *chênière* with its houses on stilts had disappeared, hidden by tall grasses. "Where is the island?" he demanded. "I thought we were almost there."

"As the bird flies, *oui*. Rest yourself, *m'sieu'*. It will return."

He wiped perspiration from his face. He was beginning to have a weird sense of unreality. The surroundings and the situation in which he found himself were totally foreign to him; he was conscious of the heat and the drone of the mosquitoes, of the salt smell of the muggy air he drew into his lungs, and of the heaviness of his unwelcome desire, as if they were elements of a nightmarish dream.

Phrases repeated themselves in his head.

But we were almost there.

As the bird flies, oui.

The girl was observing him with unnerving closeness. "You are hot, *m'sieu'*," she observed, her sidelong glance teasing. "You red as a crayfish."

He wiped his face again, fuming.

She poled the boat close to the grasses and he saw there was an edge of land beneath the reeds. Steadying herself with the oar, Coco bent gracefully over to plunge her hand into the water, and her unconfined breasts fell forward in a fluid movement that was at once an affront and a delight. It angered him that he could not control his response to it. She pulled up a metal trap, freed the dead animal from it, and flipped it into the boat at his feet.

Evan flinched and she cautioned sharply, "You mus' not rock the boat, *m'sieu'*!"

His anger flamed. He felt threatened by her exotic beauty in these unlikely surroundings, and it outraged him further that she was doing a man's bloody work. "I paid you to take me to your father," he said sharply.

"An' I take you, *m'sieu'*." There was mockery in her eyes again, and his uncomfortable suspicion that she was playing with him angered him further. He took off his straw hat and fanned the mosquitoes away while with the other hand he extracted a large handkerchief from his pocket and ran it over his forehead, down his face, and around his perspiring neck.

Coco watched him with an undisguised fascination which seemed directed as much at the pristine white handkerchief as at him. "I jus' check my traps along the way," she explained, with an air of innocence. "If I leave a mink too long, the alligators get him and I lose the fur." She pulled up another trap, but this one was empty. Again he had the impression she was teasing—or testing—him.

He simmered.

In a little while the house on stilts appeared again on the horizon, but this time it was farther away. For a long time it hovered on the horizon, now closer, now receding. Sometimes it was to their left, sometimes to their right. Sometimes it seemed to be behind them. The sun beat down on their heads, and Evan's temper rose with the heat. There was nothing he could do. No way he could return to civilization except in her pirogue. And he didn't know the way. He was a novice in the swamps. He could not tell a *prairie tremblante* from a marsh which would not support a man's weight. This slip of a girl knew, and she was entertaining herself at his expense, boiling him like a crayfish in this heat.

When she stopped again, this time to pull up a shrimp pot, he lost his temper and with it his senses. The pot was half out of the water when he leaned forward in a blind rage, shouting, and grasped her brown ankle.

It was a shout that was drowned in a mouthful of muddy water as the pirogue overturned and dumped them both. The bayou was shallow, but as he had been warned, its bottom was pure silt, washed down by the floods of many springs. Evan thrashed frantically and came up spitting grass and ooze. When he could see again his hat was floating on the water just out of his reach.

Coco was in the water three feet away, her hair streaming, her eyes blazing. "Cabbagehead!" she shrieked. She was still holding the pole, and for a second he thought she might strike him with it. "Grab the pirogue, *m'sieu'*, or we'll both drown!"

The overturned canoe was drifting away from them, one end of it already beginning to sink in the brackish water. Evan splashed toward it and got his hands on it, but found that, without a solid base for his feet, he could not move it. Coco had gained the bank, which seemed to be firm land.

She extended the pole and with it helped him drag the pirogue to the bank. His hat had disappeared. Together they pulled the heavy canoe out of the water, then collapsed side by side in the grasses under the blazing sun.

Evan turned at last to look at the girl. She might as well have been naked, he thought with a cold rage. The thin fabric of her skimpy garment clung to her body like an extra skin.

Evan rolled toward her. Of its own accord his hand curved around one dripping breast, and as he felt its warmth through the wet cotton, his arousal was instant and unbearable. He kissed her fiercely, while his hand caressed her soft flesh.

A gull's wild laughter just above them startled him and he raised his head. Coco lay beneath him on the crushed reeds, looking up at him with wide, startled eyes. For one instant it occurred to him that she was younger than he had guessed. Then he remembered the mockery in those extraordinary eyes, the terrifying suction of the mud on his legs while he thrashed to the surface of the bayou—and his rage returned.

Deliberately he lowered his head and took her ripe, fruity lips.

Chapter Two

He opened his eyes to the glare of an empty blue sky which seemed to press heavily down on them. Her head was on his shoulder and her hair smelled of the marsh. His hand lay on her bared thigh and the feel of her strong young body next to his was still pleasant and slightly erotic.

Gradually he became aware of the discomfort of his wet clothing and the drying mud in his hair. The reality of his situation became mercilessly clear, and it appalled him.

"I can't go to your Isle de Navarre like this," he said finally. "You'll tell your father I need a hunter?"

"He won't come," she murmured. "He don' care for nothing but drink."

He considered that along with the fruitless, interminable time he had spent in her pirogue as she poled it through the marshes. "You were tricking me," he accused her, but all his anger had drained away.

Her eyes slanted up at him, and he realized they were

not black but a deep, warm brown. There was something wild and unsurrendered in their beauty. "I wanted the gold coin," she confessed with a shy smile.

"And now you've lost it, and I have no more. I lost my money too." He had not expected to find her a virgin and he was feeling a remorseful tenderness toward her.

"I still have my knife," she said with quiet satisfaction.

It was her skinning knife, she had told him when she unstrapped it from her thigh. It lay on the bent grass beside them. She sat up and fastened it to her leg again.

Watching her, he asked, "How old are you, Coco?"

"Seventeen."

"If you will take me to the tavern where I left my carriage," Evan said, "I'll return there to pay you."

"*Bon,*" she said simply.

The journey back was short and silent. Coco poled close to the bank three hundred feet short of the fishermen's landing. From there a narrow path ran through the scrub oak and vines toward the clearing where the tavern stood with its back to the swamp. They parted with *au revoir*s.

Evan walked stiffly past a wide-eyed Rafe sitting on the steps at the back entrance and into a spacious kitchen with cypress walls and flooring. From beyond the door to the saloon, he heard voices and the laughter of men sharing a bottle after a day's labor. A short, stout woman stood at the fireplace, stirring something in a large iron pot.

She turned startled dark eyes toward him. "*Mon dieu, m'sieu!* You fell in the bayou?"

"I'm afraid so," Evan said ruefully. "Do you think you could do something about my clothes, *madame*? I can scarcely travel home in this condition."

"*Mais oui!* But your coat will never be the same," she

mourned, "and it was very fine, *non?*" She raised her voice and called, "Jacques!"

The noisy talk in the tavern room ceased for an instant, then began again as the big tavern keeper appeared in the kitchen doorway.

He gave a shout of laughter when he saw Evan. "What happen', *mon ami?* You look like M'sieu' Rat heself! She dunk' you, ahn?"

"I dunked us both. That damned log canoe!"

"That was a pirogue, man! The Cajun's mule. It can take you anywhere if you know how to handle it."

"I don't, as you can see. Bring me a whiskey, Jacques."

"At once, *m'sieu',* at once!"

"Jacques, you will give M'sieu' your clean shirt and trousers, no? Then I wash his suit for him. Such a fine suit, and that marsh mud, it sticks. A pity!"

"My woman," Jacques told Evan. "If anyone can remove the mud for you, it's Madame Jacques-le-grand! Come with me."

He took Evan into an adjoining room that was obviously their private living quarters. It contained a bed and a large armoire as well as table and chairs.

"Did you fin' your alligator hunter?" he asked, while he rummaged for clothing. "*Non?* I'll send someone, yes? You'll find my clothing large," he warned, "but it's all I have."

"I thank you for it," Evan said. "Send my stable boy to help me. It's time he learned to groom more than my horses."

With a tub and a kettle of hot water and Rafe's help, Evan got a bath and washed the mud out of his hair, while in the kitchen his clothing was being laundered. Jacques brought him a bottle of whiskey and a glass to help pass the time it would take Madame to iron dry his suit, and sat with him for a few minutes.

"Has the girl African blood?" Evan asked him.

"Coco? *Non!* Some sabines, *oui,* but not that one."

"What was that you called her?"

The big man hesitated. "Sabine?"

"Yes. What's that?"

Jacques shrugged. "Some swamp peoples."

"What kind of people?" Evan persisted. "Indians?"

"Oui. Coco's mother was the daughter of a Chinese fisherman and an Indian woman. Navarre is Portuguese, I believe."

"Asian!" Evan exclaimed. That explained Coco's unusual skin hue, not red nor white nor yellow but a subtle golden blend.

"It's a stew," Jacques said cheerfully, "but it comes out beautiful, *non?* It's said her mother was descended from an Indian princess. But she had a French name," he added slyly. "Now, M'sieu' Crowley, I must go back to my patrons." He drained his glass and left the room.

Evan, not wanting to join them in Jacques's clothes, drank alone, his thoughts occupied with the strangeness of his encounter with the virgin of the swamps. He was not proud of himself, and did not fully understand why it had happened. He knew some of his acquaintances among the plantation owners maintained dusky-skinned mistresses in New Orleans, but he had been faithful to Elizabeth for five years.

He wondered what their passionate encounter had meant to Coco and found himself remembering the shyness of her smile and the look of wonder in those remarkable eyes. He eased his conscience by telling himself that living as she did, unprotected except by a father who "cared for nothing but drink," she would

have lost her virginity sooner or later in much the same
way with some other man. He found that thought surprisingly unsettling.

At last his laundered clothing was brought to him,
with Madame clucking over the ineradicable stains.
Promising payment for her labor as soon as he could
return, Evan ordered Rafe to hitch up the buggy and
they drove back to Montrose, where he was received
with both teasing and commiseration over his appearance. He damned all pirogues and all alligator hunters
and laughed with them, thankful for the change of
clothing he had brought and hoping the tavern keeper
was as discreet as he was eager to help.

The following day Evan arrived at his own plantation,
which Lizzie had dubbed the Manse. Nanette greeted
him with hysterical joy. He picked her up, struck by
how little she weighed, and by the blue shadows under
her eyes.

Lizzie's look over Nanette's pale gold curls questioned him.

"A hunter will come," he told his daughter, "and he
will kill that Ol' Debbil. You'll never have another bad
dream, sweetheart."

"Were you telling her the truth?" Lizzie asked him,
after Nanette had run away to play with the servants'
children.

"I hope so. I didn't find the man I was looking for," he
admitted, "but the saloon keeper promised to send
someone."

"The saloon keeper?" He hated her raised-eyebrow
tone.

"He's a good fellow. A big Cajun."

There was another difficult moment when his valet

unpacked his valise, and took the ruined suit to Lizzie for her instructions.

"What in the world happened?" she wailed to Evan. "Your suit's not even fit for one of the gardeners!"

"It's obvious, isn't it?" Evan said irritably. "I attempted a ride in one of those Cajun canoes and fell in the swamp."

"For heaven's sake, didn't you oar in college?"

How like Elizabeth to completely miss the question she should have asked, which was what had possessed him to get into the perilously shallow boat in the first place! "A cypress-log pirogue is not one of your English shells," he snapped, "and it's not oared, it's poled!"

"Well, it's a boat, isn't it?" Elizabeth said, with her own logic.

Angrily he thrust aside a vivid memory of what had followed his overturning of the pirogue. *I am a happily married man,* he told himself, *with an adored child.* Therefore that incredible incident in the trampled reeds could not have happened if he had not been affected by the heat. He would simply erase the whole incident from his memory.

But that night when Elizabeth turned expectantly to him in the dusky privacy of the net-draped bed, the moonlight fell on her pale cheek and a strand of yellow hair, and he had a sharp inner vision of a high cheekbone of deep gold framed by black, and a slanting look from Coco's untamed eyes that made it impossible for him to make love to Lizzie. *Not tonight.* He lay very still and pretended to be asleep.

Coco lay on her back in her pirogue with her pole stuck into the bank, holding it at an angle so that the woven palmetto hat hanging jauntily on its upper end shaded her eyes. Anchored by the slight pressure she exerted, the shallow boat lay unmoving on the still, black water. As far as she could see, in any direction she looked, there was only wind-rippled grass. No human habitation was visible, nothing made by human hands except her pirogue, a burned-out cypress log made at the Indian village in the traditional way.

She watched the scarlet dragonflies darting over the surface of the bayou, and daydreamed about M'sieu' Crowley, whose eyes were as blue as the cloudless sky above her, only deeper. She had never seen eyes so blue! She looked at the ruffled grasses and thought of his fair hair, blowing in the wind when he took off his hat to fan his face that she thought so manly.

And his hands—she had never seen hands so white! As white as his coat had been before he tipped them both into the muddy water. She laughed aloud, remembering how angry they both had been.

But those hands had been gentle and sweet when he touched her, despite his anger at her teasing. His breath had been sweet when he kissed her, and his skin had a fragrance of soap and tobacco that had intoxicated her. When she remembered how he had caressed her breast, she touched it and felt again the pleasant drowsiness that had enveloped her then. Her mouth began to tingle, remembering his kiss.

Each time she had taken a catch of shrimp to the market, she had looked for him. He would return, she knew. He had promised to bring her another coin to replace the one she had lost, and he would keep his promise. He was not like her father, who would promise anything when he was drinking and never remember afterward what he had said.

Her expression darkened briefly when she thought

about her father, but he didn't worry her anymore. Not since the night she had wakened on her moss mattress to find him sliding into her bed, drunkenly whispering her mother's name. She had quietly reached for her skinning knife and laid its point against his throat, gently but in such a way that if he moved he would be cut. He had trembled and cried and swore it would never happen again, but since then she slept with her knife strapped to her thigh.

Why she had not pulled her knife on M'sieu' Crowley was a mystery that she studied constantly. Why had his touch been welcome when all other men repelled her? It was one with the intriguing mysteries of the marsh that she pondered daily as she made the rounds of her traps.

Why did that muskrat, who was sitting half hidden in the reeds watching her with beady eyes while he ate, dip his grass in water before nibbling it? Since he lived in a mud house, she didn't think he was washing it! And why did the little fellow build his house aboveground instead of burrowing into the bank among the roots as the alligator did?

Her curiosity was making the muskrat nervous. He dropped his clump of grass and dived into the water with a tiny splash. She saw the reeds around his mud hut quiver, and knew he had entered it from its submerged doorway. Another mystery, but one with an answer that she could guess—M'sieu' Rat thought it was safer not to be seen entering his house.

Very smart of him. But he was not smart enough to keep out of her traps, and he made a fine fur, although M'sieu' Weill, who bought her skins, paid her more for the sleek mink.

Coco wondered what kind of house M'sieu' Crowley

lived in. She had no notion, but she suspected it was grander than the weathered cottages along the bayou because his clothing was different and so much finer than that of the fishermen or Cajun farmers she saw at the market. She wondered if he would be at the dock when she went in again.

Evan had to make a business trip to New Orleans the following week and since Nanette had a stuffy head, Elizabeth decided not to make the two-day journey with him. Many of their friends would be vacating their *pieds-à-terre* in the city for their plantations at this time of the year, anyway.

Rafe took him over to the landing on Bayou Lafourche to catch the steamboat for Donaldsonville. He spent the night at a tavern there and the next morning boarded a more luxurious steamboat for the leisurely trip down the Mississippi River. It was a pleasant journey, with the boat furnishing all the amenities and frequent glimpses of imposing mansions on older well-established plantations along the riverbanks.

As they neared the port, Evan began to sense the excitement of change and progress in the air. He was always exhilarated by the brisk commerce in New Orleans, which seemed surprising in the city's characteristic ambience of languor and self-indulgence. Obviously its importance as a port was increasing. He noted with keen interest that several miles before they reached the landing near the Place d'Armes in the heart of the Vieux Carré, the levee was lined two and three deep with flatboats waiting to be unloaded.

Leaving his servant to bring his luggage, Evan engaged one of the hacks waiting up on the levee to take him to the garden district, a section of the city where many Americans had settled, and to the home of his old school friend from Virginia, Amos Fielding. Amos had been influential in persuading Evan to try his fortunes in Louisiana, and he and his pale, thin wife had kept Elizabeth through her confinement. They greeted him with great pleasure, both eager for news of her and Nanette.

"I'm so disappointed that they didn't come with you," Jane Fielding said. "You're bringing them for the season again in the fall, I hope?" The childless Fieldings had a fine Greek revival house surrounded by a large tropical garden, and were generous hosts.

"Lizzie is counting on it," Evan told her.

"Do you find a change in the city?" Fielding asked him, picking up a decanter.

"It seems very lively, after Bayou Black."

"You should have stayed here, Evan. New Orleans is becoming one of America's most important ports. Besides our cotton and sugar, there's more produce from the interior—hides, furs, tallow, you know the list— being moved down the river in impressive amounts. There's a lot of money to be made here in the export business."

"I'm doing very well growing sugarcane, thank you!" Evan retorted. "I'm adding twenty more *arpents* to help fill the demand for my hogsheads."

Amos laughed, and poured two drinks. "To our affluence!" he toasted. "We made a good move, Evan, when we came to Louisiana."

After a meal served in the dining room from which double doors opened on a terrace overlooking a flower-filled court in which a statue of Eros stood in the cooling spray of a fountain, the two men went for a walk, ending up in the Vieux Carré at their favorite café on Royale Street, where they ordered coffee and Amos exchanged greetings with business acquaintances, some of whom Evan knew.

"I believe there are more Americans here now than the last time I visited," Evan remarked.

"That's true of all the cafés along Royale and Chartres streets. More Americans arrive daily to engage in business. The Creoles don't like it—they claim we Americans are brusque to the point of rudeness, in too much of a hurry to conclude our business. But I notice that their more leisurely ways are affecting those of us who've been here awhile. We're learning to spend our afternoons over coffee in their cafés or over whiskey and cards in their game rooms."

"A very pleasant custom," Evan agreed.

He was surprised when Amos suggested that they walk down the street to the Orléans Ballroom "to look in" at the quadroon ball being given there. But he agreed and they walked the few blocks, mostly silent now.

Evan had attended such affairs before, and was not surprised to find the ball as elegant as any given in the city by the aristocratic Creoles or Americans. The luxurious hall was full of extraordinarily beautiful women, all elegantly turned out. The only difference was that they were all shades of brown, whereas the men were all white except for the fifteen or so musicians in the orchestra playing at one end of the long ballroom. Around the walls sat the mamas, free women of color chaperoning their daughters and shrewdly appraising the white men who asked them to dance.

Amos lost no time in approaching a stunning beauty with a glowing coffee-and-cream skin and lips colored like the blush of a ripe peach. Evan watched while they danced several times. He reflected on the frail, cool look of Jane Fielding, and wondered if his friend was tempted to take a mistress. It was a serious decision. Because their daughters could not marry a white man, those formidable mamas demanded a legal contract ensuring their fair treatment.

Evan did not dance. After a half hour Amos returned and they went out into the languorous night. "What did you think of her?" Amos asked, as they walked slowly toward his house.

"A rare jewel," Evan said lightly.

"She was educated by the nuns. She plays the pianoforte."

"Are you thinking of setting up what the Spaniards call their *casita*?"

"I'm rich enough now," Amos said, with a mixture of pride and embarrassment.

Their conversation brought to Evan's mind a vision of Coco attired as elegantly as a young quadroon, and he thought that no one in that ballroom could hold a candle to his swamp girl for sheer feminine beauty. He put the image that immediately followed, of Coco in a small elegant *casita*, out of his mind, and quickly turned the conversation back to business affairs.

In the press of his calls on the sugar and molasses buyers in the next few days, the incident in the swamp receded in Evan's mind until, passing the shop of a merchant on Rue Royale who imported objects of art from Paris, a display of jewelry on a Louis Quinze table and the glitter of a gold bracelet caught his eye.

He saw the strong, slender arms of Coco wielding the pole to move her pirogue down the bayou and knew instantly that gold had been created in order to enhance that pale copper skin. His vision was so vivid that he turned abruptly into the shop and purchased the bracelet. Then, to assuage his guilt, he bought a music box which he knew would delight Lizzie and Nanette with its tinkly minuet.

The following week when Coco took a boatload of shrimp to the market, he was there, looking more wonderful than she had imagined him, in a beautiful tawny coat over white cotton trousers. He was talking to the fur-and-shrimp trader but she knew that he was keenly aware of her as she poled up to the dock and threw her rope around a post. Yet he did not interrupt his conversation with M'sieu' Weill or acknowledge her presence in any way while she shoveled her shrimp into a basket.

Hurt, she tossed her basket on her shoulder and strode into the merchant's shed.

Evan was hoping to see Coco alone, without Weill observing their meeting, but he had asked a casual question and was interested in the information it had triggered Weill to divulge.

"It's something I would like to experiment with, if I had the capital," he was saying. "I've long been acquainted with the Houmas Indians' custom of drying seafood as well as other meats. Recently a Chinese merchant I sometimes deal with in New Orleans was here buying shrimp. He told me that his family dries shrimp for their own use. He said that the Chinese have been doing it for generations. It's the natural way to preserve food."

A sizable shrimp boat was moving silently up to the dock, and Weill raised his hand in greeting to the men reefing in its sails. Evan asked, "How much capital would you need?"

"I haven't estimated it closely," Weill replied with

surprise. "I'd have to explore the market possibilities first."

"I'm looking for an investment for a modest inheritance," Evan said. "Perhaps we can talk about it when I come down the bayou again."

"Bon!" Weill said.

In the warehouse Coco waited for the trader, her heart beating faster than usual. She burned with Evan's rejection. It was unexpected but nothing new. She was familiar with the hated appellation "sabine." She had heard the story from her mother: how her people, a gentle race, had welcomed some of the first displaced Acadians when they came to the swamps, hungry and homeless, how they had taken them into the tribe and eventually intermarried, only to have their descendants cast out of the dominant white society as illegitimate half-breeds. The new white chiefs had made mixed marriages illegal.

Her mother and father had exchanged promises in the Indian fashion, just as the Cajuns, when no priest was available, "jumped over the broomstick." But the Cajuns were allowed to make their marriages legal when the priest finally came. No priest would legalize her mother's marriage. That made her, like all mixed breeds, illegitimate. It did not make her feel inferior. Quite the contrary. She thought of most white men as *"les imbéciles."*

At last M'sieu' Weill came in to examine her shrimp and pay her for them. It was a very small amount, but Weill knew it provided her—and probably her worthless father—with a living. The merchant's calm, philosophical nature gave him a perspective on the various inhabitants of this isolated section of the new state. One of the few men who saw beneath Coco's exotic looks and respected her for her skill and spirit, he praised her catch and paid her full price.

Out on the dock Evan waited with the gold bracelet heavy in his pocket. Seeing Coco again, in the same torn dress, had made him realize the utter incongruity of his gift. In that dress she could neither wear it nor hide it. Yet how marvelously right it would look on her golden-hued skin. He must be mad. If he had any sense he would leave the coins he owed her with Jacques-le-grand and go home.

She came out of the warehouse, and he smiled at her. She was headed for her boat, but her step slowed.

"I have come to pay my bills, Coco."

He looked handsome and fit and his smile revealed his genuine pleasure in seeing her. Her heart turned over in her breast.

"I owe Madame at the tavern too," he said, still smiling, "for laundering my clothes. Will you walk over there with me?"

Coco nodded and fell into step beside him. They crossed the road and walked under the trees that shaded the tavern. Evan was leading her around the building toward the kitchen entrance.

"I believe I owe you two coins, this for the one you lost, and this for bringing me back." He gave them to her, and she lifted her skirt slightly to slip them under the binding that held her knife in place. They were hidden from the dock by the corner of the building now, and Evan pulled the gold bracelet from his pocket.

She had never seen anything so beautiful. It caught the light coming through the trees and sparkled like the sun on a leaf when the dew was on it. She could not take her eyes from it.

"I saw this in *Nouvelle Orléans* and it reminded me of

you," he said, in his strange but beautiful French. His hand was warm but it sent a chill traveling up her arm as he slipped the circlet of gold over her fingers and held them while he stood, admiring.

Her strange eyes glowed with a fire not unlike that of the bracelet. "It's beautiful, *m'sieu'*," she whispered, "but why do you give it to me?"

"You said you liked gold."

"I earned the coins. Why this?"

"Because I overturned your boat," Evan said. "Because I'm sorry for my anger and—and for what I did to you in anger."

Her eyes, gazing up at him, slowly filled with warmth.

"And if that isn't reason enough, because I knew how beautiful it would look on your arm."

She looked down at the slim gold circlet again and whispered, *"Merci—merci, mo' cher!"*

He had not intended to touch her in that way again, but when he heard the endearment his arms went around her slender body and he felt her exciting strength as she returned his embrace with passion. Their lips had barely touched when a sound warned Evan and he stepped away from her just as the kitchen door opened and Rafe came out carrying a plate of food. Madame was just behind him.

"Sit here on the steps and eat, and watch you don't break my plate," she was saying when she saw Evan. *"Bonjour, m'sieu'!"* she cried.

"Bonjour, madame, I've come to pay my debts, both to you and to Coco, whose coins I dumped into the bayou."

He walked toward Madame but Coco hesitated. The tavern keeper's wife took the coins he offered and thanked him, but he saw that her suspicious gaze was caught and held by the blaze of new gold on the girl's arm.

"You're wearing jewelry now, Coco?" she asked pointedly.

The full enormity of his indiscretion hit Evan. "It's nothing, *madame*," he said, in a friendly tone, "only a trinket I picked up in *Nouvelle Orléans* to console Coco for the dunking I gave her and"—he improvised—"the traps she lost."

"M'sieu' Crowley, there are many who would let you spill them and all their traps in the bayou for a bauble like that," Madame said severely, her shrewd eyes speculating on Coco's enrapt expression.

Evan gave her an extra coin, "for your good nature when I asked your help."

She took it but the knowing look in her eyes told him she suspected it was a bribe. He felt reluctant to leave, but there was nothing to do but order Rafe, who had swiftly cleaned his plate, to hitch up the buggy.

Walking back across the road, Coco watched the sun sparkle on the gold bracelet on her arm and recalled over and over the brief touch and taste of Evan's lips. She went into the trader's office and found him alone.

"*M'sieu'*, can I ask you to keep my money in your iron safe?"

M. Weill looked at her, his eyes seeing her ripe young beauty and understanding what she was not saying. He knew her father, and he had known her mother. If he could help her find a way out of the circumstances that bound her, he would. "But of course. I'll give you a receipt."

"No," she said. "No paper. My father must not know." She slipped the bracelet off her wrist. "Take this, too, *m'sieu'*."

"You trust me?" he asked her.

"Oui, m'sieu', because I must." Her slanted eyes were candid and amused.

Aaron Weill laughed softly and nodded. *"Bon."*

She watched him wrap her treasures in a piece of paper, which he sealed with wax, write her name on it, and place it in his safe. Then she walked out into the sunshine and stepped into her pirogue to return to Isle de Navarre with her head full of dreams.

Evan could not stop thinking of the girl. When he left the big house in the mornings to mount his chestnut bay and ride out to check on the work going on in his fields, he welcomed the opportunity to be alone and let his thoughts dwell on her. When he pictured her, it was as she stood in her pirogue, silhouetted against the sky, bare feet braced as she held her pole, with her dark hair falling down across her breasts. But that vision would soon change to the image of her beautiful face and the startled wonder in her strange, foreign eyes as she stared up at him, and he would experience again the sharp desire tinged with guilt.

He had not heard from Jacques, and Lizzie was still worrying him about the alligator who roared in the night and disturbed their daughter's sleep. He told her he must go down Bayou Terrebonne again.

"Can't you send someone?" she asked.

"Besides the matter of engaging a hunter," he told her, "I have business to discuss with Weill. I've suggested a limited partnership."

"With Mr. Weill?" Lizzie exclaimed. "Why would you do that?"

"He has an idea about preserving seafood by drying it

in the sun as the Indians do. I might invest some capital with him."

"I have never heard of anything so foolhardy!" Elizabeth declared, with color rising in her cheeks. "You must have been drinking whiskey with the man."

"Not a drop," he was able to say truthfully, for Weill was a temperate man. "He says the Chinese have been preserving food that way for generations."

"Oh, the Chinese!" Lizzie said, tossing her head.

Secretly he agreed with her conviction that nothing would come of Weill's fantastic notion. Nevertheless in a few days he was on his way down the bayou again, and again took advantage of the hospitality offered at Montrose.

He spent the next afternoon with Weill, pretending a lively interest in the shrimp boats that arrived, while looking eagerly for Coco. Near evening he started for the tavern across the way. Wagons, carts, and buggies were gathered in the vicinity and he heard a curious roar, a shuffling sound overlaid with loud voices and laughter, punctuated by an occasional shrill scream, and a burst of music.

He recognized at last the sounds of the movement of many feet over the cypress floor. A public ball! A *fais-do-do,* by God!

He'd heard about them. The 'Cadians loved to dance, and they brought the whole family, putting the babies to sleep on two chairs or on benches along the wall, which was how the affairs had acquired their name. It meant "go-to-sleep."

He felt the heat of excitement as he tried to imagine Coco in such a setting. Would she be dancing with some local fisherman or trapper? What would he do? Would he stand and watch or ask her to dance? Sensing an element of danger, he felt his excitement increase.

He opened the door. The bar was almost hidden by men jostling each other, shouting above the noise and drinking whiskey. Others sat crowded together at tables sharing a bottle. In the center of the room were the dancers, and along the far wall sat the women, one of them with a baby at her breast.

Heads turned toward the door. The laughter and rough talk ceased as Evan felt himself appraised by unfriendly eyes. A silence fell along the bar. In it Evan clearly heard the sound of an accordion and a fiddle above the shuffling feet and the whine of a crying child.

"Bonjour, M'sieu' Crowley," Jacques called in a loud, nervous voice. "A brandy, ahn?"

Silently a place was made for him at the near end of the bar. When Evan answered, "If you please, Jacques," in French, there was a noticeable thaw in the room, and conversations began again.

Jacques brought a bottle and a glass and leaned across the counter to murmur, "The girl doesn't come here."

Evan gave him a cool stare, dismayed by the Cajun's perception.

Jacques persisted, his eyes reproachful. "But the papa, he is here. See that curly head at the end? He's a bad one, that one. Gets crazy with whiskey."

Evan looked down the length of the bar at the man facing him. He was small and wiry with a badly broken nose that gave a sinister twist to his pinched features, especially when he laughed.

Coco's father? He tried to imagine the swamp virgin of his fantasies living in that house-on-stilts on the remote *chênière* with this blackguard for a father. It was incredible. Evan picked up his drink and moved along the bar for a closer look.

He stopped behind Navarre's companion. He was close enough to hear their rapid patois but understood only enough to realize that they were using words that even here would not be spoken in mixed company. Suddenly the man talking to Navarre turned to confront him. "For w'at you hang aroun', man? W'at you want?"

"Nothing," Evan said hastily. "Nothing but another drink."

Jacques moved quickly down the bar. "This is my good frien', M'sieu' Crowley," he said. "He want to buy you a drink, Navarre."

"For w'at?" Navarre said, with a scowl.

"Because your Coco give him a lift in her pirogue when he los' himself," Jacques explained glibly, filling all the glasses. "He want to give you *bien merci.*"

Navarre raised his glass and said, shortly, *"Merci."* His eyes raked Evan. "An' how you like your ride, *m'sieu'*?"

Evan forced a laugh, silently cursing Jacques for his needless revelation. "As a matter of fact, I got a good wetting."

Jacques's loud laugh drowned his. "He drip all over my floor, he so wet!"

Navarre did not smile. "So she upset you, ahn?" He turned back to the bar and said casually, "When I go *chez moi* I beat her."

"You'll what?" Evan said, jarred. "My God, no! It was my fault. I tipped the boat."

Coco's father turned back and gave Evan a long, level stare. "W'at the hell? She need a beating, that one."

"No, I said!" Furious, Evan ignored Jacques's frantic signals. "Look here, you bastard—"

Navarre said, in drunken irritation, "W'at you want I do to her, ahn?" He studied Evan for a moment, then spat in his face and burst into loud laughter.

Evan's head jerked back in shock, then he started for the pirate in a red rage. A woman in the room behind them screamed, "He's got a knife!" and came running to put her arms around Navarre's neck from behind. Someone grabbed Evan, pulling him back. The man beside Navarre grasped Navarre's wrist. Dazed, Evan saw the candlelight glitter on the steel blade that fell from the pirate's hand.

There was a swirl of movement and Navarre's ugly face was hidden from him as others pushed between them. Evan was being dragged backward, helpless against the superior strength of the three men holding him. "Steady, man," one was drawling in his ear. "You didn't have a chance against that bastard's knife."

Swearing in English, Evan was taken outside. Gradually his rage subsided, but it had been like a flame, sweeping everything before it, and it left him trembling.

He was alone in the dark with Jacques under the oak tree, breathing hard, the air filling his nostrils with the swamp smell of decaying leaves and algae.

"M'sieu' Crowley, those men save your life, maybe," Jacques was saying earnestly. "Navarre has knifed a man before in my café. Don' come back here, ahn?"

"Does he beat her?" Evan asked hoarsely.

"Non! Not Coco. She's quicker than he is, an' stronger too. He's a drunkard, that one. But if he fin' you alone—" He made a gesture and a suggestive sound. "Nobody ever know w'at happen, ahn? It's easy to hide a body in the marshes." He added, "Navarre's ugly to-

night. I better go back before somebody else make him mad."

"Coco . . . with a father like that. . . ." Evan muttered.

"Coco takes care of herself," Jacques said. "You go home, M'sieu' Crowley."

Chapter Three

Jacques-le-grand sent his friend and neighbor, Ti-Jacques—short for Petit Jacques—to kill the alligator. Ti-Jacques was a small man with a curved back and a face that laughter had visited often, leaving its footprints. Nanette adored him, even before he succeeded in eliminating the monster of her dreams.

He stalked the beast with patience and skill and for his effort Evan gave him Ol' Debbil's skin. That night the slaves made a feast with the meat, singing and dancing and rattling their bones and gourds around a bonfire far into the night.

For weeks Nanette made up little songs about Ti-Jacques and Ol' Debbil, and gradually her nightmares ceased.

Evan was playing whist at the plantation house of his nearest neighbor, Gaspard Poitevin, when he heard of the pirate Navarre's untimely end.

"Murdered," said Poitevin around his cigar. "Dis-

patched by a knife the way he sent more than one poor
soul to meet his Maker."

A cold wind passed over Evan's heart. "Who knifed
him?" he asked sharply.

Gaspard shrugged. "Who knows?"

"I don't think the law will inquire too deeply into the
matter," his brother Pierre said. "The world's a better
place without Navarre's kind."

"If he was too ugly for Lafitte's band of cutthroats,
he's certainly no loss to anyone else," Gaspard agreed,
throwing down a card.

Evan, who knew that both brothers had dealt with
the Baratarian smugglers for some of their slaves, found
an irony in that. But he did not mention it. He was
wondering what Navarre's murder would mean to his
lovely wild daughter. Was the old pirate's death a loss to
her? He remembered Jacques saying she made the living for the family, such as it was. But did Coco have
anyone else at all? He wondered if she were wearing
the gold bracelet he had given her.

It occurred to him now that the bauble could have
been a danger to her. He reproached himself for not
foreseeing that someone—including her ruffian of a father—might covet it. Or that Navarre could have
beaten her for accepting it.

Evan had not been wholly convinced by Jacques's
glib claim that she could protect herself. Navarre's reputation had probably kept other men away from her,
but now that she was alone, what would happen to her?

He was so inattentive to the game that he lost heavily
the rest of the evening.

That night he tossed and turned on the big bed he
shared with Elizabeth, unable to sleep. The next morn-

ing he told her that he must talk again with the merchant, Weill, and set off for Bayou Terrebonne.

But it was to Jacques-le-grand's tavern that he made his way when he left his guest room after a night spent with his hosts at Montrose. It was early in the day, and the saloon was almost deserted when he entered. He stepped up to the bar and Jacques left his two customers to come to where Evan stood.

"Bonjour!" He lowered his voice. "You heard, ahn?"

Evan nodded. "How did it happen, Jacques?"

"Everybody ask me how it happen," Jacques protested, with less than his usual affability. "Why should I know, ahn? I told the police from Donaldsonville w'at I know already."

"This isn't official, Jacques," Evan said.

"Navarre get in a fight here, but he lef' alone. Next day they fin' him floating in the bayou. Many times Navarre come here, he make a fight and pull his knife. One makes enemies that way, *non?* On that night one was waiting for him. He fin' out he not the only man on the bayou with a knife, ahn?"

"Coco isn't mixed up in this?"

"Coco?" Jacques's surprise was genuine. "No, I tell you for true, that one wasn't here."

"What's going to become of her now, Jacques?"

The saloon keeper shrugged, but a sharp expression in his eyes made Evan suspect the casual gesture.

"Coco can trap and cure her furs as good as any man. Navarre don't do much but fin' trouble for a long time now . . . but it's no good for a *jeune fille* to live alone in the swamp, ahn?"

"Has she relatives to go to?"

Jacques made an enigmatic noise. "A man like Navarre, he don't make friends, even wit' his own people."

He moved down the bar to refill the glasses of the two men drinking there. When he came back, he asked, "Your suit, *m'sieu'*, it was ruined?"

"Completely. I gave it to one of the field hands."

"Madame has been wondering. Come pay your respects to her, *m'sieu'*. Bring your whiskey."

Somewhat surprised, Evan picked up his glass and followed Jacques across the empty dance floor to the kitchen door. Madame was slicing vegetables at the big cypress worktable.

"M'sieu' Crowley has come asking about Coco," Jacques said significantly.

"Ah, the poor girl," Madame said, giving Evan a severe look.

"Perhaps you would like to speak to her?" Jacques asked.

At Evan's questioning glance he nodded toward the door of their private living quarters.

She was here? Evan's heart gave a startled leap of anticipation. He crossed the kitchen. Just as he reached for the doorknob, Madame murmured behind him, "She's *enceinte, m'sieu'.*"

Evan, already opening the door, felt the jar of shock. *Enceinte!*

Coco was sitting at the small table in the bed-sitting room, wearing a dress obviously not her own. It was once white, now yellowed with age, and almost demure in style, but it did not diminish her at all. Rather, the color emphasized the gleaming gold of her skin, and the incongruity of its fragile femininity called attention to her strength and the vitality of spirit that made her beauty so challenging.

She rose to her feet, exclaiming softly, *"M'sieu'!"*

God, how lovely she was! The hand-me-down dress

stirred him to imagining her in proper lady's attire. There wasn't a woman he knew who would not be eclipsed by her!

Evan closed the door, and she ran to him.

He marveled at the feel of her in his arms, not soft and yielding but alive and quick with an energy that was the most exciting thing about her. Her breath fanned his neck as she murmured, "I knew you would come."

The fragrance of her skin, earthy and clean, filled his senses and he could feel the throb of her strong life force in the beating of her heart, so near his own. And she was pregnant? With his child?

His mix of emotions was almost insupportable—a rush of primitive triumph and a surge of tenderness, coupled with sheer terror of the fate his future held. It was his daughter who leapt first to his mind, with the strange sensation that she was threatened. *My sweet Nanette, what have I done to you?*

He smoothed the heavy black hair from Coco's brow and said, "Is it true, what Madame said?"

There was a shy wonder in her expression. "Madame believes so. But I don't think she is sure."

Her innocence gave him a sharp pang of guilt. "You're carrying my child?

She drew back, reproaching him with her strange eyes. "It could be no one else's, *m'sieu'.*"

"Did you tell Madame that?"

Unexpectedly she flared, "I tell her nothing! But there has been no one else!"

"I don't question it, Coco," he said, and he didn't. "But I must think what to do. I want to take care of you," he told her tenderly. "You will not fish and trap for your living now."

"But I like what I do," she began.

"You must not go back to Isle de Navarre," he said firmly. "You are not going to live alone."

Her gaze softened; the trust he saw dawning in it was intoxicating.

"For a little while you must stay here," he said, thinking aloud. "I'll speak to Jacques and ask him to keep you while I prepare a place for you. Will you stay?"

"Oui, mo' cher." She sighed and laid her hand softly against his cheek. He could have held her forever, but he did not dare kiss her. Her allure was too potent. He forced himself to loosen his embrace and step away from her. Jacques and his good wife probably suspected the truth, and he did not know how far he could trust them. He assumed a cool demeanor.

"I'll come again soon," he promised, and paused to compose himself further before reentering the kitchen.

Closing the door behind him, he asked sternly, *"Madame,* has the girl told you that she is *enceinte*?"

"I have eyes," Madame said.

"Perhaps you suggested it to her?" Evan persisted. "Because she says she does not know it, if she is. She seems fairly innocent to me."

Madame rolled her eyes and spread her hands in an expressive gesture.

Evan turned to her husband. "That is why I think you are right, Jacques, about the folly of her remaining alone on Isle de Navarre."

"I tell you true."

Boldly Evan said, "I am disposed to interest myself in her plight. If you can keep her here for a week or so, Jacques, I'll try to find a good family who will give her a home. I'll pay you for her keep. *Madame*?" He turned back to the silent woman. "She is in need of the guidance of a woman like yourself. It is good to see her more suitably dressed."

Madame regarded him with pursed lips. "I will fix a pallet for her here in the kitchen," she said, and glanced at her husband for his approval. "For ten days. As you see, *m'sieu'*, we have little room."

"You are a compassionate woman, *madame*," Evan said, and offered Jacques some coins, which the saloon keeper took with alacrity.

Leaving the tavern, Evan walked over to Weill's office, where he sat and talked for an hour, scarcely knowing what he was hearing or what he might have promised the merchant, before he felt sufficiently calm to return to his friends at Montrose plantation.

The knowledge that he had impregnated Coco in that one violent encounter had wildly excited him. He had known it was true as soon as he saw her. He had recognized that intangible glow that pregnancy had given Elizabeth when she was carrying Nanette. It had softened Coco, adding an aura to her exotic beauty that called to a man's deepest feelings.

Lying awake in his friends' guest room, he wondered what kind of child Coco would bear him. What if she should give him a son? A big strapping son with her own strength and vitality?

A son who could never carry his name, he reminded himself; a mixed-breed son whose grandfather was a proper ruffian who had sailed with Jean Lafitte! But the reminder failed to dim his foolish excitement.

What repercussions would there likely be?

None, probably, except to his marriage if Lizzie should find out about it. Somehow the prospect of a son made Lizzie's reaction to his infidelity less threatening.

He must put his mind to the problem of how he was going to take care of Coco during her confinement. Perhaps he could find some good but poor family . . . no, he would look for a good woman—a widow, perhaps, whom he could hire to care for her. Because he must be able to see her. Already he was looking forward to their next meeting. . . . He turned restlessly under the mosquito netting.

When he recognized the desire in his joyous anticipation of caring for her, he knew it was making him take leave of his senses. What was he thinking of? If Lizzie ever found out, she would likely find a way to flee to England, taking Nanette with her. His darling Nanette!

There was no possibility of keeping Coco in the parish where they were both known, at least by reputation, he acknowledged reluctantly. Although the region was sparsely settled, the bulk of the settlers were 'Cadians, and most of them lived on the narrow strips of fertile land along the bayous, and their landholdings had been divided among their descendants for several generations. It was said that news traveled along Bayou Lafourche from the river to where the marsh began faster than a steamboat could carry it.

Gossip would travel easily as fast on Bayou Terrebonne. He would have to take Coco to New Orleans to bear his child. And that would take her out of his reach, except for those winter weeks that he and Elizabeth spent in the city.

Evan turned and tossed on his moss mattress. His life was becoming complicated, but the uncertain future promised an excitement that he realized he had not known since his courtship of Elizabeth, newly arrived in Virginia from England nearly seven years ago.

* * *

After Evan left her, Coco sat dreaming in the privacy of the tavern keeper's bedroom, reliving her shock of joy at seeing him suddenly appear in the open doorway, basking again in the glow of pleasure in his eyes as his gaze swept over her in Madame's dress with her hair pinned up.

How wonderful he had looked! Her thoughts danced over his appearance: his hair like corn silk; his eyes, so dark a blue; the gleam of white teeth when he smiled at her. How she loved his smile! It was like a torch to light up her heart.

It did not surprise her that she was going to have his child. She had divined the mystery of their mating that had come so unexpectedly, catching her unaware. It was a natural occurrence, after all, and one she had often witnessed in the swamp. She had recognized him as her mate, and accepted him. Otherwise she would have killed him. They had mated as inevitably as the animals who lived in the marsh did—and what followed naturally was the birth of the young.

And he wanted to take care of her. Love swelled her heart.

Madame knocked on the door. "Coco," she said sharply, "I could use your help in preparing vegetables for today's stew."

"Bon, *madame*," she said, and stood up and walked into the kitchen.

Madame gave her a large apron to tie about her waist. "That's my wedding dress you're wearing," she said, eyeing Coco's slender figure. "I haven't been able to get into it since my wedding *fais-do-do*. It's snug enough on you that you'll not be able to wear it long. Who's the *bébé*'s papa, ahn?"

Coco looked at her and asked, "What *bébé*?"

Madame shot her a suspicious glance. "Could be you don't know," she muttered. "Wearing jewelry, and all. Where is that circlet of gold I saw on your wrist? Did your papa take it away from you?"

Coco pressed her lips tightly together. She had told M'sieu' Crowley that she would stay, she reminded herself. She took the knife Madame gave her and tested its edge. It was not as sharp as the one she still wore strapped to her thigh.

Madame dumped a bucket of boiled shrimp in front of her. "I'll finish the vegetables," she said. "You peel these."

As Coco worked, she was remembering *"la shrimp danse"* her mother had taken her to see when she was a small child, and the strange homemade shoes her mother's people had worn to protect their feet when they spread the boiled shrimp out on a wooden platform and "danced" on them to break open the shells. Afterward they removed the meat from them and dried it in the sun. What would Madame say if Coco suggested that she dance on the shrimp? She laughed at the thought.

She would be leaving her mother's world for M'sieu's, and she had no idea what kind of world he lived in. All she knew besides the marsh and Isle de Navarre was what she had seen along the bayou and at the dock across the way—the shrimp boats and their fishermen, the trappers, and the people, mostly men, some of them slaves, who came to buy the fish and the skins.

Madame's roomy kitchen with its large fireplace, in which she prepared food for the fishermen and trappers who came to the tavern, was the largest that Coco had ever seen. She studied its array of cooking pots and tools and its shelves of dishes as she worked.

"You're a quiet one," Madame observed. "I s'pose you've had nobody to talk to. It must have been lonely for you, yes?"

"Ah, *non, madame,* not lonely. I was too busy. And there's so much to see in the marsh. Already I miss it."

"Ahn!" Madame said, disbelieving.

An African man came in to serve Madame's meal when it was ready, and a neighbor woman came to wash the dishes when it was over. Madame took Coco into her bed-sitting room and brought out a length of blue homespun cottonade. "We must make you a dress. Can you handle a needle?"

Coco nodded. "I have made all our clothes since my mother died—there was no one else to do it."

Madame looked doubtful, no doubt remembering the tattered dress Coco had worn when the two police officers who took the news of her father's death to Coco had brought her here.

"It's best if you stay in here evenings and work at sewing something for yourself. The men who come to the saloon are a rough lot. Be sure to lock the kitchen door before you climb in bed. Jacques can come through with his key when he closes the saloon."

"I'm not afraid," Coco said, smiling.

"You should be," Madame said severely.

Only once did Coco reach down under the quilt that covered her and finger her knife. That was one night when Jacques wakened her with his clumsy turning of the key, and stumbled unsteadily across the kitchen floor, sounding as her father had when he'd drunk too much whiskey. Coco lay very still, waiting to hear the saloon keeper close his bedroom door.

But he had paused beside her pallet. She could hear him breathing while he stood staring down at her.

That's when she inched her hand down toward her knife and grasped its handle.

A long moment passed, then Jacques let out a loud belch and stumbled on to the door into the room he shared with Madame. Coco sighed and relaxed.

At last the day she had been anxiously awaiting came. M'sieu' arrived with a closed carriage, in a great hurry to take her away. "I've found a good Catholic family in Thibodaux who will give her a home," he told Madame.

Madame took Coco's apron and sent her to get the small box she had packed with the extra petticoat and dress they had made her. When Coco returned, Madame wiped a tear from her eye with the apron and kissed her.

"I'll miss you, Coco."

Jacques took her hand in his big one and told her to be good.

Coco thanked them, but she was too excited to pretend she was not overjoyed to be leaving. At last she was going into M'sieu's world!

"I must go across to say good-bye to M'sieu' Weill," she told Evan, when he would help her into the carriage.

"There isn't time."

"But he is keeping my bracelet!"

"I'll buy you another. We have a steamboat to make."

"A steamboat!" she gasped.

"I'm taking you to New Orleans."

"New Orleans!" Panic almost choked her. So far? To a place so completely strange? A place from which her mother's people had fled, and where she would not be welcome. How could she leave her marshes for that?

In her dismay she let him boost her into the carriage, and he ordered the driver to be quick, then jumped in beside her, pulling the door shut. She had no more opportunity to argue about getting the treasure she had left with the fur trader, because as the carriage wheels rolled Evan pulled her into his arms and kissed her.

Gradually, as the urgency of his lips warmed her blood, she relaxed and let the waves of pleasure shudder through her body as his hands caressed her. Her response startled her; her body knew what it wanted. So this was the way it was, she thought, in wonder, and she raised her hands to bury her fingers in his corn-silk hair. She would go anywhere with him—even to New Orleans.

He was unbuttoning her dress. She gasped. "No, please!"

"I've brought you something better to travel in," he murmured, slipping the blue cottonade off her shoulders. "It's all right, *chère*, no one can see you."

She quieted and let him help her slide the dress down over her petticoats and then put the dark traveling costume over her head as the carriage rattled down the rutted road. His hands were gentle and caressing, and they warmed her skin with magic wherever they touched her. When she was completely clothed, he began kissing her again.

By the time they reached a small community on Bayou Lafourche she was rosy with his kisses, and languorous with an aroused sensuality. He had brought her a hat with a dark veil. "You are in mourning, aren't you?"

She nodded, and let him arrange the veil so that it covered her face. The driver took them to a house so large that it made her stare, a weathered house, but one such as she had never seen, with windows above windows and two *galeries*, one above the other.

"Is this where you live?" she asked, wide eyed.

"No," he said, smiling. "This is a boardinghouse. I have rented rooms for us here, a place where we can stay until the steamboat arrives tomorrow."

A dark woman with a headcloth hiding her hair met them at the door and took them up a stairway at the side of the *galerie* that led to the upper story. They followed her down a hall to adjoining rooms. Coco looked around her, dazed with happiness. There was nothing in her room but a large carved bed, an armoire, a chair, and a washstand, also of carved wood, with a basin and water pitcher, but it seemed extraordinarily luxurious to her.

As soon as the Negress had left them with Evan's money in her hand, he closed the shutters and then the doors, and began kissing Coco's swollen lips again. Slowly he undressed her, and this time she did not protest. He removed her petticoats, too, letting them fall so carelessly to the floor that Coco, who had watched Madame iron them, softly reproached him.

"You shall have a maid when we reach New Orleans," he promised, and picked her up in his arms and laid her gently on the bed.

A maid?

She did not voice the question in her mind because he was removing his own clothing, and she was too engrossed in what he was revealing. He was beautiful, she thought, so fair and golden, with broad smooth muscles and silky hair and eyes that brought the sky into the room. Sun and sky and smooth gleaming skin, and the intriguing scents of a sheltered world, so different from her own.

He joined her on the bed, and began stroking her breasts and running his hands down her long legs, and then combing with his fingers the soft tuft of dark hair that grew between them, all the while pouring out words of love and extravagant praise. He kissed her often, not only on her lips but in places surprising to her. He caressed her high instep and placed a butterfly kiss on her knee. She was becoming heated with the emotion that rose to meet his passion, and her instincts dictated the sensuous movements of her body with which she expressed her response to him.

This time when they came together it was a joining that her body was demanding quite apart from her will, and its aftermath left her shaken. Before she slept, when a faint coolness came as the night was beginning to dissolve into dawn, Coco was becoming acquainted with her own sensuality and was sure that she would love Evan Crowley forever.

For a few minutes Evan lay awake beside her. He was dazed with pleasure, but more than ever aware of the pitfalls that awaited them on the journey to New Orleans. There were apt to be acquaintances who would recognize him on the small steamboat they would take the next day up Bayou Lafourche to Donaldsonville. It was not likely anyone who had seen Coco at the fish dock would recognize her in the remarkably tall and handsome young woman traveling under his protection in a black dress that was out of fashion, but unmistakably Parisian, a dress that was one of Lizzie's discards intended for her maid.

That in itself was a hazard, Evan acknowledged.

Though Coco spoke the Cajun dialect, she could not pass for white. Her beauty was too exotically different from the dark-eyed, magnolia-skinned Creole women. Over breakfast, which he ordered brought to their rooms, he warned her that they could not be together on the steamboat.

"Why?" Coco asked him. "Is it the Black Code?"

"Yes," he said, with relief that he did not have to explain the laws regarding the segregation of races, which included the Indians.

"My mother and father were married in the Indian fashion," she told him innocently. "One does not need a priest for that."

Evan experienced a queer contraction in his chest that was probably caused by his conscience. He was surely mad! He avoided Coco's eyes as he answered, "Perhaps we can do that later, sweetheart. Now we must be careful, or we could go to jail."

He coached her in their story. She was a young orphan going to her aunt in the city, and because he was going on business she had been placed under his protection for the journey.

"I am doing it as a kindness. Tell no one anything else," he warned her. "Speak as little as possible. Do not tell anyone your name. Someone may assume that you are Cajun and ask about your lineage. You may say that one of your ancestors came from France by way of Nova Scotia, but if you are asked personal questions, apologize and say that you are not allowed to speak with strangers. Do not raise your veil. Do you understand?"

"I am not accustomed to lying, *m'sieu'*."

"Then it's easy," Evan said, smiling. "Just hold your tongue."

Coco laughed, loving him.

Chapter Four

Drunk with love, Coco stood at the rail on the steamboat's upper deck and gazed over the levee at the dazzling elegance of plantation life along the Mississippi River. Sunlight sparkled on the water splashing from the great paddles revolving below her. On the banks, huge trees dripped streamers of moss that swayed in the air stirred by the steamboat's passing. Through the foliage she glimpsed buildings of a beauty she could not have imagined.

The boat let out a hoarse blast of its whistle as it churned around a bend and a private dock came into view with a straggle of black and white children, waving and shouting as they raced down a green lawn toward the landing. Laughing, Coco waved back at them.

Behind the children was a pink house, very large, with steps leading up to a wide *galerie* supported by shining white columns. As the steamboat moved slowly down the river, other buildings behind the house wheeled into sight, one of rosy bricks with a tall chimney that Coco guessed must be a sugarhouse. Between it and the house was a village of whitewashed cabins.

She was not supposed to be on this deck. Wearing the hat and veil Evan had provided, she had crept up the stairs while a meal was being served in the dining salon, and stood entranced by this glimpse of another way of life. Nothing would ever seem so wonderful to her again.

The stately steamboat moved on, and soon both house and children vanished behind dome-shaped oaks trailing moss, to be replaced by fields of waving cane. She had seen patches of sugarcane from the deck of the small steamboat that had carried them up the narrow Bayou Lafourche the day before, but here along the river were great fields as far as she could see, the green and gold reeds rippling like marsh grasses in the breeze off the Gulf.

After them came another house—and then more rippling fields of the sweet grass—over and over again until the magnificence of all she was seeing dizzied her. It was a far cry from her marshy world, so alien that she wondered if she could ever feel comfortable in it.

But it was Evan's world, and her doubt was soon chased away by memories, as she began reliving the events of the evening before.

They had disembarked separately from the smaller steamboat at Donaldsonville, and Evan was awaiting her in a hired carriage. The coachman helped her up, and as soon as he slammed shut the door Evan had her in his arms. How sweet his kiss was! She had never been to Donaldsonville before, but she saw little of the village because the coachman drove off so smartly that Coco was not even sure in which direction she was being taken, and during the whole ride Evan was kissing and caressing her until she let her arms move up around his shoulders and obeyed the impulse to tangle her fingers in the soft fair hair at his neck.

When he let her go, the carriage had stopped in the street before a tall narrow building with a merchant's shop on the street level, and beside it a stairway going up to a second floor.

Evan whispered, "Drop your veil," and she did so. He jumped lightly down and reached up to give her his hand. "Follow me," he told her, "and say nothing."

The stair led to a small room above the shop where Evan engaged separate rooms, explaining to the gentleman behind the desk that he was escorting a young orphan to her relatives in the city, "as a kindness to the family." Coco stood behind him and slightly to his right, wondering if the man could hear the loud and fast beating of her heart.

There was a faint flavor of bitterness in all this secrecy, but she did not question its necessity. Foremost in her mind was her longing to be alone, as they had been in the boardinghouse before they caught the Bayou Lafourche steamship, with this man whom she still thought of as *"m'sieu',"* and feel again the warmth of his arms around her and his lips on hers, while she breathed in the mingled scents of his skin and his clothing.

An old colored man carried Evan's travel case and Coco's small bundle down a narrow hall and unlocked the doors of two rooms across from each other. "This one for the young lady," the Negro said in French.

Coco followed him in, and Evan stood in the doorway, inspecting her room. "You'll be comfortable here, Miss Navarre," he said, in a voice so cool that it hurt her.

The porter laid her bundle on a chair. He closed the

door when he went out, and she was alone in a room that smelled musty and stale with cigar smoke and the odors left behind by many occupants. For just a second she longed for the salt smell of the marshes. Then she heard the porter's shuffling steps return to the stairway, and almost immediately Evan opened her door.

"At last," he said, reaching for her hat and veil and tossing them on the chair on top of her bundle of belongings. He pulled out some pins and her hair tumbled down over her shoulders. He buried his hands in it with a soft groan of pleasure, and Coco leaned against him, sighing.

"Alone again," he murmured. Their hearts, close together, mingled their rhythms in an intricate beat that was background music to the sensations his touch aroused in her skin and her lips, sensations no longer strange but still delightfully new.

"Why are you called 'Coco'?" he asked her, stroking her hair. "You were not christened that, were you?"

"I was not christened, *m'sieu',*" she reminded him. "My mother called me Cléonise, but to my father I have always been Coco."

"Clay-oh-neez." He dragged out the syllables in his English voice, and she laughed.

"I shall call you Cléo, and you must call me Evan. You don't have to say *'m'sieu''* to me, Cléo."

He kissed her again and then began helping her with unfamiliar buttons. His eyes glistened as her slender figure was revealed. "I'm going to love you again, Cléo," he murmured, "in a real bed. No more rolling in the marsh grass—"

"But I liked the marsh," she confessed, just before he muffled her voice with his lips. Since he could not answer her, she did not know whether for him that familiar mixture of sea air and brine and the faint odor of decaying reeds from the mud in his hair would always resurrect the aura of their first passion.

She was less shy about looking at him, and she noticed that while his face and throat and forearms were nearly the same color as her body, he was much whiter wherever his clothing had protected him from the sun. And his hands were so smooth. . . .

Soon Coco was learning more about her passionate nature and becoming intoxicated by the pleasures of lovemaking. She thought she would never have enough of his caressing hands or the sweetness of his kisses.

It was two hours before he got up and dressed and went out to bring back some food. When they had eaten they slept, but in the night Evan wakened her and they made love again.

Warm blood coursed in Coco's cheeks as she leaned against the deck rail, remembering in vivid detail the intimacies they had shared the previous night. "Evan," she said experimentally, under her breath. He was already as necessary to her as air and water.

The sun shone brilliantly on the porticoed mansion coming into view at the end of a double row of beautiful oak trees. Flowers made bright spots of color below its *galerie*. Living on the Isle de Navarre, she had not known there was so much wealth and beauty in the world! Nor so much happiness.

The continual tingling of excitement within her was both of her mind and of her blood. She was fascinated and a little frightened by the novelty of what she was seeing, but her spirit reached out eagerly to partake of it. At the same time she was anticipating the nighttime when she would reenter that secret world she shared with the man who meant everything to her.

She stiffened as she heard his voice, and not in her imagination. Two sets of approaching footsteps told her he was with another passenger. She kept her eyes on the passing scenery, her back to the deck.

"Are you staying at the house of your friends again, M'sieu' Crowley?" the man with Evan was asking.

"I hadn't time to let Amos know I was coming," Coco heard Evan reply easily. "He and his wife may have other guests, so I'll hire a hack to the St. Charles, and send a messenger from there."

"My groom is meeting me with my carriage," the other man said. "He can drive you to the hotel."

"But I can't impose on you—"

"It will be no trouble," said Evan's companion. "I insist, sir."

Coco waited until they had passed behind her, then whirled around. Who was this friend he had never mentioned—a friend with a wife whom Coco guessed she would never meet?

Evan was looking back at her over his shoulder. He made a face of rue and mouthed *St. Charles.*

Panic seized her, as she took his meaning. He meant to accept the man's offer. He expected her to find her way in the city alone!

As soon as the two men disappeared around the curve of the salon, she quickly found the stair and returned to the lower deck where the other passengers were servants and free colored. There she paced, too agitated to enjoy the approach to the landing where the river was almost choked with boats of every shape and form, some even larger than the steamboat, or her first glimpse of the bewildering clutter of roofs that began to appear above the levee.

The whistle was blowing, bells were ringing, and people were shouting and waving from the levee and from other boats they passed. She was shaking with fright and excitement. All along the levee were landings, and tied up to them were flatboats like those they had passed on the river, and large sailing vessels, some with strange, colorful flags. Dark-skinned workers were unloading barrels of flour, bales of cotton, hogsheads of sugar and molasses, boxes and crates whose contents she could only imagine, symbols of her widening world, carrying them up to the wagons waiting on the levee.

When the steamboat inched up to its landing, all the passengers were at the railings of both upper and lower decks, and the levee was lined with waiting carriages. Coco felt overwhelmed by the crowds of people. She could not see Evan anywhere. Carrying her small bundle of clothing, trembling with an excited apprehension, she joined the line descending from the boat.

From the levee she looked across a great square at a church that to her eyes seemed incredibly high, with three sharply pointed steeples rising toward heaven. On the middle tower was the cross that told her what the building was used for. But on each side of the church was a stone building, lower in height but of an equal size and strength. Was one of them called the St. Charles?

A band was playing in the square, and blue-coated officers were marching to the music in formation. Coco joined others moving around them, wondering which direction to take.

A matronly African was coming toward her with a basket of oysters on her head, rolling the word as she sang, "Bara-tarrry-ah! Bara-tarrry-ah!" Coco's ears pricked up. The familiarity of the name and the fish odor of her produce gave Coco the courage to ask directions of the woman.

The big African looked at her curiously. "Why you want the St. Charles, *chère*?"

Her question seemed kindly, so Coco answered, "I'm to meet someone there."

The woman pointed. "Walk one square from the river and turn that way."

"Merci." Coco beamed at her.

As she walked the path of planks beside the passing carriages, she reflected in amazement that thousands of people must live in this city. The houses and shops were built cheek to jowl, with no pasture for a sheep or two and a cow, and little room for a plot of vegetables. How did they live?

Strange odors came to her as she put the river farther behind her, but among them was the unmistakable smell of the swamp, so it could not be far away, probably only as far as the foliage of distant trees she glimpsed at crossings. Here, her keen sense of smell told her, the swamp odor was tainted with the whiff of man's refuse.

She threw back her veil, the better to see the sights. The houses she passed were far grander than those on the Bayou Terrebonne, but not so grand as those she had admired from the steamboat. Many had shops on the ground floor, with intricately worked iron balconies above them, and occasionally she saw women gossiping on the *galeries*, fanning themselves, or drinking from dainty cups.

She was soon constrained to cover her face again because of the stares of the men passing her in the street. One murmured in French, *"Que vous êtes belle, mademoiselle!"* But none accosted her before she reached the St. Charles.

It was a new building of blinding elegance. A roof supported by white columns protected persons stepping down from carriages from the weather. Steps of polished stone mounted from the *banquette,* and at their summit was a man carved from stone. Behind him through an open doorway she glimpsed a ring of white pillars encircling a milling crowd of men. Loud talk and occasional shouts came to her at the foot of the steps, where she hesitated, her heart beating furiously with both fear and anger that Evan had done this to her.

After a moment she climbed the steps and hesitated, looking into the interior of the hotel. Its magnificence dazzled her. The room looked as long as the steamboat on which she had traveled down the river, and wider because it was roughly circular. Its floor was polished stone of many soft colors laid in a pleasing pattern.

At a far side she glimpsed a curious winding stairway, climbing in circles. Her gaze went up to the dome visible high above another circle of pillars. There were pictures on the walls of the dome, and from its center, suspended by a chain, was a fall of sparkling stones reflecting a hundred candles in their midst.

She stared long, entranced by its beauty. When she brought her gaze down she saw that the men immediately around her had turned from the gentleman speaking in their midst and were observing her with openly curious and admiring eyes, some of them obviously talking about her. At the same time she saw what she had missed in the crush of the gathering and the dazzle of her surroundings.

In the center of the huge room were a half dozen slaves, young and old, male and female, some with hands tied behind their backs. The man talking was quoting prices. With a shock she saw that she had

walked into a slave auction such as her father, in his
drink, had described seeing at Lafitte's headquarters on
Barataria.

"We smuggled 'em in," he had boasted, "and sold 'em
for half the price they'd bring in New Orleans."

Just then an officious man took Coco's arm and turned
her toward the door. "You're not allowed here,
ma'm'selle," he said curtly.

"I'm here to meet my friend," Coco protested. A
quick glance around revealed that as far as she could see
there was no other woman in the room. The men were
looking at her like hungry raccoons around a stray hen.

"No loitering or soliciting allowed," the officer repeated, shoving her toward the door. "You can't meet
your friends here."

Suddenly frightened again, she wondered how she
would find Evan if she were not allowed to wait for him
here.

The officer pushed her roughly out on the steps. The
sunlight struck her eyes, and she did not see Evan until
he touched her arm.

He was smiling. "I fear you have lost your way, *mademoiselle,*" he said. "May I help you?"

Her fright and humiliation turned abruptly into rage.
"*Oui!*" she said furiously. "And explain to me why—"

His hand tightened so painfully on her arm that she
gasped. "Come quickly!" he said in a soft voice. "I have
a carriage waiting."

She went with him, propelled by his arm at a fast,
unwilling pace down the polished steps. She let him
give her an arm up into the carriage, but when he
joined her and would have embraced her, she fought
him furiously, cursing him with some of her father's
language. He held her chin until his lips found hers and

kissed her until her traitorous senses were responding to him, her passion even stronger because of her fury.

"Oh, Cléo, my Cléo, you're magnificent!"

"You will not abandon me like that ever again, *m'sieu'*!" she said violently. "I will not be treated like—like—"

Evan let her go. The smile had left his face. "Like what?"

"Une sauvage," she whispered.

His eyes hardened. "What happened at the St. Charles, *chère*? What humiliated you?"

"That man—"

"He was a policeman."

"He shoved me out! He said, 'No loitering or soliciting.' What did he mean?"

Evan told her, succinctly, about the women in the little cribs near the levee on Tchoupitoulas Street, and how they were forbidden from accosting men on the streets. Every word was inscribed in pain on her heart.

"He made a mistake about you, but it was because you were in the wrong place."

"You sent me there!"

"I had no choice, Cléo, my love. There was nothing I could do except let you know where my acquaintance on the boat was taking me—"

"I would have known how to refuse a ride!"

"I couldn't refuse him." He caressed her cheek with his fingers. "I didn't make the rules," he said, "but I must live by them. I can never take you to that hotel unless, perhaps, to a quadroon ball. You are not a quadroon, but you are a 'half-breed,' which both my American and Creole friends consider cut from the same cloth."

"And you?" she asked, in a choked voice.

"I think you are the most beautiful woman on God's earth," he said huskily, "and I love you."

The carriage had stopped before a shop through whose small window she could see long loaves of bread stacked in piles on a table. Beside the shop, double doors opened from the cypress banquette onto a narrow alley. The rich aroma of baking bread spilled out through them.

Evan paid their driver, then led Coco into the alley. Ahead of them was a courtyard with a shade tree and flowering vines climbing its walls. He paused between the shop and the detached bakery kitchen and called, "Maisie?"

A very large, elderly African came to the rear door of the shop, her eyes opening wide in surprised pleasure. "Master Evan!"

"I've brought you a guest, Maisie. Her name is Miss Cléo."

"Whatever you doin' with a young gal like dat?" Maisie cried, her shrewd eyes taking in Cléo's total appearance in a flashing glance.

"She is a young woman who needs a friend."

They were speaking English, but Cléo knew they spoke of her although she did not understand a word beyond her own name.

"She will need one of your rooms for seven or eight months."

"Ah!" said the old woman, her eyes going to Cléo's waist.

"I'll explain later. Please make her comfortable, Maisie. She is very young and new to the city."

Maisie came forward, holding out her big arms. "Wel-

come to New Orleans, Miz Cléo!" she cried, her gesture
and her wide smile making her meaning clear.

"Maisie was my nurse when I was growing up in
Virginia," Evan told Coco in French.

Maisie nodded, smiling, and rocked her arms to show
that she understood what Evan was saying, but Coco
was not sure whether she was rocking Evan as a baby or
referring to Evan's seed in her womb. Through the door
of the kitchen, Coco glimpsed another dark woman in
the smoky heat. She was skinny of frame, with a sulky
face.

"Bonjour, Berthe," Evan called to her, still speaking
French. "This is Mademoiselle Cléo, who will be visiting
your mistress."

"Bonjour," said Berthe curtly. She picked up a long
wooden paddle and turned to the high brick open oven
behind her, from which she began removing the fresh-
baked loaves of bread browning beside a small fire.

"Come," said Maisie, and led them past the heat of
the kitchen into the court, shaded by its high walls and
an overhanging balcony. It was ablaze with bright
flowering vines. In a far corner was a small lean-to building.

Behind the kitchen was a stairway to the balcony.
Maisie led the way up the stairs, which quivered under
her weight. Several rooms opened off the *galerie,* and
Maisie took Cléo into one. It was much like the bed-
rooms she and Evan had occupied the past two nights,
holding a poster bed draped with netting, an armoire,
and a table and chairs. It was a very pleasant room,
shining clean, with glass doors opening on the balcony
and wooden shutters that could be closed over them at
night.

"You will sleep here," Evan told Cléo, translating

Maisie's foreign talk. "I'll be in the room next to yours. If you need her she will be in the shop or in her room, which is at the head of the stair."

"Where does Berthe sleep?" Coco asked.

Evan, who was just outside the door on the balcony, pointed down to the shed in a corner of the court. "Berthe's room is there where the house servant sleeps. She is also Maisie's slave."

"Maisie's slave?" Coco repeated in astonishment.

"Maisie is a free Negress. I brought her with me when I came from Virginia, but I freed her here because she didn't want to leave the city for the frontier."

It had been Elizabeth's idea. She had resented Maisie's familiarity, born of caring for him since his infancy. He was counting much now on the hostility between the two women and his old nurse's fondness to help him keep this new love secret.

"I gave her the money to acquire this property and buy a good bake-woman. When I have business in the city, Maisie has a spare bedroom for me."

Maisie nodded happily.

Coco looked at him in wonder. How much more was there that she did not know about this man she loved so wholeheartedly and with such passion that she could be ready to claw out his eyes when he angered her as he had this day?

"Anything you need, tell the servants and they will tell me," Maisie assured Cléo as Evan translated for her. "Now I must return to my shop."

"I'll be down directly," Evan told his old nurse, and she left them.

Alone, they fell into each other's arms. "Your kisses are like brandy," Evan whispered. "They intoxicate me, and I crave them. I can never get enough of you, Cléo."

He ran a hand down the curve of her bodice and over her hip. "I must arrange for a dressmaker, *chère*. You are too lovely for hand-me-downs and cottonade."

They spent the warm afternoon making love, slowly and drowsily, under the mosquito netting. When they wakened, dusk had fallen outside their shutters. "I have business to attend to," Evan told her. "I must leave you for a few hours."

He went to his own room and rang for the servant. Cléo, as she was beginning to think of herself, lay abed in a delicious languor and listened to the sounds of his bath coming through the wall between their rooms.

He came in to kiss her good-bye and told her to get some more rest. Soon after he left, Maisie brought her a simple supper. Her warmth was soothing even though her language was foreign, and the new bread was delicious.

Cléo did not think she could go to sleep in a strange room without Evan holding her, but the excitement of the last two days had tired her and she slept soundly all through the night.

The next morning Maisie's house servant brought her hot water for a bath and some breakfast, and later in the morning Evan brought a light-colored woman who carried a large bundle. "This is Madame Barnet," Evan said. "She is a dressmaker."

Madame Barnet unrolled her package on the bed and displayed a rainbow of fabrics such as Coco had never seen before.

"How beautiful!" she exclaimed, lovingly touching one after another.

The dressmaker smiled. "This one came from Paris— and this one . . . Ah, this would be lovely on you, *madame*!"

She held the samples beneath Coco's chin, so that Evan could choose for her. He had made Coco aware of her body, and she examined herself critically in a looking glass, understanding for the first time what fine clothes could do for her. She could hardly speak for the excitement choking her throat. She stood still, adoring Evan with her eyes while the woman took a string and measured Coco—her bodice, her waist, the distance of her shoulders from the floor, even placing a string around her wrist, and marking her measurements with a knot.

Evan ordered many dresses, some to be made now, and others later, since "Madame" was *enceinte.*

When the seamstress had gone, they made love in the drowsy afternoon with the shutters drawn, and then went downstairs to eat a delicious meal served in Maisie's kitchen.

The days fell into a delightful rhythm. Every morning Evan went to the Merchants' Exchange in the rotunda of the St. Charles—where slave auctions were held only on certain days—while the seamstress came with her work for fittings. In the afternoons Evan came to spend several hours with her in the shuttered room. Sometimes he told her how he had spent the mornings bargaining with the traders in sugar and molasses. Or he told her about the city and its busy inhabitants bustling outside around their quiet island of delights. Another large hotel was being constructed across the street from the St. Charles.

"It will be even more magnificent," he told her, "and there is nothing in New York or Boston as grand as the St. Charles. New Orleans is rolling in wealth," he said with pride.

Sometimes they did not talk at all, but just made love.

Afterward in the dusk of the evening he sometimes took her for a ride in a hack through the narrow streets, some of them paved with stones, pointing out various buildings of importance. The wealth of the city was obvious on those rare evenings when they walked, and looked through iron-barred windows at the imported furniture, the ornaments and jewelry and books, among the fine things merchants had for sale.

The books fascinated Cléo. "Do you mean that if I could read, I could learn all about New Orleans?"

Evan laughed and squeezed her arm. "You would learn more about Paris."

Weeks passed in a pleasant dream. One afternoon Evan mentioned his sugarcane plantation on Bayou Black. "It's nearly cutting time," he said drowsily.

"Sugar is a valuable crop, isn't it?"

"The most profitable of all."

"Who tends your sugarcane?" she asked.

"It's being looked after. I have an overseer and many slaves."

She said no more but while Cléo drowsed beside him, he thought about home. He should be back there now, checking the color of the tasseling, seeing that the sugar mill was in good repair, since it had not been used since last year's crop was cut. He wondered about the condition of his workers. Had they escaped the summer scourges of yellow fever and cholera that occasionally attacked even the best-run slave quarters? Lizzie would be wondering why he was staying so long in the city without her. What was she telling Nanette, who must be asking for her beloved papa?

He should pack up and go. He had narrowly missed having to bow to Jane Fielding yesterday when her carriage turned into Rue Chartres just as he walked out of Maisie's.

It was time to go home—but he was entrapped in a cocoon of earthly delights:

—of nights of love in the secluded room fragrant with the scent of the jasmine blooming just outside, and filled with the magic of the mockingbird's songs;

—of Cléo's eyes, mysterious in the moonlight filtering through shutter and gauze;

—of waking in the mornings with her satin body in his arms, while into his senses stole the fragrance of Berthe's baking and the chants of the fruit-sellers:

"Canta-lope-ah! Verrry fine canta-lope-ah!"

—of opening his eyes to see Cléo's dark eyelashes drooping on her golden cheeks; or watch them swoop up to reveal her golden brown eyes with consciousness and love dawning in them. . . .

Cléonise! He could not tear himself away from her and the part of himself that she carried in her womb. The weeks became a month, and he stayed on, unable to leave her.

Chapter Five

On a fine morning in August as Evan entered the rotunda of the St. Charles, someone grasped his arm and he turned to face Amos Fielding.

"I've been expecting you, Evan!" his friend exclaimed with a broad smile. "Why haven't we seen you?"

"Amos!" Evan took his friend's proffered hand and forcibly conquered the threat of panic. "I've been going to call on you." It was remarkable that he had not encountered Amos before. It would have happened sooner if he had not been scrupulously avoiding Maspero's and the other exchanges where he knew Amos did much of the bartering involved in his brokerage business.

"You remember I purchased a house to provide a home for an old servant?"

"Your old nurse, wasn't she?"

"A fine old woman, but she didn't suit for Nanette. I wanted to see to some maintenance of the property, and since I came alone, I'm staying in one of her rooms. It's not a fashionable house, but she makes me comfortable."

"Then you must come and dine with us. Jane will want to hear news of your family."

"I'd be happy to, but I'm leaving the city soon. My cane is getting high—I don't like to leave the plantation during the summer growing season, you know." He broke off, with the fear that he was talking too much. He had left during the growing season. . . . What was it Amos had said?

"You were expecting me?" He wondered which of their mutual friends had seen him, and if he had been seen with Cléo. Those of his Creole friends who had quadroon mistresses were undoubtedly more discreet than he had been but even Amos would think nothing of his taking a half-breed mistress; it was the fact that he was passionately in love with her that would cause talk. And talk had a way of reaching the women—through the servants, probably.

"Yes, we thought you must have arrived in the city," Amos answered, "because a letter for you from Elizabeth was delivered to my house."

"From Lizzie!" Her name, spoken aloud, came to him out of a world he had emotionally abandoned, a place he had been deluding himself existed somewhere in his past, but had little to do with his present. Now small details of that life rushed into his memory, bringing a painful guilt.

He realized that he had let Lizzie assume he would be with their friends because of his guilty knowledge that he would have Cléo with him at Maisie's. A vivid picture of his sunny-haired daughter running toward him with outstretched arms flashed to his mind, and he heard her childish voice crying, "Papa, Papa!"

"I see you're anxious," his friend said sympathetically, with a glance out the doorway to judge the length of the shadows cast by the sun. "I have an urgent appointment and I fear Jane is not at home at present. Can you dine with us tonight, then?"

"Yes, of course, thank you." Evan changed the subject quickly before Amos could inquire how many days ago he had left Bayou Black. "I've been occupied with numerous business matters. I've been approached by some local men who are organizing a new railroad company. They plan to install a track between New Orleans and Nashville. I think it could be a good investment. What do you think, Amos?"

Amos was diverted. "There are half a dozen such companies being formed in the city, and most of them will go bankrupt!" he snorted. "I'll take a paddlewheel and its amenities over rail travel any day myself. Have you seen the track they laid from the Pontchartrain landing? The bed is laid over swampland so soft that the track is sinking and the rails work loose. One recently was jammed up through the floor of a car!"

"Without that four and a half miles of track, more Gulf steamers would risk going aground in the tricky passage up the river channel instead of coming into Pontchartrain," Evan reminded him, "because the carriage road their passengers must take from the lake is a quagmire every time it rains."

"You think rail is safer than water travel? Only last month news was published of a locomotive boiler exploding, badly burning the engineer. I wouldn't advise risking your money in railroads. I suggest we dig canals instead."

While Evan listened to his friend, his thoughts were busy with questions. It was not a simple matter to send mail from Bayou Black. If Lizzie had sent a courier over to the steamboat landing on Bayou Lafourche with a letter, something must be wrong on the plantation. The possibility that Nanette was ill occurred to him. Summer was yellow fever season, although it was less prevalent in the interior than it was in the city. His Creole neighbors in Terrebonne and their slaves seemed mostly to escape it, but everyone said Americans were more vulnerable. A terrible fear seized him, and he had an urgent need to see the letter awaiting him.

Then he realized how long he had been away and saw that Lizzie had good cause to worry. It was surprising that she had not written before. Six weeks had slipped by like a dream. It was time to go home.

The mere thought of a separation from Cléo was so bleak that he broke off his conversation with Amos—after promising to present himself at his friend's house after the afternoon siesta—to hurry back to the rooms above Maisie's bakery where they had been so happy.

As he walked the few blocks from the St. Charles, the noises of the city streets accompanying his steps—carriage wheels grinding over the paving stones, bursts of laughter and oaths from the cafés he passed, a woman chanting the virtues of the ginger cakes she carried in a basket on her head, and shrieks of playing children from an open court, all punctuated by the complex beat of trotting horses' hooves—were sounds already affecting him with nostalgia. He had been living in Eden, and he was being driven out. How he would miss it all!

On his way he passed a jewelry shop he had walked by with Cléo one evening. Lying in the window was an unusual ring set with a large topaz of a color that reminded Evan of her eyes in bright sunlight. He went in and bought it for her.

Cléo was in the shady court, dressed in a soft yellow muslin with a low *décolletage* which compensated somewhat for the extra warmth of the petticoat it required. She was picking dead blossoms off the crimson bougainvillea vine.

She turned when she heard Evan's step. He opened his arms and she went into them with a glad cry, thrust unexpectedly soon out of her throat by his fierce embrace.

"Evan!" she protested, laughing. "You squeeze the breath out of me!"

"Come, what are you doing here, *chère*? Someone else can pretty the vines."

"Maisie doesn't want me in her kitchen, and I have too little to do."

"You have something to do for me," he said, nuzzling her neck, "but not here. Come upstairs where Maisie's customers passing by can't ogle us while I kiss you."

Smiling, she took his hand. He knew her well now, and yet her eyes still seemed excitingly mysterious when she smiled at him. She led him to the stair, where she immediately tripped on her skirts. "Why must I wear these petticoats?" she complained.

"A lady pulls them up in front when she climbs a stair. Like this." He reached around her waist and lifted both her skirt and petticoat and looked down at the graceful bare foot he had revealed. "Cléo!" he scolded, secretly moved by the sight of it. "No shoes or stockings?"

"I didn't wear them in the marsh, and it's even warmer here." But she grasped her skirts and, holding them high, ran ahead of him up to the *galerie*.

In the shuttered room, he took her hand and ordered,

"Close your eyes." When she obeyed, he slipped the topaz on her finger.

Her eyes flew open of their own accord when she felt the metal slide over her finger. She gasped with pleasure, then, holding her hand out before her, whirled around in a circle, admiring it. "Oh, it is so lovely!" she cried. "And you are so kind to give it to me!" She turned her hand this way and that to catch the light, then examined it more closely. "You spoil me," she said finally. "I am so lazy that my hands are getting soft."

Evan laughed and hugged her. "You're supposed to be lazy when you're *enceinte, chère.* Do you like the ring, then?"

"I never hoped to have anything so beautiful!" She threw her arms around him in a fervor of gratitude and he began kissing and caressing her with a desperate passion born of his knowledge of their impending separation. Even while he held her, his thoughts were winging ahead to the letter awaiting him at the house of his friends, and he was praying nothing had happened to Nanette.

He wondered if Lizzie had written to Jane Fielding, as well. Jane would be sure to suspect something was amiss if she discovered how long he had been in the city without getting in touch with them. Would she write to Lizzie?

Creole wives, he had noticed, were expected to close their eyes to the quadroon mistresses and half-breed children of their husbands, but he knew instinctively that neither Lizzie nor Jane Fielding ever would. They were scandalized, they often said, by the tolerance of infidelity in French Creole families.

Legally, he had absolute ownership of his wife and daughter and could do as he liked. But if Lizzie took it into her head to go back to England while he was away, taking Nanette with her, it would be a fait accompli that would be difficult to undo. It would leave him free to live with Cléo, but he could never marry her nor could her son carry his name, whereas Lizzie still might give him an heir. And his adorable golden-haired Nanette— he could not face losing her!

Of course, he reassured himself, if Jane wrote to Lizzie she could very well ask him to carry the letter back with him, since the mails were so uncertain! Only last week the *Louisiana Gazette* had published a story about a post rider whose horse had drowned fording a bayou, and warned patrons that a bag of mail lost in the incident was unrecoverable!

He breathed in the clean earthy fragrance of Cléo's skin and put his lips to her breast. How could he leave her? Resolutely he banished all thoughts from his mind that could interfere with their mutual pleasure.

"I have an appointment this evening," he told her, after they had made love. Drawing apart from her, he felt a deep heaviness of spirit, as though they were already separated by miles instead of inches.

She merely fluttered her eyelashes at him and was dropping off to sleep, wearing nothing but the ring on her finger, when he left her to go into his own bedchamber to bathe and dress. The child was already making his existence visible in the rising mound of her abdomen.

He hailed a hack to take him to the Fieldings' well-furnished house, where Amos and Jane greeted him affectionately and poured him a sherry before handing him Lizzie's letter. Evan broke the seal and unfolded it with a slight tremor in his fingers.

My dear husband, [he read silently]
  Our tender regards and wishes for your continued health, and we send affectionate greetings to Jane and Amos. All is well here, but we anxiously await your return. Your overseer tells me the cane is tasseling nicely, and will be ready for the cutting soon. Nanette has been crying for Ti-Jacques because she wants him to find her papa. I believe she is persuaded Ol' Debbil got you, so if it please you to hasten your return, it will make your daughter very happy.
                                        Your loving wife,
                                        Elizabeth

"I trust Elizabeth and Nanette are well?" his hostess asked.

"Yes, thank you, and they send their affection to you both." He refolded the letter and placed it inside his waistcoat, grateful that Jane had received no missive of her own, and hoping she was not wondering why Lizzie had assumed he would be staying with them, when he was at Maisie's.

He knew that his idyll was over. Elizabeth's careful reminder about his crop made him wonder how much she had guessed about his unusual return to the city in summer. But it only pointed to what he was trying to ignore. He must leave Cléo now or lose everything he had worked for since arriving in Louisiana.

They were lying naked under the mosquito netting, barely touching because the heat was heavy in the room, when he finally found the strength to tell her that he was leaving.

"Maisie will see that you have everything you need. I

trust her completely. You can talk with her through Berthe, who speaks both languages."

"But you'll be with me," Cléo said, bewildered. Shock had kept her from understanding his incredible words.

"I must go to my plantation on Bayou Black," he repeated. "I must be there this fall for the cutting and grinding of my cane."

"Then I'll go with you."

"No, you will stay here with Maisie. That is why I brought you here," he said patiently. "I'll be back after the grinding to sell my sugar and molasses."

"You are going back to Terrebonne parish without me?" Coco shrieked, sitting up in the bed. "Then why did you bring me here to this stinking city? You said you were doing it because you wanted to take care of me!"

"I brought you here to have our baby where Maisie can look after you when I'm busy, here where there are good physicians. Surely you know that all Creole ladies come here for the last months of their lying-in, in order to have a good physician?"

"Indeed I don't! I'm no Creole lady! The women I know have their babies with the help of a neighbor!"

"Cajuns?" he said. *"Sauvages?"*

He laid a hand on her stomach, which was nicely rounded now, and tried to kiss her, but she jerked her face away. "I could have stayed in the marsh!" she said angrily. "Having a baby is a simple thing there, and you would be near—"

"My child will not be born in a swamp."

She glared at him. "Why not? His mother was born in a swamp."

"Cléo, you can trust me. I brought you here because I don't want you to be alone when your time comes. I've told you I'll be back after the grinding. I love you, I adore you! When the baby is here, I'll buy our own little house on Rampart Street. I've arranged for everything, Cléo, even for a doctor when the time comes—"

"I won't stay behind!" The look in her slanted eyes, blazing at him in the shadowed room, reminded him of the eyes of a fox his dogs had once treed. "If I'm to be alone, I'll be in the marsh, which I know!"

"You would prefer that miserable stilt-house of your father's to this pleasant room?"

"Yes, if I must be alone!"

"You won't be alone here. I've told you. Maisie is here to serve you—"

"—a woman who doesn't understand my talk, and is too busy—"

"Berthe understands—"

"—a slave who resents my being here!"

"Nevertheless you can learn much from her. She can teach you the ways of the city—" He broke off because Coco was pounding her fists on his shoulders and chest in a passion, crying, "Why should I learn the ways of the city, if you're not here? I'm going with you—I don't want to stay here without you—"

She stopped when she saw the agony in his eyes. He put his arms around her lovingly, and held her close.

"I'm going to miss you, too, *ma chère,*" he said miserably.

Cléo would have felt completely abandoned, if Evan had not brought her, on the day he left, a young servant. She was very black with big round eyes and she stood shyly just inside the door while Evan told Cléo, "This is Esther. She will dress you and coif your hair. I have seen that Maisie and Berthe are too busy in the shop to do those things for you, and Maisie's house servant can't.

But Maisie is responsible for your well-being. I've asked her to see to it that Esther accompanies you when you go out."

"Why do you put all these people around me?" Cléo flared. "I feel trapped! I can't breathe!"

"A lady is always accompanied when she is out on the street."

"Have you made me a lady, then?" she mocked him. "Do you forget that I fished and trapped alone? And took my catch alone to market in my own pirogue?"

The little slave blinked, hearing her.

Flushing with annoyance, Evan said, "This is a city, Cléo. There is more wickedness here than you could possibly know. I've asked Maisie to take care that you never leave the house alone."

"She was your nursemaid, *m'sieu'*," Cléo retorted. "She's not mine."

"Esther, please leave us," Evan said. When they were alone, he asked Cléo unhappily, "Do you love me?"

She chewed her lower lip. "That is why I must go with you, Evan. Haven't I said I will go where you go? And haven't you said you would take care of me?"

"I thought we had settled the matter," Evan said. "You are making it very difficult for me, *chère.*"

She beseeched him with her eyes, and recognized the helplessness in his. "I will be very busy soon with the cutting and grinding of my crop. It will be impossible for us to be together, and I'll worry about you and the baby, unless you are here with Maisie. Please do as I ask, *chère.*"

She could not deny his pain at leaving her, and she saw that she was adding to it. She fell silent. There was a stone in her breast, and she felt sickness beginning in her stomach. "When do you go?"

"In an hour."

She drew in her breath sharply, her eyes squeezed shut in denial. He kissed her again and again, then tore himself away, muttering, "I'll be back as soon as I can," and fled the room.

She sank down on the bed and sat there, frozen in misery. After a few minutes she realized the little black maid was still standing just outside her door.

"Esther?"

The girl appeared in the doorway. Cléo made an effort to control her trembling mouth and asked her, "Where did M'sieu' find you?"

In soft French, Esther answered, "At the auction, *m'dame.*"

"He bought you!" Cléo's attention was diverted from her own pain, as she remembered the shock and humiliation she had experienced at the St. Charles rotunda her first day in New Orleans, and thought how it must have felt to this young girl to be displayed there. "But why were you at the auction?"

"My mother was a *femme de chambre* and her *m'dame* was training me, but when *m'dame* died of an ague, *michie* sold us both."

"I wonder why M'sieu' Crowley didn't buy your mother, if she was more experienced?"

"She was not taken to the auction. One of *m'dame's* friends offered to buy her."

"Without you? Then you are lonely too," Cléo said, feeling the stone in her breast grow heavier. "I, too, have no mother. We must comfort each other, Esther."

"Yes, *m'dame.*" The young girl's eyes shone with warmth. "*M'dame* is *enceinte,* no?"

"*Madame* is *enceinte,* yes," Cléo said, and admitted, "I don't think much about it yet."

It was strange, but true. She had been so absorbed in her lover, she had scarcely realized she was carrying his child until now, when he had made it plain that was what had separated them.

"M'dame can't be lonely, if she think about her *bébé."*

Cléo was looking down at the topaz on her finger, but she heard clearly what her maid was saying, and she knew it was true. If she were home in her own world, the child in her womb would keep her from ever being lonely. She wanted to go home.

She was twisting the topaz again. It must be a valuable ring, she thought. Was it valuable enough to buy her a ticket on the steamship Evan was taking? But he had asked her to do what he thought was best for their child. And he had said when the child was born he would buy their own little house where they could be together. For always, she assured herself. For now, she would do as he asked. But if he stayed away too long— she had the ring!

She had felt gloriously well until now, but as soon as Evan left her she began to suffer from the nausea and backaches that Berthe told her unsympathetically were to be expected in her condition. Maisie's bake-woman added to Cléo's misery with a few warnings of her own.

"Take care you don' look on a body who lose a leg or arm, or," she predicted darkly, "your *bébé* be born a monster."

Maisie clucked over her in her strange tongue, her eyes communicating the warm interest that her little command of French could not. But it was Esther who coaxed Cléo to eat in those first weeks after Evan's departure when she often paced her room like a caged wild animal. The little maid entered at first light carrying a tray holding *café au lait* and one of Maisie's fried dough rolls dipped in sugar, which, if they stayed down at all, sat heavily on Cléo's stomach. The maid never asked Cléo if she slept well. She came in chirping, *"Le bébé*, he is already awake?"

Constantly she reminded Cléo that she was not entirely alone as long as she carried Evan's child.

The days were sweltering and the city's inhabitants were overcome by languor. The men moved slowly on the *banquette* past the bakery in the mornings, while on the balconies overhanging the street the women fanned themselves and gossiped. Both streets and balconies were deserted during the heat of the afternoon, when nothing moved except at the river's edge where the dockworkers were unloading the boats that nearly choked the channel. Sometimes when the breeze blew from the river with a slight coolness, it carried snatches of their musical chants to Cléo's ears in the room above Maisie's shop.

She missed Evan with a physical ache. She heard nothing from him, but she could not have read a letter, whether it was written in French or English. Neither could any of the other women in the house read.

One day her hunger to hear his voice was so great that she gave the topaz ring to Esther and told her to go to the jewelry shop where Evan had bought it and sell it for her so they could take a steamboat back to Terrebonne parish. Berthe, who had stepped out of the kitchen and was standing under the *galerie* below them, overheard her.

"Are you crazy?" she yelled. "He'll call the police and accuse Esther of stealing it. Then you'll have no ring and no servant! What you need money for, anyway?"

"To go home, to M'sieu'."

Berthe brought Maisie and with Esther they made a

ring around her, their talk swirling about her, until it crowded her into her room.

"You think you can get a cabin on one one of them fancy steamboats without *michie*? You be put below with Esther an' the other servants on bunks."

"I've still got my veil!" Cléo told them.

"It cost you plenty money to hire a carriage. An' where you stay when you get to Donaldsonville? You know any colored peoples there?"

"And don't it take two days and more to get where Master Evan lives?" Maisie asked. "What you goin' do when your money run out? Even if you can sell your ring, it's not goin' make you rich. You're dreamin', sugar."

"They'll think you an' Esther both runnin' away," Berthe added to her translation of that.

"You could lose *le bébé*," Esther put in.

In the end it was her concern for the child growing in her womb that made her give in. She reminded herself that Evan had promised they would be together in their own house after the baby came, and she sank into a dreamy preoccupation with the physical changes taking place in her body and a vision of future happiness.

She was large with his child when Evan returned in late fall.

There was nothing to announce his arrival; no carriage stopped in the street, nor did Maisie call up to warn her. There was just the familiar step on the stair from the court, followed by his deep, glad voice.

"Cléo! Are you there?"

She had sent Esther out to buy some fruit, and was lying on her bed. A few short months ago she would have leapt up and run to meet him. Now she separated the mosquito netting on the barre and got clumsily to her feet just as he opened the shutters that kept the afternoon sun out of her chamber.

He looked wonderful. His blue eyes contrasted brilliantly with the bronze tone of his normally fair skin, which in fact showed evidence of sunburn and peeling. The love and anticipation she saw in his gaze was blinding. Her heart pounded with joy.

He put his arms around her and they kissed hungrily. A warm, tingling happiness spread from his lips on hers through her entire body, as welcome as water to a desperate thirst. She sighed as he led her blindly to the bed behind her and they sank down on it, still joined in an embrace. When they lay side by side, he caressed the mound of her distended abdomen just as the child moved within it.

"How is my son?" he asked.

Chapter Six

Jane Fielding and her houseguest were enjoying their ten o'clock coffee on the upper veranda overlooking the rear garden, shaded from the sun partly by the large magnolia tree that grew close to the squared Greek revival house. A neatly uniformed maid brought a tray of sweet cakes and as Elizabeth Crowley selected one, Nanette dropped Jane's kitten and came running to join them.

"Only one, darling," her mother cautioned. "And what do you say?"

"Thank you, ma'am," Nanette caroled, and ran after the kitten who had leapt to the railing and was trying to climb the bougainvillea vine winding up a pillar to the roof.

Elizabeth was thinking how very pleasant it was to be back in New Orleans for the season. She munched cake and listened with pleasure to the muted sounds of the city's activity—the brisk thud of horseshoes and creak of carriage wheels on the street mingling with the dis-

tant ringing of the cathedral bells and faint hoots from
the river traffic. It was an exciting urban symphony,
suggesting important things going on and a foretaste of
the round of balls and entertainments she anticipated
during the remaining winter months.

Amos kept horses at a nearby livery stable. Early that
morning she and Jane had gone riding on the bayou
road and a house she had seen kept returning to her
mind. They had left the city at daybreak, with a groom
following them. It was just as the sun emerged above
the oaks and magnolias to the east to throw brilliant rays
of light across the bayou, that she saw the old mansion,
its roof rising from the mists obscuring the overgrown
jungle of its garden. The sudden radiance and its distance gave the weathered structure an illusion of great
elegance.

Elizabeth had reined in her mount, exclaiming, "Is
that beautiful old house across the bayou still uninhab-
ited?"

"It was abandoned long ago, I fear."

"What a pity! In this light it has a certain grace, don't
you think?"

Jane, sitting erect like the excellent horsewoman she
was, agreed.

It was a two-story house of the raised-basement Acadian style, its *galerie* lifted off the ground with brick
pillars that became slender wooden columns supporting a second *galerie* that was also wrapped around the
main structure. Floor-length windows with shutters
closing over them gave access to the *galeries* from each
room.

The simplicity and graceful proportions of its style
were impressive even though the effects of weathering
and neglect were clearly visible and its gardens were

choked with long unpruned shrubs, and vines almost obliterated its trees.

It must have been the scene of many a wonderful ball, Elizabeth thought, and demanded, "Who owns the property?"

"Jeff Archer."

"An American! Do you know him?"

"Yes, indeed. He's our lawyer. Haven't you met the Archers?"

"I don't believe so. Why aren't they living in the house? How could anyone allow such a beautiful home to fall into such ruin?"

"They live in Bellemont, just three miles away. Jeff's wife inherited both plantations. Bellemont is a splendid house. Jeff has no need of Sorcellerie."

"Sorcellerie," Elizabeth breathed. "What a beautiful name!"

"They say the crystal chandeliers still hang from the ceilings, and the fireplaces are of the finest marble," Jane mused, "but I've never been willing to risk my horse meeting a snake in that unscythed grass in order to explore it."

That conversation had taken place as they reined in their horses on the bayou road, and watched the mists half concealing the decaying old mansion dissolve in the morning sun.

There was something haunting about the image. Now Elizabeth brought the subject up again, as she sipped the strong black Creole coffee Jane's cook had brewed.

"Wouldn't it be pleasant if Evan could buy Sorcellerie and restore it?"

"Restore Sorcellerie?" Jane shook her head doubtfully. "I'm certain the plantation isn't for sale. Jeff has it under active cultivation."

"Sugar?"

"What else? The Archers raise sugarcane on both plantations."

The two women looked at each other.

"Do the Archers have children?"

Jane smiled slightly. "Indeed they do. Alex, their youngest, is two years older than Nanette. A charming little boy."

Elizabeth looked over at her daughter's golden curls and selected another cake. After a moment she asked, "Do you think Mr. Archer would restore his house if Evan took a long-term lease on it for a winter residence?"

Jane stared at her. "I doubt it. Anyway, why should Evan go to that expense, when we always enjoy your company for the season?"

"Evan can certainly afford the expense." There was a bitter flavor to Elizabeth's words. Evan had surprised her this winter with his total involvement in business. Always before, their sojourn in the city after the grinding was over had been a time of relaxation and the pursuit of pleasure. This year, Evan was spending all his time at the exchanges or coffeehouses, no longer just a planter in the city to trade his crop and enjoy a season of opera and the theater, but an investor, always talking about a consortium to build a railroad or a big hotel.

"It's most enjoyable being with you, dear Jane, but don't you think it's time we had a place of our own where we can entertain the many friends we've made here? Nanette is growing up so fast—"

"Nonsense. You're free to entertain here." Jane's eyes twinkled, giving her rather severe face a hint of humor. "I can certainly arrange for you and Evan to meet the Archers. I'll give a dinner party! I think I can fit it in between the Poydras's ball and the opening of that new play at the American Theater. You'll like Melodie and Jeff."

"Mama!" Nanette wailed shrilly. "Kitty scratched me!"

"Well, stop squeezing her," Elizabeth scolded, and Jane went to rescue her kitten from Nanette's excessive love.

But the kitten leapt out of Jane's hands and scampered up the vine, scrambling at the eave and, after a hair-raising flirtation with death, at last attaining the relative freedom of the roof.

"Oh, dear!" Jane said. "Now I'll have to ring for a footman to climb up and bring her down. She'll never be able to do it without breaking her neck. Nanette, darling, let me look at that scratch."

All day Cléo had paced the *galerie* clenching and unclenching her fists. When Evan finally came up the stair at the siesta hour, she turned on him like a trapped mink. "Where do you sleep?"

He stopped on the top step, his fair skin showing the rush of angry blood to his face. "Where I always sleep. At the home of friends."

"I haven't seen you in three days!"

"I'm a planter and a man of trade, Cléo." His voice was dangerously quiet. "I can't spend all my days and nights lying about in your room with you."

"One time you were happy doing that! Before you went back to Bayou Black! What happen' there, ahn?"

She stood at the door of her room, wearing a loose white garment that accented the gold of her skin. Her hair shone like a blackbird's wing in the sun, and light glanced off the high bones of her cheeks. He thought she had never been more beautiful. In spite of her awkward figure he felt the exciting vitality that emanated from her. The air on the *galerie,* fragrant with baking aromas from the kitchen below and vibrating with birdsong, was alive with it.

He wanted nothing more than to stay the night with her, and he was tempted until he remembered that Jane Fielding was entertaining for him and Lizzie at dinner that evening. Lizzie was keeping their social calendar so filled that he wondered sometimes whether she suspected that he had a mistress.

His anger was dissipated by Cléo's nearness, as always. He said more gently, "Nothing has changed, *chère.*"

"Everything has changed!" she insisted, her dark eyes flashing. "It's because I'm big with child, *non?*"

At this expression of her insecurity and what he realized was her boredom with her enforced lack of activity, he felt an overwhelming love for her. "You're still the most beautiful woman in the world, and I love you."

Cléo heard his words, but they were robbed of their gloss by passing through her strong emotions. It was not true, she thought, but she looked into his blue eyes and believed that he thought her beautiful. Then why did he always leave her to sleep at the home of his friends? Did he have another woman?

He opened his arms, smiling. Slowly she came toward him and, without embracing him, put her forehead against his shoulder and inhaled the smell of starch and damp wool and tobacco from his clothing. It felt cool. She was dizzied with the excess of her emotion, and the strength of his arms around her was enormously comforting.

He began rubbing her aching back. "I love you," he

crooned. "This is my true home, and you are my true love. Even when I can't be here, I'm with you. I always want to be with you. Will you remember that, Cléo?" He found her hand and touched the topaz ring on her finger. "This stone tells you of my love, when I'm not here—"

"I want more than a ring from you," she whispered.

"What we want is impossible," he said sadly.

He stayed for an hour, talking to her and petting her, but not trying to make love to her.

Soon after he left, Berthe came upstairs with a tray of food for her and found her sitting forlornly on the edge of her high bed, with her feet on the little step stool beside it. She waved the bake-woman away, uninterested in food, but Berthe ignored her refusal and set the tray on her lap, saying, "He comes late and leaves early now, ahn?"

Cléo gave her a black look, but Berthe went on, "That's the way of it when a woman's *enceinte, non*? *Mais,* ever'thing different this time 'cause his family with him."

Cléo came out of herself, and asked sharply, "His family?"

"You don' know 'bout *michie's* wife, ahn?" Berthe straightened up and Cléo saw that the bake-woman's face was alive with an amused malice. "You don' guess why he bring you here? He tell Maisie to train you in city ways so he can put you in a little house on Rampart Street like those uppity quadroons and keep you for heself."

Cléo's blood froze. She stared at Berthe, not speaking. So that's where Evan was sleeping. With his wife!

It was not the cane harvest that had pulled him back to Bayou Black, leaving her here alone. He had a wife there. Evan was already married. It explained so much that she had not understood. His insistence that she must have their baby in New Orleans. His refusal to take her back to Bayou Black with him. After the baby came, Evan had said, he would buy her her own house on Rampart Street, and she had pictured them living there together with their baby.

Rampart Street! That street of neat little cottages, Berthe and Esther had told her, was where white men kept their quadroon mistresses. White men who made "arrangements." Like buying a hogshead of molasses!

And he had let her dream of marrying him in an Indian ceremony, like the wedding her mother had described, a simple but beautiful exchange of vows. It was that promise that had blinded her to the truth—she had refused to see what was plain before her eyes, because she had not wanted to see. How foolish she had been! Like the mink that swims, trusting, into the trap.

"Maisie say she a British woman with yellow hair. There's a pretty child, with yellow hair." Clearly Berthe was enjoying this.

Cléo picked up the tray with one hand, pushing herself to her feet with the other, and flung it and its dishes straight at Berthe's face.

The slave dodged and screamed, and the crockery made an uncommon racket as it crashed to the floor and broke, scattering food and shards everywhere. Esther, who was in the courtyard washing some of Cléo's clothes, came running up the stair. Berthe's cheek was bleeding where the coffee cup had struck it and spilled hot coffee down her bosom. She continued screaming when she saw blood on the hand she put to her cheek, but Cléo knew she was not seriously hurt.

"You stinking cabbagehead!" she screamed after her, as Berthe ran down the stairs. "You snake-in-the-grass!"

Esther was crying, *"Madame, madame!"* adding to the uproar. Then Maisie came lumbering up the wooden stair, shouting in English. It took her huge strength as well as Esther's gentle voice to calm Cléo and persuade her to let them help her into her bed, where she lay alternately hating Evan and longing for him to return and deny Berthe's scalding words.

She ached all over and there was a terrible pain in her heart. Another woman. All the while, another woman who had borne him a child. Lies. Lies. Cléo tossed on the bed, perspiring and in pain. Esther crooned soothing endearments as she cleaned up the mess, alternating with scathing comments about Berthe, all in a soft loving voice.

Cléo felt a sharp cramp. The pain had moved down her body to where her baby lay, heavy and swollen. Pushing. She lay quiet for a few moments, feeling that something was different, something had changed in her world that only that morning had been happy and secure.

When another knifelike cramp seized her, she sat up and gasped, "Esther!"

The maid came to the bed. *"Madame?"*

Instinct told Cléo what was happening. She grasped Esther's wrist and held tight. Her time was approaching. She wanted Evan, and she didn't know where he was. Except that he was with his wife! He had always said, "When the time comes, Maisie will find me." She resented that. Maisie knew more about where he went from here than she did. She hated him for not being with her now when she needed him.

"The baby, *madame*?" Esther whispered, her eyes wide.

"But yes! Tell Maisie M'sieu' must come, quick."

The old woman climbed the stair again on her overburdened legs and took charge, talking volubly. Cléo understood nothing beyond the soothing tone of her deep rich voice, but she trusted her, because she sensed that Maisie knew what she was doing. Berthe and Esther had followed her up, and she barked orders in English to all of them.

Berthe repeated them to Cléo and Esther. "She say *madame* mus' get up and walk the floor while we fix your bed. Then I go for the doctor. She say don' worry, she send Esther with a message for *Michie*, and he come. She say calm yourself, madame. It won' be soon, and she know what to do."

All the while Berthe was telling Cléo this, Maisie was nodding her head and smiling at her. She knew, Cléo thought. She knows where Evan sleeps.

But another sharp cramp came, and she let her thoughts go to the child who had signaled his coming, a child who would not be born in the swamp as she had been. What would his life be like, with a father who could not give him his name—and who had another family!—and a mother who was called *"une sauvage"*?

A fierce, protective emotion blossomed in her heart.

The message reached Evan as he and Elizabeth were dressing for Jane's dinner party. Elizabeth's mood was scarcely suited to her festive appearance in the new gown of emerald velvet with silver braid trim that she had engaged a popular *modiste* to make for her. She was angry with him because he had rejected outright her suggestion that they buy some abandoned house she had seen out on Bayou St. John and restore it for a winter residence.

"In the first place, Lizzie, I don't want to live out on the bayou. I must be in town. Secondly, if I wanted a showplace I would prefer to build it on Bayou Black. All we need in the city is a *pied-à-terre*!"

"Think of Nanette," she urged. "We must have a place where we can entertain properly in order to find the most eligible husband—"

Evan exploded. "My God! She's not yet four years old! There's time enough to think of a husband for the lass! You will not let me hear any more such talk!" The very notion outraged him.

"Evan, you know yourself that in New Orleans most important marriages are arranged between children. By the time Nanette is sixteen every eligible young gentleman will be contracted to some Creole girl he's known since childhood!"

"I won't hear any more, Lizzie!"

At that moment there was a knock on their door.

"What is it?" Evan snapped.

A footman opened the door. "Beg pardon, *michie*, but it's a strange woman at the servants' door with a message, she say from Maisie."

"Oh, that tiresome woman!" Lizzie exclaimed. "Say she is to tell Maisie the master will come around tomorrow."

"Have her wait!" Evan ordered, in an icy tone that halted the servant. "I'll come down."

"Jane's guests are due in half an hour!"

"Kindly hold your tongue, *madame*! I intend to find out what's happened." He strode angrily after the footman, leaving Elizabeth seething.

A few minutes later the footman returned to tell her

michie had left the house but would return in time for dinner.

Furious, Elizabeth called her maid in to touch up her coiffure which the woman had carelessly disarranged when she was pulling out the puffed sleeves at her shoulders. "This time, do keep an eye on what you're doing!"

Evan had not returned when she heard the sounds of a carriage in the courtyard. She left her chamber to walk down the stairway and joined Jane and Amos in their drawing room. A few moments later the butler announced Monsieur and Madame Archer.

Elizabeth saw a nicely rounded young Creole woman with skin like a magnolia blossom, and a sparkling smile enhanced by laughing black eyes. She was dressed simply but elegantly in deep rose wool. Behind her came a lean man with golden-brown hair. He had a friendly American face, and the eyes, as blue as Evan's, that met Elizabeth's gaze as she was introduced were alight with frank curiosity.

A most attractive man, Elizabeth thought, and an American, a man she could understand. She would find a way to have his house!

Amos ordered sherry and explained that Elizabeth's husband would join them for dinner.

Jane broke the ice by inquiring about Melodie's children, and Elizabeth was soon trading anecdotes about Nanette with the attractive Creole mother. Tactfully she inquired about the education planned for the Archer children.

"When they are old enough to leave home," Melodie said, "the girls will go to the Ursuline nuns, as I did. Alex"—she hesitated—"I would like Alex to go to Paris, as most of his friends will. But Jeff would be happy if

Alex decided to go to Harvard to get a law degree so he can join his father in the firm." She chuckled. "Alex is a little young to make the decision, so at present, we've agreed not to discuss it."

Time passed and Evan did not return. When Elizabeth exclaimed that he was being inconsiderate to his hosts, Jeff Archer said, "I trust you are not concerned for your husband's safety, *madame*. If you are, Amos and I will go looking for him."

"No," Elizabeth said. "He has gone because his old nurse, whom he freed when we came to Louisiana, sent for him. It's probably nothing. She has a little bakery, and is always having some crisis in her business affairs. Very tiresome."

"But it's admirable of him to show his concern for her," Melodie Archer said with a warm smile. "Please don't imagine that we are offended."

They had another sherry, but still Evan did not come. Finally Jane's butler appeared in the doorway. "Beg pardon, *madame,* but cook says dinner will be ruined if it's not served."

"Very well." Jane took Jeff Archer's left arm and asked him to offer his right to Elizabeth, Amos offered an arm to Melodie, and Jane led her guests into her dining room.

Elizabeth found herself facing Melodie across the table and as the meal was served could not resist telling her how she and Jane had come upon Sorcellerie during an early-morning ride. "It looked so beautiful, rising from the bayou mists."

A shadow crossed Melodie's face. "It was once very beautiful."

"I've been wondering ever since then why it has never been restored."

Melodie was silent.

"It is too fine a house to let fall into decay—"

"My wife does not wish to discuss Sorcellerie," Jeff Archer interrupted quietly.

Elizabeth was surprised, but she smiled at him. "I'm sorry. Apparently this is not the right time to speak of it, but I had thought perhaps you could be persuaded to sell or lease it."

"No!" Melodie's easy warmth had vanished. "I do not wish the house restored," she said, softly but firmly. "Nor do I wish it occupied."

Elizabeth turned a puzzled look on Jeff, looking for support from him, but he changed the subject to her husband's failure to appear, and she was obliged to think quickly how to avoid the possibility that the Archers might consider her persistence an affront.

Jane's guests departed early to drive back to Belle-mont, and so left without meeting Evan. Lizzie was so furious that her hands trembled and her voice shook when she bade her hostess good night and climbed the stairway. She was convinced that he had stayed away because of their quarrel about the old mansion, and his distress at her talk of a marriage for Nanette.

She went into the adjoining nursery and leaned above a sleeping Nanette in her gauze-draped crib. Such a beautiful child! She must have the best. It was not too soon to begin thinking of her future.

"I could tear his hair out!" she muttered, going into the adjoining room she and Evan shared. Her maid had helped her out of her emerald velvet and into her night-robe when Jane tapped at her door.

"Are you concerned about Evan?" she asked when Jane invited her in. "Amos says he will go out with a couple of the servants if you wish him to make inquiries."

"Thank you, dear Jane, but I don't think it will be necessary." She dismissed the maid, and when they were alone continued, "I don't think Evan wanted to meet the Archers. Perhaps I'm misjudging him, but I feel as if I'm being punished for suggesting that we think about Nanette's marriage prospects."

Jane said wryly, "I think it's not unlikely, my dear. Evan is a doting father, and Nanette is very young."

Elizabeth sighed. "One must look ahead. But perhaps it is foolish of me to think of buying a deteriorating old house. It does look uninhabitable."

"Amos says it's built of cypress, which never decays. But he doesn't think Jeff will sell it as long as Melodie feels so strongly about someone living in it."

"How long has it been vacant?"

"Ever since the tragedy. It's a shame too. It must have been quite a lovely house at one time."

Elizabeth's interest was pricked. "Tragedy?"

"Have I never told you about that? There was a shooting. I'm not sure just what happened, because my Creole acquaintances don't gossip when an American is present. They're very clannish, you know."

Elizabeth's curiosity was fully aroused now. "But what happened? Do sit down for a moment and tell me! I won't fall asleep until Evan returns."

Jane sat on the chaise longue and Elizabeth got into her bed and sat up against her pillows.

"It was quite a scandal at the time," Jane began. "A young man—titled, by the way—was accidentally shot by his mother."

"Melodie's mother?" Elizabeth exclaimed, shocked.

"No, but the the marquise Angèle de l'Église, who

raised Melodie, was a cousin of her mother's. Her own mother died in childbirth. The shooting happened before we came to New Orleans, of course, but there were still all sorts of rumors passing through the servants' grapevine."

"What kind of rumors?"

Jane hesitated. "Well, apparently a story was going round the cafés that Jean-Philippe was not Angèle's son at all, but the marquis's illegitimate son, who was furious at being denied his inheritance. I don't know whether it's true or not, but Angèle de l'Église went into the convent after it happened. They say she tended the nuns' kitchen garden until her death."

"And Melodie inherited," Elizabeth said thoughtfully.

"Exactly." Jane sat with a musing look on her face. "I met an old gentleman once who went to all the public balls of Melodie's first seasons. He said she was the belle of all the balls. He told me that Melodie and Jeff and her cousin, the young marquis, were a threesome, always together, and known in society as the Triad. He said she seemed equally fond of both young men and didn't agree to marry Jeff until after Jean-Philippe was shot."

"It must have been dreadful for her."

"I'm sure it was. People talk so! "Jame paused and lowered her voice. "They even whisper about mixed blood, you know? Not to an American, of course, but the servants talk."

"Oh, Jane!"

"Well, you know, my dear—some of these Creole families—not the Archers, of course! Melodie herself is half American," she reminded Elizabeth. "Her father was a gentleman from Philadelphia. Her mother's people were French aristocrats who fled the revolution, but

I believe Jeff's father came to Louisiana after the war with the British. Jeff was sent to Harvard to study law, and he has a fine practice. Amos says he's highly respected by both the Creoles and the Americans. Of course, marrying a popular Creole heiress helped."

"You said she inherited both plantations?"

"There were two Roget brothers who escaped the Terror. Melodie's grandfather built Bellemont. His brother, whose only daughter was Angèle, *la marquise* de l'Église, built La Sorcellerie. Melodie's mother died when Melodie was born, and after her father was killed fighting the British, her mother's cousin Angèle raised her. It was Angèle's father who is rumored to have had a colored mistress and half-breed children."

"I see."

Jane gave an embarrassed laugh, and got to her feet. "I'm ashamed to have repeated such rare gossip, Elizabeth. I love Melodie and Jeff, and I would defend her if anyone else—Creole or American—repeated the things I've told you. But I thought you should know as much as I do. Which is very little."

Elizabeth said, "Thank you, Jane. I'm so annoyed with Evan for missing such an enjoyable evening. He could as easily have responded to Maisie's request tomorrow." She fell into a brown study, from which she emerged shortly to ask, "How old is the Archer boy?"

"Five, I believe." Jane's pale eyebrows arched above her amused eyes. "Just the right age for Nanette."

Elizabeth laughed. "We shall have to see that they meet," she declared with pretended lightness. "Can we call on Melodie with Nanette some morning, do you think?"

"An excellent idea." Jane rose. "And now, dear Lizzie, I'm going to bed."

Soon all the candles in the garden district house were extinguished except for the candelabra left burning for Evan in the entry. But Elizabeth lay awake with thoughts blacker than the night beyond her shutters, remembering all the times this winter Evan had pleaded business, prevented a social engagement she wished to accept, and urged her to go with Jane and Amos.

All at once there were a host of memories plaguing her mind and forestalling sleep, all wanting to be taken out and examined closely—a glimpse of a turbaned coffee-colored woman coming out of a *modiste's* shop with a darker woman following her carrying her purchases, another passing by in a carriage, a gleaming jewel in her *tignon*; a sudden silence in a conversation, a look exchanged between two women—or two men—or a lifted eyebrow, all silent comments on the canker that ate at the heart of Creole society, acknowledged by all but spoken of by none.

Evan too?

Her milling thoughts coalesced into a fierce denial. Not Evan!

It had been dusk when Evan rode up the street to the bakery on the horse he had borrowed from Amos's stable. The lamplighter was running down the street with his torch and a flickering yellow light burned in the lamp on the post at the intersection. Evan's heart gave a thump when he saw the doctor's carriage and team in the passage to Maisie's courtyard. He dismounted and led his horse past the carriage and tied his reins to a post supporting the stairway.

Light streamed out of Cléo's room onto the *galerie* above him, but it was quiet . . . too quiet. One of the doctor's horses neighed nervously, making Evan start. He ran up the stairs.

Cléo was sitting up in her bed only partially screened by the mosquito barre, her face wet, her eyes wild, her hands gripping Maisie's on one side and Berthe's on the other. A shawl was wrapped around her shoulders. Esther leaned over her, momentarily hiding her face from him as she wiped perspiration from it. The room was quite cool, and the doctor, at the foot of the bed, was shrugging back into his caped greatcoat.

"Ah, M'sieu' Crowley!"

"I'm glad to see you, doctor." Evan motioned Coco's servant away from the bed and parted the mosquito netting. He bent and kissed Cléo's damp forehead and stroked her hair back from it. "I came as soon as I got your message, *chère,*" he murmured.

She nodded, but did not smile. When she tensed with obvious pain, her eyes went blank as if she were no longer seeing him, and he was gripped by a sudden fear of losing her.

"Cléo?" He turned to the doctor. "Is she all right?"

"I see no problems, *m'sieu'.* She is just going about her work." The doctor added cheerfully, "She can go about it better without us, I think. The baby will not arrive before midnight. Come, you can give me a game of *écarté* while her women help her."

"Yes, go," Maisie said in English. "Ever'thin' be fine now you here."

Feeling somewhat dazed, Evan found himself engaged in a game of cards with the doctor by the light of an oil lamp on the table on the *galerie* outside Cléo's door. In spite of the cool weather, a cloud of small gnats hovered about the light. In the room behind them the silent struggle went on. Below them the patient horses champed occasionally at their bits, or moved, jostling the carriage tongue, and the doctor's groom spoke quietly to them.

At intervals the doctor excused himself to go in to Cléo, or Evan put down his cards and went in to press her hand. Toward midnight Cléo screamed. The doctor rose immediately and went to her. Evan stood, too, but the doctor closed the shutters between them, saying, "We do not need you now, *m'sieu'.*"

Evan clenched his fists and paced up and down the *galerie.* Cléo was still screaming, and he did not know how much he could stand. Nanette had been born in New Orleans while he was preparing a home in the wilderness of Bayou Black, and he wondered if Lizzie had screamed like this. He knew he would never forget the sounds he was hearing now.

The doctor was talking softly, much as a groom talked to a mare foaling. Maisie was crooning encouragement too. Through the sound of their voices he could hear Cléo's gasps. Then one long, piercing shriek assaulted his ears, and set the horses to neighing and thrashing in their harness and the mockingbirds to screeching.

With sweat starting on his face and hands, Evan wrenched open the shutters in time to see the doctor lift his daughter in his hands, turn her over, and spank her gently, and then to hear her mewling cry.

He turned to Cléo and she met his gaze with a glow of triumph illuminating her weary face. He sank to his knees beside her bed, and laid his head on her breast. Cléo's hand touched his hair.

Maisie was washing the baby. She brought the tiny body, swathed in fine blankets, and placed it in Cléo's arms. Still on his knees beside the high bed, Evan examined the small face and touched the tiny fingers.

"She's beautiful," he marveled. "As beautiful as her mother." Silently he observed, *As beautiful as Nanette!*

The doctor was speaking to him. "Now you must leave us for a while, *m'sieu'*, if you please."

He got to his feet. Maisie put the baby in his arms and said, "Take her to your chamber, Master Evan. We has work to do in here."

Evan carried his burden as gingerly as if it were a basket of eggs. In his own chamber he sank carefully into a chair and inspected his daughter, marveling at the fuzz of fine hair on the small head. It was dark gold, its ends drying to the color of pale sunlight on a cypress floor. The tiny features were perfect. She opened her eyes, a dark cloudy blue, and looked at him. Blue eyes, like his own? His heart swelled. But, like Cléo's, in that faintly alien almond shape.

She would be a unique beauty, like her mother. As her eyes closed again, a great tenderness welled in him.

Sometime later Cléo's maid came for him. *"M'sieu' le docteur* is leaving."

The doctor met him on the *galerie*. "She should be fine," he told Evan briskly. "It was a relatively easy birth. Send for me if there is bleeding or fever, but I don't think that will happen." He turned back and said to Cléo, lying drained of her energy and half asleep behind the mosquito barre, "It might be well to see if you can feed her."

Cléo, smiling, reached her arms for her baby, and Evan went in to put the infant in her arms.

"Rest, now, *madame,"* the doctor said behind him. "I will call on you tomorrow."

Evan followed him down to his carriage. "The hour is late, doctor."

"Much of my work occupies me past the midnight hour."

"I thank you for your concern. I wish to pay you generously. Send me your bill."

"My thanks to you, *m'sieu'*," said the doctor with Creole courtesy. "It isn't always that I have a challenging game of *écarté* to help pass the time of waiting."

It was when Evan returned to the room and saw that Cléo had opened her night-robe and offered a breast to the infant that he noticed how very white his daughter, still rosy from the ordeal of birth, looked beside the golden tan of her mother's skin. She would be even more beautiful than her mother!

He stayed until Cléo fell asleep, when Maisie took the baby and sent him away so Cléo could rest. He was not in the least sleepy himself, although it was near morning when he cantered through the dark streets to the garden district and the livery stable that cared for Amos's horses.

He was in a state of euphoria, still riding high with excitement when he entered the Fielding house quietly with his key. He picked up the candelabra left for him on the table in the entry and it lit his way to the nursery room adjoining the chamber he shared with Lizzie. In the light of the guttering candles, he bent over his sleeping child, Nanette.

He admired but did not touch her golden curls; he observed the golden lashes lying on her rosy cheeks, the perfect rosebud of a mouth, parted to show white baby teeth. Little Nanette had a sister she would never know, a sister who he knew would rival her beauty. That they would never meet did not strike him as of much import. He was filled with love for both of his children. He had created two perfect human beings. He felt like a god.

He removed his clothes in the dressing alcove, pinched the candles and quietly parted the mosquito barre, and slid into bed beside Lizzie, who was deep in sleep. He stretched his legs, enjoying the rasp of clean linen sheets against his skin. Lizzie's fragrance stole into his senses. He was still not sleepy; he was conscious of an irrational desire to share his momentous news with her.

She stirred in her sleep and turned toward him, her hand brushing the mat of hair on his chest. The pitch of his excitement was so high that he felt the contact through each individual hair.

"Is that you, Evan?" Lizzie murmured, half waking. "Isn't it very late?"

"Ah, Lizzie, Lizzie!" he said, and took her in his arms.

No, she thought, still barely awake but feeling a response to his mood and his touch course through her veins, there could be no other woman.

Chapter Seven

Cléo's child was a source of constant wonder and delight to her. She spent hours just gazing at her, touching her tiny fingers or feet and smoothing the golden fuzz of hair. But her delight in their child did not wipe out the sense of betrayal she felt because Evan was living with another woman who was his legal wife. She had said nothing of it to Evan during those hours of labor when nothing else mattered but the arrival of their child. But Berthe's revelation lay in her mind like a coiled serpent while she recovered her strength. When Evan came back two days after the birth of their child, she struck at him.

"You lied to me!"

He was leaning over her bed, gently touching the baby's face. His head came up and the bemused smile left his face. "What? What's that?"

"You said you loved me, but Berthe told me you have a wife and a child. Is it true?"

His eyes hardened briefly. "Berthe told you that?"

"It's true, isn't it? You lied!"

"Cléo, *chère!*" He leaned over and kissed her forehead. Her senses were filled with fragrances that, mingled, made up his special scent, and his touch on her breast, bared for the baby, was warm and familiar. That she could still respond to it gave her such pain that tears started to her eyes.

"Everything I have told you is true, *chère,*" he said. "I do love you. Too much! You are the most beautiful woman I know, and you have given me the most beautiful girl-child in the world. I would spend all my nights with you if I could. That is true, *chère.*"

"But you didn't tell me the truth!" she said fiercely. "You didn't tell me that you already had a wife, and a child!"

"Because I couldn't change anything."

"You let me speak of an Indian wedding!" she reproached him, angrily brushing the moisture from her eyes. " 'Later,' you said. You were lying then."

"I'll go through any ceremony you want, Cléo," he said. "It won't be legal and it can't make us any more married than we are now, but if you wish it—"

She shook her head, and two tears rolled down her cheeks. She had thought he was a perfect man because he seemed so far superior to her father and other men she had known in the marshes. She had believed that his love was as pure and as self-effacing as her own. Now that belief was shattered.

She remembered how angry she had been because he abandoned her the day they arrived in New Orleans, throwing her on her own resources in a bewildering new environment, and was humiliated because she had not guessed sooner why he had not wanted to be seen with her.

"You knew we could never legally marry," he reminded her, his hand caressing the infant's head and incidentally brushing her exposed breast with tender little strokes. "If I hadn't married before I found you, it still wouldn't be possible. This is the only way we can be together, Cléo, and that hurts me as much as it hurts you, *chère.*"

She didn't believe that, but she forgave him because his pleasure in the perfection of their child was so great and so obviously sincere. She forgave him—but there was still an unhealed wound.

He came every day after that to admire Aurélie, as they named her, and to enjoy watching Cléo bathe her and then expose a golden breast and give her a nipple. Aurélie sucked with greedy tranquillity, occasionally slanting an incurious glance at Evan, but clearly absorbed in nothing but taking nourishment. Cléo laughed when Evan tried and failed to distract her.

Evan had brought a beautifully crafted wooden cradle. When Aurélie was asleep in it, Cléo hovered over her, studying the tiny features, seeking evidence that she would have the high cheekbones of her mother and grandmother, seeing her Chinese grandfather in the almond shape of her eyes, which Maisie claimed would not remain blue like Evan's.

"All newborns blue-eyed," Berthe quoted her. "It don' mean much."

Every day Aurélie grew more beautiful. She smiled. She waved her arms when Cléo laughed and teased her. Sleeping, she looked like a little angel. No unhappiness could mar Cléo's pleasure in her daughter in those weeks following the birth of Aurélie.

The golden fuzz rubbed off her little head, and when new hairs began appearing, they were definitely rusty in color. "She's going to be a Titian," Evan said, with delighted awe. "She will be a great beauty, Cléo."

Cléo agreed.

The days passed rapidly, marked only by Aurélie's first smiles, her first genuine laugh, her growing strength to raise her head to peer at her surroundings, her ability to sit up against a pillow and to respond to voices. She seldom cried, but she had a will of her own, especially when she wanted to be fed, and young as she was, was developing ways to express it.

The days grew warmer, and Esther carried Aurélie's cradle down the stairs to the flower-fragrant courtyard where Cléo sat beside her in the welcome sunshine, sewing on tiny garments. Cléo's longing for the vast reaches of the marsh, silent but for the high cries of migrating geese or the soft splash of diving water mammals, came less frequently now but when it did, she dreamed of taking her daughter home and introducing her to that beautiful, lonely world that had shaped her.

She would teach Aurélie the ways of the creatures who lived there, how to recognize the home of the muskrat, where to set a trap for the more highly prized mink, and where the best oysters grew. She would show her the beautiful snowy egrets who made their home in the marsh, and the shier wading birds whose feathers were streaked to look like the reeds they hid among. When she rocked Aurélie's cradle she crooned Indian songs her mother had sung to her about the Great Spirit and their brothers, the eagles, and all the other creatures that shared the earth.

Evan ordered Esther to gather up all the gowns Cléo had worn while *enceinte* and carry them away. Then he brought the *modiste* back and selected imported

French silks for new gowns. The first to be made was a pale gold silk.

"Madame's figure has changed," the quadroon *modiste* observed, and Cléo studied her reflection in the looking glass.

She was slender but her body seemed to have acquired subtle curves, and her breasts were full and round. When the new gown was finished, and Esther had pulled her hair up on top of her head with two pins for the last fitting, she thought that Madame Jacques-legrand would not know her. Or M'sieu' Weill, who kept her money in his safe, or the shrimp fishermen who brought him their catch. She hardly recognized herself.

Evan came that afternoon and watched Esther dress her and put up her hair in an elaborate coil. "I have a carriage waiting downstairs to take us for a ride, *chère.*"

Cléo clapped her hands and ordered Esther to wrap Aurélie up against the changeable spring weather, but Evan said, "Leave Aurélie with Esther."

"But I must feed her again in three hours," she protested.

"I promise I will bring you back before she starves," Evan teased her. "This is an outing just for you and me."

Cléo wondered if she could bear to leave her daughter, but Evan said, "She can't go everywhere you go. She must get used to that."

So they left Aurélie in her cradle in the courtyard with Esther sitting beside her. "Already my arms feel empty," Cléo said. But the day was fine and she had been confined to the bakery house too long. She was already enjoying herself when the carriage moved down the brick-paved street.

"Where are we going?"

"To the lake."

With their horses trotting briskly, they passed other carriages drawn by lively pairs with gleaming silken coats, and silver ornaments adorning their bridles. They admired the gardens of the houses along the Bayou St. John. The coachman turned in to a large lakeside house and stopped before its raised entrance. With obvious pride in her, Evan handed Cléo down from the carriage and they went up the stairs and were admitted by a deferential liveried servant.

Inside, Cléo looked around a room more beautiful than anything she had seen before, except perhaps the rotunda of the Hotel St. Charles. There were velvet chairs and chaise longues. The walls were covered with red fabric and looking glasses with gold frames. A curved stairway led to a circular *galerie* with the doors to upper rooms opening from it. An enormous chandelier holding a myriad twinkling candles was suspended from a domed ceiling.

A door opened on their right and she had a glimpse of a large room with men standing around large tables.

"What are they doing?"

"Playing roulette. That's the gaming room. This is a casino."

A well-dressed black man approached and guided them through a door to their left. They walked into a larger salon, also decorated with red damask and mirrors but furnished for dining. A long oval table was set in the middle of the room, as yet not in use, but a scattering of diners sat at small tables against the walls.

As Cléo followed a waiter to their table, feeling lithe and graceful in her new slenderness, she became aware that she was attracting attention; men were turning to look at her. She lifted her head with new confidence. Evan was not the only man who found her attractive.

She said little, but observed everything, especially the women and their gowns and their jewels. One thing was very obvious. Not one of them was white.

"Do you bring your wife here?"

Evan flushed, but said lightly, "Respectable American and Creole ladies do not usually visit casinos."

She absorbed that inwardly, without revealing its sting, but raised her eyebrows. "Then these fine ladies are not respectable?"

"That's part of their charm."

I am learning, Cléo thought. But the learning process was painful.

A distinguished-looking man came in the door and walked around the room, stopping at different tables to greet the diners. When he approached them, Cléo felt a wave of emotion. Although he was much younger, he reminded her of her grandfather, her mother's Chinese father, dead now but beloved in her childhood.

He was nearing their table; his eyes were on her and she felt his sharpened interest as he recognized her Chinese blood. "M'sieu' Crowley," he murmured in French. "Thank you for bringing your lovely young friend—she adorns my establishment."

Evan nodded rather coldly and said, "Mademoiselle Cléo, this is Lee Hing, who is our host," and explained, "He owns the casino."

"Are you enjoying your dinner, *mademoiselle*?"

"The food is very good, M'sieu' Lee," Cléo said, feeling a natural liking for the man.

"Ah, you are familiar with Chinese customs, *mademoiselle.* Most of my French and American guests make the error of calling me M'sieu' Hing!" He laughed, and told Evan, "That, in our culture, is my personal name."

Cléo flushed. "My grandfather was Chinese," she explained. "He was not educated, *m'sieu'*— just a fisherman. But he was a kind man."

"He gave you a fine heritage. This is your first visit to my casino, is it not?"

"Yes." She said shyly, "I think this is the most beautiful room I have ever seen."

Lee Hing bowed. "It doesn't match your beauty, *mademoiselle*. I hope you will come again."

Evan's eyes, across the table, were glowing with pride. "Haven't I told you that you are beautiful?" he murmured after Lee Hing had moved on. "No one here can hold a candle to you!"

Cléo glowed with pleasure. But afterward, on the drive home, he put his arm around her and told her that he would soon be returning to his plantation for the summer.

"So soon?" she cried.

"I must see to my crop."

She bit her lip, holding her wave of rage and grief inside. This time, she reminded herself, she would not be alone. She had little Aurélie for company.

"When do you go?"

"By the next steamboat to Donaldsonville."

"And she goes with you? And *her* child?" The questions burst out of her mouth, in spite of Cléo's resolve.

"Of course. She is my wife." Evan added coldly, "We will not speak of her again, Cléo."

His tone hurt, and her fragile control burst. She lashed back in fury. "I speak when I wish—of anyone I wish! My grandmother was a Houmas princess! She knew four hundred herbs that cure illness! What do *you* know?"

She was sitting erect on the carriage seat, as straight and arrogant as she had stood in her pirogue the first

time he had seen her. Memories of that fateful day
flooded him and his desire flamed.

"Cléo, listen. I will be back on business, frequently. As
often as I can. When I come, I will come alone, and we
will be together again as before. I'm going to buy you a
house of your own, *chère,* where I can be with you."

She continued as if she had heard nothing.

"You think you know everything because you are
American, but you are less than the French and you
know nothing of my people and our ways! You treat us
like you treat your African slaves, but we are more than
half French! My grandmother told me how her people
took the homeless Cajuns in when they were starving,
how they lived together in those early days like brothers, and how some of them married—I am as white as
your wife, and I have the royal blood of my mother's
people!"

"Cléo, Cléo," he said, his voice going as deep and
thrilling as the deepest note of the steamboat whistle.
"Do you know how much I'm going to miss you and
little 'Rélie? I wish I could take you with me, so we
could relive that first night we spent together. I would
like to teach you all over again how to love me. Do you
remember how we lay awake all night long, talking and
making love? It's been so long since I've loved you like
that—"

His hand brushed her cheek and caressed her jaw as it
slid down to lay fingers against her throat. She shivered
under his touch, which was bringing back the wonder of
those first nights in his arms when she learned about her
own body and the pleasures of love. How innocent she
had been! And how tender Evan had been with her!

She raised her gaze to his light-streaked hair—like
the colors of the bittern who hid in the reeds—and his

blue, blue eyes, and put her hand on his chest, letting it find the smooth, lean muscles filling his soft shirt beneath the soft hairs. She felt a tremor of desire, remembering how strong and silken those muscles felt when she lay naked in his arms.

"There are other places besides the casinos where I can take you," he murmured. "You will not stay home all the time now that 'Rélie is born. I want you to be admired. I want my friends to say, 'Your woman is the most beautiful woman in the city.'"

"Like the shrimpers say, 'I brought in the biggest catch'?" she asked wryly.

"Cléo!" he reproached her.

She laughed, and he captured her laughing lips in his kiss, ignoring the tears that lay in her eyes.

As soon as the carriage stopped in the passage beside Maisie's bakery, she heard Aurélie crying, and realized that her breasts were aching with milk. She stepped down and hurried to the cradle. "She is hungry, *madame,*" Esther said softly.

Cléo picked her daughter up and crooned a promise to feed her. Holding Aurélie in her arms satisfied a yearning that had been growing all the way home from the casino. It was joy to hold her and smell her baby fragrance, and feel the surprisingly strong grasp of her tiny hand around one finger.

"Let me carry her upstairs," Evan requested, and she gave 'Rélie into his arms with a little stab of reluctance.

When Evan left her, later that night, she was again holding their daughter. He stood beside her and fondly touched Aurélie's cheek. Cléo kissed him and wished him a good journey, and kept to herself her bitter curiosity about the wife and the child he was taking with him. It was not his fault that the Americans honored the

Black Code that France had imposed on Louisiana, was it, or that her people were unfairly included in its prohibitions?

Evan's last words to her were "Take good care of little 'Rélie for me."

Aurélie was waking up every three hours and crying to be fed. Cléo was always sleepy, but she had little to do but bathe and feed the baby. It was a sultry afternoon three days after Evan took her to the casino that she left Aurélie in her cradle in the courtyard with Esther watching her, and went upstairs to take a nap.

Going up the stair she could hear Maisie and Berthe in the kitchen, talking in English. Through the gate to the courtyard she heard the usual sounds of carriages, and men on horseback, passing on the street. The heat made her feel languid and very drowsy. Below her, Esther was humming a lullaby and pushing the gauze-draped cradle to and fro with her bare toes.

Cléo dropped off to sleep as soon as she slipped under the mosquito barre and it seemed only minutes later that she was awakened by Esther's screams. A mocking-bird screeched and a carriage started up on the street with a brisk clop-clopping of the horses, but Esther's screams did not stop—she was running and screaming as she ran.

Cléo leapt out of bed, her first thought of Aurélie. Something was wrong; something dreadful was happening. She ran out on the *galerie*, saw with a lurch of her heart that Aurélie's cradle was empty, and caught a glimpse of Esther running through the open passage to the street. Terrified, Cléo ran down the stairs and after her.

Aurélie! My baby!

Berthe and Maisie came out of the kitchen, clucking like two hens. "What is it?" Berthe cried. "What's happened?"

Cléo ran by them without stopping. When she reached the *banquette*, Esther was far ahead of her, running like a deer after a carriage that was half a block ahead of her and being carried rapidly away by its trotting horses.

With pounding heart, Cléo ran after her.

Horses clip-clopped behind her and a groom shouted at her to make way. Carriages moved between her and Esther but she swerved and ran on, keeping her eyes on her maid. She was gaining on Esther, but the carriage Esther followed was pulling away. Somehow Cléo knew, without understanding what had happened, that Aurélie was in that fast-disappearing carriage. She must catch it! Nothing else, no one in her way, mattered, only her baby.

Far down the street, at the second intersection, the carriage stopped. Cléo strained to see around the other vehicles and the pedestrians between them. She had a glimpse of a veiled woman in black who stepped down from the carriage, carrying a bundle.

Aurélie? Ah, *dieu, dieu,* give me strength to catch her!

The carriage started up. The woman was on the *banquette*. Just then a pair of horses pulled a carriage out of a courtyard a half block away, hiding the woman from Cléo's view. Clutching her side, gasping for breath, Cléo ran desperately on.

She caught up with Esther, who was heaving like a winded horse. "Where?" she gasped. *"Where?* I must catch her. *Mon dieu,* I cannot believe this! She has *my baby*!"

"Ah, but, *madame*—she disappear!" Tears were

streaming down her maid's ebony face. "She go roun' the corner—or maybe in a door—I couldn't see!" They were still running, and Esther's breath was coming in sobbing gasps. *"Madame*, I left the cradle—only one minute! To get a crust of bread—from the kitchen. When I come out, the cradle—she is empty. Then I see the woman —an' she is climb into a carriage—"

The image of the empty cradle was like a gaping wound; Cléo felt as if Aurélie had been torn out of her flesh. "I will—find her," she gasped, her chest heaving, "and I will—tear her eyes out!" They raced on to the intersection. There they paused and looked both ways on the crossing street. They could see no veiled woman.

But at least the woman in black was now on foot. Cléo drew great gulps of air into her hurting lungs. *Ah,* mon dieu, *let me find her!*

In her terrible urgency Cléo began asking people passing on the street breathless questions. "Did you see a woman in black? Get out of a carriage? Carrying a baby?"

The passersby looked at her blankly. She sent Esther across the street to inquire of people passing there or coming out of the shops near the intersection. One man said he had seen her, but he did not notice where she went.

She could not lose Aurélie . . . sweet Aurélie! Growing bolder as she grew more frantic, Cléo began going into the shops, and knocking on doors, asking urgent questions. "Did a woman come in here? Carrying an infant? A woman dressed in black? A baby in her arms?"

No one had seen such a woman. She had alighted from the carriage and disappeared. Cléo was exhausted from running, but desperation drove her on. When she was near collapse, a woman leaned over a balcony and called down, "What have you lost?"

Cléo gasped out her question. "Did you see a woman in black—carrying a baby—get out of a carriage?"

"Ah, that one. Yes, I thought it was strange."

Cléo's breath choked. "Why? Where—?"

"She got out of a carriage here, walked around the corner, and hailed another."

"Which way?" Cléo cried urgently, hope leaping up and giving her strength.

"That way." The woman on the balcony pointed in the direction of the levee.

Cléo swayed, her fear was so great. The levee road led out of the city, whether up or down the river. Or to a steamboat landing. Or the carriage could have turned to the right or the left at one of several intersections before it reached the levee road. She must hurry to catch it! *Sweet Mary, Mother of Jesus, help me find my baby!* Dieu, I can't bear this! she thought as she and Esther ran on. At each intersection she asked bystanders about a carriage with a veiled woman in black as passenger. Did it go straight or did it turn? They looked at her as if she were a woman demented. *Help me!* She cried out to the unfeeling sky. *Someone help me find my Aurélie!*

They came at last to the levee. The river was crowded with sailing vessels at anchor or tied up. A steamboat was moving downriver, toward the Gulf. A Gulf steamboat, a man told them, bound for Texas ports. *Aurélie! How can I go on living if I don't find you?* Up and down the levee they ran, asking their questions at various landings.

A woman in black. Veiled. Carrying an infant.

No one had seen her. The trail was getting cold. Too

much time had been lost. Distraught, they retraced their steps and began knocking at doors on the route. Cléo was shaking so that she could no longer speak. Nor could she think, except to tell herself over and over, *I can't let this happen. I can't lose Aurélie. How can I go on living without her?* She stood trembling beside Esther as the maid asked the servants who answered the door, "Please, is there a new baby in this house?"

When Cléo was too exhausted to go on, she leaned against a lamppost and said, "Esther, we must think where to go now." If only Evan were here, he would know what to do.

"Oui, madame."

"Who would steal my baby?" A suckling babe! Aurélie would be hungry for the mother's milk that was painfully swelling her breasts. Who would feed her?

She needed Evan. But he was already too far away to help. Or was he? He had said, "by the next steamboat." Was there a chance there had not yet been a steamboat to Donaldsonville?

She drew in great lungfuls of air, then said, "Esther, you took a message when I delivered Aurélie. You must take me to that house."

Esther looked alarmed. "Berthe say I mus' never—"

"We must get word to M'sieu' Crowley. He will know what to do, if he is not already too far away to help." Cléo had forgotten everything but her terrible need to find her child. She was willing to do anything, go to any length, if it would bring Aurélie back to her breast. "Esther, who else can help me? Aurélie is so little. She needs me."

"Ah, *madame,* the poor babe!" Weeping, Esther led the way.

By the time they reached the garden district, walking

because neither of them had brought a coin for a carriage, Cléo was near collapse. Esther insisted that Cléo stay concealed behind a small myrtle tree while she went to the servants' door at the rear of the Fielding house.

A young black footman opened the door. "So, it's you again," he said in a friendly way. "Is Maisie in trouble again?"

"Yes, please. Will you tell *Michie* Crowley it's urgent?"

"You can tell Maisie that *Michie* Crowley took his family an' lef' for his plantation two days ago." He was grinning. "Maisie'll have to wait a long time to keep him all night again."

"Is there a new baby in this house?" Esther asked him.

His mouth fell open. "You crazy? They's no chil' a-tall in this house. This a chil'less house 'cept when *Michie* Crowley visit with his family."

"He was telling the truth," Esther said when she reported the conversation to Cléo. "Little 'Rélie's not in that house."

"I never thought she was here," Cléo said. Evan would not have told his wife about her baby.

How could she get word to him? He had left New Orleans the day after they said good-bye. What was she going to do? How was she going to find Aurélie without his help?

And how could she ever tell Evan she had failed to keep their baby safe?

Chapter Eight

Cléo could not sleep. The empty cradle stood beside her bed, a yawning reproach. Her breasts ached with the milk she could not give her baby and it was like a knife in her heart when she pictured Aurélie in some strange woman's arms, crying to be fed. How could such a thing happen? Who would wish an innocent babe harm? No one, no one!

"Aurélie, Aurélie!" she sobbed.

Through her misery ran the baffling questions, repeating themselves over and over: Who would do such a thing? And why? She could not think, she was crying too hard.

She had told Maisie that Evan must be told. He must come.

"Tomorrow," Maisie had promised. "Tomorrow we find someone to write a letter for us."

Evan would come. But a letter would take forever to reach him. And when he came, how could she explain what had happened? *Ah,* mon dieu, *how could you let this happen? I can't bear it.*

Toward morning her shocked mind was able to begin seeking realistic answers. Who knew of Aurélie's existence? There were few people in Aurélie's young life. Cléo could count them on her fingers: she and Evan, the doctor, Maisie and the servants, the *modiste,* a few of Maisie's customers.

In her seven weeks of life, Aurélie had never been taken out of Maisie's house or its courtyard. She had never been out of Cléo's or Esther's sight except for those few minutes when she was stolen.

Aurélie was such a beautiful baby! Cléo could easily imagine someone falling in love with her and impulsively picking her up. But the second carriage waiting around the corner for the woman in black meant the crime had been carefully planned. Was it possible that someone would pay money for a baby?

She had trusted the doctor. Was her trust misplaced?

Suddenly feeling nauseated, she rolled over, clutching herself. *Aurélie!* If only Evan were here! He would know what to do, where to look. She must let him know! But how could she tell him that she had failed to keep Aurélie safe? His last words to her had been "Take good care of Aurélie for me." He would despise her. But she must get word to him.

She got up and went out on the *galerie.* Dawn was breaking; the crescent moon was fading in the gray sky, from which the stars had already disappeared. Mists from the river hung over the city, muffling the hoofbeats of a single trotting horse somewhere in the fading dark. In her night-robe Cléo knocked on the door of Maisie's room.

"It's Cléo."

"Poor chile! You can't sleep? I'll give you some laudanum."

Cléo heard the rustle of her mattress as the big woman left her bed and the stump of her bare feet across the floor before she unbarred the shutters. The room behind her was still in shadow, but Maisie's face shone with warm sympathy. She took Cléo in her arms, patting her back as if she were a child, and murmuring English words whose warm sympathy Cléo understood.

"It's morning, Maisie. You must send a message to *M'sieu'* for me," Cléo said in a flood of French. "He must be told that Aurélie has been stolen. He will come and help me find her."

But how long would it take?

She did not know whether the old woman understood or not. Maisie nodded, still patting Cléo and murmuring comfort in her own language, but she led Cléo back to her own room and urged her into bed. Then she went out on the *galerie* and called sharply down to Berthe and Esther to waken to a new day.

They wanted Cléo to eat something, but she could not. She dressed in a simple morning gown and, as soon as it was light, took Esther with her and went to Jackson Square, where the carriages for hire often waited for patrons. She and the maid went from hack to hack, as the drivers arrived at their stations, asking if they had been hired the day before by a woman in black carrying a baby.

None had.

When they had finished there, they inquired at the livery stables. But they could not find a driver who admitted carrying such passengers.

"His lips are sealed with money," Esther suggested. "Perhaps *Madame* should go to the police."

"Not the police!" Cléo exclaimed.

The only encounter she had had with the law was with the officer who had shoved her out of the rotunda of the Hotel St. Charles on her first day in New Orleans, and the humiliating experience had convinced her that the police would not listen to her story.

"They could make those drivers talk," Esther argued. "An' they maybe send a message to *Michie* for you. The police help you fin' her."

But Cléo was trembling with exhaustion, and Esther took her back to the bakery. The fragrance of fresh-baked bread drew them into the kitchen, and Esther persuaded Cléo to sit at Maisie's worktable and brought her coffee and a warm crust of fresh bread spread with butter and gingered pear preserves.

Berthe was kneading a batch of dough. "Maisie asks did you find the coachman?"

"No," Cléo said despairingly. "Ask her how long it will take the letter to reach le Terrebonne."

The two women spoke in English, then Berthe said, "First she must find someone who can write a message, then it have to be carried on the steamboat to Donaldsonville. From there"—Berthe shrugged—"she don' know how long it take, or how long before *M'sieu'* can return."

"It's a two-day journey," Cléo said. "He will come at once."

"More likely a week or two," Berthe said.

Cléo touched her painfully swollen breasts and noted, "Aurélie will be hungry."

When Berthe reported that to Maisie, Evan's old nurse began talking volubly and making cupping gestures at one massive breast.

"She say someone feed her," Berthe said. "Whoever

take the baby will have a wet nurse, Maisie say. She say
she bind your breasts so the milk won't give you pain."

"No!" Cléo said sharply. "I must have milk for Aurélie
when we find her. Tell her I want her to send for the
doctor."

"Why you want *Michie le Docteur?*" Berthe asked
suspiciously.

"Because I don't know where to go next. I must ask
his help because I can't wait for *M'sieu'* to return," Cléo
said wearily. "I will ask the doctor to go with me to the
police, so they will believe me."

Berthe said in English, "She is going to the police. She
wants the doctor to take her to the police."

Cléo understood two words, *doctor* and *police,* and
she understood Maisie's sharp tone and shake of her
head. Evan's old nurse was saying *No!* It was the wrong
thing to do, she was apparently saying, Master Evan
would not like it.

"Tell her it is what *M'sieu'* would do, if he were here,"
Cléo told Berthe sharply. "We can't wait for him. We
must find Aurélie now, today!"

"Non!" Maisie shouted, trying to express herself in
French, and succeeding only in confusing Cléo. "Police
not need to know!"

When she realized what Maisie was saying and saw
how upset she was, Cléo felt a sickening suspicion.
Someone must have signaled the woman in black that
Aurélie was unattended. Who outside the house would
know that Esther had left the cradle?

"You know something about this, don't you, Maisie?"
she said, her voice breaking. She saw the expression
that crossed the bake-woman's face, and accused her
angrily, "And you, Berthe!"

She had always known Berthe resented her presence

in the house because of the extra work, perhaps, but she had trusted Maisie. Now she had a growing conviction that the old Negress knew something about that mysterious woman in black that she was not telling. She had given herself away by her fear of the police, and by her insistence that Aurélie would be fed.

Cléo felt betrayed, outraged by this criminal act that was so terrible, she could not face its consequences. "You had something to do with this, didn't you?"

Maisie looked at her in blank apprehension, but Berthe turned sulky.

"Both of you!" Cléo cried. "Did you do this for money, you bitches?" Her whole body flushed with rage.

"No, no, we wouldn't harm your baby. No one would hurt Aurélie!"

Cléo understood nothing of what Maisie was trying to say except "No," and she didn't believe her protests. She walked around the table toward the older woman, her hands clenched into fists. "Where is Aurélie?" she demanded.

Maisie backed away from her, her eyes distended, protesting, "No, no! Not harm baby."

"Tell me where she is! If you don't tell me, I will kill you both!" Cléo said, in a fury.

"She doesn't know!" Berthe shouted, in French.

"She knows! *You* know." Cléo thrust her face close to Berthe's. The bake-woman backed around the table, and Cléo followed her, her head thrust forward, her hands balled into fists. "Where's my baby? What have you done with her? Tell me, or I'll split your cabbagehead!"

Berthe grabbed a butcher's knife from the table and raised it.

Esther screamed.

"Berthe! Put the knife down!" Maisie ordered.

They paid no attention to her. A quick pluck at her skirts, and Cléo's hand came up with her slender skinning knife in it.

"*Voilà!*" Berthe said under her breath.

Esther shrank against the wall, whimpering, as Cléo and Berthe circled the table silently, knives raised, their eyes wary, but Maisie jerked forward, her big arms reaching for Berthe.

She was too late. The bake-woman lunged toward Cléo, who dodged, backing through the door into the shop. A woman customer waiting there for Maisie screamed and fled into the street.

"Police! Police!" she shrieked. "They're fighting with knives!"

A crowd quickly gathered, taking up her cry for the police and blocking the entrance to the bakery. They screamed as Berthe's knife came down. Cléo ducked and slashed open Berthe's skirts, exposing her legs. The crowd screamed again, in delighted fear. Cléo's sleeve was ripped and her arm bleeding, grazed by the tip of Berthe's formidable weapon.

The crowd parted and she edged through the open door into the street, dropping her arm and concealing her knife in the folds of her skirt. A man grabbed at her, but everyone fell back as Berthe charged out of the shop, her big butcher's blade flashing in the sun.

A police officer, arriving on the run, grasped Berthe's arm, and immediately two men jumped forward to help him subdue her. Cléo slipped through the momentarily diverted spectators who were blocking the passage of a fine carriage-and-pair passing the bakery.

The carriage door opened, and a man who looked

vaguely familiar beckoned Cléo. "Quickly!" he said, extending a hand.

She stared into the shadowy interior of the carriage. It was M'sieu' Lee Hing, the Chinese casino owner. His face was calm and kind like her grandfather's.

"Do you want to be arrested for disturbing the peace by fighting in the street?" he asked her. "Or for assault with a deadly weapon? Come!"

With a sob of relief Cléo gave him her left hand and let him pull her up into the carriage. Closing the door hastily, he motioned her to crouch on the floor. With his walking stick he rapped sharply on the ceiling, and the coachman whipped his horses, forcing them into the crowd of spectators blocking the way.

Men shouted imprecations at him, but let the horses through. Cléo could not see what was happening but she heard Berthe's shrill curses as the officer and his helpers overcame her.

Cléo looked up at her rescuer. "Where are you taking me, *m'sieu*?"

"Where the police will not find you."

"I must find my baby," she said weakly.

"Baby?"

In a few halting sentences, she told him what had happened the day before. "Now I can't ask the police to help me find her," she said in despair, "or they will arrest me."

"Leave that to me," he said.

She was shaking, and he asked, "Are you feverish?" and reached out to touch her forehead. His fingers felt dry and cool. Then he exclaimed, "You're hurt!"

She lifted her hand and stared at the blood running down over it from under her ripped sleeve. "I'd have cut more than her skirt but for this!" she muttered.

The wound was in the hand holding her knife and Lee Hing reached for it. Instantly she flipped the blade toward him.

"Give it to me," he said calmly.

"You'll not take my knife without a fight, *m'sieu'*! It's been my protector since I was thirteen." The hand that held it trembled violently, but the pain in her arm was nothing like the pain in her heart.

"I am your protector now," he said, and gently took the weapon from her.

Chapter Nine

Faces appeared in the darkness above her bed, then faded away. At times she thought she heard voices whispering over her supine body in a darkened room—her mother's quiet voice, her grandfather's deep tones—and she strained but could not see them.

At other times she tossed restlessly, hearing many persons, but at a distance, laughing and talking all at the same time in a distressing gabble of noise. Once she thought she heard angry shouts and the sharp thuds of a horse's hooves as it galloped away.

Then she opened her eyes and looked around an unfamiliar room, opulently furnished. Many objects in the room were strange to her, and she felt confused. But one had a wrenching familiarity. She was looking at a tall blue-and-white jar with a design very like a small soup bowl that her grandfather told her he had brought with him from China and that as a child she had desired passionately.

"Madame!" It was a voice she recognized—Esther's

voice, ringing with joy. The little maid came to the bed, lifted the gauze, and laid a soft dark hand on her forehead. "You wake!"

"It was you," Cléo murmured. "I thought you—were my mother. I thought—I was dead."

"Ah, *madame,* no!"

"Where—?"

"We're at *Michie* Lee's casino. You don' remember coming here?"

"I remember—his carriage," Cléo said weakly. "But not you—"

"He come back for me."

"Aurélie?" She could only whisper the name, as the pain of remembrance seized her.

Esther shook her head. "No. But there's much to tell when you stronger, *madame.* You been ill with the fever."

"She—lives?"

"I'm sure," Esther said, stroking her hair. "*Michie* still looks for her."

Despairing, Cléo slid back into her dark sleep.

She slept and wakened several times before she again saw the man who had rescued her from the police. When Esther admitted him to her room, Cléo looked at him with cleared vision and saw a man younger than she remembered. She had associated him in her mind with her grandfather because of the racial features they shared, but he was a man in his prime with a smooth skin of pale olive, dark hair, and sleepy eyes. She sensed a quiet power in the way he carried himself. He would be a dangerous enemy, but perhaps a powerful friend.

"How are you feeling?" He was speaking French, and his voice had a deep, mellow tone.

"Weak as a baby raccoon," she murmured, "but strong enough to thank you, *m'sieu'*, for what you did."

He smiled. "You are too young and lovely to fall into the hands of the police."

"How long have I been ill?"

"Nearly two weeks. Your wound became infected and you were feverish. According to my physician, you were suffering from exhaustion and the grief of losing your baby."

"I told you—?" Memories were coming back in painful stabs.

"You told me many things in your fever, *madame*, and I promised to help you. I'm making inquiries, and perhaps I'll have something to tell you soon."

"You are a kind man, *m'sieu'*," Cléo said. "I don't want to be a burden. Esther and I will leave as soon as I'm fit."

Fit and able to take a steamboat and return to le Terrebonne. She must see Evan, and tell him how this had happened. The fingers of her right hand felt for the topaz ring on her left middle finger, and his voice spoke in her memory. *This ring will remind you of how much I love you.*

"That would be unwise, I think," M'sieu' Lee said. "The police are looking for you on charges of assault and disturbing the peace brought by the bakery owner—"

"Maisie? Do the police know what she did to me?" Cléo demanded weakly.

"—and Esther is listed as a fugitive slave, by her owner, Evan Crowley."

"By her—owner?" The perspiration of weakness was breaking out on her body. Cléo knew that her start on hearing his name told M'sieu' Lee everything, if he had not already known that Evan was the father of her child. "He knows, then?"

"He knows at least that you and your maid have disappeared. The police can be rough on a runaway slave, so I have thought it best to keep your whereabouts secret for the time being."

"But—but has M'sieu' Crowley been told that my baby was stolen?" she persisted.

Lee Hing was silent for a moment, regarding her with what she thought was a strange expression. "He knows," he said at length. "I sent one of my employees to Bayou Black. He has not yet returned."

A warm flush of gratitude coursed through her veins. "You are truly kind, *m'sieu'*!"

Evan would come, she thought, closing her eyes. He would come and take her away from here and they would find Aurélie. . . . She slept again.

Each day she was able to take a little more food, and each day she was stronger. From Esther, Cléo learned that during the week, Cléo and her maid and the other servants and some rather burly men Esther called "the guards" were the only occupants of the mansion on the Bayou St. John near its junction with the lake.

"This casino open only on weekends," her maid said. "*Michie* own a bigger casino in the city, an' it stay open twenty-four hours. He and his body servant stay in the city all week, his men say."

As Cléo began feeling stronger, Esther took her down to the garden that stretched from the bayou in the front to the beginning of the swamp behind the big house. There a cypress grove grew in stagnant water, great trees whose foliage provided perpetual shade and whose roots, pushing their knees up through the shallow water, were convenient perches for water snakes and turtles and the large birds that fed on the insects and tiny marine creatures living in the swamp.

It was not her marshy Isle, but it was still and lonely and home to familiar wild creatures, and she felt more at ease in M'sieu' Lee's mansion because of its nearness. Looking at the size of Lee Hing's house from the edge of the swamp, she thought it was as impressive as the great houses she had admired from the Mississippi steamboat. "I never thought I would be staying in so grand a place," she told Esther.

"You should have a house like this of your own, *madame*," her maid said.

Working as gardeners a few paces away were the guards, two large, silent men who followed them at a discreet distance whenever they went out of the house, supposedly to prevent them from being surprised by someone who might report their whereabouts to the police. If the sound of a carriage or horseman came to their ears, they hurried Cléo and Esther into the house and up by a back stair to Cléo's rooms.

She had not seen M'sieu' Lee for several days when he unexpectedly appeared at the mansion in midday in the middle of the week. Esther reported the arrival of his carriage, and a few minutes later a servant came to summon her to his office, next to the gaming rooms downstairs.

Cléo went down the grand staircase and knocked on his door. The lower floor was silent, both the gaming and dining rooms closed.

"Enter," she heard, and went in to find M'sieu' Lee seated at a huge polished desk.

"Sit down, *madame*," Lee Hing said, in French, indicating a chair facing him. "Are you feeling stronger?"

"*Oui, m'sieu'.*"

"You look much better. You walk like a queen."

Instinctively Cléo lifted her chin. "My grandmother was a princess."

"Of what race?"

"Of the Houmas tribe. We are the swamp peoples. The Cajuns call us *'les sauvages'* but my grandmother was of French blood too. My grandfather was a Chinese fisherman who left a sailing vessel and came to the swamp to fish for shrimp and oysters."

"That explains why I was so strongly drawn to you," Lee Hing exclaimed. "That and your beauty, *madame,* which is like a flower too lovely to be picked."

She flushed at the extravagant compliment, but it was spoken in the tone of one admiring the beautiful Chinese jar in her bedroom.

"Who were your parents?"

"My mother was the fisherman's daughter. My father was French and Portuguese. A former Baratarian."

"Ah! With Lafitte?"

"Oui, m'sieu'."

"You combine the best of many races, *madame.* That's why your beauty is as moving as the lotus blossom beloved by our people."

She looked into his eyes, shaped like her grandfather's and reflecting the same inner strength. What she saw in them made her heart skip a beat. "You have news for me, *m'sieu'?*"

"Yes. I have not found where your baby was taken, but I believe I know who is responsible."

Cléo drew in a gulp of air, but when her voice came out it was only a breath. "Maisie?" she said. "And Berthe?"

"They didn't plan the abduction. I don't believe they know where your child is. I have had Maisie watched and followed. The woman in black has not been seen in the neighborhood except that once. Maisie has had no contact with her or whoever has your child now. But I think she knows who planned the crime. It was planned by the father of your child."

Cléo stared at him. *Evan?*

"That's impossible, *m'sieu*!" she said, in instant, violent denial. "You're mistaken."

He didn't contradict her. He sat silent, regarding her with compassionate eyes.

A chill entered her heart, slowly congealing her blood. She had a sharp, anguished memory of Evan's arms holding her in the embrace of love's ecstasy, a stabbing recall of the taste and smell of him and of the magic touch of his hands. . . .

"No!" she cried. *"M'sieu',* she is his child, the child of his love! He adores her! Why would *he*—?"

"I don't know why, and I haven't found out yet where she is, but I believe he arranged for her to be taken." There was regret in his eyes and in his voice.

"No, no," she insisted. "It's impossible!"

"It was Esther who led me to suspect—"

She was shaken. *"Esther* believes this?"

"She was alone in the bakery when I went there to see the women you had been living with, and to find out what I could about your differences with them. The bake-woman was in jail and her owner had gone to try to free her, and left Esther in charge. The owner had talked carelessly to her servant in front of her after you disappeared, thinking Esther would not understand their English, and she told me what she suspected. Fortunately, I was able to persuade her that you needed her. She came and brought your personal belongings. She has nursed you back to health."

"Esther accuses M'sieu' Crowley of stealing his own daughter?" Cléo cried. "Why would he do that? He had left New Orleans—we went to his house—"

"Why?" Lee Hing asked quietly.

"To see if perhaps he had not yet left—to tell him—to get his help—" Her voice choked up. If Aurélie had been there, the servant would have known. Esther had been certain that he was not lying. No! Evan was not— *could* not be responsible for that crime.

She sat very erect in the chair facing Lee Hing. "I must go back to Terrebonne parish immediately!" she said, with her mother's royal arrogance. It was imperative now. She had to see Evan.

Lee Hing was watching her face as if he could see her thoughts parade across it. "Monsieur Crowley does not have your child at his plantation on Bayou Black. I've been able to discover that much."

"Of course not," Cléo said with scorn. "But has he been told she was stolen?"

"He planned it. He knows where she is."

"I don't believe that!" Cléo shouted. "He loves me— he wouldn't—it isn't true!"

He stood up and came around his desk. "Go back to your rooms now, *madame*. Esther can tell you what she told me, and you can judge for yourself. We can talk later." He touched her hand. "I'm still trying to find your baby. I have men in the city looking for the woman who stole her and the coachmen she hired. We'll find her."

A great lump moved up in her throat, making it impossible to say more. *You are my true love,* he had said. *I would spend every night with you if I could.* His blue eyes incandescent with love, his hands worshiping her breasts. The man who had loved her like that could not have wounded her so cruelly. . . . She stood and walked, in a daze, to the door. It wasn't true. It couldn't be.

"One more thing," Lee Hing said behind her. "I suggest that you and your maid remain on the upper floor of my house on the weekends when I am entertaining my gambling friends here. During the week while I'm away at my casino in the city, you will be guarded. You needn't worry about the police molesting you here."

It amounted to imprisonment, Cléo thought as she climbed the stairs to her rooms. Already she was wondering how she could escape both Lee Hing's guards and the police and take a steamboat to Evan. She needed him. Together they must find their child.

Esther was in her sitting room when she entered.

"Has he paid you to blacken M'sieu' Crowley's name?" Cléo demanded. "It's all lies, isn't it?"

Esther faced her, trembling. "No, *madame*. I tell you true, I heard Maisie talk to her servant after you left. Maisie took fright of what *Michie* would do to her when he found you gone."

"*Oui?*" Cléo asked stonily.

"I couldn't understand all the talk but I knew they spoke of the *bébé*. I think Maisie say she must tell *Michie* that you blame her. Then Maisie told me I must stay in the shop to sell her bread. I ask why I must, it not my work. And she make signs to say she have to send a letter to tell *Michie* you gone. While I'm alone in the shop *Michie* Lee come in and I recognize him."

"You knew M'sieu' Lee?" Cléo asked with cold suspicion.

"I saw you get in his carriage, *madame*," Esther said, her voice soft with reproach. "I would've run after you but another policeman come, and I was afraid he follow me and find you!"

"And then?" Cléo asked, in resignation.

"*Michie* Lee say my mistress very ill and need me. He ask me to get your things and meet him in the street. So I leave Maisie's servant in the shop, and I pack your things and go."

"And now you're a runaway slave."

"*Oui, madame.*" Her eyes were wide with fear. "If the police find me, I be flogged."

Cléo put her arms around the trembling girl. "I won't let that happen, Esther."

Her whole being protested against the direction her thoughts were taking her. What Esther had overheard didn't prove Evan was guilty of having Aurélie taken away, did it? Why had M'sieu' Lee arrived at that answer? He must be wrong!

But as Cléo pondered the scene Esther had described —Maisie in a panic because she had accused her of knowing something about the abduction—she asked herself why Maisie had been so quick to send a message to Evan after she left. Neither she nor Berthe had been anxious to send the message that Aurélie had been stolen.

She could think of reasons for Maisie's urgency the next day. Berthe had been arrested. She herself had disappeared. Maisie would not dare fail to tell Evan that. But why had she demurred the night Aurélie was taken unless Maisie knew that her former master already knew something about the abduction?

Once the thought had entered Cléo's mind, it would not go away. If Maisie had made some criminal deal to sell the baby, would she have rushed off to send a message to Evan saying that Cléo was blaming her? Cléo did not think so.

She was filled with despair. Esther's words had been simple and true, but what they said didn't make sense.

Maisie had doted on little Aurélie—but Cléo knew also that Maisie would do anything Evan asked of her. Yet she could not be mistaken about his feeling for his daughter. He loved Aurélie! Why would he send her away? Aurélie, born of their love! How could he do this to her? Didn't he know he would be tearing out part of her flesh?

Hour after hour she paced the *galerie* outside her rooms. She could not eat or rest. Where was Aurélie? Into whose hands had she been entrusted? Maisie had as much as told her that Aurélie had a wet nurse—that, as much as Esther's transparent goodness, convinced her that Maisie knew who was responsible.

But she still could not believe it was Evan. *Why* would he do such a thing? She would not believe it unless she heard it from his own lips!

Lee Hing had not gone back to New Orleans. He sent word that he wished her to join him at dinner in his private dining room in his apartments that evening. Esther brought her a dress.

"Whose is it?" Cléo asked indifferently. It was a buttery yellow color, of simple cut with a high waist, bouffant skirts, and small puffs for sleeves.

Esther shrugged. "*Michie* wishes you to wear it."

Since she had nothing else but the clothes she had worn the day he had helped her into his carriage and the necessaries Esther had managed to bring with her, Cléo allowed Esther to dress her in the borrowed gown.

"Oh, *madame,* how beautiful you are!" Esther exclaimed when she had arranged her long hair in a swirl of braids and curls and tucked gardenia buds into its ebony strands.

Cléo scarcely heard her. She felt dead inside. She walked down the upper hall to Lee Hing's private dining room, turning over in her mind the things she wanted to say to him. Lee Hing met her at the door. "You are a poem about a water lily in that dress, *madame*," he told her, bowing and smiling. "I knew it would become you."

She could not even smile. He escorted her to the far end of the long table, and instructed the servant who appeared to serve their meal. When the man had gone, he said, "Have you talked with your maid?"

"Yes, *m'sieu'.*"

"Well? Do you believe she is telling the truth?"

"Yes," Cléo said painfully, "yet I can't believe it. I must go to Terrebonne parish, *m'sieu'.*"

"Why?"

"I must see him, and ask him if he has done this terrible thing to me!"

"And you will risk going to jail and having Esther picked up as a fugitive slave in order to confront him?"

"I have to find the truth, *m'sieu'.* I have to know why my baby was taken and where she is. I can't bear this hurt—"

"Do you think he will tell you where your baby is?"

She put her hands in her lap, dizzied with pain.

"What if he refuses? What will you do then? Pull a knife out of your skirts?"

"Mon dieu, non!" she cried in despair. "I could not—not against him!"

Lee Hing studied her with concern in his face. After a moment he said, "I have another suggestion for you. Stay here and make him come to you."

She looked at him, silent with her misery.

"I can give you work that will make you independent. Meantime I'll keep my men searching for your child."

"Work?" Her lips were trembling.

"You could be very valuable to me if you would act as hostess to my gambling friends."

She stared at him through tear-filled eyes. "Hostess?" she repeated dully. "What would I have to do?"

"Greet my guests. Make them feel privileged to be admitted to my gaming rooms. They are open only to a favored few, and only from Saturday noon to Sunday evening, when a complimentary dinner is served in the restaurant. You would be an adornment, to add to their pleasure. I will pay you well."

He had pricked the shell of her despair, aroused her interest but also her Cajun suspicion. "What privileges would they expect of me?"

"Absolutely none," he said. "In fact, my guards will see that you are not molested. My idea is to make you unapproachable. Do you understand me?"

She nodded. She had learned a great deal from Evan.

"An exotic, unattainable beauty! I can make you the toast of New Orleans."

She shook her head. "Why would you do that?"

He was silent for a moment. A servant entered carrying a soup tureen, and another followed him with a tray holding bowls. The tureen was placed on the table, the bowls were set before them and filled.

When they were alone again, Hing said, "I will do that for two reasons. Your beauty would bring me business. And you are a descendant of my race. . . . There are not many of my race in this city."

He waited for her response. When she said nothing, he said, "If you haven't thought about your future, *ma-*

dame, consider it now." He picked up a spoon and began on his soup.

She did not know what to say. Until now her future had held Evan . . . and Aurélïe.

"And my baby?"

"I will continue searching for her. When we find her she will live with you here, and Esther can be her nurse."

When she still did not reply, he spoke again. "I know this is a difficult time for you. You want to *do* something, but you are helpless. That's why you pace the floor and wish you could confront Crowley."

Would she never be able to hear his name again without feeling a quiver of emotion?

"It isn't good for you to be inactive at a time like this. While you are regaining your strength and considering my proposition, I suggest that you study both French and English. You should learn to read and write both languages, and to speak both correctly."

For the first time a flicker of interest broke through the darkness of her despair. "Could I?" she asked. "Learn to read and write—and speak English?"

Lee Hing's smile gave her a glimpse of white, even teeth and made his unemotional face look almost handsome. "Of course, if you really want to. I will find you a fine teacher, who will open the world to you. The love of learning, *madame,* is one love that will never betray you."

Chapter Ten

The clothes he had selected for Cléo still hung in the armoire. Maisie, her heavy, dark face contorted with outrage, flung its doors wide to show him, and Cléo's scent drifted out, bringing her essence back to Evan so clearly that he felt a sharp pain. Maisie pulled out a drawer and he looked down at the folded shifts and petticoats lying there.

"She take only the clothes she had on the day she attack' us."

"Comme une sauvage!" Berthe, behind them, added viciously. He had left the river steamboat less than an hour ago and had gone straight to the police to pay Berthe's fine and arrange her release from jail. The city was not yet solid beneath his feet.

"Tell me again what happened."

"She chase us roun' an' roun' the kitchen table," Maisie said. "Berthe snatch up a knife from the table an' she pull one out of her skirts. My customer see 'em fightin' and scream *'Police!'* an' police come an' arrest Berthe."

"And Madame Cléo?"

"She just disappear in the crowd what gather in the street. Somebody say while all this arrestin' goin' on, she step into a carriage, and it carry her off."

Evan had been trying to imagine the scene ever since he received Maisie's cryptic message. "Was it a hired carriage?"

"Nobody say what kinda carriage, but they's a man in it."

It was a stabbing pain in his breast now. "And her servant?"

"Next day Esther take off. And she take Miz Cléo's hairbrush and pins with her."

Evan waved them from the room. He sank into Cléo's chair and stared at the bed where they had spent so many hours in loving, and at the empty cradle beside it, and the misery of his loss flooded him with memories.

The image of Cléo behind the mosquito barre with Aurélie's perfect little head nestled against a golden breast, sucking greedily, materialized before his eyes, so real that his hand jerked toward her pillow. But other memories crowded it out. He averted his eyes from the empty cradle, and his mind carried him back to the first time he had taken Cléo, after he had dumped them both in the muddy bayou.

She was a virgin but she had not resisted him, and her response to his lovemaking had stunned him with its natural passion. There had been something wild and alien in the unsurrendered beauty of the eyes that gazed back at him in that moment when they looked at each other after their gasping breaths had slowed—a strongly felt presence, alien to his way of life but something he knew he would never be able to forget.

Cléonise! . . . with another man?

No. It couldn't be from her choice. He was sure of Cléo's love. She was a wild, free spirit, and she had given herself utterly—but only to him! She was not a child of the city streets. The city confused her. She must have been frightened away. But where could she go? Where was she now and how was she living?

She had escaped the police, while Berthe had spent thirty miserable days in jail before he'd arrived to pay her fine and get her out. It had not been easy for him to leave the plantation so soon after their return, and during the growing season, with Elizabeth putting every possible obstacle in his path.

He experienced a return of the rage that had consumed him when he learned Berthe had raised a kitchen knife against Cléo. But she claimed Cléo had pulled her knife first. He didn't believe her, but it did not surprise him that Cléo had taken to strapping her knife to her thigh again after he left. And in all honesty he could not blame her.

He sighed and got to his feet. He turned his head slowly in one last look around the room where he had known genuine happiness, then left it.

Maisie was waiting for him in the courtyard at the foot of the stair. "What do I do with her clothes?"

"Leave them," he said curtly. "I'll find her."

"And the baby clothes?"

He made an impatient gesture. "She didn't go to the police?"

"No. She scared of the police. She and Esther go running around—they go to your house, but you gone. Then she get the notion we done it."

"Why?" he asked sharply.

Maisie rolled her eyes.

He didn't know where to begin. At the police station he had questioned the policeman on duty the day of the "disturbance" at Maisie's bakery. He was a young Cajun from upriver with a stocky frame and roses in his cheeks. He had been the first officer on the scene, he told Evan. He had heard a woman screaming for the police and, running to the spot, had seen Berthe run into the street with her big kitchen blade raised above her head, and tackled her. Two men passing by had come to his assistance.

"She claimed the other woman had a knife, but I saw no other knife, *m'sieu'*. A carriage, he was stop' in the street, *oui*, because of the crowd, but me, I don't recognize it, *m'sieu'*, and I don't see it leave."

The police captain had not been able to help Evan either. They were no longer interested in finding the other woman in the domestic dispute, although they promised to keep an eye out for his fugitive slave. Maisie and Berthe had been of little help. Maisie brought in a neighbor who was another witness, but it seemed all eyes had been on Berthe's knife.

Evan bided his time, keeping his ears open as he went from coffeehouse to saloon, certain that Cléo's unique beauty would not allow her to remain hidden for long in New Orleans, and listening for talk about a missing child.

As he frequented the cafés and exchanges in the days that followed, he looked at each man he encountered with suspicion and a dark question in his heart. *Was that Cléo's new lover?* The thought kept him continually on the verge of rage.

Meanwhile he checked his investments and listened

in the cafés to newly arrived Americans complain about the leisurely way of doing business in a young state that still had the flavor of a foreign colony.

"We're changing that." Amos Fielding chuckled. "Can't you just feel the American bustle in this balmy air? Look how fast the St. Louis Hotel is rising!"

The dome of the new hotel was going up in a novel way and Evan spent one afternoon drinking coffee with Amos while they listened to the French architect discourse on his method of lightening the weight of the building, which threatened to sink in the swampy land of the Vieux Carré. He was using a unique hollow tile instead of bricks to build up the walls of his curved dome, something that had not been tried before.

Evan was staying with the Fieldings in the garden district. He had accepted their invitation because the rooms at Maisie's were full of disturbing memories. The Fieldings, of course, had read an account in the local papers of the arrest of Maisie's bake-woman for "disturbing the peace" and assumed he had come back to the city in summer to procure the slave's release, which was true. He had accomplished that within a few days, but he stayed on, even though it was the growing season on the plantation, ostensibly in concern about his hotel investment, but actually hoping to uncover a clue that would lead him to Cléo.

One evening, at Maspero's, he heard a man praising the beauty and sexual skills of a new girl at a certain house of revelry discreetly run by a notorious quadroon whom men called Madame Joy, and he turned cold with dread. *Cléonise?*

How else could she support herself in New Orleans?

He forced down the murderous rage that boiled up to conquer his chill, and managed to meet the man and inquire about the girl. "She's beautiful, you say. In any different way?"

"In a way that's perfect," the stranger, who was slightly in his cups, insisted. "Bee-yootiful!"

"Black?"

"No. Very light."

"What do men call her?"

"Colette. Or Coquette? Something like that. But the name isn't the thing, my friend. The thing is, she's— she's bee-e-yond compare."

Evan bought him several drinks but could get no more specific description out of him. It could not be Cléo, he told himself, but several nights later, he visited the house of Madame Joy and stayed until he was satisfied that Cléo was not one of her women. Nor did the women he talked with know of her.

For two weeks, he followed up every bit of talk he overheard about a new beauty among the "ladies of the evening," without finding a hint to Cléo's whereabouts. Occasionally he and Amos visited one or another of the many casinos for an evening of gambling. It was on one of those evenings that he overheard two Creoles talking about the Chinese gambling lord's new hostess at his exclusive weekend casino on the Bayou St. John.

"A stunning beauty, *m'sieu'*!"

"His new mistress?" his friend asked.

"Oh, without doubt."

"Who is she?"

"I heard no name. In fact, she spoke scarcely a word except for a prettily parroted greeting. He probably imported her. She looks a bit Chinese herself."

It was that last remark that stayed in Evan's mind. He was reminded of Cléo's almond-shaped eyes, revealing a trace of Oriental blood. He had heard mention of the gambler's new mistress before, but no one had commented on her race, and when he tried to imagine Cléonise mistress to Lee Hing, he failed. It could not be his Cléonise!

Nevertheless, he couldn't dismiss the conversation from his mind, especially when he remembered how the Chinese had complimented her the night he took her to the casino to dine. When the weekend came, he hired a carriage and, without inviting Amos to accompany him, rode out on the Bayou St. John road.

It was a balmy night in late April when he drove along the waterway that was a small finger of the lake. Moonlight silvered the streamers of moss hanging from trees along the way. It had rained recently and the washed-clean moon was reflected in drops of moisture in the grass edging the road.

The casino was a large house built, like the Fielding residence, in the Greek revival architectural style much in vogue, with a triangular gable and portico above the entrance, supported by columns with decorated plinths and capitals. Evan turned his carriage over to a groom and mounted the torchlit steps to the double doors.

He was reliving the night he had brought Cléo here for her first dinner that was really *ton*. He had introduced her to Lee Hing that night. Did that have any significance? His heart was pumping a little faster than usual as he entered the casino.

There were late diners in the salon on his left, but he gave his coat and hat to the attendant and entered the gaming room through a door to the right. The gamblers, all men, were gathered around two large roulette wheels. When the door had closed behind him, the room was quiet except for the whirring of the wheels, the tinkle of ice in glasses, and the polite voices of the croupiers—said to be imported from Paris—as they made their calls.

Evan circulated, speaking to one or two men he knew. He went into the adjoining room where there were tables of blackjack and *écarté*. Here, too, there were only men at the tables, and the servants in livery carrying trays of drinks were all male. He returned to the roulette tables and bought some chips at the rear table.

"Where is Lee Hing's hostess?" he asked casually of the man next to him.

"You missed her? She may not return tonight. She usually makes one *sortie* through the room, welcoming the players, and then disappears upstairs."

Upstairs. Evan's heart contracted. *To Lee Hing's residence.* "Is she as beautiful as men say?"

"*Oui,*" the man said simply. "Like an exotic animal. Beautiful and dangerous, because she is unattainable. A powerful combination, no? She is the woman men only dream of having."

"I must see this apparition," Evan said, affecting an ironic tone. But she did not reappear, although he stayed until he had lost almost all of the money he had brought with him.

"*Bonsoir,* M'sieu' Crowley." It was Lee Hing's suave voice beside him.

Evan felt a sharp thump in his chest. He turned and met the enigmatic gaze of the Chinese casino owner. "*Bonsoir,* Lee."

"How is your luck this evening?"

"Not good," Evan returned, probing the calm, expressionless face for a clue. Was this the man who had taken his place?

"But your family is well?"

"Mais oui," Evan stammered, startled by the question. What did it mean? Was Lee asking about Cléo? He had never met Elizabeth.

"Then you are not unlucky, *m'sieu'.*" Lee moved on to the other table, greeting someone else.

Evan left shortly after that.

But he could not stop thinking about Lee Hing's woman. Exotic. Unattainable. Words he himself might have used to describe Cléo. But not his Coco-of-the-swamps, surely! Yet a faint question plagued his mind. He knew he could not give up his search and return to Bayou Black without seeing Lee's woman. So on the following Saturday night he hired a carriage and was again driven out to Lee Hing's weekend casino.

This time the air was heavy with moisture, presaging another deluge, and in fact the moon was hidden by dark clouds. He was earlier, but the gaming rooms were as crowded as they had been on the last evening he was there.

He moved without apparent haste through both rooms, but the elusive hostess was not present. The shutters on the doors opening to the galerie were all closed and barred, with louvres open to let in a barely discernible breeze from off the lake. Too keyed up to be interested in gambling, Evan soon found the smoke of numerous cigars, trapped by the heavy air and hanging motionless in the room, was giving him a headache.

He decided to step out into the hall and as he did so, someone was descending the stair. He looked up and experienced a wave of dizzy disbelief.

An exquisitely beautiful young woman was coming down the steps on the arm of a young man about her own age. She was wearing a gown such as he had seen only in a Chinese painting on the casino wall. Her golden arms were bare, but a high little collar encircled her slender neck. The gown hung straight from her shoulders over her small breasts, so incredibly narrow it made her look tall and very thin. There was a breathtaking slit up one side, as shocking as the ragged garment he had first seen her wear. It was a style completely at odds with the current Parisian fashion of flowing skirts and exposed bosoms below tiny bouffant sleeves, but it was exquisitely right on Cléo.

It really *was* Cléo, although Evan scarcely recognized her.

He sucked in his breath as he remembered what the sight of her brown thigh revealed by that ragged slit had done to him. This gown was of a China silk so luxurious that it needed no decoration beyond the subtle designs woven into its silvery green folds, almost the color of his sweet cane that had brought him such riches. He knew exactly what effect it was going to have on the men in the gaming rooms. The young man whose arm she held was gazing at her with a look of stupefied admiration.

It recalled the look of more than approval in Lee Hing's eyes the night he had brought Cléo here to dine. Had both men had her? His flood of rage was too powerful to harness. He lunged toward the stairway, shouting her name.

Immediately his arms were seized by two men who seemed to have materialized from somewhere behind him.

"No one approaches her, *m'sieu'*," one of them said in his ear.

"Take your filthy hands off me, you ruffians!" Evan shouted, struggling against their hold.

His eyes had not left her. She had paled, and even

from this distance he could see that she was trembling. Who was that young jackanapes whose arm she clung to? Evan fought to get loose, his thoughts murderous.

Cléo felt the shock of seeing him travel through her body and immediately all her reluctant belief in Lee Hing's outrageous accusations against him fled. Looking at him, his light hair disarrayed by the struggle, his dear face contorted with rage, blue eyes blazing with passion, she imagined he was angry at her for not keeping Aurélie safe. She trembled, unable to speak or move, and clung to the young man at her side.

Evan's head was pounding. He was furious, not only at the manhandling he was receiving, but at the sight of Cléo dressed like that in this house full of men. Now that he had found her, he wanted to grab her and throw her over his shoulder. That was impossible, thanks to Lee Hing's two ruffians, whose iron grasp still held his arms behind him.

Lee Hing emerged from his office to the rear of the stairway, his Oriental face calm but his eyes swiftly raking the scene.

"Take him into my office," he said.

Evan was hustled into Lee's private office and then, to his surprise, left there to cool his heels, while he composed the deadly insult he would fling at the Chinese man. He would have liked to provoke a duel with pistols so he could kill the man. But one did not duel with one's inferior!

"By God, I'll find a way to get him!" he muttered.

The door opened and Cléo entered, alone.

For a second they stood in tense silence. She made a tiny movement toward him and hesitated—and he flung his rage at her.

"So it was the Chinaman who carried you off!"

"M'sieu' Lee rescued me from the police."

"Are you his mistress, as men say?"

She recoiled. "No!"

He ached to touch her. The urge to hold her was so strong that he pulled out a cigar, but his hands were too shaky to light it.

"He just happened by," he said, with irony.

"Oui!" A mocking look came into her strange eyes, the look she had given him in the pirogue the first time he had seen her. He had not seen it since they had become lovers. "He just happened by, and offered me work."

His hand closed on the cigar so tightly that it broke and he flung it on Lee Hing's carpet. He saw her through a red haze. "Was the young man who brought you downstairs part of your work?"

She stiffened, her eyes turning cold. "I prevented M'sieu' Lee from having you thrown out just now for one reason: to ask you if what he said is true. Was it you who had my baby taken from me?"

"Our baby," he said, his voice softening.

She looked at him with hatred and grief. "It *is* true, isn't it? *You* had her taken away from me. Where is she?" Her voice broke, and there was such agony in it that he took a step toward her, lifting his arms. But she stepped back, striking at his arms and crying, in a fury, "Answer me! *Where is she?*"

"She's well cared for, Cléo. I promise you—"

"How can she be well, away from me, her mother?" Cléo shrieked.

He said coldly, "Who is that young man who brought you downstairs? Are you sleeping with him?"

She shook her head, tears sliding down her cheeks, and demanded, "Tell me where 'Rélie is!"

"Were you with him just now?"

"No! No!" she shouted. "He's my tutor!"

"Tutor!" He gaped. "What in hell—"

"If you ever loved me, Evan, tell me where my baby is! What have you done with her? I thought maybe Berthe and Maisie had sold her. Or that your wife wished her harm."

His face closed against her as it always had whenever she mentioned his wife. "She knows nothing of Aurélie."

Cléo's eyes flashed. "Then maybe *she* will help me!"

Evan groaned. Her distress was so obvious that he could not but be moved by it. He had not foreseen all the consequences of his decision and his rage was dissolving into an appalled realization of the upheaval that he had brought about, and the danger to his daughter that it could bring about.

"Cléo, *chère,* if it's possible to love anyone more than I love you, it's what I feel for our Aurélie. I've done what I thought best for her. Aurélie is with a wet nurse in a good Catholic family where she is receiving excellent care. They think she's an orphan."

"An orphan?" she cried in horror.

"Cléo, I told you she is well—"

"Why?" She pummeled him with her fists. "Why did you do this terrible thing to me?"

"They think both her parents were white."

Cléo stared at him in shock.

"Don't you see?" he pleaded. "She's such a beautiful child! She will be as lovely as her mother. I don't want her to grow up in the *demimonde,* which is what will happen if she remains with you. This daughter of ours must have the best."

She said slowly, "*You* decided what was best for her—without asking me?"

"It was too dangerous. The fewer people who know of her existence, the safer she will be. No one must know of her origin."

"Of her mother, you mean." The hurt was so deep, she felt ill. "You despise me, don't you?" she whispered.

"Cléo, no!"

"All this time when I thought you loved me, you've secretly despised me."

"Don't you understand? There's nothing I can do to take the taint of the half-breed from you, no matter how much I love you. But our daughter is as white as I am. I'm going to educate her and give her a dowry that will enable her to marry in the highest ranks of society. You do see, don't you? I'm going to make it possible for her to go wherever she wants."

"With you, you mean!" Cléo cried. "Away from me, her mother! You're a stupid man, Evan. I thought you were different, but you're like all the white men who can't see beyond their own skins! My mother's people are superior to your race in all the ways that matter."

"*Chère—*" He tried to take her in his arms, but she pushed away from him.

"My people are a gentle people who were forced into the swamps by warrior tribes. The first whites who came to the bayous, the mistreated Cajuns, were starving. My people took them into their village. They gave them food, and they gave them their prized daughters in marriage. Even my mother's grandmother, who was a princess, was given to a Frenchman. This was my mother's race, and you think I'm not fit to raise our daughter? That's something I can never forgive!"

He was pale, but he didn't yield. "I didn't make the rules, Cléo, and I've never said they were fair. I just want our daughter to have her chance. She will have the things I'm not able to give you—a good marriage, a fine home, children who can go anywhere in the world and achieve anything they want. Don't you want that for 'Rélie? I know it's hard, I miss her too. If you love our daughter unselfishly, you will understand why I'm doing this."

"Understand?" She flung herself at him, shrieking, "You have no understanding! You don't even know what you do to me! My own flesh! You don't know anything! You're a monster!"

"Come back to me, Cléo!" he begged. "Together we can watch over our daughter from a distance—"

Her voice rose. "You said you bought Esther for me, but you told the police she was a fugitive slave. She is the woman who nursed me back to health after Berthe knifed me!"

"She is yours," Evan said hoarsely. He snatched up paper and the pen in Lee's inkwell from the desk behind him and scribbled a bill-of-sale note. He put it in her hand. "Will you come back to me? I'll make it up to you, *chère*—"

She tucked the note between her breasts. The look in her eyes suddenly chilled him. "You talk of love," she said in a low, furious voice. "When I loved you, I gave freely, asking for nothing. I held nothing back. When you said you wanted to take care of me, I thought it meant you were giving of yourself in the same way. But it was only part of yourself, wasn't it, Evan? The most important part you had already given. What you gave me was half a man!"

"Cléo, I love you!"

"It was your love that gave me Aurélie, and she is everything to me. But you stole her from me!"

"Cléo, my love, please . . ."

She said deliberately, "I'll come back to you, Evan . . . when you bring me 'Rélie safe and well. If you don't, I'll maybe kill you, but I'll never love you again."

"Bring 'Rélie here?" His tone was scathing.

In her rage and frustration, she fell on him, beating her clenched fists on his chest in such a furious onslaught that he staggered back and fell against the door. It opened behind him, and Lee's two guards had him again by his arms.

Lee stood just behind them. "Put him out," he said quietly. "He is not to enter this house again."

The guards began dragging Evan backward down the hall toward a rear door. From the dining room in the front came the sounds of low talk and laughter and the discreet clatter of dishes. Behind the closed doors of the gaming rooms the roulette wheels whirred.

"Cléo!" He gasped, struggling. *"Cléo!"*

She watched him go, standing with her head thrown back and her legs slightly apart as if she were bracing herself in her pirogue. "I'll find her!" she shouted after him. "You can't hide her forever!"

Part Two

Aurélie

Chapter Eleven

New Orléans. 1856.

At the Ursuline convent it was playtime for the orphans. Aurélie, who at seventeen was the oldest, was supervising the games of the youngest ones on the lawn behind the orphans' building.

The day was pleasantly warm, with the scent of jasmine and lime blossoms in the balmy air. Surrounding the clearing where they played were groves of pecan trees and flowering shrubs, with a few palm trees throwing a spiky silhouette against the blue-and-white sky.

A hundred yards away was the riverbank, and above the levee Aurélie could see the masts of a variety of vessels, but the ships themselves were hidden from her. Their bells and mournful whistles and the chants of the cargo workers unloading them came to her ears in the intervals between the children's shrill cries, but they were muted by the levee and the convent wall, and their reedy tones gave her a mysterious mood of nostalgia for things she had never known.

Was she doomed always to hear the intriguing activities of a great city from a distance, and never to experience their mysteries? When, oh, *when* would she begin to live in the real world? When could she start on the quest that obsessed her thoughts by day and her dreams at night—the acknowledgment of her birth by her real family?

She had always known that she was not really an orphan, not like these children at play whose parents were victims of the yellow fever or some other disaster such as shipwreck or fire. The secret knowledge that she had a family somewhere had come to her so early that she was not sure how she knew, and it was something she had never told anyone, but she was always on the alert for corroborating clues, and there had been some important ones.

Not far away two nuns in dark habits were working in the vegetable garden while keeping an eye on Aurélie's tutelage.

"She is so pretty!" one of them murmured. "I fear her beauty will endanger her soul. Last week I caught a young man sitting on a friend's shoulders with his elbows on the wall for a glimpse of her playing ball with the littlest ones."

"Aurélie's soul is strong," the older nun said confidently. She stood, straightening her stooped back for a moment's rest, and her companion imitated her. They stretched their tired muscles, watching the children run about in circles.

A young nun came walking toward the group from the main building, moving so swiftly over the grass that her long skirt seemed to float above it. "Aurélie, *chère,"* she called, "you're to go to the mother superior. I'll stay with the little ones."

"Yes, Sister."

The two nuns in the garden looked at each other with questioning glances, then bent again to their weeding.

Aurélie fairly flew over the distance to the main building and through its lush garden court. She had received a summons as suddenly as this before, and nearly always it had signaled the arrival of her mysterious friend, Monsieur Crowley, who brought gifts for her and money for the Sisters.

Because of him she was given more privileges than the other orphans. But she still must live in the orphans' building and, except in some of the classes she attended, was never in the company of the daughters of wealthy planters who were sent to the convent during the winter months for their education.

One or two of them had become friendly, but for most of the time Aurélie was outside of the circle of young women boarders who were allowed to go home for Christmas festivities and for summer vacations on their parents' plantations. From overhearing their talk of the Christmas balls and summer hunts and picnics they enjoyed while at home, she had fashioned an image of the plantation from which she was exiled. Someday, she vowed, she would find her mother and her father and force them to acknowledge her as their child!

Before she reached the rear entry she paused to pluck a yellow trumpet flower to carry with her as her own gift. The convent, with its terraces and colonnades and the delicate fanlight over the double doors, was a far more interesting building than the orphans' residence. It housed not only the office of the mother superior, the refectories, and the classrooms, but rooms for the nuns and dormitories for the regular students. Aurélie went with quiet speed down the hall—sparsely furnished, its walls decorated only with a few pictures of the saints—and knocked on the office door.

"Come in, Aurélie," called a quiet voice.

She opened the door and looked eagerly around the room. It was empty except for the mother superior, seated at her desk and awaiting her with a look of concern.

The nun extended a hand and said gently, "Come, sit at my feet, Aurélie. I have had some distressing news."

Aurélie's disappointment turned to apprehension, so strong that it pushed her heart up into her throat, giving her a feeling of suffocation. "Is it about M'sieu' Crowley, Reverend Mother?"

"Yes." The nun took Aurélie's suddenly cold hands and gently urged her to the stool at her knees. "He will not be coming to visit you again. He has been taken to Our Lord."

Aurélie's hand closed on the trumpet flower, crushing it, but she could say nothing. Her throat felt paralyzed.

"Our good friend suffered a hunting accident, and his horse fell on him. We shall miss him sorely. He was a kind and generous man, not only to you but to the Order. We will offer prayers for him in chapel this evening."

Aurélie drew a deep breath and blurted, "He was my father, wasn't he?"

For a fraction of a second the mother superior looked startled. She hesitated, then answered, "He told me that he was acting for your father in paying for your education and bringing you gifts that made your life here more like that of a boarder than a recipient of our charity. That, of course, will stop now."

"Then who was my father?" Aurélie said, her throat still so tight, it rasped her words. "Surely you can tell me now?"

"Monsieur Crowley would not reveal his name, and he gave us sufficient reason to respect his refusal." The mother superior placed her fingertips gently on Aurélie's hair. "You are nearly eighteen, aren't you? I think you are old enough to be told what we know, which is very little. You will have to make a choice soon, Aurélie, between joining our Order or letting us arrange a marriage for you."

"A—a marriage?" Aurélie faltered.

"I have been expecting Monsieur Crowley to bring an offer for you these past two years. He told me there would be a dowry for you when the proper husband was found, but none has been provided. . . .We would welcome you as a novice, Aurélie, if you choose Christ."

She paused again, but Aurélie was still numb with shock.

"If you ask us to find a husband for you, we will do our best to find a good man, but you must realize that he will not be a man of wealth. With such people, family counts for a great deal."

When Aurélie still did not speak, the mother superior said gently, "That is the situation. In order to help you make your decision, I am going to tell you what I was told when Monsieur Crowley brought you to us as a very young child. It's a tragic story, but not an unusual one. Do you want to hear it now, or shall I let you go to the chapel first to pray?"

"Please tell me now, Reverend Mother," Aurélie whispered.

"*Bon.* Your first years were spent with Marie and Joseph Boudin on a modest plantation on False River. Do you remember anything of them?"

"Only like a dream," Aurélie said slowly. "A wooden floor I played on. A large dog that frightened me. A woman who rocked me to sleep on her lap."

The nun nodded. "You cried for her when you first came to us. Apparently you were well cared for. But Monsieur Crowley told me you were an offspring of highborn families. An illegitimate offspring, unfortunately."

Aurélie listened tensely, her breasts rising and falling with her breathing.

"Your mother was a young woman of society who fell in love with a young man of whom her parents disapproved. He was also highborn, of a very wealthy family, but he was fond of women and gambling and had a rakehell reputation. His offer for your mother in marriage was rejected, and when it was found she was *enceinte,* her father took a horsewhip to him. You were born secretly and your mother was persuaded to give you up to Marie and Joseph Boudin, a humble Cajun family."

So Boudin was not her name. *I knew it!* she thought. She asked painfully, "Who named me Aurélie?"

"I don't know the answer to that, my child. According to Monsieur Crowley, your father changed his ways after losing the woman he loved, but he couldn't acknowledge you without ruining your mother's reputation. He arranged with his friend, Monsieur Crowley, to act for him in providing you with an education. He wanted you taken away from the Boudins when you were old enough, and brought to us for the training proper to a young lady of your breeding. He promised, when the time came for you to marry, to provide you with a dowry. Alas, he has not come forward with either husband or dowry."

"Because he does not exist?" Aurélie ventured.

The mother superior regarded her thoughtfully. "It has occurred to me that he may be dead, and that Monsieur Crowley was continuing your support out of pure kindness."

Aurélie's eyes were dry, but intense. "Who is my mother? Do you have no clue?"

"That," said the mother superior, "was Monsieur Crowley's most stubborn secret. He said he would protect that young woman's reputation unto his death . . . and he has."

A slow burning anger was taking root in Aurélie's grief. Her mother had stolen her birthright by refusing to acknowledge her birth. The blood of two good families was joined to pulse in her veins, yet she could use neither her mother's nor her father's name.

"They sinned," she said intensely. "Once I was conceived, a marriage should have taken place. I should have been given my father's name."

"It is for God to judge," the mother superior reproved her, and Aurélie was silent.

But her thoughts were not silenced. She should have been given her rightful place in her father's family. Or her mother's. Instead, she had been given to foster parents as an infant and forced to grow up as an orphan, an object of charity!

Discarded like an unwanted kitten. It was unforgivable!

And now Monsieur Crowley, who had been so good to her, had died without providing the dowry that had been promised, the money that could make all the difference in her future life, because it would determine the kind of man she would marry. Was he her father or not? Perhaps that hope had bloomed simply because he was the only friend she had outside of the convent.

Her only friend. Gone.

"May I go to the chapel now, Reverend Mother?"

"Yes, Aurélie. Pray for guidance. And pray for his soul."

A few miles away Cléo read the notice of Evan Crowley's death in the *Times-Picayune* brought to her at noon by Esther with her morning *café au lait*. She was sitting up in her silk-canopied bed, with pillows at her back, her shoulders bare above the light cotton coverlet, her hair plaited in a thick, lustrous braid—black and still untouched by silver—which fell across her bosom.

> Word has reached the office of this newspaper of the tragic death by accident on his plantation in Terrebonne parish, of Monsieur Evan Crowley, sugar planter, financier, and patron of the opera. . . .

A wave of intolerable sadness flooded her eyes with tears. She had not spoken to Evan for sixteen years, although she had once seen him at a distance during the winter social season. She had recognized his corn-silk hair from half a block away when he doffed his hat, and stopped, dizzied by an old pain, while he walked on with his yellow-haired English wife and daughter out of her sight.

Evan had been her first lover, and the magic of those months was an ineradicable memory. She had never given herself with such abandon again. He had taught her to love, but he had also taught her to distrust.

She had not lifted the ban against him in the casinos after she inherited them from Lee Hing. She could never forgive him for what he had done. Yet ironically, she had come by herself to the supreme sacrifice he had demanded of her. Although she had found Aurélie she had never revealed herself to her daughter. Perhaps because of that, Evan's love had haunted her all these years, even though she had shared a deep love and friendship with Lee Hing and still mourned his passing.

If she remains with you, she will inevitably be a part of the demimonde. . . . Cléo had come painfully to the acceptance of that truth, and kept her distance since she had discovered that her daughter was with the nuns. She had done it to protect Aurélie. But what would happen to her darling now that Evan was gone?

Her thoughts flew to her daughter in a turmoil of longing. Should she try to claim her now—and perhaps destroy her? Wouldn't Aurélie hate her if she learned the truth?

There was a knock at her door. Esther looked at Cléo. Cléo nodded and said, "Stay with me."

It was Michel. He came in, fully dressed, bringing a blatantly male and youthful vitality into her feminine *chambre de lit*. Bending over the bed, he kissed her. *"Bonjour, chère."*

He glanced at the newspaper in her hands, then looked sharply at her. "Tears for Monsieur Crowley?"

"Why should I weep for him?" Cléo asked lightly. "But it's unfortunate, all the same."

"Most unfortunate," he agreed.

He sat on her bed and let his dark eyes rove over her morning dishabille with proprietary admiration. Cléo was not sure how it had happened that—after remaining celibate for two years after her protector had succumbed to the yellow fever in that terrible summer of 1853—she had taken Michel Jardin for her lover.

Notorious in New Orleans as Lee Hing's concubine, and heiress to his gambling empire, she must have turned aside the advances of a dozen men who were eager to take Hing's place and share his wealth. Michel was half Hing's age and, at twenty-eight, seven years younger than she, but his youth had called to something still eager and unsatisfied in her, after her years with the shrewd, calm Lee Hing. Lonely and facing her middle years, although she was still toasted for her beauty, she had opened herself to Michel.

Now she wondered if she had been wise. Disquieting bits of information about his gambling had been brought to her ears by her other employees; Esther warned her that Michel would expect her to pay them. As her closest business aide, he was not supposed to gamble at all.

Cléo put down the newspaper and studied his handsome face. "Were you an acquaintance of Monsieur Crowley, then?" she asked him.

"Oh, yes. He was very rich, and I was one of the young hopefuls who offered for his daughter during the season last winter."

"You?" Cléo said. She was conscious of his desire to hurt her.

He shrugged. "If a Creole doesn't inherit, he marries money. It's the accepted way for a man of my class to achieve wealth."

She knew what he was doing—testing his power over her. Her eyes mocked him. "And you're still looking for an heiress?"

He grinned. "Purely of necessity." Unexpectedly he pounced. "He was your lover, wasn't he?"

"Evan Crowley? You're daft!" But she turned her face away.

"Am I? Then why do you weep?" Her quick flush of anger and the rapid pulse in her throat told him he had touched a nerve. She smiled as he bent and kissed that pulsing spot.

"What brings you here so early?" she asked him.

"I invited myself to have breakfast with you, *chère.*"

Her shrewd business instincts, honed by Lee Hing, warned her that he wanted something from her. Probably money. "I'll have our breakfast brought to the office," she said, in the firm tone that brooked no dissent.

That tone always annoyed him. It was equivalent to an order, and it should not have come from a woman. "I was hoping for something more intimate," he said, brushing a strand of hair from her cheek.

She shook her head away from his sensual touch. "Esther, choose a gown for me. I think blue this morning." She had made her distinctive mark the Chinese-style costume Hing had designed for her, and wore no other fashion. "Leave us now, Michel. I want Esther to dress me. I'll be down in fifteen minutes."

Michel left, disgruntled. Her choice of trays in the office told him she had guessed he wanted money. He wondered about that trace of tears on Cléo's smooth cheeks. What did it mean?

He knew his mistress was a woman of iron. She had to be to keep control of the money and the casinos Lee Hing had left to her. She was still the most beautiful woman in New Orleans, and probably the shrewdest. And one of the wealthiest. He was greatly set up by his conquest of her, but her power made him uneasy. He was constantly probing for a weakness in her armor.

He went down the stairs and, meeting a footman, sent him to the kitchen with an order to the cook, then continued on to the office door. It was locked.

Michel seethed. This was the last straw. It told him she had heard of his gambling debts. She knew what he was after this morning.

In spite of his triumph in winning Cléo over his many rivals, his position with her was an unenviable one, demeaning for a man of his family background and social standing. When he became her lover, he had thought to take control of her gambling casinos. Instead, he had the status of her principal employee. She controlled her wealth, and he had none.

The law forbade marrying her, which was the only way he could gain control of her fortune, because even though she had allowed him into her bed she kept the reins of business tightly in her own hands.

While he waited for her, he considered his strategy for the coming confrontation. Since she had foiled his attempt to mix business and pleasure, he considered his secret weapon. He had long since guessed that Cléo had a daughter in the Ursuline convent, and had often speculated about the girl's father.

Cléo kept a fine riding horse in town, since she spent only weekends at the house on Bayou St. John, and she loved a morning ride. Michel rode with her most mornings. The popular ride in the city was on the levee road and their access to it was along the rue Ursuline past the old convent, now the archbishop's palace, and by the dirt road along the barracks to the levee, which took them by the new convent.

When they were on the levee road, they could look

over the convent wall. Often they saw the orphans marching in a double file to the refectory in the main building for their breakfast.

He knew where they were going because Cléo had commented once on what was happening, and he had wondered how she knew. She was not convent-educated herself. She did not attend mass, and he knew that Lee Hing had hired a tutor to teach her English and her letters.

There was a tall girl with tawny hair who seemed to be in charge of the younger orphans. Even from the distance of the levee road she had attracted his interest. She looked as if she were developing into a real beauty. Like her mother? It was a wild guess, but he could pursue it.

Cléo came down the stairs, looking elegant and self-possessed, just as the footman entered from the rear of the house with a covered tray, the fragrance of strong hot coffee drifting before him.

"*Bonjour,* Pierre," she said cheerfully, and with a key unlocked the office door and preceded Michel in, taking the chair behind the desk, indicating to Michel that he should take the visitor's chair across from her.

So strong was his conviction that *he* should sit in the seat of power that she occupied that a quick rage darkened his thoughts. He controlled himself immediately, but Cléo had seen the flicker in his eyes. She felt regret, for she knew what she must do.

Pierre set the tray down beside her, picked up the two small silver pots, one of black, black coffee and the other of hot milk, and poured the two liquids together into their tall cups. Then he uncovered the plates of rolls and butter and sausages and fruit and set their morning meal before them.

"Enjoy your breakfast, Michel," she said softly when Pierre had gone. "After you have eaten, I want to hear the truth about the gambling debts you have run up."

He flushed. "So you put your spies on me!"

"That is just one of the things Lee Hing taught me."

"I'm grateful for your trust!"

"I learned long ago not to trust a man who said he loved me—but not from Hing. He was my friend, more than my lover."

She picked up her *café au lait* and drank while Michel stared sulkily at her. "Whom do you owe, Michel, and how much?"

"I owe Marigny two thousand dollars, and Guererro three thousand."

Cléo dug a spoon into a slice of early melon. "You gambled rather extravagantly, didn't you? Yet you knew it was against my house rules for any of my employees to—"

"Don't treat me like one of your footmen!" he said intensely. "Are you going to pay my debts or not?"

She sipped her coffee, her gaze on him speculative and sad. Once again she had made a wrong choice. Lee Hing had been the best thing that ever happened to her, but their relationship had not been what she had once thought she had with Evan Crowley, or had foolishly hoped to find again with Michel Jardin.

"I'll pay your debts, Michel," she said quietly.

His face had begun to clear when she added, "But you are through here, as of today," and his expression altered into a confused and angry disbelief. "I'll ask Pierre to pack your things."

He felt such rage that he could have struck her, but he was aware of what would happen to him if she signaled her guards. Nor could he cajole her, as once would have been possible. The coldness in her eyes told him that.

Michel flung his serviette down on the tray and stood up. "Damn you!" he said bitterly. "Damn you to hell!"

It was the following week when Aurélie had another summons. This time she was told she had a visitor, a male visitor, and she was taken by a novice to the small visitors' building. There were three rooms. The two inner rooms were connected only by a device similar to that used in the confessional.

In the wall of each room was an opening two inches square, screened by a grid. The openings were opposite each other, separated by six inches, thus allowing the nuns or their charges to communicate with callers from the outside who remained largely invisible.

With high excitement Aurélie moved close to the small opening. In spite of the sharp disapproval she sensed from the novice watching her, Aurélie stooped a little to peer briefly through it, but she could see only red lips parted in a smile that showed a gleam of white teeth, and above it a black mustache.

"Bonjour, m'sieu'," she said softly, into the grid. "I'm Aurélie."

"Aurélie Crowley?" the deep voice said incredibly.

She gasped. "You know me—I mean, know my name?"

"Yes." Her answer filled Michel with elation. He had put together the tears Cléo had denied when she read of Crowley's death, and her interest in the Ursuline orphans, and *mon dieu*, had come up a winner!

Aurélie wished she could see his eyes. "But you are not my father!" she exclaimed. "You're too young!"

He laughed. His laughter had a joyous, reckless sound

that touched something unsuspected in her nature. "Far too young!" he said. "Evan Crowley was your father. Didn't you know?"

Aurélie took a deep breath. "I guessed it might be so. But who are you? How do you know this?"

"My name is Michel Jardin. I am a friend of the family. I came to express my sorrow at your loss and to see what your situation is now."

"That is very kind of you, *m'sieu'*. My situation here has changed, because M'sieu' Crowley was paying for my education, although I was placed here as an orphan."

Her voice was enchanting. He wished he could see her, but the stern old nun who had escorted him to the visiting room stood just behind him, her arms crossed with her hands tucked into her sleeves, and he dared not stoop to put his eye to the grid.

"You are not an orphan, *mademoiselle*. I personally know that Evan Crowley planned to include you among his heirs, but he was taken so suddenly, God rest his soul, that he may have neglected to do so. If you don't have a lawyer to represent you, you may be overlooked in the probate of his estate."

"I have no lawyer," Aurélie said. "M'sieu' Crowley was my only friend."

"That is not true, *mademoiselle*. I wish to help you."

"Why?"

"Because of my friendship with your father."

"M'sieu', I am illegitimate," she said, in a low, shamed voice. "How can I claim a share of my father's estate if he did not choose to name me?"

"I can testify as to your father's wishes. I know your half sister, and I do not believe your father meant for her to inherit his total estate without sharing it with you. There's ample money for you both."

"My—*half sister?*" She put her hands against the wall on each side of the grid to steady herself because the spare, unfurnished room was suddenly spinning. Her heart was beating rapidly. She wondered if the man on the other side of the wall could hear it.

"You didn't know about her?" he asked.

"*M'sieu'*, you bring me the first word I have had about my family. I—I am overcome by emotion. Please forgive me."

"I'm sorry if I've upset you, *mademoiselle.*"

"I'm so grateful to you!" she exclaimed fervently.

"Your half sister and her mother are in Terrebonne parish, two days' journey southwest of here. My advice to you is that you go immediately to call on them and make your claim on your father's estate."

"I have no wish to make such a claim, *m'sieu'*. But the mother superior did say he promised a dowry for me."

"Then it is urgent that you make your claim now before the estate is settled."

"But how can I? I'm penniless, *m'sieu'.*"

She saw his smile again. "But potentially rich. And that is almost as good as being rich."

"I fear they won't welcome me."

"You have the support of friends. I'm prepared to advance money for the journey."

Her head was whirling. "*M'sieu'*, do you also know my mother?"

"No, *mademoiselle*, only that she was a lady."

"Would Madame Crowley know who she was?"

"Undoubtedly she knows," Michel said. "Unfortunately I can't accompany you to Terrebonne parish, but I will find an older woman of impeccable respectability to go as your companion. And if it becomes necessary to go to court, I'll testify on your behalf."

"Go to court? M'sieu', finding my mother is of more importance to me than any inheritance. The mother superior is seeking a husband for me, because I have no calling to spend my life as a nun. Before I can marry, *m'sieu',* I must know about my family background."

Michel sucked in a quiet breath. He had done well to move quickly. He had made an immediate trip to Terrebonne parish to call on Crowley's lawyer, and his inquiry as to whether provision had been made in Evan's will for an illegitimate daughter had jolted Alex Archer considerably. Back in New Orleans, he had visited the convent to put his story before the mother superior and obtain her permission to speak with Aurélie, whose name he hadn't even known. His position in New Orleans society, and his open pursuit of Nanette Crowley the season before, had made his claim of friendship with her father credible even though Nanette had chosen another.

"You needn't be in a hurry to marry, Mademoiselle Crowley," he said. "I daresay you'll have many opportunities to wed when you come into your inheritance. If you agree, I'll seek a very proper lady who is willing to accompany you to Terrebonne parish, where the Crowleys are spending the summer, and then we can discuss your journey with the mother superior."

"Oh, yes, *m'sieu',* I agree!" Aurélie said eagerly.

"Then I will go ahead with the arrangements and return in a week's time. *Au revoir, mademoiselle."*

"Au revoir, m'sieu'." She peered through the grill, but he had moved out of her sight, and she could see only the dark habit of the nun who had brought him in.

Aurélie made the sign of the cross and bowed her head. The Virgin had answered her prayers! She was going to find her real family, and prove her right to their name.

Chapter Twelve

Madame Duclos was a delightful traveling companion. In public she was ramrod straight, her expression dour and forbidding, discouraging any casual conversation. But in their private cabin she chattered away in French, saying the most droll things about their fellow passengers and teasing Aurélie about the various men who tried to outwit her chaperone in order to speak to her.

Aurélie walked demurely beside her as they circled the deck of the river steamboat, but she was fizzing inside with excitement, and the glow in her eyes as she risked a sidelong glance at an admirer gave her away. This journey was not only fulfilling her lifelong dream of finding and confronting her true family, but after her cloistered life in the convent, it was high adventure.

She was enjoying the luxury of her surroundings, the pleasure of having Madame's maid help her with her new gowns and her hair, the polished wood and brass of the salon and its velvet chairs, the deliciously rich food served the passengers. Besides all that, between meals she was viewing what was reputed to be the most beautiful river shore in the country. But best of all, she had a new friend in Michel.

Michel had brought them and Madame Duclos's servant, Julienne, in his carriage to the steamboat landing, had come on board with them to inspect their cabin to see that they were comfortable, and had personally asked the captain to extend them every courtesy. He had even inspected the servants' quarters belowdeck and made sure Julienne could come to their cabin to attend them. Michel was wonderful!

He was younger than she had thought, when she first spoke with him through the visitors' grill—only about ten years her senior. He was handsome and worldly and he had predicted just what was happening, by telling her while escorting her and Madame Duclos on board— gently pressing her hand on his arm—that she was pretty enough to turn a man's head!

"All the young men will adore you. But don't go falling in love," he'd warned her teasingly, "without giving me a chance first to make you fall in love with me."

She had blushed, and he had laughed at her. So she assumed he was teasing her. He couldn't mean he loved her!

As Aurélie gazed on the oak-shaded lawns of the beautiful plantation houses they were passing, she imagined the scenes of Christmas revelry and summer hunts she had heard girls in her needlework and deportment classes at the convent describe after they had attended the holiday house parties.

Aurélie had never been invited to a house party. She understood why. She had no family and no money, and could return no invitations. Living in the orphans' building instead of sharing a dormitory in the convent prevented her from becoming intimate with the boarders, although some of them were friendly.

"Besides," one of the young novices had said, trying to comfort her, "you're prettier than they are, and some young women can't abide that."

Understanding had not lessened the hurt. But now she was going home, to assert her rightful identity as a Crowley.

"They call it the Manse," Michel had told her. "They're English Americans, you know."

Well, she could speak English, although she was more comfortable with French. She looked at the house on the bank sliding by as they moved upstream, and wondered if the Manse were like it—shining white with wrought-iron railings joining the pillars supporting the wide overhang of roof shading the *galeries* that overlooked the river. There were women sitting on the upper *galerie*, tiny colored figures lifting a dot of a teacup to an invisible mouth. Women living in a world she had never known.

Was one of them her mother?

She would find out. Surely her father could not have conceived an illegitimate child with a woman of his class without his English wife knowing about it! And then she would confront her mother. It was her mother who had rejected her. She would never forgive her for that. But it was her father's name she needed. To have her blood recognized and acknowledged, even if she would always be tainted by her illegitimacy.

I'm no orphan. I have a family. I am a Crowley.

"It's a roundabout way to go southwest," she observed to Madame Duclos. "Anyone can tell by the sun that we're traveling *north*west."

"We'll turn south at Donaldsonville," Madame said.

They left the steamboat at Donaldsonville, stayed in a hotel, and in the morning took a smaller vessel down Bayou Lafourche on which the plantations grew smaller and many modest farms appeared, with kitchen gardens and farm animals, and always a rustic pier with a pirogue or a cypress-log canoe tied up. The farmhouses were all built with a steep roof extending over a wide front *galerie* on which could be seen a table and chairs and sometimes even a dresser holding dishes. Often at one side of the *galerie* an outside stair ran up to the second floor or attic.

"Sleeping rooms, I believe," Madame explained.

There were always children running about the yard or playing at the water's edge, pausing to wave at the travelers passing by.

In the afternoon of the second day, they left the bayou steamboat and, after another night spent in a rented room, hired a carriage to take them from the Bayou Lafourche landing on a road built across a swamp to "le Terrebonne," as their driver called it. It was Madame Duclos who found the pension run by two elderly maidens beside the Bayou Terrebonne.

They were a faded, kindly, but shy pair of maiden ladies who talked of a revolution in faraway France that their parents had fled with nothing but their jewels long before Aurélie was born. Why did they think she would be interested? It was now, today, that was exciting. So many questions about the Crowleys bubbled on her tongue, but Madame had advised discretion, and with difficulty she repressed them.

Tomorrow! Tomorrow she would see her ancestral home.

Madame Duclos had arranged for a hired carriage for the next morning, and before ten o'clock they were dressed in their best mourning black and heading for the Manse.

"What would I have done without you, *chère madame*?" Aurélie said, barely managing not to bounce on her seat with excitement. "I have learned much about how to get along in the world from you."

"Have you, indeed!" Madame gave a dry chuckle.

"I have! I think I could make that journey by myself now."

"Not unaccompanied," Madame Duclos said severely.

The carriage was taking them along a quiet stream, the road shaded by magnolia trees with great white blossoms and spreading oaks with streamers of moss swaying gently in the breeze. A pair of birds, one prettily colored in earth tones and the other a bright scarlet, swooped low over the road, and disappeared into the lush shrubbery that edged the black water.

They came to a stretch of the bayou where the bank had been cleared of brush and smooth green grass grew right down to the water's edge, under some magnificent oaks. A drive wound up from the road, and their coachman took it. Aurélie leaned out of her window, to stare at the house set back in a garden that was a burst of riotous color against the smooth lawn.

It was as white as alabaster, with large round pillars rising magnificently from the lower *galerie* to the roof's edge, with long windows reflecting gold from the morning sun, and a brick chimney rising high above its dormered roof. Her heart was beating heavily. At last! At last!

This was her father's home, this was where she really belonged. Her heritage had been denied her, but it was real. Tears stood in her eyes, tears for her father in his grave, a marble crypt on his own land, Michel had said —but tears of happiness too.

As the carriage swung around the curved drive, other buildings came into view, a long row of whitewashed slave cabins with smoke rising lazily from one of them and beyond that the sugarhouse with its tall brick chimney reaching even higher than that of the Manse.

"Are you ready?" Madame Duclos asked in her flat voice.

"Oh, *madame*, I'm so excited—"

"Take a deep breath," the older woman advised.

The coachman stepped down and gave his reins to a black groom who had run up. He opened the carriage door and said, "This is the Manse, *madame.*"

"Wait, please," Madame Duclos said, as he helped her down.

Aurélie took his hand and stepped down to the stool he had placed for them and then to the ground. She stood there gazing up at the magnificent house with its pillared double verandas and its slanting roof pierced with three dormer windows. Magnolia trees flanked the verandas, dark green starred with huge waxy blossoms. Beyond the sugarhouse the fields of sweet grass began.

This was her real, her rightful home, and it was beautiful.

A dignified black butler opened the door. *"Madame?"* he said politely.

"Please tell Madame Crowley that Madame Duclos and Mademoiselle Crowley are here," Aurélie's chaperone said.

"Crowley?" the man said, blinking.

"Announce us!" Madame Duclos said, in a no-nonsense tone.

"Yes, *madame.*" He nodded and withdrew.

Aurélie looked at the beautiful double staircase curving to rise against the walls and meet at the upper landing, which was lit from floor-length windows at its rear. The light streaming through them was caught and flashed from a dozen lovely surfaces—a mirror, a crystal vase holding a bouquet of spring flowers, the gold frames of portraits on the walls . . . *my ancestors*! Aurélie thought, her heart swelling.

A slender, yellow-haired young woman ran down the stairs, stopping when she saw the two of them standing in the hall. "Oh!" she said. "I didn't know—" A puzzled look came into her face. "Who are you?"

Aurélie was taking in every inch of her figure in fresh white mourning, the pert face under the fashionable curls, the cleft chin and the blue eyes she would have known anywhere. Her father's eyes.

A rush of emotion made her forget everything Madame Duclos and Michel had told her. Shyly, she said, "I am Aurélie, your half sister, and this is Madame Duclos, my chaperone."

Nanette's mouth dropped open. "I have no sister," she said, blinking. "You must be mistaken, *mademoiselle*."

"I thought *I* had no sister," Aurélie said. "It seems we were both wrong."

Nanette's pretty face hardened. "You've heard that my father died. He was very well known. You must be an adventuress!"

The butler coughed and said, "I've sent someone to notify your mother, *mademoiselle*."

"Thank you, Radcliffe."

They stood in a wary circle, observing each other, while they waited. Aurélie's heart filled her ears with its pounding. An adventuress, was she? This was her home

and someday she would make this cold half sister acknowledge her!

Alex Archer sat behind his desk in his brand-new law
office in the small town that was the heart of le Terrebonne and listened to the complaint of a grizzled old
Cajun from Bayou Lafourche who wanted to file suit
against his neighbor for allowing his goats to stray into
the old man's vegetable garden.

"They trample my corn, they bring down the tomato
vines, they eat everything, even my peppers. My wife
don' cook without peppers, ahn?"

Alex thought that his father, who had wanted him to
join the family law firm in New Orleans, would have
been amused, but Alex was not easily amused these
days. He was feeling discouraged and very conscious of
the black band worn around his sleeve as a courtesy to
his future bride.

He had expected to marry Nanette Crowley this summer. He had set up his own law practice here in the
Lafourche *Intérieur*, not only because of the scarcity of
lawyers in the gulf parishes but because Nanette
wanted to live on her father's plantation, which she
would one day inherit.

"It's such a wonderful place to raise our children,
darling," she said. "We can always go to New Orleans
for the season as Mama and Papa do." It was not going
to be that easy to leave his practice once he had built it
up. A planter could always leave his work to a hired
administrator, but how to explain the difference to
Nanette?

Now the plantation was hers, but they could not
marry. Instead of a wedding there had been a funeral
for Evan Crowley, and it was over before the news of his

death could reach Bellemont, Alex's family plantation near New Orleans. His parents and his sisters would not be coming to Terrebonne parish now. The wedding was postponed for the year Nanette and her mother would be in mourning.

A whole damned year.

"You're *anglais, non?*" the old farmer was saying. "But you speak French."

"My mother is French."

"Ah, that explains it. A Creole, ahn?"

"Yes, a beautiful Creole lady," Alex said. Melodie Archer, his mother, was still pointed out as one of New Orleans's beauties, to the secret delight of her son.

The Cajun beamed. "Then you take after your father, ahn?"

That made Alex laugh in spite of his gloomy mood.

"Ah, now you look more French!" the old man exclaimed. "If you laughed more, you could maybe win the heart of a Cajun belle."

"I'll remember that," Alex said, and stood up to end the interview. "I'll look into this matter for you, *m'sieu',* and give you my advice when you return to town."

"Bon! You have the physique of a fencer," the old Cajun said, eyeing the narrow hips and strong arms and shoulders of young Archer in his Parisian-cut frock coat.

Alex laughed again. "A lost art, *m'sieu',*" he said as he walked the farmer to the door.

Alone, Alex went back into his inner office, but did not sit at his desk. He smoothed his brown hair, which had a tendency to tumble down his forehead, and then put his fingers at the nape of his neck, throwing his head and shoulders back, and stretched prodigiously. He had an invitation to the Manse for dinner, and he decided to close the office, since no other customer had appeared.

He walked to the Pension des Avignons, where he had rented rooms from two elderly sisters, the remaining members of an aristocratic family that had fled the Revolution. All that was left of the grant of land their titled ancestor had been given by the Spanish government but was too inexperienced a planter to maintain, was the weathered two-story house with its comfortable *galeries*, its separate kitchen and servants' quarters, and a stable. The town had grown up around it, as the sisters' father had sold off chunks of land, and the house was only a short walk from his office.

Alex had come to le Terrebonne, as the natives called the parish, with two slaves, one a groom to take care of his carriage team and his hunter, the other his personal servant. As a child he had teasingly called him Lafitte, and the name had stuck. He rang for both of them, ordering his groom to saddle his horse and his servant to prepare his bath. An hour later, he was mounted and riding out on the Bayou Black road.

The Crowley mansion, set down with its gardens in lush fields of cane, combined elements of the simple Cajun plantation home with the Monticello-inspired style popular in Virginia. Its fat, round pillars with their carved plinths gave it an air of grandeur that the Acadian houses disdained. It was a fine, impressive residence which would one day be his and Nanette's home.

But it was not as beautifully proportioned as the Acadian plantation-house his mother had inherited and allowed for some mysterious reason to fall into ruin. When Alex thought of La Sorcellerie, his heart softened with a painful affection. He had loved the old ruin since he first discovered it in his boyhood ramblings on horseback over his father's land, and could not understand his mother's refusal to put a halt to its disintegration.

Even in complete decay La Sorcellerie compelled admiration. Like the face of a truly beautiful woman, age could not ravage the beauty of its bones.

A groom took his horse, and the butler opened the door to him. He handed his hat and whip to the African Nanette's mother called Radcliffe.

Nanette came down the curved mahogany stairway just as Alex was turning into the living room. He paused to admire her coloring. She was wearing deep mourning today, although local custom demanded only *demideuil* from her. The black gown emphasized her light skin and fair hair—and just at that moment the light behind her head from a round window in the stairwell above her was making a golden halo of her hair.

"Oh, Alex, I'm glad to see you!" she exclaimed, holding out her hands to him. "Something dreadful has happened, and Mother has taken to her bed with her *femme* putting cold cloths on her forehead."

He took her hands and gave her a chaste kiss on her cheek. They had been friends since childhood, and their marriage had been taken for granted by their parents ever since their teens. "What's the trouble?"

"A young woman came to call on us, claiming she was my half sister!"

"The devil!" Alex said, jolted. "What did she want?"

"Some of the estate, of course! She admits she's illegitimate, but says my father has had her educated at the Ursuline convent, and promised her a dowry."

Alex immediately doubted the story. Evan Crowley had been a Protestant, an obstacle he and Nanette had faced when they decided to marry. As a Protestant, Nanette had not been sent to the Ursuline nuns, but had been tutored by an English governess her mother had asked her London relatives to find for her.

"It's ridiculous, of course, but Mother is extremely upset. She asked me to bring you to her as soon as you arrived."

Alex thought, seriously concerned, that Nanette could not possibly foresee the legal problems that immediately came to his mind. But he said only, "Please tell her that I am at her service."

"Come, she's expecting you."

Alex followed her as she turned and started back up the stairs.

Madame Crowley was in her bed, sitting up against a pile of pillows with a mauve shawl thrown about her shoulders. She looked pale and drawn, almost ill.

"Bonjour, madame," Alex said, and without waiting for her reply turned to her *femme de chambre.* "Please get another shawl for your mistress. Something with more verve! That one is extremely unbecoming."

Elizabeth glared at him, but Alex said with a smile, "It has washed all the color out of your face, *madame.*"

"Oh, Alex!" she said testily. "You *are* more French than English, aren't you?" Since her husband's death, Elizabeth Crowley seldom spoke French. But a faint smile had lightened the misery on her face.

"You do look much better, Mama." Nanette cried when the maid had wrapped a rosy length of knitting about her. She sat on the stool beside her mother's high bed.

"Charming!" Alex agreed, settling himself in an upholstered chair. "Now tell me about your unexpected visitor."

Elizabeth fussed with long, thin fingers at the quilt covering her. "I was told she was very young with exquisite manners and was properly chaperoned, so I agreed to see her. A mistake! A formidable Creole woman accompanied her as chaperone, but the girl did the talking."

She hesitated so long that Nanette burst out, "She told of a cock-and-bull story about my father and a young woman of society who was her mother!"

Elizabeth raised a hand to silence her. "Her birth was kept a secret, she said, and she was given away. She claims that Evan took her from her foster parents and put her in the convent of the Ursuline nuns, which she has just left."

Nanette cried, "Alex, she calls herself 'Mademoiselle Crowley'!"

"What does she want? Money?"

"Oh, undoubtedly!" Elizabeth said with contempt. "But that isn't all. She wants to be recognized as my husband's daughter."

"Can you imagine the effrontery of it?" Nanette asked, two spots of color appearing in her cheeks.

"Who does she say was her mother?"

"My husband gallantly protected her mother's name, according to her," Elizabeth said, in tones of outrage. "I don't believe a word of it! Alex, you have Evan's will. I saw nothing in it about an illegitimate child. Was there a secret codicil that I don't know about?"

"Of course not. Forgive me, Madame Crowley, but as your lawyer I have to ask you this. Do you know of any liaison of your husband's that might have resulted in—in this situation?"

"No! It's fraudulent, completely fraudulent! She had the appalling taste to ask *me* for her mother's name! Should I notify the authorities, do you think?"

"I shouldn't like to have you experience the talk that

would cause, *madame.* Leave this to me. Does this person have an address?"

"Oh, yes, indeed. She and her duenna have moved into rooms at your pension, Alex. They are staying with the Mademoiselles d'Avignon, where they will await word from us. I do believe she expected to be invited to stay at the Manse!"

"That makes her easy to find," Alex observed. It was not surprising. The pension run by the two elderly aristocrats was the only place in town where one could obtain a room and meals in an atmosphere congenial to respectable ladies. "Please don't worry about this, *madame.* I'll have a talk with her tomorrow."

Nanette said uneasily, "Couldn't we just ignore her?" and Elizabeth shot a quick look at her.

"I'm afraid not, Nanette," Alex said. "I'll have to look into this before we can finish the probate of your father's will. It will be very easy to check her story with the Ursuline nuns. Don't let it concern you. I'll make an investigation into her claim."

"Do you think she can actually make a claim against Evan's estate?" Elizabeth exclaimed, aghast.

"Since she has raised the issue with you and we don't know who else, I may have to satisfy the judge that M'sieu' Crowley left no promise to the girl in writing."

"She's a bloody thief, isn't she?" Elizabeth said under her breath.

Blushing, Nanette protested, *"Mama!"*

Alex remained discreetly silent.

Riding home late that evening, he speculated about the new boarders in his pension. Since he took his breakfast in his room, and his other meals elsewhere, often at the Manse, he had not seen them. Indeed, he had been aware of their presence in the pension only because now and then he had heard the sound of feminine voices from somewhere down the hall, one young and fluty, the other with the deep, reedy tone of an English horn.

The pension was dark when he arrived except for a faint glow showing through the moonlight. He gave his horse to his groom and entered. The light he had seen came from the candle his servant held at the top of the stairs.

"You still awake, Lafitte?"

"I heard your horse, *michie*."

Inside his bedchamber, Alex sat and lifted his booted feet, one at a time, for his servant. "Have you seen the new boarders, Lafitte?"

"*Oui, m'sieu'*." His servant gave a grunt as he pulled off Alex's last boot.

"What are they like?"

"They are two women alone. One is very young." Lafitte hesitated. "I don't think they are related, *michie*."

"Why do you say that?"

"Perhaps they are related, but have been separated for some time. The *jeune fille* talks of little else but the Sisters, as if she were just home from the convent."

"I see. What does she look like?"

There was a silence. Then Lafitte said, with careful restraint, "I think you will be pleasantly surprised, *michie*."

As he was helped out of his clothes and into a thin cotton nightshirt, Alex wondered, *An adventuress? Or the offspring of Crowley's dalliance?* It was not impossible, although he had known Nanette's father since his childhood, and was unaware of any extramarital alliance. Their families had spent much time together during the winter seasons which always brought the Crowleys to New Orleans. He searched his mind for any clues, any gossip that might suggest a liaison with a "young woman of society." But of course, it would have to have happened while he was still in the nursery!

The next morning while Lafitte was shaving him, he was more aware of the feminine voices from across the hall—the young voice with the clear flutelike tones, and the deeper counterpoint of her duenna's aristocratic rasp, indistinguishable words, but a constant rise and fall of sound. What did they find to talk about so animatedly?

The presence of the girl in his pension made him a bit uncomfortable. He decided it would be wiser to go to his office as usual, and than return to formally call on her in his role as the Crowley women's lawyer.

Accordingly he lifted the door knocker at the pension at ten o'clock.

The maid who opened the door exclaimed, *"Michie* Archer, did you forget your key?"

"This is a formal visit," Alex said. "Please tell Miss Crowley that Monsieur Archer, attorney, wishes to see her on business. I'll wait in the salon."

"Oui, michie."

Alex smiled at her. "Can you see that we are not interrupted for a half hour, more or less?"

"But yes! Just close the doors."

"Merci."

In the shabby, spacious drawing room, Alex remained standing, going over in his mind the line of questioning he had worked out that morning. He planned to give her plenty of rope with which to "hang herself" and then he would tell her how long he had known Evan

Crowley and how close he was to the family. He hoped that would throw her off balance. He would be alert to catch any slip she might make.

Then the door opened and he gaped, as a vision walked in.

She was defiantly in mourning, wearing a stark black dress that revealed the lines of a superb young body. Alex's first stunned thought was that, on her, mourning was a weapon, while Nanette was vanquished by it, made pale and unconvincing. This girl had a heart-shaped face with high cheekbones, tawny hair, strangely different greenish eyes with gold lights in them. There was an older woman in black hovering behind her, made almost invisible by the blazing beauty of the young girl.

Alex fought his purely physical response, which was understandable but quite unexpected in the circumstances. While he groped for the questions he had painstakingly devised, his innate good manners took over. He bowed and introduced himself.

In a clear, musical voice, the girl replied confidently, in French, "I am Aurélie Crowley, and this is my chaperone, Madame Duclos."

"*Enchanté, madame, mademoiselle,*" Alex said. They took chairs, but he felt more comfortable standing. "I am an attorney representing Madame Crowley and her daughter, Nanette." He was looking at the girl's eyes, fascinated. It was their unusual oval shape that made them seem exotic. *Cat's eyes.* He felt a warning prickle that said danger.

"You have made an extraordinary claim to membership in the Crowley family," he said. "Do you have any proof of this relationship?"

She was looking him over with frank curiosity. "I

expected Madame Crowley to send someone to interrogate me, but I didn't expect you to be so young."

Alex flushed. "I have a degree in law from Harvard, if you're questioning my credentials."

"Oh, no, *m'sieu'*! Please continue."

"I repeat, *mademoiselle*, what proof can you produce?"

"My father, Evan Crowley, paid for my education by the Ursuline nuns—"

"In what way?"

Her eyes widened slightly. "By contributing money to the Order—"

"Monsieur Crowley contributed to many charities, both Catholic and Protestant. The nuns and their hospital are greatly appreciated by all New Orleanians."

"He visited me at the convent from time to time and brought me gifts."

"I don't think you understand the nature of proof, *mademoiselle*," Alex said. "Do you have anything in writing? Any letters from him?"

"No," she admitted.

"Did he tell you he was your father?"

She shook her head. "Someone else told me."

"Who?"

"A friend of his. He knew my father planned to give me a dowry and find a husband for me. But my father died so suddenly—" Her extraordinary eyes filled with tears and her voice faltered, causing Alex to feel a dangerous impulse to move to her side and comfort her. He repressed the wrench of sympathy he felt and asked sharply, "What is this friend's name?"

Her full lower lip pushed out stubbornly and her eyes grew wary. "I'll tell you if it becomes necessary. He's willing to testify in court, if I am forced to bring suit."

His heart hardened. "Have you ever asked yourself whether such a suit would cause embarrassment to innocent members of the Crowley family?"

Her eyes flashed a hot golden light. "Do they know the pain and ignominy of being rejected by one's family?"

In spite of the outrageousness of her demand, he found himself admiring her spirit. "Is it blackmail, then? What do you want? Is it money?"

Her chin lifted. "Not the money, but what it would signify, M'sieu' Archer. What I want is to be acknowledged by my family. I want them to admit that I am not Mademoiselle No-Name!"

"And incidentally share in Monsieur Crowley's estate," he said cynically. "You think you can appear from nowhere—"

"From the Ursuline convent, *m'sieu',*" she corrected him quietly.

"—and get part of the Crowley estate by threatening to bring suit against my clients? Without producing a birth certificate or a will or any written proof, with only the threat of an unnamed witness? You are very young and very naive, *mademoiselle.* Filing a hopeless suit would only provoke a scandal which would bring disgrace upon yourself as well as calumny on M'sieu' Crowley's name. I don't believe you will do that, Mademoiselle—whatever your name is."

"Crowley!" she said, and now her eyes blazed with an intensity that both alarmed and fascinated him. "The mother superior will tell you I do not lie! It was she who told me that my father had promised to provide a dowry for me!"

Alex was shaken. He looked at the girl's chaperone. "Is this true, *madame?*"

"I believe so, *m'sieu'*," Madame Duclos answered with lifted eyebrows.

He looked at her with sharpness, recognizing in her that quality of social arrogance that marked the older Creole families, an arrogance that usually accompanied a biting contempt for anything American. She was saying little, but she was not to be underestimated. He wondered where she fitted into this conspiracy, if conspiracy it proved to be. He was fairly certain that's what it was.

The mother superior, no less! His jaw knotted. "Believe me, I'll ask her. *Bonjour, madame, mademoiselle!*"

He bowed and left the room.

Outside, he headed for his office, walking very fast. After half a block, he realized that he was very angry and, wondering at himself, slowed down. He did not ordinarily get emotionally worked up over his cases. Was his loss of control because this girl threatened Nanette?

Then he realized that he had not once thought of Nanette during the interview, and yet his mind was filled with visions of the girl who threatened her. The proud, slender neck, the luxurious fall of tawny hair, the warm peach of her skin, undiminished by the somber black costume, the lovely shape of her mouth speaking those outrageous lies. And the power of those strange eyes!

Danger. The warning was only a flash of intuition, but it was there. And not only to Nanette's inheritance.

Chapter Thirteen

Aurélie wakened from a dream that was fast slipping away from her, leaving only a desolate feeling of rejection and loss. She grasped at the receding image, and succeeded only in recalling the blinding white of the imposing columns of the Manse, and the impression that she had been turned away from that coldly impressive entrance.

She heard a step in the hall and struggled up against her pillows, expecting Julienne with the breakfast tray. But the step halted just beyond her door, and she heard a man's voice.

"—and saddle my horse at about four o'clock, Lafitte. I'll be riding to the Manse tonight."

She knew that voice! Snatching her light cotton robe, Aurélie ran on bare feet to the door and opened it cautiously. Peering through the crack, she saw two men in the hall; a black servant standing just outside an opened bedchamber door, and a young man in a beautifully cut brown frock coat and trousers. Could it be . . . ? Yes, it was Monsieur Archer, the young lawyer who had called on her, representing the Crowley family.

A gasp escaped from Aurélie's lips. Monsieur Archer had rooms in her pension? The enemy was sleeping in a bedchamber across the hall from her own? Hastily she closed the door.

She listened to his steps running lightly down the stairway to the front door, her indignation growing. When Julienne arrived with their breakfast trays, Aurélie tied her robe securely around her and knocked on Madame Duclos's connecting door. "May I take my *café au lait* with you, *madame*?"

"*Oui, ma chère.*"

Madame was sitting at the small table in her room enveloped in a flowing blue robe. "*Bonjour.* Come in."

"*Bonjour, madame.*" Aurélie sat and folded her hands tensely in her lap while Julienne set the trays down before them. When the servant had been dismissed, she hissed, "He's here."

"Who is here, *chère*?"

"M'sieu' Archer, the lawyer. He stays in a room across the hall. I saw him leave this morning!"

"So?"

"He is the enemy. He spies on us!"

"Ahn?" Madame replied in her deep, rich voice. "And who was doing the spying this morning?"

Aurélie flushed scarlet.

Madame laughed. "The enemy is handsome, no?" she asked slyly.

"He is not nearly so handsome as Michel," Aurélie retorted. "And Michel is on my side!"

"I was teasing, *m' petite.* Where else would a young

bachelor find a room with breakfast? This is probably the town's only pension. Come, drink your coffee and eat your rolls. And remember that Michel expects you to be dutiful and discreet, as becomes a convent-trained young woman. Today we must look in your wardrobe and decide which *deuil* gown you will wear to mass on Sunday. Everyone will be there, and everyone's eyes will be on you. Don't imagine that the servants have not carried the tale of our arrival in town to every house."

"You are right, *madame*, as always," Aurélie said meekly. But her thoughts continued to dwell on the disturbing presence of the young lawyer in the pension, sleeping not over thirty feet away from her own bed!

Alex attended eleven o'clock mass at the Terrebonne parish chapel the following Sunday and was startled to see the young adventuress in the congregation. He did not notice her until he was filing out after the services. The girl and her chaperone were just ahead of him in the line waiting to greet Father Vigeaux. He recognized her by the brilliant fall of auburn hair beneath her smart little black hat.

With murmured apologies Alex pushed through the worshipers between them in time to overhear part of her conversation with the priest.

"Welcome to Terrebonne parish, Mademoiselle Crowley," the father was saying warmly. "Are you related to the Crowleys of the Manse, on Bayou Black? They are in mourning, too, I understand."

"I'm from the Catholic branch of the family, Father," Aurélie told him with perfect composure.

The priest beamed. "May God ease your sorrow," he said, adding a blessing in Latin as Aurélie bowed her head submissively.

Alex suppressed the bubble of laughter that rose in his throat, both cynical and amused, at her brashness.

Where had she come from? He had to find out.

He watched her as she descended the steps, demure and lovely, not ignoring the stares of the regular worshipers, yet not challenging them either. She was a credit to the nuns. His sisters could not have handled themselves better.

He resolved to make the trip to New Orleans to speak with the mother superior about Mademoiselle Aurélie. But first he would call on Aurélie and her dragon again, and this time he would control his emotions and not leave in anger. This time he would be more wily.

The next morning when he presented himself at the door of his pension, again as a visitor, the elderly sisters' maid let him in with a little conspiratorial smile. "Ah, *michie,* you call on Ma'm'selle 'Rélie again?"

"Please tell her I await her pleasure," Alex said a bit stiffly.

"Oh, *oui, oui, michie!*" caroled the maid. She fairly ran up the stairs, all smiles.

Alex paced the beautiful old Turkish carpet in the salon, turning words and phrases over in his mind. He was more respectful of her as an opponent since seeing how she handled herself in public. She was a determined young woman and a threat to Nanette and her mother that should not be taken lightly. He was resolved to get the name of her "witness" before he left for the city to check her story.

She came through the door, a vision of loveliness in the black that merely focused attention on her lively face. Her dress was of sheer cotton, which revealed the warm tones of her arms and upper bosom through the sleeves and yoke. Velvet ribbons tied in tiny bows were fastened randomly on its full skirt, with a larger bow at her modest neckline. Madame Duclos followed her in and, with a dour nod to him, settled herself in a chair.

Aurélie's eyes sparkled with green lights. *"Bonjour, Monsieur Archer,"* she said, with every indication of being delighted to see him, except for that glint in her eyes.

Alex responded to her subtle challenge with a quickened pulse. *"Bonjour, mademoiselle."*

"You have more questions for me?" she inquired sweetly.

"A few." He could not keep the sarcastic edge from his tone. "You attended mass Sunday morning."

"But, naturally."

"I happened to overhear your invention of a Catholic branch of the Crowley family. That was an inspiration of the moment, I take it, since I happen to know such a branch doesn't exist."

"How do you know?" she inquired, with bright interest.

Alex's cheeks warmed. "As an old friend of the family. In fact, as the betrothed of Mademoiselle Nanette Crowley—" He did not know why he volunteered that bit of personal information unless it was in self-defense against the lure of her beauty. He was angry with himself at once.

There was a little silence.

"Are you, indeed? Then you knew my father too!" She was regarding him with intense interest, looking as if she were bursting with questions.

Again he had misjudged her. His revelations had not dented her composure. "Very well! I know that he was a Presbyterian who chose to have his daughter tutored at home instead of sending her to the convent."

"Perhaps," Aurélie said thoughtfully, "because I was there?"

Alex stared at her.

She grinned. *"I* am the Catholic branch of the family, *m'sieu'."*

Flushing, Alex said sternly, "I came, *ma'm'selle,* to advise you that I intend to journey to New Orleans to speak to the mother superior about your claim—"

"Ah, bon!"

"—and to urge you to give me the name of Monsieur Crowley's friend and any others I might talk with while I'm in the city. I'm sure you realize that any information you can give me will help us resolve your case more quickly."

"But, of course!" she said, surprising him again. "It was his friend Michel who told me about my dowry. Michel Jardin."

Alex's jaw dropped. "Jardin?"

"You know him?" she exclaimed, warm peach washing into her cheeks.

"Oui, mademoiselle. I know him." He tried to hide his surprise, not only at the name but at her willingness to reveal it, sparing him all the devious moves he had planned in order to get her fellow conspirator's name.

"No one else?" he asked.

"Perhaps some of the nuns, but the mother superior will speak for them."

"Then I will speak with Monsieur Jardin as well as the mother superior. *Adieu, mademoiselle. Madame,* I shall make inquiries about you, also, while I am in the city."

"You will find I am well connected, *m'sieu',"* Madame Duclos said with a wintry smile.

He bowed and turned to the door. Well connected? So was Jardin, but a scoundrel just the same!

He walked back to his office in confused thought and sat at his desk. The girl had the most amazing ability to scatter his thoughts. She could not possibly know how much doubt Michel Jardin's name alone had cast on her story. Yet there was a crazy kind of logic to it.

Michel Jardin had been one of his rivals for Nanette before their informal understanding was made generally known in New Orleans the previous winter. But Jardin had been just one of several impoverished young Creoles who hovered around the eligible heiresses like bees in a blossoming orange tree. Alex had not been aware of any close friendship between Jardin and Nanette's father, although Jardin had been one of the regular callers at the Crowley house.

Was it blackmail, then?

He reminded himself again that Aurélie must have been conceived when he and Jardin were both in the nursery. If Jardin had proof she was Evan Crowley's daughter, how had he come by it? And how did he hope to profit from sponsoring her claim?

Marriage? To an illegitimate daughter who was using blackmail to procure a dowry? Was the money that important to Jardin?

Yes, possibly. But not to Jardin's aristocratic family! They would fight such a union, unless Michel were already disgraced and they had turned him out.

There was much to be learned in New Orleans, and some of it—whatever was local public knowledge—he could get from his parents or his sisters. The opportunity for the visit with his family that he had hoped would occur at his wedding added a strong appeal to the necessity for journeying to the city.

When Alex closed his office, he ordered his horse saddled and once more set out for the Manse.

The butler admitted him. Alex said, "Will you tell your mistress that I would like to speak to her in private, Radcliffe?"

"Oui, michie."

"If it's about that adventuress, I want to hear it," Nanette announced from the salon door. She was wearing a touch of white at her throat, but no jewelry, and she still looked pale with little lines of restlessness around her blue eyes. She missed her father, who had doted on her, but also her mother's withdrawal from all social activity where she might encounter music or entertainment was hard on Nanette, he knew, for while a young woman was not so restricted by the conventions of mourning, there were many things she could not attend unchaperoned.

Alex put his hands on her shoulders and gave her a chaste kiss first on one cheek and then the other. Since the postponement of their marriage, he would not steal a kiss of passion even when he had an opportunity so tempting—there was too much frustration in his present situation. "Forgive me, Nanette? This is something I must discuss with your mother alone."

"You'll have to tell me, sooner or later," she pouted. "Why not now?"

"Indulge me in this, darling. Your mother and I will both speak more comfortably if we are alone. How is your mother?"

"Still grieving. She worries about those dreadful people—"

Alex had a clear image of glinting green eyes. "Not dreadful, Nanette. Just—very clever."

She shrugged. "It's all the same. Very well. I'll take you upstairs and leave you with Mama."

Madame Crowley received him on the upper *galerie*

outside her bedchamber, dressed in unrelieved black. "Alex! What would we do without you?" she exclaimed. "You are such a comfort to me. Would you like a whiskey, or some tea?"

"Tea would be welcome, *madame.*"

"I'll order it, Mama," Nanette said, and left them.

Alex sat across the tea table from Nanette's mother and said, "I have something to tell you before Nanette returns. I talked with the young woman who calls herself Aurélie Crowley again and obtained the name of her 'witness.' She claims it was Michel Jardin whom Evan told he had promised her a dowry."

Elizabeth straightened. "Michael?" she exclaimed in disbelief. She had always insisted on using the English version of Jardin's name, he remembered. "That proves she's a liar! Evan wouldn't have told him anything, not even a joke!"

"I thought as much," Alex said.

"He disliked the man intensely. Michael had the effrontery to offer for Nanette, did you know that? Offer! He had nothing to bring to the marriage. He was simply asking us for her hand filled with money, that's what it amounted to."

"It's an old Creole custom," Alex said, with a flash of humor.

Elizabeth was not diverted. "Naturally, Evan rejected him out of hand. Is he back of this preposterous story, Alex?"

"She claims that he has offered to testify for her if she sues," Alex reminded her.

"Sue!" Elizabeth repeated, in outraged tones.

"The mystery is this. If there was a—an incident in your husband's life that we know nothing about, where did Michel Jardin learn of it?"

Elizabeth's pale cheeks began to show mottled spots of color. "There was no incident, Alex! That story is a monstrous, impudent lie. If Michel is involved, it's sheer vindictiveness on his part because he was so summarily dismissed by my husband when he sought to become a member of our family! He has found some strumpet—"

Alex winced. Whoever she was, Aurélie "Crowley" was no strumpet. He said, "We must remember that she is convent-reared, *madame*. I think I should go to New Orleans and find out if her story that Monsieur Crowley paid her expenses at the Ursuline convent is true, and also to find out, if possible, how Jardin got mixed up in this. I go as your representative, of course, if you authorize it."

Elizabeth sighed. "What do you expect to find?"

"Proof that she's lying."

"Of course she's lying! She should have to prove *her* story, instead of—"

"I want to be prepared, in case it becomes necessary to prevent her from going to court with her story," Alex said patiently. "I fear that would be most unpleasant for you and Nanette, especially at this time. There would be a lot of speculation, absurd rumors . . . people tend to say, 'Where there's smoke,' you know."

Elizabeth sat in mutinous thought for a moment, but finally said, "I suppose I must tell you to go, and that I will pay your expenses. We won't get any answers here, will we?"

"I'm afraid not, *madame*."

"Very well, Alex. Now let's forget the creature! You'll stay to sup with us, won't you?"

"Delighted to, but now I'll have some of that tea."

The footman was just coming out on the *galerie* with the big silver tray. It held three cups and a plate of cakes as well as the teapot and sugar bowl and creamer. Nanette appeared in the doorway behind him. "Can I come out now?"

"You were listening!" Alex accused her.

"I didn't hear a word," she said mischievously.

Laughing, Alex stood up and pulled out a chair for her.

Aurélie had become very conscious of Monsieur Archer's presence in the pension. She listened every morning for his running steps on the stairs. He was always running! He left before she arose, apparently after breakfasting in his rooms. He returned between four and five in the afternoon, and for a half an hour there were voices, his and that of his servant, who ran downstairs for hot water and hurried back.

After the sounds of a quick toilette—the splash of water, the rapid footsteps and the creak of floorboards, sometimes the explosion of a mild oath, then the slam of his bedchamber door—she heard him on the stairway again. The front door banged shut and Aurélie, who had likely been sitting frozen above her book or her embroidery, straightened her tilted head and again began listening to Madame Duclos.

One morning later than usual, Aurélie heard them both leave, Monsieur and his servant. When Julienne brought her *café au lait,* she volunteered the information that Lafitte and his master had left for New Orleans to be gone for several weeks. Oddly, Aurélie continued to listen for those light running steps each morning upon first awakening, and life in the pension seemed dull without them.

Madame Duclos took paper and pen and ink and wrote a letter which she arranged to send by the weekly post to Michel Jardin. "Do you wish to send a message, *chère*?" she asked Aurélie.

"Yes, please tell him that I am well."

"Is that all?" Madame Duclos asked, with a teasing smile.

"—and that I think often of his kindness and generosity. And—I hope he remains well."

"And is *that* all?"

"—and—and—that I look forward to our next meeting?"

Satisfied, Madame Duclos said no more.

Aurélie thought, "It's strange, but I've missed those running steps on the stairway more!" But she did not say so. She told herself that she was obsessed with the idea Monsieur Archer had been spying on her. That was all.

He's a handsome enemy, no? her mind said, mimicking Madame's teasing voice.

But not as handsome as Michel, she told it. And not nearly as kind!

Nevertheless, there is something about him—

He is betrothed to my half sister!

Naturally he would be protective of her, but does he really love her? Would a man in love look at you the way he does, sometimes? As if he wants to hate you, but cannot?

He is my enemy!

That night Aurélie dreamed about the Manse again. Again she presented herself at the beautiful door with the graceful fanlight above it, but she was alone and much younger. She knocked repeatedly, growing more and more anxious. At last the door opened. Her father stood there, smiling down at her.

She cried, in anguish, "Why didn't you let me in?"

He kept that familiar quizzical smile on his face, saying nothing, and she wakened with moisture on her cheeks and a dull headache.

Chapter Fourteen

Alex arrived at Bellemont in a hired carriage just at dusk. The "big house" gleamed whitely in the fading light. Windows glowed in the original plantation home his mother's grandfather had built and the two graceful wings his father had added. The gates of the drive were closed, but a straggling line of black youngsters came running over the grass and had them open before the coachman could dismount from his high seat.

"Michie! Michie Alex!" they shrieked in chorus, seeing him at his window.

He laughed and waved at them. Their welcome at the gate was something that never changed at Bellemont.

The coachman, caught up in their excitement, flicked his team and they galloped up the drive with style, the children running after the carriage, and came to a dramatic stop in front of the *galerie* where Alex's family were gathered to greet him. Standing beside his mother and father was his sister Antoinette, her fine red hair caught up with combs above her ears. She was holding her infant son, and her husband, Robert Robichaux, and Alex's younger sister, dark-haired Thérèse, stood near her.

Alex jumped out and ran eagerly up the steps to embrace them all, leaving Lafitte to put the excited youngsters to work unloading and carrying up his luggage. Everyone was talking at once, asking about Nanette and Madame Crowley, expressing their sympathy, and quizzing him about his trip up the bayou and down the river.

"Next year we'll have a cross-country railroad completed to those parishes," Jeff Archer predicted.

"Across those *prairies tremblantes?*" Alex scoffed. "You haven't seen them working on it, Papa. I have. They lose tools and mules and even workers in the swamp. The first locomotive to cross it will sink!"

"I hope not," his father said mildly. "I'm heavily invested in it."

"We're *so* disappointed about the wedding," Antoinette, his married sister, told him. "We were all looking forward to a trip to the Terrebonne to see where you and Nanette will be living."

"It's terrible to have to postpone it," declared Thérèse, who, Alex observed, was beginning to rival their mother's beauty. "Nanette's wedding dress will be out of style."

Melodie waited silently, a loving smile on her face, for her son's hug, and a kiss on each cheek. "Have I time for a bath and change before dinner, *maman?*" Alex asked her, and they finally let him escape to his old room on the upper floor.

That evening he devoted to his family, hearing about his young nephew's first words and Thérèse's suitors and saying nothing about the reason for his visit. In the morning he rode with his father when Jeff went to his law offices in the city, rapping on the ceiling to stop the coachman when they neared the Ursuline convent and telling his father only that he had business with the mother superior. A few minutes later he was admitted to the office of the nun who administered the convent.

"M'sieu' Archer," she greeted him, smiling. "How are your sisters?"

When he assured her of their health and happiness, he said, "I am representing the Crowley family in an investigation of one of your former students, a Mademoiselle Aurélie—"

"Aurélie Boudin?" she said, her expression lightening as soon as she heard the name. "A charming young woman, sweet-tempered and generous. She was good with the young orphans we placed under her care. We miss her, *m'sieu'*."

"Boudin?" Alex made note of the name. "She is calling herself Aurélie Crowley, Reverend Mother."

The nun's expression altered subtly. "Ah, yes, she believes herself to be M'sieu' Crowley's illegitimate daughter."

"Do you believe this, Reverend Mother?"

The nun made a steeple of her fingers. "She is illegitimate, yes. We don't know who are her parents. M'sieu' Crowley brought her to us, but he told us he was acting for her father, who wished to remain anonymous and would not reveal her mother's name. A tragic story."

"Is it true that M'sieu' Crowley promised to give her a dowry when she married?"

"He said that her father would provide a dowry when the time came," she corrected him gently. "But no marriage was arranged. After his death, M'sieu' Jardin came to tell us that M'sieu' Crowley had confided in him, and he offered to take the responsibility for finding a husband for her."

"Jardin," Alex repeated heavily. "And you allowed this, Reverend Mother?"

"Madame Duclos has impeccable qualifications for chaperoning the girl until her marriage, *m'sieu'*."

"But Jardin! I'm sorry, Reverend Mother, but he is a notorious rakehell, and a heavy gambler—"

"But he did bring Madame Duclos when he came to offer his assistance, and we entrusted Aurélie to her, not to him. We must not discourage M'sieu' Jardin if he has decided to atone for past sins by a generous act. Remember, Aurélie is of age. We couldn't keep her here when she wanted to go."

"She is threatening to sue for a share of the Crowley estate," Alex said bluntly, "which will cause a pretty scandal. I wouldn't be surprised if Jardin suggested it to her."

The mother superior shook her head. "I'm sorry to hear this, but you may be wrong, *m'sieu'*. Aurélie has a quick mind and a strong character, and she also has a deep need to be acknowledged by a family she thinks abandoned her. It amounts to an obsession with her, I fear." She made a gesture with her expressive hands. "It is sad, no? Because her illegitimacy will prevent her from finding the acceptance she needs."

Alex did not dare consider his feelings at that moment. They were becoming more confused rather than clearer. He took refuge in formality. "I am directed by Madame Crowley to investigate this matter for her so her husband's will can be probated. I think it will be necessary for me to question the family that gave Aurélie her name. What can you tell me about them?"

The mother superior signaled to her assistant, and the young nun brought her a large ledger. It was cool in the gray room with its stone walls and stone floor, but the sun shining in through high windows threw a flood of light on the mother superior as she turned pages of fine script.

"Aurélie Boudin . . . was given to the Joseph Boudin family of False River soon after her birth. She apparently stayed with them until M'sieu' Crowley brought her to us as a boarder on the third day of August, 1842. She was with us for nearly twelve years, *m'sieu'*."

She raised her head, her gaze going past him to a painting of Christ on her wall. "She was a spirited child —and she grew into a lovely, dutiful young woman . . . I shall pray for her soul."

Alex thanked her and left, walking slowly through the busy morning streets of the city to his father's office. There he greeted his father's employees and answered their eager questions about the interior and marveled with them at the changes in the bustling port since his departure. It was not until he and his father left the office to lunch at Jeff's favorite café that Alex revealed the reason for his visit.

"The mother superior supports the girl's story that she was placed in the convent by Evan Crowley, and that he visited her there when he was in the city, bringing gifts. But she says Crowley claimed to be acting for an anonymous father. You've known M'sieu' Crowley for a long time, Papa. Do you know of any adventure he had with a young woman of society?"

"No," his father said without hesitation, "and I know of no scandal of that sort in our set that could involve him. If he fathered a child, he was very discreet about it.

But Evan had many acquaintances in the city, and I suppose he could have been acting for one of them."

He was silent for a time, as they entered the café, looking troubled. He asked for a table in a corner that gave them some privacy and, when they were seated, asked, "Is there a possibility the girl's mother was an octoroon?"

Alex started. "The idea had not occurred to me! No!" he said almost immediately. "No, it isn't possible. If you could see her—!"

"Ask your mother to tell you about her cousin Jean-Philippe," his father said cryptically. "How old is the girl?"

"About eighteen. She was brought to the convent as an orphan when she was six, close to twelve years ago."

"Eighteen," Jeff mused. "That would have been about the time we first met the Crowleys." He leaned back to allow the waiter to put their luncheon plates before them, heaps of golden fried shrimp with a bowl of tangy sauce as accompaniment. "I should have said when we met Madame Crowley. Evan failed to show up at the dinner in their honor to which we were invited by the Fieldings. It was some trouble involving his old family nurse, I remember now, a slave he brought from Virginia and freed. He had bought her a bakery on Chartres Street. It's still there, I believe, but she would be ancient now, if she's still alive. If she is, she might know something. It may be worth a try."

"I'll walk around there this afternoon."

Alex was silent for a few moments while they ate their shrimp. He was thinking about Aurélie as a six-year-old girl, taken from the only home she knew and placed in the convent's orphanage. He felt again that wrench of sympathy for the beautiful, misdirected young woman, and a distaste for what he was doing. "I'll have to make a visit down False River," he said. "But first I think I'll call on Mike Jardin. . . . What's this about *maman's* cousin?"

"That will be difficult," said his father. "I believe Jardin left the city on the steamboat going upriver yesterday. I happened to be at the landing when he boarded it with luggage."

Alex swore softly, and for the moment forgot about Cousin Jean-Philippe. "What has Jardin been doing since I left? The usual rakehell rousting?"

"Gambling," his father said. "At least, gossip has it that he has sustained heavy losses and his father has threatened to disown him."

"Where is he getting his money? He was always strapped."

His father shrugged. "From friends, no doubt."

"He's on his way to Terrebonne parish now—to press his blackmail against Nanette and Madame Crowley, no doubt," Alex said gloomily.

"You don't have proof of that yet," his father reminded him.

But Alex was sure Jardin was involved. And that Madame Duclos hoped in some way to profit from her chaperonage of the girl. He could see no way they could profit except by a marriage between Jardin and the girl, and the way they were using her depressed him. What move were they making in his absence? He should be in the parish where he could keep his eye on them. He resolved to finish his business in the city as quickly as possible.

He parted from his father when they left the café and walked out on the rue Chartres until he came to a bakery in the ground floor of a nice little property with an entrance running back beside it to a small court.

He went into the shop and was greeted by a young mulatto. *"Du pain, m'sieu'?"* she asked amiably.

"No, thank you. I didn't come to buy bread, but to inquire who owns this property."

"M'sieu' Evan Crowley own it," she answered with no hesitation.

"Does his old nurse still live here?"

"Pardon?"

"The old woman who once ran the bakery, is she still here?"

"Ah, *non, m'sieu'*. That old woman, she been dead before we come here."

"We?"

"My mother and me. M'sieu' Crowley hire us after the old woman die."

Alex thanked her and went out into the street. A beggar sitting on the *banquette* with his back against the house next to the bakery squinted up at him, and held up a shaking palm. The sun on his face revealed many deep wrinkles around slitted eyes with a gleam of humor in them. "You don' like her bread, *m'sieu'*?"

"I was buying information," Alex said, on an inspiration. He took a coin out of his pocket. "Did you know the old woman who used to make the bread? The old one from Virginia?"

"The old one who died? *Oui, m'sieu'*, but she don't make *le pain*. The other one bake it, the one the police took away."

"What for?" Alex asked quickly.

"She chase somebody out of the shop with a kitchen knife!" The old man cackled. "I tell you for true, people scattered."

"When was that?"

"Before your time, *m'sieu'*." A sly grin lingered on his gray lips. "These old eyes have seen much, much, *m'sieu'*."

A knifing on his property could have taken Evan away from a dinner party in his honor and kept him most of the night, Alex thought, amused to think that he could clear up that old mystery for his father. He tossed the beggar a coin and went back to his father's office.

On the next day he took one of the family carriages and a groom and set off for the plantations lying along a former finger of the river that was now cut off from its main course, resulting in one of the region's loveliest bayous.

He found the Boudin plantation without difficulty. It was a small one, prosperous in a modest way. Madame Boudin was a plump Cajun housewife who readily answered his questions.

"I had lost a baby, *m'sieu'*, and I had much discomfort with my abundance of milk. We lived in the city then. I complained, and my doctor, he said he would ask if someone was in need of a wet nurse. That was how it happen' that one day a woman wearing a veil appear' at my door with a month-old girl. M'sieu', it was a blessing from the Virgin! The money I was paid made it possible for my husband to buy this land on which he cultivates sugar, and we prosper. But it was hard-hard to give up little 'Rélie when her father decide' she must be taught by the nuns. We had her for six years, *m'sieu'*."

"You say she was brought by a veiled woman?" Alex asked her. "Was she a white woman or a woman of color?"

"She was white, *m'sieu'*. Oh, yes, I could see that. She

was no black nurse. But she was not the child's mother. I knew that for sure."

"And who took her away from you? Was it her father?"

"It was M'sieu' Crowley. He said that her father wanted her educated. M'sieu', I miss' her so much! At first I went to the convent to visit her, but the nuns said it upset her much and that M'sieu' Crowley advise' against it." Tears suddenly appeared in her eyes, and Alex felt pity for her.

"Who was the doctor who arranged this for you, *madame*? Is he still living?"

"Ah, no. I've had to find a new physician these many years ago."

She could tell him no more. Alex made the long drive back to Bellemont feeling discouraged.

On the Sunday after Alex left, a stylishly dressed Creole lady approached Madame Duclos as she and Aurélie were leaving the church, and introduced herself. "I am Claire Poitevin. Father Vigeaux is coming to my house Wednesday morning to take coffee with my family and a few women who are my neighbors. We would be so happy if you and your ward"—she hesitated delicately —"would join us."

"You are very kind," Madame Duclos replied, "but we are in mourning, as you see."

"You need have no fear, *madame*, there will be no entertainment of any kind. It will merely provide an opportunity for you to become better acquainted with Father Vigeaux, and to meet some ladies of the congregation, who are most sympathetic."

"In that case," Madame Duclos said graciously.

"At ten o'clock, at Rosewood," Madame Poitevin said, and walked on.

As they took the carriage they had hired back to their pension, Aurélie said, "I wonder if Madame Crowley and Nanette will be there?"

"I don't think you need to worry about their coming to meet with Father Vigeaux, since they are Protestant."

"But my half sister is to marry M'sieu' Archer, who is Catholic."

"I don't understand that," Madame Duclos admitted. "Some adjustment has to be made in a situation of that kind. Yes, you're right. The Father might very well be involved there."

But Madame Crowley and Nanette were not among the small group on the *galerie* of Rosewood plantation taking coffee that Wednesday morning. There was another man besides Father Vigeaux among the company, however. Madame Poitevin's son, Charles, passed the cups for his mother and then took a chair next to Aurélie.

"Have you felt my eyes on you in church?" he asked her, smiling. "Last Sunday I missed most of the sermon, looking for you."

"For shame!" Aurélie said sternly, but she felt laughter rising to her throat. She repressed it, but murmured, "I know that feeling, *m'sieu'*, I often found my mind wandering in chapel at the convent when the sermon was long."

"If you were not in mourning, I would prevail upon my mother to send you an invitation to her ball next month. Is the one you mourn a very close relative?"

"Quite close, *m'sieu'*. I fear it is too soon for me to attend a ball."

"Will your dragon permit me to call on you, perhaps?"

"I think not just yet," she said gently, eyeing him with a tilted glance from her almond-shaped eyes that brought a dazed expression to his face. He was quite nice-looking but very young and impressionable compared to the men in her life so far, her father and Michel Jardin. Even young M'sieu' Archer was more worldly. She felt very mature.

A pair of butterflies fluttered erratically across the *galerie* and through the open shutters into the rooms behind them. The breeze carried the fragrance of the flowers blooming beyond the wrought-iron rail. The small cup in Aurélie's hand was of delicate French porcelain, and the coffee was hot and strong. This was her mother's world, the world that her mother had denied her by refusing to admit her birth. For the first time she felt that she was where she belonged.

She smiled at young Charles Poitevin and watched the rosy color deepen in his smooth young cheeks, while she parried the probing of the ladies of the congregation into her genealogy, claiming only a distant relationship to the local Crowleys, who were "not Catholic."

Going back to their pension in the hired carriage, Madame Duclos said, "Well, now we know to whom we owe the pleasure of that invitation."

"Who, *madame*?"

"That young man who became smitten with you in church. He probably browbeat his mother into inviting you so he could be properly introduced, and ask if he could call."

"Do you really think so?" Aurélie said, delighted.

But when they arrived at the pension, they found

Michel Jardin awaiting their return in the downstairs drawing room, and she forgot young Poitevin.

Alex wakened early the morning after his journey to False River. His sleep had been broken by a confused dream and he opened his eyes with his father's words repeating themselves in his head: *Ask your mother about her cousin Jean-Philippe.* The admonition had not had much impact at the time. Now he wondered about it.

Jean-Philippe was the cousin who was buried privately in a marble tomb near the old mansion on his father's other plantation, the one called La Sorcellerie. Alex had stumbled on it on one of his rambles on horseback while a boy. It was an untended grave, as neglected as the old house, with ugly, aging vines covering most of the incised inscription.

With his pocketknife he had cut back the foliage until he could make out the letters:

Jean-Philippe de l'Église
né à Paris, France, 5 Mai 1804
mort 23 Septembre 1822

Later he had asked his mother why Cousin Jean-Philippe had not been buried in the St. Louis cemetery with the rest of his family.

"He died young. His mother wanted to keep him at La Sorcellerie."

"How did he die?" At age eleven, Alex was more interested in the how than the why of death. But he had not expected his mother's reaction or the answer she gave him.

She had gone very still and waxy white, and for a long

moment did not answer. Then she said in quick bursts of words, "He was accidentally shot by his mother for an intruder—when he brought home a—a rowdy group of friends."

"By his mother?" Alex was horrified.

Melodie had quickly hugged him. "Oh, *cher*, she was *very* sorry. That was why Cousin Angèle went into the convent, you see."

Alex sensed that there was more to the story of Cousin Jean-Philippe's private tomb, but he had not asked a second question because of the obvious pain it caused his mother to speak of it. It had left an uneasiness in his mind, and changed forever his feelings about Cousin Angèle, who had raised his mother.

Now his father had suggested that he ask her about it, and he still felt a reluctance to do so.

He went down to the dining room, and as the Fates would have it, found his mother alone at breakfast. She greeted him warmly and rang for fresh coffee. "Your father's gone into the city, and Thérèse went for an early ride. She wanted to wake you to go with her, but your father said to let you sleep."

"I'm grateful for that," he said, kissing her cheek, "and I'm glad we have a chance to talk alone, *maman*."

"So am I, *cher*. I've missed you."

Alex told her about the girl who was calling herself Aurélie Crowley. When he had finished telling her about his interviews of the past two days, he added slowly, "Papa told me to ask you about your cousin, Jean-Philippe."

Melodie said, after a hesitation, "Does this young woman have colored blood?"

"Impossible! But"—Alex felt the chill of shock travel

over his skin—"are you saying that your cousin . . . ?"
His lips felt too stiff to form the question.

Melodie nodded. Her fingers had tightened on the
handle of her cup and she set it carefully down, then
twined them together. "I've known since you and your
sisters were born that someday I would have to tell you
the story back of that marble tomb at Sorcellerie. Apparently your father thinks the time has come."

He was very conscious of her twisting fingers.

"You asked me about it once, do you remember? But
you were so young. I couldn't—Antoinette is the only
one I have told. She and Robert had to know the truth
before they married—"

Seeing his stricken expression, she said swiftly, "Not
because there was anything that could prevent their
marriage, Alex! Only because someday someone would
tell Robert a distorted version of what really happened.
I know there is still gossip, occasionally resurrected by
someone who wants to wound me. Most of the gossip is
untrue. Very few people know the truth."

She looked at him so sadly that Alex reached for one
of her hands and held it tightly. "What is the truth,
maman?"

"I feel desperately sorry for your young woman who
is claiming her father's name, because, like her, I am
'illegitimate.' But instead of abandoning me, my
mother married another man who died in the Battle of
New Orleans thinking I was his daughter."

It was not what Alex had expected to hear. He could
see how difficult this was for her, and he exclaimed,
"*Maman, chère,* how can that matter now?"

"It is sad, but it really doesn't matter beside the
greater tragedy dear Cousin Angèle suffered. Hers was
a family of mixed race. Her mother died after they

escaped the Negro uprising in Saint Domingue in 1791 and her father took the black servant who saved their lives as his mistress. You remember old Mimi, don't you, who was nurse to you and your sisters when you were small? She was like a mother to Cousin Angèle—and to me, when I lived with them. Our Ouma is Mimi's son, half brother to Cousin Angèle."

"Ouma," Alex said numbly. Ouma was a free colored, hired by his father to manage the sugar plantings and the grinding, and paid a good wage. Alex had idolized the big gentle man as a child, and still respected him. Ouma was one of the family? The ground seemed to have shifted beneath his feet. But he knew there was more.

His skin felt icy cold. "And Cousin Jean-Philippe?" He heard his voice as if it came from someone else.

"Was *my* half brother," Melodie said, so low he scarcely heard her. "I learned the truth the same horrible night that he learned he was not white, that he was not Cousin Angèle's son as he had been brought up to believe, but the son of Mimi's daughter and my real father, who was the *comte,* Cousin Angèle's husband—and that Ouma, whom he had once whipped, was his uncle—and that he could not inherit La Sorcellerie, which we both loved. He—he . . ." She paused and drew a deep breath to control her shaking voice.

"This is difficult for me to tell you, my son. He had asked for my hand. When he was denied everything, he tried to take it by force. That's the real reason Cousin Angèle shot him."

"Mon dieu!" Alex breathed.

"I've shocked you, Alex. I'm sorry I was so blunt, but even now I can't—I can't bear to—"

From beyond the open doors to the *galerie,* they

heard Thérèse's clear voice. Melodie rose from the table. "I can't talk to her just now," she said. "Alex, I will never speak of this again, don't ask me—" Swiftly she left the dining room.

Alex sat in a daze of disbelief and confused emotions. Mimi, Ouma's mother, had loved him and his sisters like her own children, but she was gone now, taken to her well-deserved rest while he was at Harvard. She had been like one of the family; she had earned the place that had been hers by birthright.

I wish I'd known while Mimi was still alive.

"Why are you sitting there letting your coffee get cold?" Thérèse asked him, in an amused voice. "If you weren't such a sleepyhead, you could have gone riding with me this morning." She poured herself some coffee at the server.

"I wish I had, *chère,*" Alex groaned.

"What a head you must have!" she said unfeelingly. "Who were you carousing with last night?"

Chapter Fifteen

"M'sieu' Jardin!" Aurélie exclaimed warmly. "We were not expecting you."

It had been two months since he had escorted her and Madame Duclos to the steamboat landing in New Orleans and charged the captain with providing them with every courtesy. Now he stood in the drawing room of the pension, his elegance in the dark frock coat and white waistcoat in gleaming contrast to the shabbiness of the worn damask covering the delicate French chairs and the faded velvet window drapes with their faint smell of mold.

His smile was the one Aurélie remembered framed by the visitors' grid at the convent when all she could see were those curved lips parted to show beautiful white teeth. Now she could see his eyes, smoky dark with violet smudges—of dissipation?—beneath them. There was something in them that made her feel a woman, and at the same time a little uncomfortable with him.

A look passed between him and Madame Duclos that Aurélie caught but did not understand. It left her with the impression that they knew something she did not, and her heart leapt with impatience.

She had extended her hand, and M'sieu' Jardin took it in his and brought it to his lips in a practiced gesture that both pleased and embarrassed her.

"I've come to see what progress you are making with the Crowley family."

Aurélie stopped smiling. "They were very cold." In spite of herself, her voice faltered as she remembered the cool contempt in her half sister's eyes when Madame Crowley asked her butler to show them the door.

"They have hired a lawyer," she told him, "who has called on us twice. He doesn't believe my story."

Again Michel looked at Madame Duclos, who nodded her head.

M'sieu Jardin looked older than Aurélie remembered. He must be older than M'sieu' Archer because his dark hair was silvering at the temples. A handsome man, all in black and silver-white, with a strong nose and jaw, and youthful color in his olive cheeks. A mature and experienced man who would be able to prevail against a cocksure young lawyer who thought he was protecting her half sister from a thieving imposter.

"The lawyer has gone to New Orleans," Aurélie continued. "You didn't see him there, *m'sieu'*? He intended to interview you, as well as the mother superior at the convent. His name is M'sieu' Archer. He said that he knew you."

"Oh, yes, I know him."

"He is affianced to my half sister."

"I know," Michel said, and again Aurélie had a sense of being left out of things. "I'll be calling at the Manse."

"Where are you staying?" Madame Duclos asked abruptly. "Not here!"

"No, *madame.* I am a guest at a plantation up the bayou from here. Friends I've stayed with often before."

"*Bon,*" Madame said. "When do you call on the Crowleys?"

"Tomorrow."

They were arranging the next step of her campaign without consulting her. Aurélie suppressed her annoyance, knowing she could not have made her claim for recognition without Michel.

She turned her thoughts instead to her half sister, remembering the fair, curling hair piled stylishly on top of her head, with little tendrils of gold on her forehead, the pale skin, and the blue eyes, round and wide open like their father's. Her own eyes must have been given her by that mysterious mother who had rejected her. Nanette and Madame Crowley had rejected her, too, but that was more understandable than that her own mother—

Aurélie's heart contracted with a longing that was painful in its intensity. If only Nanette Crowley had accepted their relationship—if they could be sisters, really sisters! Her need for family was so great she ached for it.

"I'll come again or send word in a few days," Michel told them. "After I've talked with Madame Crowley." He took his leave, refusing any refreshment, but taking Aurélie's hand in his again with a lingering pressure.

"They should welcome a lovely young lady like you with open arms. I would!" he said with such sympathetic regret that Aurélie felt a flush rising from her bosom up her throat to her cheeks.

"He has a *tendresse* for you," Madame Duclos told her as they ascended the stairs to their private quarters.

"Oh, no!" Aurélie exclaimed, but the flush of heat remained on her cheeks.

Alex shunned the game room on the steamboat churning up the Mississippi to Donaldsonville. He had no interest in playing cards. Instead he walked the deck, avoiding other travelers, his head filled with the enormity of the implications in the brief story his mother had told him. Old Mimi and her son Ouma, blood relatives of the Rogets! He'd heard such stories before, but . . . his *mother's* family?

Old Mimi had been his mother's nurse, and had ruled the nursery at Bellemont when he and his sisters were young. He had followed Ouma around the plantation like a half-grown puppy. He had taken them pretty much for granted, as he had the presence of slaves on the plantation.

But Mimi and Ouma were *gens libres*— free people of color. There was a whole substratum of them in New Orleans—merchants, artisans, and workers, with its own society, rich and poor, and its own leaders, a society of mixed blood.

He had always known of its existence, but it had not had this reality for him before. Now he saw its relationship to the Creole society he had been raised in, like a shadow population composed of unacknowledged cousins of the Creole families that made up his world. He had never really thought about it before, but it had scarcely left his mind since his mother had told him about her cousin—no, her half brother!—Jean-Philippe.

A phrase she had dropped into the story would not go away. *He wanted to offer for me.* It had clanged like a gong in his head, scattering his thoughts. He could not forget it.

He looked down at the paddles of the huge wheel slicing into the dun-colored water, throwing up muddy droplets and trailing foam. The river was still high, and now and then a log could be seen floating downstream, submerged except for part of its corolla of roots, the only warning to unwary navigators. How did the helmsman manage to avoid such monstrous menaces?

He could have been born into that circumscribed underworld whose inhabitants were forbidden by the Black Code to bring suit against a white person, or to represent themselves as equals of white persons, as in marriage, whose women for a hundred years had been forced to cover their hair with a *tignon* because the Spanish governor's wife had been envious of the stunning beauty of the quadroons and their elaborate hairdress. . . .

Maman had loved Jean-Philippe. He had heard it in her voice. *He tried to take what he wanted by force—* his half sister, the heiress Melodie Bellamy too?—*that was the real reason Cousin Angèle shot him.*

He could so easily have been one of the subworld, Alex thought. Or perhaps could have successfully passed as white and never known he was doing it? Which must have been Cousin Angèle's intention in the beginning, when she took that illegitimate son of her husband's for her own. But she had not known then that her husband was also Melodie's father!

What a rake that man who had made Cousin Angèle a countess must have been! What a quicksand life was!

He thought about Cousin Angèle in the convent, working in the nun's kitchen garden as weed-woman. There must have been talk, not only about the tragedy, but about his great-uncle's black mistress. He wondered bitterly which of his parents' generation had whispered behind his back all the while he was growing up in innocence.

He had been an infant when Cousin Angèle died, but he had heard about her all his life. She had raised *maman*. They had lived at Sorcellerie when it was one of the loveliest plantation houses on Bayou St. John, when its balls were legendary, when his father was courting his mother. And the unhappy Jean-Philippe had lived there . . . died there in his own blood. No wonder his mother would never listen to talk of restoring La Sorcellerie!

He would still like to do it.

Nanette's mother had long coveted the place, he knew. He was not sure how Nanette herself would feel about living in the old ruin.

The girl who called herself Aurélie Crowley stole unbidden into his thoughts. He considered her beauty, her spirit, the delightful innocence that made her demand to be acknowledged in Evan Crowley's estate seem more pathetic than greedy.

He remembered Nanette saying, "Those dreadful people!" and thought that he must have fallen under the girl's spell, because he thought Aurélie Boudin—or Crowley, if that was her name—far from dreadful.

A passenger walked the deck behind him, throwing out a tentative remark about the rain clouds gathering overhead, but Alex ignored the invitation to converse and answered tersely. He wanted to be alone with his thoughts, which were dwelling on the character of his late father-in-law to be. He had never been entirely sure of Evan's approval of him as a husband for Nanette, although he had Madame Crowley's full cooperation.

He was aware of Michel Jardin's ignominious rout from the field of Nanette's admirers. And if Aurélie was Evan's daughter, as he was beginning to think likely, Evan must have felt a similar reluctance to arrange a marriage for her.

That procrastination in finding a husband for an illegitimate daughter for whom he had not provided was strange—unless Evan was a man who loved his daughters overmuch.

A few hard drops of rain fell on the cypress deck. Evan shook away his uncomfortable train of thought, and turned into the saloon where the other passengers were gathering.

Waiting was hard for Aurélie because she had been used to being so busy at the convent, up at dawn to get the little ones dressed and lined up to march to the refectory for their breakfast, and then alternating lessons and duties hour after hour until after vespers in the chapel when she helped supervise in the dormitory until the candles were doused.

Here there was nothing to do but climb the levee across the main road which ran through the village, and walk along the bayou. It was so different from the Mississippi River, whose muddy brown current boiled between the levees behind the convent in spring, its high water lifting the sailing vessels so high they seemed to float above the convent. The Bayou Terrebonne was still and black with fallen trees lying half submerged on which one might see perched a little blue heron, or a turtle sleeping in the sun with its head tucked under its shell.

Aurélie missed the care of the young orphans she had mothered, and the companionship of the young nuns.

No one called at the pension except Charles Poitevin. Aurélie would have seen him out of sheer loneliness, but Madame Duclos sent Julienne down with regrets.

"The young scalawag presumes too much!"

There was no one else in the pension but the two reclusive owners, who twittered like birds behind their closed doors while their pert maid and their cook and Julienne took care of their tenants. Mademoiselle Claudette presided at the dining table, but her sister appeared only at a distance scurrying through the halls, and never spoke to them.

One afternoon Aurélie heard a commotion in the stable yard back of the house. A carriage had arrived, and was being unloaded. Horses whinnied, there was the jingle of harness, and the voices of the grooms calling to each other as they slapped the horses' flanks.

Footsteps sounded on the back stair, running up lightly. Heavier steps followed—someone carrying trunks. Aurélie laid down her embroidery and went to open her bedchamber door a crack. It was Monsieur Archer, back from the city. He was unlocking his door across the hall as his servant set down two traveling cases.

"Home again, Lafitte!" Aurélie heard him say.

"Oui, michie."

The young lawyer turned his head, just as if he felt her surveillance, and his gaze fell directly on Aurélie's slightly opened door.

He bowed elaborately. *"Bonjour, mademoiselle."*

Aurélie's start jerked her hand and the door closed with a little click. Beyond it, she heard a chuckle and she clapped her palms to her burning cheeks. Could he have seen her? Or had it been a lucky guess? Now his servant began to laugh. They were laughing at her!

And now that he was back in the pension, sleeping in his rooms just across the hall from her, she would again be waking early and listening for his step on the stairs as he ran down them to go to his office and study ways to protect Nanette Crowley from her. She would be alert for his arrival home between four and five—it was maddening to be so aware of his movements!—and his preparations to go to her half sister.

Well, Nanette was welcome to him!

But that evening, he did not leave the pension, and Aurélie persuaded Madame Duclos that they should take their evening meal in their rooms.

"Darling!" Nanette cried. "When did you arrive?"

"Last evening." Alex held out his arms and she flew into them.

"I've missed you," she whispered.

"And I, you."

Nanette clung tightly to him until Alex, hearing Elizabeth Crowley's step in the hall above them, reluctantly put her away from him.

"Well, Alex?" said Elizabeth, from the top of the stair.

He lifted his head. "You are looking well, *madame.*"

She snorted. "I am a scarecrow in black." She came down the stairs. "Mike Jardin is here."

"I know," Alex said. "I missed him in New Orleans because he was on his way here."

Elizabeth's face looked pale under her silvered blond hair. She gave him a powdered cheek to kiss, then told the servant who had let him in to bring tea, and led the way into her drawing room. She took her chair before the tea table and Nanette sat beside her.

"Michael sent a note around asking for an appointment," she said. "I refused to receive him. Told him he must see you."

The doors to the *galerie* were open, letting in a breeze carrying the fragrances of the garden, but the shutters were closed to deflect the strong rays of the spring sun. The rays filtering through them were reflected in bars of light on the polished surfaces of rosewood tables and the parquet floor. Over the fireplace, its black hole concealed by a mahogany-framed needlepoint fire screen, was a portrait of Elizabeth with Nanette as a golden-haired child at her knee.

"Michel called at my office this morning," Alex said.

"What does he want?"

"A dowry for the girl."

Elizabeth demanded, "Why? Does he mean to marry her?"

"Mama!" Nanette cried.

"That thought had occurred to me," Alex said, after a glance at Nanette's annoyed expression.

"Leave us, Nanette," Elizabeth ordered.

"This concerns me, Mama."

"Excuse me, Alex. I will not discuss this matter further in front of Nanette. You will please go to your room at once, my dear."

"Mama, I am not a child—"

"Please do as she asks, Nanette," Alex said.

Nanette's blue eyes flashed. She tossed her head and went out, closing the door with unnecessary force.

In the hall she walked crisply away on the parquet flooring, then paused and, stepping on the Turkish carpet, crept back on tiptoe to listen at the door.

Alex was still on his feet, having not yet been invited to sit. "Jardin told me this morning that it was something he had to do for Evan, who confided in him—to carry out what was Evan's intention."

"Michael owes my husband nothing!" Two spots of color blazed in Elizabeth's pale cheeks. "Evan would never have confided *anything* in him. If he says so, he's a liar. . . .Well, what did you find out in New Orleans? Did you go to the police?"

"Yes, but not to check on Mademoiselle Aurélie. She is not the type—"

Elizabeth said coldly, "I had hoped your investigation would uncover some facts, not just personal opinions."

"Yes, well . . ." Elizabeth Crowley was making him feel uncomfortably defensive. "I checked the police records and found the arrest of the baker in Evan's property on rue Chartres about eighteen years ago. Apparently she chased another woman out into the street with a knife. Do you remember that incident?"

Elizabeth frowned.

"Evan apparently went down to the police station and paid a fine for her. She was listed as a slave."

"Maisie's slave," Elizabeth said.

"The police assumed she got into an argument with a customer. They were never able to question the other woman involved."

"I suppose that's what happened. I remember the incident vaguely. It was a foolish bit of philanthropy on Evan's part, setting his old slave up in a bakery. Maisie was always sending for him—such a nuisance . . . but what has that to do with this, Alex?"

Instead of answering he asked, "Would you be willing to meet with Jardin in my office?"

"Why should I?"

"I went to the convent. The mother superior confirmed that Evan paid the girl's expenses there for the past twelve years, during which time he visited her often and brought her many gifts."

Outside the door, Nanette put her hand to her mouth. It couldn't be true! Papa wouldn't—!

"Twelve years?" Elizabeth repeated, stunned. "It can't be. I would have known—"

Alex said gently, "He told the mother superior that he was representing the girl's father, who wanted to remain anonymous to protect the woman who bore their illegitimate child. A tragic story, she said. He told the same story to the woman who kept the child for her first six years. It was Evan who took her away from there and placed her in the convent." He described his visit to the Boudin plantation on False River.

Elizabeth's face was gray. "He was a fool to foul his hands with someone else's dirty linen! It must have been Amos Fielding. I've always suspected that Amos was one of those men who kept a quadroon mistress on Rampart Street—"

"The girl is white, Madame Crowley."

"Are you sure about that?" Elizabeth asked, with an edge to her voice. "Amos was always fascinated by those pretty creatures and the outrageous balls where they parade their bodies—"

"And convent-bred," Alex pointed out firmly, swallowing his surge of anger. "If Jardin didn't have some evidence that her mother is white, he couldn't threaten a suit. The law expressly forbids it. I suspect that Jardin knows who the girl's mother is. Would you be willing to meet with him and Madame Duclos in my office to discuss what evidence he has?"

"I'll not stir out of my house to meet Mike Jardin anywhere!"

"Then you must allow me to bring them here to you,

madame. I think our next step should be to have a dialogue with them to discover what they plan to do—"

Elizabeth's voice was like ice. "Are you suggesting that I pay blackmail, Alex?

"No, *madame.* As your lawyer, I'm saying that you may find it expedient to negotiate a settlement in order to keep this matter private and prevent them from blackening your husband's name. A suit would stir much interest. Are you willing to give the girl a dowry rather than face the scandal her public demand for recognition as your husband's daughter could create?"

"Admit that Evan is her father?" Elizabeth said. "And have her coming back again and again for more money?"

"I can draw up papers for her to sign that will protect you—"

"Evan would throw you out of the house for such a suggestion!"

"You are free to consult another lawyer, *madame,*" Alex said stiffly.

"Then I shall do so! Good day, Alex!"

He bowed, furious. *"Adieu, madame!"*

Nanette was waiting for him in the central hall with fury in her eyes. "You believe that girl's story!" she accused in a harsh whisper.

His anger increased as he realized that she had been listening at the door. Alex clenched his jaw with the effort to get control of himself. "She does strike me as a truthful person."

Nanette spat, "She's a *mannelouque!*"*

"She's white!"

---

*A *mannelouque* is one-sixteenth black. Beyond that point racial color virtually disappears.

They were suddenly hissing at each other—like two snakes, Alex thought, appalled. Nanette's pretty face was twisted with jealous fury. "You would naturally be sympathetic! After all, your mother's family is notoriously color-blind!"

Alex drew in his breath with a hiss. This was why his parents had wanted him to hear Jean-Philippe's tragic story. They had known something like this would happen, sooner or later. But that the attack should come from Nanette was totally unexpected.

The angry hurt spread like ink through his heart. "If you object to my mother's family, how could you consider marrying me?" he said coldly. "I release you from your promise, *mademoiselle!*"

She put a hand to her lips. "Alex, I didn't mean—"

"You made your meaning very clear, Nanette. You are *not* color-blind, and my family offends you."

Just then Radcliffe entered the hall from the rear of the house, carrying a heavy silver tea tray. A maid followed, with a linen tea cloth folded across her arms. Nanette's supplicating hands fell to her sides.

The butler stopped in dismay. "You're leaving, *michie?*" But before he could set the tea tray down on a hall table, Alex had taken his hat from the hall tree. He bowed to Nanette and said, "I'll let myself out, Radcliffe."

As he strode through the front door, he heard Nanette cry angrily, *"Mama!* Now look what you've done!"

Chapter Sixteen

Dark clouds were moving down from the north, carried by a chill wind, as Alex rode back to the pension. He left his horse with Lafitte and walked to his office. When a *coup de nord* met the warm, moisture-laden air off the Gulf, it meant rain. A few large drops fell just as he unlocked his door. By the time he had reached his desk, rain was running in sheets down his front window facing the emptied street. Alex grabbed paper and pen and ink and began furiously compiling a statement of his expenses and services, including his trip to New Orleans, to present to Elizabeth Crowley.

When he had finished, the rain had spent itself and so had his anger. In its place was a desolate sense of loss and a throbbing homesickness for Bellemont and his family. He felt as if something had been amputated. He and Nanette had taken their eventual marriage for granted for so many years that he was scarcely able to contemplate any other direction in his personal life. But his break with her was final. To marry a woman who had revealed those hidden feelings about the mixed blood in his mother's family would be a disaster.

He thought with regret of his father's invitation to join his New Orleans law firm. Alex had chosen to come to Terrebonne parish because it was Nanette's home, to which she was attached, and because it offered him frontier territory in which to establish his career as a lawyer and perhaps later in state politics. With his unannounced betrothal at an end, the prospect of a career outside the city was no longer attractive.

He crumpled the statement of expenses and discarded it. Then he put on his hat and walked to his rooms. That evening, for the first time since the two women had arrived at the pension, he went downstairs for his evening meal.

The dining room, like the rest of the old mansion, retained a faded splendor. The crystal chandelier, which hung above a long rosewood table, was sparkling clean, but its candle holders were scantily filled. The diminished light softened the shabbiness of the royal-blue damask covering the walls and the scars of wear and weather on the painted ivory moldings trimming doorways and windows and the plaster rosettes and cupids decorating the ceiling. The stains on the ivory marble that framed the fireplace and supported a rosewood mantel were almost invisible.

Seated at the long table were Madame Duclos and her beautiful ward, who looked down at the service plate and gleaming silver at her place, acknowledging his entrance by only a faint blush.

He felt an unreasonable resentment of her extraordinary beauty. It was not only alluringly exotic, but it was based on a bone structure that he knew—and also resented—would remain beautiful long after Nanette's prettiness, like her mother's, had faded.

"Good evening, Madame Duclos." Sheer perversity led him to add, "—and Mademoiselle Boudin."

That name opened her almond-shaped eyes abruptly to stare at him with frank dislike.

He bowed and slipped into a place across the table from the women. Mademoiselle Claudette usually presided at the evening meal, but on that night her chair was empty. There were only the three tenants at table. Alex sat morose and silent while bowls of crayfish bisque were placed before them.

Aurélie stole looks at his face, wondering what had brought that somber expression to it. He was not as handsome as Michel Jardin, but his features were deceptively pleasant, and tonight she thought she read a surprising vulnerability in them. In spite of his disapproval of her, she admitted that it could be a likable face . . . his eyes, a deeper blue than her father's, held a steadiness that would have inspired confidence in anyone else, but only warned her not to be beguiled by his appearance into trusting him.

"I assume your trip to New Orleans was successful?" she asked him, with an ironic edge to her young voice. "At least you learned the name of my foster parents."

"Yes, *mademoiselle.*" He added impersonally, "The mother superior sent her love and blessings. She seems genuinely fond of you."

Her expression of distrust wavered. "I—*merci, m'sieu'.*"

"A question remains in my mind," he said, lifting his spoon, "and that is how a girl spoken of so highly by the mother superior of the Ursulines has been persuaded to engage in blackmail."

"Blackmail!" Aurélie gasped.

Madame Duclos snapped, *"M'sieu'*, I will not allow you to insult Mademoiselle Crowley!"

"Oh, come now, Madame Duclos, you must admit that her threat to make her claim to M'sieu Crowley's estate public if she is not paid off is immodestly mercenary, if not actually criminal."

"M'sieu', you will apologize!"

Color stained the girl's high cheekbones. "Is it criminal to want to be acknowledged by my family?" she demanded, her voice steady in spite of the moisture that had sprung to her eyes. "I would forego any amount of inheritance if only I could know my mother!"

"But it was your father's estate that brought you to le Terrebonne, yes?"

Aurélie put down her spoon. A servant had just brought in a roast of game and set it on the serving table, where he was preparing to carve it. The warm, spicy fragrance of the Creole gravy made in the roast juices brought her an expected wave of nausea. She rose and pushed back her chair.

"I knew my father, *m'sieu'*. I couldn't mistake his love for me. But I know nothing of my mother, and my heart is sore because of that."

Alex rose, too, shamed by her simple dignity. He had an uncomfortable vision of his mother's distraught face when she said, "I will not speak of this again," and a flood of the painful love her look had brought to his heart. He was dismayed at his roughness with this lovely young woman, who also was marked by someone else's sin, and in his remorse had grasped her arm to stay her. "Please accept my apologies," he muttered.

She tried to withdraw her arm, very pale.

"M'sieu'!" Madame Duclos was on her feet, too, her voice like the crack of a whip.

Alex let go of Aurélie, and bowed.

"Mademoiselle and I will take our dinner in our rooms," Madame Duclos told the servant, and her skirts rustled starchily as she swept Aurélie ahead of her to the stairs.

Elizabeth Crowley could not sleep that night. Nanette had had hysterics after Alex left, and had to be given a dose of laudanum before she could be quieted. But that was not what kept Elizabeth awake. Her thoughts had been sent back in time by Alex's story about the arrest of Maisie's bake-woman for attacking a customer with a kitchen knife. She remembered the incident. They had barely returned to the Manse and settled down for the summer that year, she recalled, when Evan had had to return to the city to arrange for the release of Maisie's slave and to pay her fine. She had protested bitterly.

The winter before had not been a particularly happy time. That was the year when Evan had been summoned continually to settle some problems at Maisie's bakeshop. He had had an unusual amount of other business to attend to that year, often pleading important meetings when she had planned some diversion, or had accepted an invitation. Often she had gone out with Jane and Amos without him.

His investments had prospered, but could there have been another reason for his many absences? Could there actually have been another woman? One of the black women at Maisie's? Her stomach clenched with a sick rage. That had been seventeen or eighteen years ago. The girl Marie Duclos was sponsoring at the parish chapel and at the best houses this summer could have been born that winter.

A "Catholic Crowley," indeed!

It had been clever of Michel Jardin to enlist Marie Duclos. What was Marie hoping to get out of this? Her family name was powerful enough to get the girl—aided by her incredible good looks!—into the houses of all the *nouveau riche* sugar planters in Terrebonne—at least those with an impressionable son of a certain age!

She was not allowing the girl to accept all invitations, maintaining her ridiculous show of mourning Evan, which was clever of her. Elizabeth knew exactly which of her neighbors had invited Marie Duclos and her charge for morning coffee and small gatherings. All had reported the girl "genteel and charming." Although they avoided the subject with her, Elizabeth knew that behind her back they were speculating about the identity of the highborn woman Michael Jardin claimed had been Evan's mistress.

Well, those Creoles with their greedy hands reaching for part of Evan's estate had met their match in her. Michael Jardin obviously planned to marry the girl if they succeeded in prying a dowry out of Evan's estate, and Elizabeth was sure Marie had been promised some kind of payment. Her name might be a powerful one, but she herself lacked money.

As a widow, Elizabeth could accept no invitations which included music and dancing, but she could spread her version of the girl's origins over the coffee cups at her own home and those of her women friends. She would be believed. She lay awake until the birds began their morning twitterings and squawkings, formulating the story.

Turning over restlessly, Elizabeth admitted to herself

that she had lost her temper and treated Alex badly. She was going to have to mend fences there, somehow patch things up between him and Nanette. She had planned their marriage for too long to allow it to go up in the smoke of a hot quarrel. Nanette was a little fool to listen at doorways. If she had known her daughter was overhearing, she would have minded her own tongue!

Just what had Nanette said? Elizabeth wondered. Tomorrow she would wring the truth out of Nanette. She was not a liar, but she was capable of twisting things to put herself in a better light. Elizabeth needed to assess how much damage had been done.

But it was already tomorrow, she realized with helpless anger, and she had not yet had her sleep.

On the following weekend Aurélie attended her first ball. The invitation had come from an aunt of Charles Poitevin's who had a plantation on the Bayou Cane. Aurélie's dress—in *demideuil,* which Madame assured her was *de rigueur* for young women in mourning—was a gray silk which looked bluish when it caught a certain light, with touches of cream lace at her throat and wrists. Its demure design had been chosen by Madame Duclos, who thought now that its conservative lines only underscored the exotic element in Aurélie's beauty.

Michel came for them in a rented carriage. His eyes caught fire when he saw Aurélie coming down the stairs. "Charming, *chère!*" he exclaimed.

"Thank you, *m'sieu',*" she said, taking his proffered hand.

He brought it to his lips for a lingering kiss, then said in concern, "Your hand is cold. It seems a warm night to me."

"I am very nervous, *m'sieu'*. I've never attended a ball before: Will my half sister be there, do you think?"

Michel's face hardened almost imperceptibly, and Aurélie had the strong impression that he disliked Nanette. "Madame Crowley, of course, will not attend," he said, "but her daughter could very well come with one of her mother's friends. You have no reason to be anxious. No one there will be more beautiful or charming."

He complimented Madame Duclos, who was resplendent in a violet satin, which was quite becoming to her pale, powdered complexion and the pink rose paste she used on her cheeks.

It was dusk of a balmy evening when they set out. The road, which followed the bayou, was bordered with trees, some of which were adorned with creepers. There was a strong hint of honeysuckle in the air.

"Where is the Bayou Cane?" Aurélie asked.

"It's one of five bayous that spread out like fingers from this region," Michel explained. "All sugarcane country, very prosperous."

He and Madame gossiped about some of the guests she would meet, but Aurélie sat silent for most of the hour's ride, enjoying the passing scenery, her head filled with a mix of exciting anticipations and worrisome alarms.

The carriage turned down a long dark lane overhung with oaks and tupelo and magnolia trees, with a myriad of fireflies twinkling under their branches. At its end their coachman pulled his horses to a stop and young black servants ran up holding torches to light their way as they stepped down from the coach and climbed the short flight of steps to a spacious veranda where their host and hostess stood to meet their guests.

Both Madame Duclos and Michel were known to them and they greeted Aurélie with a gracious curiosity. Almost as soon as they entered the house, a young woman rushed up to Aurélie, exclaiming. "It *is* you, 'Rélie! I couldn't believe it when I heard!"

Aurélie had scarcely had time to examine her surroundings, but her nervousness evaporated. It was Seraphine, a bouncy, cheerful girl who had been a boarder at the convent and a fellow student in her needlework class. Seraphine was one of the few boarders who had been friendly to the orphans. Now she greeted Aurélie like an old friend.

"I'm so glad you're here! There's no one else my age within miles. I've been hearing intriguing things about you, 'Rélie. *Maman* says that Charles Poitevin has a *tendresse* for you. I'm not surprised. You're so pretty!"

"I've only just met him," Aurélie protested.

"Well, he insisted that his aunt invite you. *Maman* says that there's some mystery about you, but that Michel Jardin is telling everybody that your family bloodlines are the best and you are likely to be declared an heiress. That's so exciting, 'Rélie! I *love* a mystery."

"I don't," Aurélie said. "I want to solve it."

"You mean you really *don't know who you are?*" Seraphine cried. "How exciting! And I was just complaining that nothing ever happened in le Terrebonne."

Her interest and enthusiasm did much to make Aurélie feel secure and accepted, which was a comfort when very soon after that she glimpsed her golden-haired half sister across the room. Nanette was talking earnestly with Alex Archer, who looked surprisingly handsome in his dark frock coat and trousers, but quite miserable. They were arguing about something; Nanette seemed to be pleading with him. Aurélie was sure Nanette saw her because she immediately lifted her chin and turned her back. It was an unmistakable cut, and it hurt. Her half sister was rejecting her just as her mother had.

Just then Charles Poitevin reached Aurélie and claimed a dance. Smiling, she accepted, and after that she was besieged for dances. The next hours had a dreamlike quality. She had indulged in fantasies of being the belle of the ball, lying on her cot in the dormitory in the orphans' house, but she had known that it was only a fantasy. And here she was living it!

Her dream had literally come true, thanks to Michel Jardin and Madame Duclos—but there was an element of nightmare in it, because whirling in the waltz, or bowing and curtsying in a reel, she was always aware of Nanette in the background, watching her with malice in their father's blue eyes, but never meeting her gaze —and whispering, always whispering to someone.

Finally, feeling warm and mindful of Madame's injunction to remember that she was in mourning and not to be too enthusiastic in dancing but to remain modest and unassuming, she begged off a third invitation from Charles and went up the stairs to the ladies' withdrawing room.

As she entered quietly, a woman was saying, "—she says Michel Jardin wants to get his fingers on some of the Crowley estate. He offered for Nanette last year, you know, and was rejected."

Aurélie stopped. Michel had wanted to marry her half sister?

"I had coffee at the Manse last week," the other woman replied, "and Elizabeth tells a different story from what Michel is peddling."

Aurélie knew that politeness required that she make

her presence known, but she was paralyzed by what she heard next.

"She says the girl is not only illegitimate, but that"— her voice dropped—"apparently Evan was able to fool the good nuns with his fantasy about a society belle's adultery, because the truth is she's a *mannelouque* trying to pass as white."

Feeling faint, Aurélie backed out of the room as quietly as she had come in. A *mannelouque?* They were saying that she was the daughter of an octoroon? Instinctively she sought the darkness of the *galerie* until she could control her shaking.

Across the room, Alex Archer was talking with one of his former clients when Aurélie bolted for the *galerie.* "What do you think, *m'sieu?* Jardin is telling friends he's going to marry her."

"He has good taste," Alex murmured, and excused himself to slip out of one of the floor-deep windows standing open. He had been watching Aurélie's triumph, and listening to the currents of gossip that drifted through the room as she became the most watched and most discussed young lady on the ballroom floor, and noticed how Jardin also stood aside, watching her.

He had indignantly denied it when Nanette had accused him of falling under her spell, but perhaps there was reason for Nanette's jealous notion. He admired the way Aurélie handled herself, her quiet self-confidence. She must know everyone was watching and talking about her, but she behaved with a modest dignity. The nuns had trained her well. She was too good for Jardin.

Something had upset her, and he thought he knew what it was. He felt a pang of guilt because he had seen Nanette at work among the older women and knew he had contributed to her anger because he had spurned her overtures to make up their quarrel.

He walked along the shadowed *galerie* until he saw Aurélie standing, hands clenched on the *galerie* rail, and looking out at the garden which sparkled with darting fireflies. Moving up beside her, he said quietly, "*Bonsoir,* Mademoiselle Crowley."

She drew a deep, ragged breath and made an obvious effort to control her emotions before she turned to face him. "You call me by my father's name, M'sieu' Archer," she challenged him. "Does that mean that you believe my story?"

"I believe Evan Crowley was your father," he said. "But I don't believe Michel Jardin's story about Crowley's lover being a mysterious member of high society who bore you clandestinely."

"Why not?" she demanded.

"There has not been the slightest rumor of a particular scandal that would support that story. It would be phenomenal if such a thing could happen without arousing any suspicion among the gossips here or in New Orleans."

"I would expect my father to have been very discreet," Aurélie said coldly. "And I would not have expected you, *m'sieu',* to speak socially with one you accused of engaging in blackmail!"

"I think you are being exploited, *mademoiselle.* You have said that what is of prime importance to you is finding out who bore you, *non?*"

"Do you have a mother, *m'sieu'?*"

The question pierced him, coming as it did so soon after his mother's confession. "But of course!"

"Can you imagine how much it would hurt," Aurélie rushed on, "to have been rejected by her? I long for a family, but my half sister also rejects me. Yes, I want to know who bore me!"

"I should very much like to know, myself. will you allow me to help you?"

Aurélie exclaimed, "But you are my half sister's lawyer!"

"Not any longer. I've been dismissed."

She hesitated, surprised and put off by his admission. "Then why are you still interested in finding my mother?"

"I have my own reasons for continuing my investigations, *mademoiselle.*"

She was disturbingly aware of the warmth of his body beside her and the scent of bay rum. "I don't know if I can pay you for your services, *m'sieu'*. I have no money of my own—"

"Jardin? I thought as much. What is he to you?"

"He was my father's friend."

"Is that all?" His tone was suddenly sharp.

She tilted her chin and gave him a look of such hauteur that he could only think of it as royal. "You have no right to question me!"

"You're right," he said, both touched and amused. "Please accept my apology, Mademoiselle Crowley."

Hearing him use again the name that meant so much to her softened her indignation. "M'sieu' Jardin has been a good friend to me—because of my father," she told him, and he saw that she believed that.

"May I ask what disturbed you so just now?"

She shook her head, her throat closing.

"I saw you come rushing down the stairs looking as if someone had kicked you. I assumed that you heard some of the gossip that is being spread here tonight. Am I right?"

She looked stricken. "Are people really speculating that my mother was an octoroon? That is pure nonsense. I am not a fool, *m'sieu'l*!"

"Neither is Madame Crowley," he returned, with a wryness that Aurélie found only more puzzling. "She knows a free person of color can't sue for equality with whites. But since you can't produce your mother, *mademoiselle*, perhaps Madame Crowley has found her defense."

Aurélie was speechless. She had sensed the reactions of shock and disbelief when Nanette and Madame Crowley learned of her existence, and had understood their dismay—but this kind of hostility was frightening. In her innocence she had not foreseen such hatred from her father's legitimate family.

"I think your duenna is looking for you. I don't want to compromise your good reputation. It *is* good, *mademoiselle*," Alex said very seriously, "far better than that of Michel Jardin. Don't lose heart."

Leaving her greatly confused, he slipped into the ballroom and disappeared among the dancers. Presently Madame Duclos found her. "Michel has been looking for you, *chère*. He is ready to take us home."

In the carriage, Michel took her hand and patted it. "You were a great success tonight, Mademoiselle Aurélie."

"But you didn't dance with me, *m'sieu*." She had expected him to claim a dance, but he had not. Neither had Alex Archer, but she had not expected him to.

Madame Duclos chose that moment to give a great sneeze, and Michel murmured in Aurélie's ear, "I cannot trust myself to hold you in my arms, *chère*."

Startled, Aurélie looked quickly away from him and said, "*Madame*, are you taking a chill?"

"No, *chère,* it is something that grows along the bayou that tickles my nose." She sneezed again.

Michel was still holding her hand, and it had grown uncomfortably warm. Aurélie pulled her hand away. Involuntarily she wondered why Alex Archer had not asked her to dance. Was it for the same reason?

A slow, sweet flush warmed her whole body and she was glad for the darkness that hid it.

Chapter Seventeen

Alex Archer's law office in the growing community along the bayou consisted of two small rooms, one behind the other in half of a frame building. His practice had not yet required him to hire a clerk. When he was not closeted with a client the door between the waiting room and his inner office stood open, making him accessible and allowing him to lift his eyes from his work and look through the front room window to what was happening on the street.

On that Monday morning, he was closeted with a M'sieu' Chachère from Bayou Lafourche who wanted him to file a suit against his next-door neighbor, a widow who had a habit of walking out into her backyard in her night robe in the early morning to pluck a clean housedress off her drying line.

"It's indecent, *m'sieu'*!" Chachère sputtered, in the Cajun patois. "She offends me! Everyone knows she's taken that scoundrel Jean-Baptiste for a lover!"

"That's what offends you, *n'est-ce pas*?" Alex asked, smiling.

"W'at she do in her bedroom is her business, but w'at she do in plain view of her neighbors in something else, ahn? W'at would you do, *m'sieu'*?"

Alex advised Chachère how much it would cost him to bring his suit to court and told him to go home and think it over. When he escorted the irate old man to the door, Michel Jardin was tying his horse to the hitching post.

"*Bonjour*, Archer," he greeted Alex affably, coming up to the door. "I saw you enjoying yourself at the ball Saturday night. It was a pleasant diversion, no?"

"A fine ball," Alex agreed. He stepped back, inviting Michel into his inner office, and indicated the chair facing his desk.

Michel turned it sidewise so that he could lounge in it with his legs stretched out in front of him, and placed his riding crop across his knees.

"Although I couldn't help but notice that most of your attentions were lavished on Bizet's excellent punch bowl."

"I didn't see you behaving as if you were at a *fais do-do*," Alex retorted.

"I don't care much for the dancing. But Mademoiselle Crowley—*Aurélie* Crowley, that is—made quite a favorable impression with those who do, no?"

"I agree."

"Are your clients ready to talk about a settlement on her?"

"No," Alex said. "In fact, they adamantly refused to meet with you, Jardin, here or at the Manse."

"That's regrettable." Jardin began idly flicking his

riding crop at the floor. "I assume you're prepared to defend them if we decide to go to court?"

"No. But I've no doubt someone will. Possibly a lawyer from Donaldsonville."

Jardin's hand stilled on his whip as he stared at Alex.

"I've been dismissed from the case for suggesting a settlement with you." Alex took a mild satisfaction in telling him that. "The next move is up to you, Jardin."

"So that's why you didn't dance with Nanette at the ball!" Michel exclaimed. "You've quarreled about this."

Alex returned his look in noncommittal silence.

Jardin began to laugh. "Well, I'll be damned. What about your betrothal?"

"What betrothal?" Alex asked blandly. "Madame Crowley and her daughter are in mourning, you may remember."

"True, true." Michel stood up. "The banns were never published, were they?"

"They were not. Since we're no longer adversaries," Alex said, "will you satisfy my curiosity, Jardin? Do you really not know the identity of the woman who bore Aurélie? Or did Crowley tell you?"

Michel's eyes gleamed. "Crowley didn't reveal her identity. Not to me, nor as far as I know, to anyone else. But anyone can see that Aurélie is quality, ahn?"

"Everyone? Aren't you forgetting my former clients?"

Michel shrugged. "It's in their interests to deny it."

"Obviously you don't believe the story they're circulating, since I understand you're telling your friends you're thinking of marrying the young lady."

Jardin hesitated. "Well, that was somewhat premature," he said lightly. "A remark I didn't expect to be

repeated." He turned to go. "So you're out of it now?
Wish me luck, Archer."

"Bonne chance!" Alex said agreeably. He rose and
walked with Jardin to the door, and watched while he
mounted and flicked his horse into a trot, thinking, *He
was lying.* Crowley may not have told him who Aurélie's mother was, but Michel Jardin knew.

Thoughtfully Alex turned back to his desk. He had
always doubted Jardin's claim of a close friendship with
Evan Crowley. But if Jardin's knowledge of Aurélie's
relationship to Crowley had not come from the planter
himself, then how had he come by the information?
Perhaps, Alex told himself, he should have spent more
time in New Orleans investigating Jardin.

He cleared his desk of papers, picked up his hat, and,
locking the office, walked to the pension, where he told
the maid to set a place for him at the luncheon table. He
was already seated there at Mademoiselle Claudette's
right when Madame Duclos and Aurélie entered the
dining room.

He stood and bowed, and they murmured greetings.
Mademoiselle Claudette spoke to her servant and the
soup was served. The proprietress sat at the table's head
with her rather heavy features fixed in a frown, which
Alex had guessed was more a sign of her shy reserve
than of displeasure, and they ate in silence.

Alex wondered if Jardin had bought the gown Aurélie
was wearing. She looked very lovely in its low décolletage and loose sleeves in a mourning white that made a
sparkling background for the golden-red lights in her
hair and her tawny eyes.

Her face was beautiful from any angle, he thought in
wonder. An artist would be enthralled by the fine arch
of her eyebrows above those elongated eyes, by her

high cheekbones and the sweet curve of her cheek sweeping to the firm chin with its tiny hint of a cleft. And the way her head sat on that long, slender neck, graceful as the stem of a flower. . . .

He caught himself up. The girl was inducing fantasies in him; he was imagining himself an artist painting her portrait! He realized that he was aroused, and was irritated.

Aurélie stole looks at him, remembering their astonishing conversation at the ball. She had not told either Madame Duclos or Michel that Alex was no longer the Crowley's lawyer or that he had offered to help her find her mother. She suspected that it was a trick to disarm her and that if she repeated it, Michel and Madame would think her a gullible fool.

"*Mademoiselle*, may I have a few words with you after lunch?"

Before Aurélie could reply, Madame Duclos asked coolly, "What do you wish to know this time, M'sieu' Archer?"

"I have some information about *mademoiselle'*s early life that she may find interesting. Also some questions," he said candidly, "raised by my investigations in New Orleans. Since this is rather personal, if we might meet in the drawing room—"

"Business is best conducted at your office, *m'sieu'.*"

Alex hesitated before the hauteur of Madame Duclos's expression. "Would three o'clock this afternoon be convenient?"

"Very well, *m'sieu'.*" Her curtness discouraged further conversation, and the proprietress made no effort to revive it.

Upstairs, Madame Duclos commented, "You obviously made a good impression at the Bizets' ball."

"Don't you mean 'notorious'?" Aurélie asked wryly. "Everyone was gossiping about me."

"That's to be expected. But you ignored it and kept your head high. It was wise to go quietly about making friends and not putting pressure on the Crowleys. I have been expecting an overture from them. Perhaps this is it."

Aurélie looked out of the open window at a cardinal that had just alighted on the railing of the upper *galerie* and was regarding her with a bright eye. "I don't think so, *madame.*"

"Why not, *chère*?"

"Because M'sieu' Archer is no longer Madame Crowley's lawyer."

"What?" Madame cried, in an outraged tone. "How do you know this?"

"He told me so at the ball."

"And he presumes to question you again? He has no right! We'll not go to his office this afternoon, Aurélie. Why, he's a scamp!"

Aurélie longed to believe that the lawyer's offer to help her find her mother was genuine, but she kept her own counsel, still uncertain whether or not she was the victim of some cruel trick.

"I'm going to take a nap," Madame announced, "and I suggest you do the same. I shall tell Julienne we are not to be disturbed."

Aurélie agreed to take a rest, but since she wanted to read, decided to go down to the library to select a book from the bookcases there.

The library was the most impressive room in the old house. The walls were lined with beautifully crafted bookshelves and age did not diminish their contents. The size of the Mademoiselles d'Avignon's collection of books suggested more than anything else vanished days of prosperity and leisure. When she entered, Alex Archer rose from a chair by the cold hearth.

She stopped in surprise. "I beg your pardon, *m'sieu'*. I thought you had returned to your place of business." She turned in retreat.

"Please, *mademoiselle*! I've been hoping to see you without your dragon." Actually, his hope had been little more than a fantasy. He was filled with delight at this unexpected opportunity.

His smile was hard to resist. Face-to-face with him, he looked so honest and trustworthy that her doubts about his offer to help seemed foolish. But she steeled herself against his charm. "There's no need for that. I have no secrets from Madame Duclos."

"But does she have secrets from you?"

Aurélie frowned. "I think you had better explain yourself, M'sieu' Archer."

"I intended no hidden meaning," he said. "I am simply asking—as a disinterested lawyer—if you completely trust Madame Duclos and Michel Jardin?"

"I have no reason to distrust them."

"They believe you are a potential heiress. Your father left a great deal of property in his estate. That's reason enough to distrust anyone, *mademoiselle.*"

"I am not so cynical as to be suspicious of my friends!"

"You know, then, that Michel Jardin has threatened Madame Crowley with a suit for a share of your father's estate?"

"Not a share, *m'sieu'*. I want only the dowry he promised me," she said, with spirit. "It's only fair, *non*? Otherwise no one will marry me, and I shall be forced to become a seamstress to gentlewomen in order to support myself!"

"So you *are* planning to marry Michel Jardin?"

"Marry Michel? Oh, no!" she exclaimed.

"I hear that he is telling his friends he will share in the Crowley estate."

Her eyes flashed golden fire. "Rumor and gossip! *Mon dieu!* Is there no end to it? The inheritance is not my chief concern, *m'sieu'*. I want the right to use my own name, *oui*, but more than anything, I want to find my mother—or, if she no longer lives, to know of her family. Is that wicked of me?"

"I'm properly chastened!" he said, his blue eyes twinkling with enjoyment of her spirit. "It's my training in the law that bids me warn you. But I'm asking myself why you think your mother's family will give you a warmer welcome than you received from the Crowleys?"

"Because I am her child," Aurélie said bravely.

His heart ached for her. "Please be seated, *mademoiselle*," he said, indicating a comfortable velvet-covered chair.

"I don't think Madame would approve," she began, knowing well that Madame Duclos would severely disapprove of her lingering in the room with him without a chaperone.

Alex interrupted her. "While in the city, I made a trip to the False River plantation of your foster parents, the Boudins."

"Oh!" she exclaimed, feeling a tremor of painful emotion.

"Would you like to hear about my visit?"

"Very much, *m'sieu'*." Aurélie sank into a faded satin chair. She could not let this opportunity pass, no matter what her chaperone would think.

"I found them well. They have prospered, thanks to

M'sieu' Boudin's industry and Madame Boudin's thrift. She still misses you. She said you took the place in her heart left empty by the loss of her own daughter, and she still feels hurt that she was not allowed to visit you at the convent."

"Not allowed?" Aurélie faltered. "I didn't know—I cried because she didn't come."

"The mother superior said it was M'sieu' Crowley's wish that she not be encouraged to visit."

Aurélie looked so distressed that he hurried on to his next question. "A white woman who said her name was Marie Legarde brought you to the Boudins as an infant. Does that name mean anything to you?"

"No."

"You never made her acquaintance as a child?"

"Not to my recollection, *m'sieu'*."

"I wasn't able to find any trace of her . . . Madame Boudin said that she and her husband were paid handsomely for taking you. Because of the child she lost, Madame Boudin was able to nurse you. She said the fee enabled them to buy a plantation on False River. Moving there from New Orleans was part of their bargain."

Aurélie's heart was pounding against her ribs. A great deal of money must have been paid to the Boudins for the care they gave her the first six years of her life if it had provided them with a plantation. It seemed to substantiate Michel's claim that her mother was also from an important family.

She said slowly, "M'sieu' Jardin never told me—about the Boudins."

"How long have you known Jardin?"

"He came to the convent to find me after my father died." She had not questioned his story, but surely the mother superior had. She wondered if Madame Duclos knew about her father's transaction with the Boudins.

"You knew my father well, M'sieu' Archer?"

"I'd known him for as long as I can remember, but that's not saying I knew him well."

"Did he tell you these things?"

"No, indeed. I learned them from the mother superior and from Madame Boudin herself. Your father had many secrets. One of them, *mademoiselle*, is why, after spending so much money on your care and providing you with an education, he did not name you in his will, or at the very least provide a dowry for you."

"M'sieu' Jardin said it was procrastination, an oversight. He said no man really believes he will die."

"A rational answer," Alex said, thinking . . . *and a clever one.* "But if it was an oversight, it was a serious one for you."

She was silent for a moment. "I was born in the city?"

"Probably. But there is no church record of your baptism there."

She sighed. "What else did you learn in New Orleans, *m'sieu'*?"

"That Evan Crowley was a kind man—he freed his old African nurse and set her up in business—but not a loyal one—he was married and had one daughter, your half sister Nanette, when he loved your mother."

And that was why she was illegitimate, Aurélie thought. A resentment took root in her heart against those long-ago lovers who had considered only their own pleasure. She wanted to confront them and cry, *What about me?* She hoped her mother was still alive. If she were, someday she would find her and fling that question at her!

"You learned nothing about her—my mother?"

"Nothing. But I will. I want to know, for your sake. I very much want to know." *And I want to expose Jardin for the schemer he is!* he thought, with anger.

Aurélie saw the flash of ire in his eyes and, not understanding it, stood up. A disturbing tension had come between them. She imagined what Madame Duclos would say if she knew about this private conversation.

"Thank you for what you have told me, *m'sieu'.* I—I came downstairs to select a book."

"May I help you?" He loomed above her, taller by half a head, and followed her to the bookshelves. There was strength and grace in his carriage and walking beside him she was aware of his masculinity in a way that made her feel strangely excited.

He was smiling down at her. "In French or in English?"

"French, please."

"I'm afraid the *mademoiselles'* selection is somewhat dated." His gaze was raking the shelves, and he reached for a volume. "Here is Rousseau's *Julie, ou La Nouvelle Héloïse.* Have you read it?"

"No, *m'sieu'.* In the convent we read our prayers and the Bible."

"You may find more pleasure in the English novels of Jane Austen. You do read English, don't you?"

"Yes, sir. Quite well." Her smile and the accent she gave the English words were so enchanting that he caught his breath. He reached for another book to hide what his eyes could be revealing. "Here's *Pride and Prejudice!* Do you know it?"

"*Non, m'sieu'.*"

"Then I promise you have a treat in store." As he put the two volumes in her hands, his fingers brushed hers and she caught her breath. How oddly sensitive her skin was! It was as if it had a memory of its own, holding the warmth of the touch of his hand long after he had withdrawn it.

She thanked him, and went quickly upstairs, relieved to find that Madame Duclos was fast asleep in her room. Her cheeks felt hot, and her heart was still beating too fast. *He is Nanette's fiancé,* she reminded herself.

In the library, Alex stood a minute in bemused thought. Aurélie Crowley's quest was a poignant one, and almost hopeless. But what a charming creature she was! The sympathy he felt for her, and the mystery of her origins, were helping him to forget for a time the emptiness of his own future now that he had severed his almost lifelong connection with Nanette. He let his mind wander over the information he had about Aurélie, wondering what other avenues he could have explored while in New Orleans.

He was convinced Jardin had the information Aurélie wanted and Jardin was right here in Terrebonne. Michel had friends with whom he had stayed for several summer seasons when he was dancing attendance on Nanette, to Alex's distress and that of her parents. There must be a way to get at Jardin, some leverage he could use either to get his information or to prove him a liar and his charming protegée an unwitting fraud.

He took his hat from the hall tree and set off for his office, feeling an exhilaration that he had not recently known.

Later that afternoon, he looked up from his desk and saw the Crowley carriage pull up in the street outside. Nanette and her maid were handed out by the Crowley coachman, and crossed the *banquette* to his door. With a heavy heart he rose and went to greet them.

"Bonjour, chère," Nanette said, with a brightness that betrayed her nervousness. "Wait here," she told her maid, and walked into Alex's inner office. "Close the door," she ordered in a low voice.

Alex ignored the command. "What is it you want, Nanette?"

"I came to end this foolish misunderstanding between us." She raised a moist, entreating gaze to his eyes. "You love me, Alex, and I love you. Why should this—this pipe dream of Michel's little friend separate us?"

She moved out of the doorway to where she would be out of her maid's sight, and held out her arms, her lips parted in a tremulous smile and her blue eyes sparkling with unshed tears.

Alex took a step toward her, profoundly moved, as memories slid over each other in his mind like a scattered deck of playing cards: the golden-haired little girl he had first seen as a shy boy, his secret dreams of her as an adolescent, her trembling lips under his first kiss, the mad season of balls and hunts and other entertainments in the season after he came back from Harvard when a half dozen other men were competing for her attention . . . and his joy when he won her promise.

And then a perverse voice in his mind repeated, *Your mother's family is notoriously color-blind!* with that tone of malice he had heard in Nanette's voice, and an icy snow drifted around his heart.

"You haven't taken back what you said, Nanette," he reminded her, in a low voice.

"What did I say?" she asked, smiling. "I spoke in anger, Alex. I don't even remember!"

"I can't forget that easily," he said. "I wish I could." The image of his mother's face when she told him of the shooting of her half brother was painfully clear between them. It had changed everything—himself and his future—forever. "Words spoken in anger speak the truth."

Nanette's smile crumpled. "Alex, please—!"

He put his hands on her shoulders to turn her toward the door, but she threw her arms around his neck and pulled his head down, raining kisses on his face.

"Mon dieu, mon dieu, Nanette!" he cried in anguish, trying to avoid her lips.

"You love me, Alex," she insisted, beginning to sob. "Say you love me!"

He managed to unclasp her arms from his neck and move her into the doorway. Her maid was on her feet, her face crinkled in alarm.

"Take your mistress home," Alex told her.

The dark woman put her arms around Nanette, giving Alex an accusing look and crooning endearments to her sobbing mistress.

Alex walked them out to their carriage and handed them in. Then he went back into his inner office, closed the door, and put his face in his hands. "Ah, *dieu, dieu . . .*"

Chapter Eighteen

Cléo rode out with her groom in the early New Orleans morning, taking her usual route past the barracks and the Ursuline convent to the levee road. She was wearing a bottle-green riding habit trimmed in black braid, and a smart little hat of the same color perched on her smooth black hair.

It was barely dawn. Lights at the tips of masts on the unseen vessels at anchor shone palely through the mists rising from the river. The odor of dark roasting coffee beans permeated the damp air, already sweet with the fragrances of lemon blossoms and jasmine.

As she rode, Cléo thought about Michel Jardin with a constriction in her breast. She was alone again, a woman without a lover. She still missed Hing, who had been lover and friend and wise teacher, and she regretted ever giving herself to Michel Jardin, but she would miss his skillful lovemaking. He knew too well not only how to arouse her passion, but how to keep her at an edge by denying her.

There would never be another man like Lee Hing, she thought sadly. He had known exactly what she needed and had waited until she was ready to receive what he had to offer her. She had lived in his house for a year before they became lovers. It had taken her that long to recover some kind of sanity after her painful break with her first love and the grief and disillusion that accompanied it. She had never recovered from the loss of her child. It was still a bleeding wound in her heart.

Hing had opened a new world to her, the world of books and music and history, and their mature love had been enriched by all that he had taught her. But he had schooled her in other things, as well: how to judge men, especially the men who gambled; how to know who could be trusted and who to refuse her hospitality. When Hing had died of the yellow fever that dreadful summer, she had been equipped to take over his gambling kingdom, and his well-trained employees had transferred their loyalty to her.

She had managed well, until she had succumbed to Michel Jardin's seductive attentions, in an ill-chosen attempt to find the happiness and content that had eluded her. It had been an unfortunate choice. But she had put an end to it. Now she was no longer in bondage to passion. She was alone and independent, as she had been alone on her Isle de Navarre in the marshes before Evan Crowley had come into her life.

She had a sudden longing to be back in those wide, wet reaches of land that were half water, where the inhabitants grew webbed feet, as M'sieu' Jacques-le-grand said. She wondered if the old Cajun was still shelling oysters for his drinking friends in his tavern bar while Madame cooked up spicy jambalaya to serve them.

A homesickness grew like an ache in her. What was she doing in Hing's casinos in this bustling port city that had never been home to her? She was a swamp woman of the Houmas tribe. She wanted to go back.

But she had Aurélie to hold her here—Aurélie, who did not know of her existence, and would never know her. Her love for Aurélie was all she had left.

As she cantered up the rise to the levee, Cléo turned to look over the wall of the convent garden. The orphans were trudging over the wet grass in the mist from their building to the convent refectory with a black-clad nun at their head, and another following the last child.

Where was Aurélie? Why was she not leading them with her spirited step? Cléo searched the straggling line and could not find the tallest orphan in it. Was Aurélie ill? Fear crawled in Cléo's veins. Dared she go to the convent and ask about her?

But how would she explain her interest? She did not even know if she were still called Aurélie.

One day she had recognized herself in the tall colt of an orphan and knew that she had found her daughter at last. Evan had hidden Aurélie in the convent right under her eyes. It was so logical that she had known she was right. An education by the Ursulines was a ticket to the world Evan wanted his daughter to enjoy.

After wrestling with herself for long days and nights, Cléo had made the decision to stay out of her daughter's life, and give her the chance in the privileged white world that her father had made possible.

She must not weaken now. No matter how discreet she was, or how much the nuns could be trusted to keep her questions confidential, if anyone—*anyone*—suspected that Aurélie was a half-breed, it could ruin her chances if she should fall in love with a man of position. Cléo had denied herself too long to jeopardize her daughter's future happiness now. But, ah, *dieu*, she could not lose Aurélie too!

How could she know what was the right thing to do? Perhaps Evan had already arranged a marriage for her. Perhaps that was why she was no longer at the convent. Perhaps he had left instructions in his will for their daughter. Assuredly he had done that! What reason was there for all the pain he had caused, if he had not provided for her?

How could she find out? As she rode along the levee with her groom following her, watching the port waken to activity on the docks below her as the sun rose in the east, Cléo felt a troubling unease. She was remembering that Michel had asked her once about her interest in the convent garden. Had he guessed it was centered on the tallest orphan there, the auburn-haired girl with the lilting walk?

Michel was shrewd. It had taken only a tear and a glance at the newspaper in her hands to make him jump to a conclusion that Evan Crowley had been her lover. Or had it been only a malicious jab?

When she returned to the casino, she called her assistant manager to her office and said, "Find out for me where Michel Jardin is now, and what he is doing."

The young Creole's face took on a guarded look as he said, *"Oui, madame."*

Cléo laughed at his obvious distress. "He will not be coming back here, Louis, never fear."

"Oui, madame," Louis said again, discreetly.

That Sunday evening, as she strolled through her exclusive weekend casino on the Bayou St. John, she saw among her guests a distinguished planter who had been absent from the gaming rooms for some time, and experienced a flush of pleasure. Paul d'Estrahan was a man of many interests, from architecture to hunting to opera, a gifted conversationalist with charming manners. "Paul, *mon ami!*" She extended her hand. "I thought you had forsaken us."

"Never, *madame,*" he said, bringing her hand to his lips.

Hing had enjoyed a quiet friendship with the Creole, an example, Lee Hing had claimed, of all that was fine in Creole society, both honorable and gracious in his business dealings, and generous to a fault with his friends. Since Hing's death, she had seen Paul rarely.

She looked at him now, observing the streak of white in the mass of dark hair rising from his brow, the new lines around his silver-gray eyes and his strong, sensual mouth. He was still as slender as a much younger man and easily as erect.

"I lost my wife after a long illness," he said in explanation, "and for the past year I've been busy with family and estate matters."

"I heard of your loss, Paul. I'm so sorry."

"Thank you." He was still holding her hand, and he raised it to his lips again. "It has made great changes in my life. I've just completed the necessary legal actions to turn the management of my plantation over to my two sons."

"And what will you do then, Paul?"

"You may see more of me, because I intend to look for a *pied-à-terre* in the *quartier.* But first I plan to spend a year or two in Paris."

"Ah, we'll miss you."

"Will you, I wonder?" he asked, with a fond, faintly ironic inflection that made her look sharply at him. "Your assistant has been questioning me about my late wife's nephew—"

She stopped him, saying, "I feel a need for fresh air. Will you walk with me on the rear *galerie, m'sieu*?"

"Delighted, *madame.*"

He offered his arm and they left the roulette players and walked down the center hall past the stairway and the door to her office and went out through the French windows opening on the *galerie* overlooking the rear garden. The air was warm and redolent with heavy flower scents overlaying the odors of decay from the swamp beyond the garden. Fireflies darted in zigzag fashion under the trees, and unseen frogs filled the night with an unceasing trill.

"I'll miss this lush tropicality," Paul mused. "But Paris has its charms, too."

Cléo was wearing her customary mandarin gown, tonight in a jade brocade with a deep cream satin lining showing at the neckline and the slits in the skirt. She saw admiration in Paul's eyes for the picture she made as she leaned against a white pillar, and was stirred by a feeling something like regret.

Paul said gently, "So you booted Jardin out, and now you want him back?"

"No, Paul, it's over. Michel was a mistake. One of my mistakes," she added ruefully.

"But you want to find him." His tone was skeptical. "Do you know people are saying he has found a young protégée? They are saying he found her in the Ursulines' orphanage."

Aurélie! With an effort she kept her face expressionless.

"No, I don't want Michel back. But I think"—she hesitated—"that he may have taken something of mine with him. Do you know where he is?"

"Oh, yes. I heard he had gone to Terrebonne parish to visit relatives." He was watching her closely, but she did not speak.

She was thinking, *I must go after her. Michel has done this to hurt me. I must save her.*

"What are you thinking at this moment?" Paul asked her.

She had the strongest impulse to confide in him, but her resolve to keep the taint of her heritage from Aurélie was stronger. "Of Paris," she lied. "I've never seen it."

"Then come with me, Cléo."

The *galerie* was in darkness except for the candlelight flickering through the French windows. Through the dusk his silver-gray eyes shone steadily. She repressed the light retort on her lips and gasped, "You're serious!"

"Yes, *chère.* Didn't you guess that I was in love with you? That's why I've stayed away. But now . . ." He moved closer, imprisoning her between his body and the pillar, but not forcing her. Instead he slowly lowered his head until their lips touched.

She took his kiss with passive wonder, letting the taste and feel of his mouth flow into her consciousness. Slowly her tingle of response grew into a warm glow, and she raised her arms and put them around his neck and gave him her mouth. When they drew apart, they looked into each other's eyes. What she saw mirrored there startled her.

"Does that mean you could care for me?" he asked.

"I've always thought of you as a very dear friend," she said slowly.

"Friends we will always be. I'm not a young man. My passions are not easily aroused, and my love is not lightly given. What I'm offering is more than a trip to Paris, Cléo."

"I know," she whispered.

"Then . . . ?"

"Then give me time, dear friend," she said, and to her surprise heard a tremor in her voice.

"How long?"

She paused, silent. Finally she said, "I must go away for a few weeks, Paul."

He looked at her with irony and such sadness that she felt a pang, and reached out to touch his cheek.

"When I return, I'll give you my answer."

He brought her hand to his lips, and this time he pressed a soft kiss into her palm and closed her fingers over it. Then he offered his arm to escort her back to the gaming rooms.

Alex Archer could not get Evan Crowley's illegitimate daughter out of his mind. For days he had deliberately thought about Aurélie and her obsession to find her mother in order to keep from dwelling on his break with Nanette. Now he had forgotten Nanette, and Aurélie haunted him.

He tried to banish her from his thoughts, but it was not easy when he knew she slept behind a closed door across the hall. He spent as little time as possible in the pension, but that did not help because everywhere he went men were talking about her, and speculating about Evan Crowley's *grande passion.* Who was the highborn woman who had borne him a child, and how did they get away with it, ahn?

*It happened in the city, that was it. These little affairs
are more easily managed there, ahn?*

But his bastard, she is a little beauty, non?

But an unfortunate position for une jeune fille.

*Me, I think she should have a dowry. She was a child
of his blood, ahn? And she is* très gentile.

Alex listened in silence, surprised to find himself
wanting to close their mouths with his clenched fist.
Aurélie should not have been exposed to such loose talk.
It was not her fault. Obviously Jardin was directing the
conspiracy. His disgust with Michel Jardin grew.

The first of the week he took a boat to Donaldsonville,
where he was helping a local attorney defend a wealthy
but hotheaded planter accused of assault and battery
resulting from a quarrel with a neighbor. It was a not
uncommon case and in this instance resulted in a fine
for his client, who did not take his defeat graciously.

Alex accepted the invitation of the other attorney to
dine at his house that evening. M'sieu' Latour was a
widower living alone in a substantial house with several
servants to keep him comfortable. He was a noted rac-
onteur and entertained Alex, his only guest, throughout
the meal with amusing anecdotes about his long experience in the practice of law.

"My clients are largely my friends and neighbors,
most of them descendants of the original 'Cadian settlers, just as yours will be. The Cajun is an individualistic
human with some lovable traits. He is highly litigious,
which is fortunate for our profession, *non?*" He chuckled, and rose from the table. "Shall we have brandies in
my study?"

Alex found the cool leather of his heavy chair facing
another like it near the hearth very comfortable.
M'sieu' Latour poured two brandies from a decanter on

a small table and carried them over to where Alex sat. He offered a cigar, which Alex refused.

"To success in your profession," he proposed, and Alex lifted his glass to him before drinking.

"You will find differences in character between these bayou 'Cadians and the clients of your father in the city," he rumbled, "especially in your end of the parish." He seated himself in the opposite leather chair and settled his head into his heavy shoulders, obviously preparing himself for a comfortable chat. "But the racial mix gets fuzzier the nearer one gets to the Gulf, have you realized that? It's not too many miles as the crow files from your office to the headquarters of the old privateers down in those marshes. And they were as colorful a mix of smugglers as has ever been assembled in this country, *non*?"

"I suppose that's true," Alex said, swishing the brandy in his goblet and quietly inhaling its rich aroma.

"The pirates came from the Caribbean, the Mideast, and the Far East, as well as all the countries of Europe. Many bloodlines have been mingled down in the swamps. Including *les sauvages*. The Baratarians brought no women with them, and the aborigines were their neighbors. When smuggling was no longer countenanced by the government, some privateers turned to trapping and fishing and joined the Indian tribe."

He relit a fat cigar lying in a crystal dish beside his chair. "A curious thing, M'sieu' Archer—I've observed that those racial mixtures produce the most beautiful women on earth. Pirates are not marrying men, I grant you, but they procreated. I've met women living in the swamp, daughters of the original inhabitants of the parish, *les sauvages*. Some of their children, by French and

Spanish and God knows what other race of fathers, are among the most beautiful women I've seen."

"Are there still aborigines here, then?"

"Oh, yes. Some of them are of pioneer Acadian stock!" His rumbling laughter rose in his throat.

"What tribe, *m'sieu*?"

"The Houmas. Not a warrior tribe. They were driven into the Attakapas region by tribes to the east, who were being forced west by our encroaching white civilization." Latour sipped his brandy and settled deeper in his chair. "The Houmas were welcomed by the local tribe of Indians, who befriended them, and the two tribes lived in peace for a time. Then, unexpectedly, the resident tribe rose up and attacked their guests. Those who escaped the massacre fled south toward the Gulf, choosing land so deep in the wetlands no one could covet it, and there they have subsisted ever since on the fishing and trapping offered by the marshes."

"How did you learn of the massacre?" Alex asked. "Do you know the swamp people?"

The older attorney removed his cigar. "About twenty-five years ago I had a close friend who married a Houma woman. Not officially, of course, since the Black Code forbids it. But they produced a number of children. My friend acquired quite a lot of property, and he was concerned because his children were not legitimate, and feared they would not be allowed to inherit when he died. He came to me for help, asking me to act with another friend as guardians to his children if he should die young. I helped him write a will."

"That must have been difficult," Alex observed wryly.

"Ah, *oui*, since legally he had no children and no spouse. I listed his children by name, thusly: 'Joseph, child of Félice Viger, *une femme sauvage*; Elise, child of Félice Viger, *une femme sauvage . . .* ' "

" 'A savage woman!' " Alex repeated gloomily.

Latour nodded, puffing on his cigar. "It was Félice who told me about the massacre. She was more than half French, actually. Viger, her father, had 'married' a Houma woman, who could have had French blood too. The Houmas befriended the early Acadians who came to Louisiana a hundred years ago with nothing, and from the beginning they have lived together, some of them intimately."

The most beautiful women in the world. Inescapably Alex thought of Aurélie's beauty. Was it the shape of her eyes? Or the full ripeness of her lips? He wondered what racial strains in her heritage had given her those remarkable eyes and that faint golden cast to her skin. What blood had mixed with Crowley's English blood to form her unique appeal? Her beauty was different from the classic ideal, with a faint exoticism that made her look like no one else.

Here in le Terrebonne, an affair with a woman of the best society could not easily have been kept secret, Alex thought. But if Crowley had had an affair with a Houma woman such as Latour had described, one who was more French than Indian—he stopped there, thinking of how patrician Aurélie's beauty was. He called up the image of her lovely face, and was stunned by how vividly he saw her.

"M'sieu' Latour, what is the ideal of beauty among aborigines?"

Latour looked at him with a quizzical surprise in his expression, but answered after a thoughtful moment, "The prettiest Indian *jeune fille* I ever saw had a face as round as the moon, with high cheekbones and large, round eyes. I remember her soft, shy voice."

Alex let out his breath and leaned back in his chair. That was not a description of Aurélie.

But a seed had been planted.

Aurélie was going to be taken to her second ball. Julienne was working on her hair with Madame Duclos standing by, supervising the disposition of each lock. Aurélie's gown was a demure white—she was still in mourning, after all—with a bewitching décolletage, which Madame declared was the best of costumes because it gave men conflicting signals.

"The bosom says, 'Come, love me!' and the color says, 'I am innocent.'"

"You're wicked," Aurélie declared, laughing. "You must have been a very forward young woman."

"I was very popular," Madame Duclos admitted, with brazen lack of shame.

Aurélie watched as they dressed her hair. She was thinking about what Alex had told her about the gossip about her and Michel. "Have you heard talk that Michel intends to offer for me?" she asked Madame Duclos.

"Of course he will offer for you if you are named an heiress," Madame said matter-of-factly. "So will a dozen other young gentlemen rakehells."

Aurélie laughed.

But when Michel called for them in a somber mood, she could not believe the rumors. Aurélie sat quietly between him and Madame Duclos in the carriage, listening as they discussed what they called her petition.

"We may *have* to get counsel and threaten suit," Michel said. "Madame Crowley still refuses to see me, and Archer told me he's been let go. Until she hires another lawyer with whom we can deal, we have no recourse but the courts."

"That will cost you," Madame Duclos observed bluntly.

"*Oui,*" Michel said, and sighed.

"Please, Michel," Aurélie said, "do not even think of bringing suit on my account."

"How else can we force her to deal? It is the only way we can recoup our losses, *chère,*" Michel said reasonably. "Money has been spent for your gowns and your pension, to say nothing of what we owe Madame for her services."

"Oh!" Aurélie said, feeling all at once very gauche and immature. Growing up in the convent, she had never seen or handled money. She had simply never thought about it. She realized that she had incurred some impressive debts by thoughtlessly accepting Michel Jardin's generous offer of help and wondered how she would ever repay these two people who had befriended her, if she were not granted a dowry from her father's estate. She was very quiet for the rest of the drive.

Once again, after introducing her to their hostess, a Madame Ensenat, Michel left her to her own devices. Seraphine, her fellow student at the convent, was present, looking very pretty in a pale blue gown. She embraced Aurélie and teased her about Charles Poitevin.

"He's hopelessly in love with you, 'Rélie! His sisters have told me how he writes poems to you, then tears them up. It's so bad that his mother is trying to persuade his father to send him to Paris so he will forget you. It's so romantic! Do you care for him?'"

"He's very young," Aurélie said. "Perhaps a year in Paris will help him grow up."

"Oh, it's a real-life romance, isn't it?" Seraphine cried.

Several young men presented themselves to them for dances, and they had no further chance to talk. Aurélie had no lack of partners and was enjoying herself until she saw Alex Archer coming toward her with the obvious purpose of asking her for a waltz.

He had been away from the pension all week, and she had not seen him since their conversation in the library when he had told her about his visit to the Boudins. Her throat went dry as he bowed before her. For a few seconds she could not speak. He took her silence for acceptance, and put his arm around her.

An interior trembling seized her as she followed his first steps and she wondered if he could feel it. But she was a natural dancer, her body trained by the games and folk dances she had supervised and entered into with enthusiasm in the convent garden, her movements graceful and well coordinated. He whirled her around the ballroom.

"You've been away," she said breathlessly.

"I'm glad you noticed." His eyes were soft with an amused understanding that was so intimate, she could not face it, and aimed her gaze at the dark hue of his frock coat.

Alex was struck by the easy way she reacted to the slightest movement of his body, the softest pressure of his hand. It was a physical rapport that dazzled him. Involuntarily his arm tightened around her waist. Her questioning gaze lifted from his shoulder to his eyes, and a long, deep look passed between them.

Slightly dazed, Alex thought, *Am I falling in love?*

Aurélie, feeling penetrated by his look, turned her head away from its intensity and was startled to see

Michel standing against the wall talking earnestly to her half sister. What was more astonishing was the little smile of satisfaction on Nanette's lips as she listened to him.

Remembering Nanette's ugly whispering campaign against her at the Bizets' ball a few weeks ago, Aurélie wondered what Michel could be saying to bring that look to her half sister's face, when her mother would not even receive him.

Just then Nanette looked up and for an instant their gazes met. Even at that distance Aurélie saw the jealous anger that contorted Nanette's pretty face, and then in horror saw her half sister running toward them, zigzagging through the surprised couples waltzing on the floor.

"Alex!" she breathed in warning, just before Nanette grabbed her hair. It was the first time she had spoken his name. That was the thought that thundered in her mind in the few seconds she was under attack, with tears of pain springing to her eyes.

"Nanette!" Alex's voice was sharp with reproof.

As the winds of shock blew silence through the elegant ballroom, Aurélie heard through her pain her half sister's low, furious words, addressed not to her but to Alex. "How dare you do this to me?"

Alex reacted quickly, using his two hands to grasp Nanette's wrists so tightly he forced her fingers to relax and loosen Aurélie's hair.

"You're just like your mother, aren't you?" Nanette said, in a low, furious voice. "Well, I won't be shamed in public, do you hear?"

He whirled Aurélie away and waltzed her toward a floor-length window opening on the *galerie*. The distressing scene had lasted only a few seconds, but the last glimpse Aurélie had of her half sister was astounding. Michel had somehow reached her and with an arm around her was forcing her into a waltz. The silence in the ballroom exploded with whispers and conversation that almost drowned the music the black musicians were still playing.

Did you see?—What did she say?—Could you hear?

Then they were outside and Alex was dancing Aurélie down the *galerie* to a shadowy corner. He stopped there. When he saw the gleam of tears in her eyes, his arms tightened around her. He bent his head until his lips captured hers in a gentle kiss that sent an explosion through the guilty confusion of her emotions. He was Nanette's fiancé, after all.

But what had she done to provoke such a primitive attack?

Still dazed, she was scarcely aware that her hands moved up his shoulders and around his neck, but when it was happening it seemed utterly right to be holding him and caressing his hair while she drank in the sweetness of his kiss.

When the kiss ended he was laughing softly. "I should thank Nanette. I've been wanting to hold you like this for so long." He drew back and looked at her critically. "Your hair is falling down, *mademoiselle*. Will you trust me to replace some pins?"

"You?" she gasped, breathless with the emotions warring within her. The kiss had been a cataclysmic experience for her, but not for him, He had laughed! Yet it had been a loving laughter, and the implications of that were cataclysmic too.

"I have two sisters," he told her, turning her around to assess the damage. The Grecian knot on the crown of her head had been loosened and was coming unwound.

He took the tail of a coil that had fallen out of it gently in his hands and tucked it back in, replacing the tortoiseshell pin that had held it. "Such beautiful hair," he murmured. As he took his fingers away they traced the curve of her long creamy neck below her hairline.

Aurélie shivered with guilty pleasure at the touch, light as the brush of a butterfly's wing.

"I've asked to be released from my betrothal to Nanette," he said conversationally. "It was never made official because her father's death interrupted our plans to announce it."

"But she loves you," Aurélie protested tremulously. The intimate touch of his fingers had rendered her helpless. "I shouldn't have accepted your invitation to dance—"

"Sometime I'll tell you why I could never marry Nanette. The postponement for her year of mourning has spared us both unhappiness. I think she will understand when she recovers from her hurt pride."

"There you are, *mademoiselle*!" It was the voice of Madame Duclos, unusually sharp. "You will return to the ballroom immediately!"

"Mais oui," Alex said smoothly. "I didn't think she wanted to return with her Psyche knot undone. Perhaps you can improve on my handiwork, *madame*."

He bowed and left them.

"How audacious he is!" Madame Duclos seized Aurélie's arms and spun her around to inspect her coiffure, her deft hands smoothing a hair here and there. "Amazing! It's perfectly secure."

"He has two sisters," Aurélie said demurely, wanting to giggle. She had never been happier.

Chapter Nineteen

"You're so beautiful," Alex said, under his breath. "I wonder if a man can die of love?"

"You're mad to say such things to me," Aurélie whispered, her cheeks glowing. "I won't listen!"

They had met in the library before the shelves of old books belonging to the ancient *mademoiselles,* and this time it was not by accident but by unspoken agreement. Aurélie was aware of his efforts to see her alone, and had made it possible.

Their stolen time was short. Madame Duclos was quick to forestall any opportunity for private conversation between them. The sharp way she watched them was an indication to Alex that she was a confederate of Michel Jardin.

"Does Jardin say such things to you? Does he speak of love?"

"Sometimes," Aurélie admitted, "—but it's only in jest," she finished quickly, as she saw the anger that darkened Alex's open countenance.

She couldn't believe that Michel was serious when he claimed to be in love with her, or assumed a proprietary air and warned her not to fall in love with anyone else. Perhaps it was because, although he escorted her to parties, he never claimed her for a dance, and seemed pleased when she was besieged by young admirers.

"He wants me to make conquests," she confided. "He says I need friends. But he is my best friend. Besides you," she added softly.

"I am your conquest," Alex corrected her firmly, "and one conquest is enough."

He put his arms around her and she laid her cheek on his breast. His strong heart was beating as rapidly as her own.

"Has Jardin kissed you?" he demanded jealously.

"Ah, non, non!" she whispered, lifting her head.

Their lips met, and Aurélie felt the touch of a heavenly fire that traveled straight to her heart and made it swell almost to bursting. She imagined it glowing in her breast like the last coal in the fireplace when the candles were snuffed out.

Alex groaned. "Say you love me, Aurélie. I'm out of my mind with wanting you!"

"An illegitimate adventuress, with no dowry?"

"Do you think that matters to me?"

"What would your sisters say?" she teased.

They heard a step on the stair. "Aurélie?" Madame Duclos called.

"I'm coming, *madame.*" She snatched another English novel from the shelf and flew to the door, pausing only to check her upswept hair in the large mirror across the room over the mantel, and to blow a kiss to Alex.

"I have a new novel for you, *madame*," she called, and went into the hall, closing the door behind her.

Alex remained motionless until he heard the two sets of steps ascend to the upper floor. Then he quietly left the house. There was no longer any question in his mind. He had fallen deeply in love with Evan Crowley's illegitimate daughter.

He loved the courage and the honesty with which she faced her situation in life and the pride that made her assert her rights in the face of social stigma, and force local society to take notice. Her inner strength illuminated her remarkable beauty.

But his love was more than admiration. His need to be with her was so deep and fundamental that he felt diminished by her absence. He wanted to take her home to Bellemont. He wanted to marry her. But first he must dispel the mystery surrounding her.

He stopped by the general store, which was the postal drop, to pick up his mail and found an answer to a letter he had sent asking his younger sister, Thérèse, for some information about Michel Jardin's connections.

Why this sudden interest in Michel's affairs, dear brother? [Thérèse wrote.] *Gossip links him with the notorious Cléo, who inherited the Chinese gambling houses from her former lover. But Michel is no longer there, according to Robert, who answers my improper questions but staunchly refuses to take me to the casino. He says that respectable women are not admitted because they have no money to lose. Since I'm a woman and still respectable, I can't do your sleuthing there. Mama and Papa send love to you and to Nanette.*

Your ever loving sister

Thoughtfully Alex folded the letter and walked back
to his office. He believed Jardin knew who had borne
Aurélie, and had hoped Thérèse would unearth some
old gossip that might provide a clue as to where he had
gotten his information, but she had come up with nothing more than a current rumor about Jardin's latest
mistress.

He dismissed the idea of beating the truth out of
Jardin, which had its attractions. For one thing he could
be wrong. Jardin could be bluffing. It was possible he
knew nothing more than that Crowley was Aurélie's
father, and had invented the story of her birth out of
whole cloth.

Before he could propose marriage, for Aurélie's
peace of mind and for the sake of her future relations
with his family, who were all fond of Nanette, he must
solve the puzzle of Aurélie's origin. He believed that
Evan Crowley was her father, but who was her mother?

Nanette had made it clear that she believed Aurélie
was the child of an octoroon passing for white. Although
he knew it would make no difference in his love for her,
Alex rejected that. But the possibility made him understand his mother's pain more fully, for he was well
aware that to most Louisianians it would make a great
deal of difference.

When he thought of Nanette, it was with a troubled
heart. Even though he knew he was right in ending
their understanding, her unhappiness concerned him.
Now that he was truly in love, he saw clearly how he
and Nanette had been maneuvered almost to the altar,
mostly by Elizabeth Crowley, and he felt that Nanette's
mother had done them both a disservice.

Had Elizabeth instilled that poison about his mother's

family in Nanette, or had it come from Evan, her father?

He was so deep in thought he failed to see a former client approaching him until the man clasped his shoulder and spun him around, saying, *"Bonjour, m'sieu'!* Do you walk with your eyes closed, ahn?"

"Pardon!" Alex exclaimed, tapping his forehead. "I must remember to do my thinking in my office."

"You should go fishing," the Cajun said. "I've just come up from my fish camp in the marshes. It clears a man's mind."

Alex laughed. "I'd lose myself in the marsh."

"Go to the Indian village down the bayou and hire a guide. No one should go into those waterways alone."

"Thanks for the advice," Alex told him, shaking his hand. "I may do that."

When they parted, Alex was thinking again about Michel Jardin.

So Jardin's mistress had been the exotic Cléo! Alex had never seen her but he had heard men claim that she, too, was Chinese, that Lee Hing had brought her from China. He had always doubted that, assuming that she was probably a local woman of mixed blood.

But if that were true, Creole New Orleans would know exactly who she was, which quadroon mother was her mother, and what arrangement she had made with the Chinese gambling czar. Such information traveled quickly over the grapevine of the city's black servants. If the notorious Cléo were an octoroon, she would not be an enigma.

Walking on to his office while turning these thoughts over in his mind, Alex recalled his conversation with Latour about the Baratarians, the privateers who were adventurers from many nations, including those of the

Orient. Perhaps the "Chinese" mistress of the late Lee
Hing had been spawned in that den of rogues. If she
were the source of Jardin's information, wasn't it possible Crowley's mysterious mistress was from the same
lawless community? It was a community long trained in
keeping its secrets.

Men said it was worth a man's life to ask a Baratarian
too many questions. But the Indian fishermen and trappers who shared those fecund lakes and complex waterways that were such a boon to the smugglers might be
induced to talk. Perhaps a fishing trip with an Indian
guide was not such a bad idea. It was a long chance, but
he had no other clue to follow.

On his first free day, Alex ordered his horse saddled
up after breakfast and rode down the bayou road below
the town. He had not been able to see Aurélie alone but
he announced in the dining room that he was going to
arrange a fishing trip.

It was not a long ride to the end of the road, where
stood Weill's fish market and warehouse dock. From
there he would have to catch a ride with a fishing skiff to
the Indian village.

The dock was a busy place. Several shrimp boats were
moored there, as well as the pirogues of oystermen
unloading their haul. Beyond the warehouse was a
shrimp-drying platform where men raked layers of
boiled shrimp in imitation of the Indians, who tradition-
ally dried shrimp for the lean months. A strong odor of
fish permeated the humid air. Servants of local planters
were buying fish just off the boats for their masters'
tables.

Alex gave a big-eyed black boy some pennies to hold
his horse and walked into the office of M'sieu' Weill, the
merchant who operated the dock and its related busi-

nesses. Weill was a dignified white-haired man, somewhat bent and shrunken by his years, but with sharp eyes and a gentle voice.

After exchanging greetings, Alex told him he was looking for a ride down the bayou to the Indian village.

"You'll find the fishermen who've unloaded their catch over at the tavern across the road," Weill told him. "You can probably find someone there who will give you a ride."

"Can I leave my horse at the tavern?"

"*Mais, oui,* Jacques-le-grand has a stable. He'll take care of it. I haven't seen you around here before, *m'sieu',*" Weill said, his keen gaze appraising Alex.

"Alex Archer, lawyer." Alex offered his hand. "M'sieu' Weill, were you acquainted with the late M'sieu' Crowley?"

"*Ah, oui,* an unfortunate accident that, *non?* A fine horse was destroyed too. That was a fine hunter Crowley had."

"Most unfortunate," Alex agreed. "Recently, a young woman has approached Madame Crowley claiming to be his illegitimate daughter."

"Ahhh!" the merchant exclaimed. His thick white eyebrows lifted, for a moment showing more of his sharp eyes. "And who does she say is her mother?"

"That is what I'm trying to find out. She doesn't know. She was given to foster parents and then placed in the convent."

"That's why you want to go to the Indian village?"

His leap of thought interested Alex. "One must ask many useless questions in many places in order to hit on the right one."

"True." The elderly merchant frankly studied Alex's face. "How old is this daughter?"

"Seventeen or eighteen years."

"Ahhh," said the merchant again, and lapsed into a brief silence. "There was a young woman, but she was not from the Indian village. An extraordinary *jeune fille*. When you go over to the tavern, ask Jacques-le-grand about the one called Coco."

"*Merci*. I will."

"He'll remember her," Weill said. "She was not a *jeune fille* a man could forget. She had a rare quality of beauty."

A pulse leapt in Alex's throat. He could say the same about Aurélie. It seemed like an omen. "*Merci*, M'sieu' Weill," he said again, and went out into the broiling sunshine of the dock. Motioning the boy to follow him with his horse, he walked across the road and through some scattered trees to the tavern.

Inside the weathered building the fishy reek of the dock was layered under a strong odor of beer and whiskey. The bar was lined with fishermen, and the sounds of their laughter and Cajun patois filled the room. Behind the bar was a husky man with grizzled hair and beard and a booming voice. "*Bonjour!*" he greeted Alex heartily.

"*Bonjour, m'sieu',*" Alex returned, and asked in French, "Am I speaking to Jacques-le-grand?"

"I am that man, *oui*. What can I do for you?"

"Pour me a whiskey and give me a few minutes of your time."

"*Pou'quoi?*" the man asked, splashing whiskey into a glass.

"Perhaps we could speak in private?"

"Perhaps," the man said, his gaze wary. "As you can see, I am busy with my friends."

"I can wait," Alex said, and lifted his glass.

"What is your business, *m'sieu'*?"

"I'm a lawyer."

"Ah," Jacques said enigmatically, and walked to the other end of the bar.

Alex waited, sipping his drink, while the big man joked with his patrons. Presently he returned and leaned over the counter. "Is this a matter of law, then?" he asked in a low voice.

"Not yet. It's a personal matter with me. Did you know the late M'sieu' Crowley?"

"Everyone know him," Jacques said carefully.

Alex took a gamble. "I have met a charming young woman," he confided, in low tones, "a *jeune fille* straight out of the convent, who claims to be his illegitimate daughter."

"Ahn," Jacques said noncommittally. "M'sieu' Crowley was a man like other men, *non*?"

"She never knew her mother. Only her father."

"And you want to know where M'sieu' planted his seed, ahn?"

"It is his daughter who wants to know. M'sieu' Weill said I should ask you about a young woman called Coco."

"Coco? Ah, that one!" Jacques moved down the bar again in answer to a signal. When he came back, he said, "He told you to ask me about Coco? That was a long time ago, *m'sieu'*. My wife, she say Coco was *enceinte*, but me, what do I know about these things?"

"Was it Crowley's child?"

"How do I know that? Coco's father was knifed one night when he lef' my bar, and my wife say the girl, she can't live alone on that *chênière*, so we take her in. Then M'sieu' Crowley take an interest. He say he find a good family what give her a home. We never hear from her after he take her away."

Alex lifted his glass and took a gulp of whiskey to dull the excitement pounding along his nerves. He knew he had found something, but he was not sure it was something Aurélie would want to hear. "Was Coco from the Indian village?"

"*Non!* Her mother, *oui*, but she live on Isle de Navarre. Her *père* was a Baratarian, as ugly a man as I've seen in my three-score years. But Coco, she was something, that one! She fish and trap and keep the old scoundrel in whiskey. That's all he care about."

Alex finished his drink in another gulp. How could he tell Aurélie this?

"You mus' talk with my wife, *m'sieu'*. She can tell you more about Coco. Coco help her in the kitchen, and they sew clothes for her."

"Jacques, may I bring Crowley's daughter to see your wife?"

Jacques shrugged. *"Pou'quoi non?"* He moved down the bar toward a customer who was lifting his glass for a refill.

Alex threw some coins on the bar, lifted his hand in a salute which Jacques answered with a wink, and left.

He had lost his desire to go fishing. One day he and Aurélie would visit the Indian village. First he must talk with her. He was convinced that he was on the right trail, but he did not know yet what awaited them at the trail's end. He thought it a distinct possibility that the Coco of Jacques-le-grand's story was Aurélie's mother, and it was very probable that Michel's knowledge had come through his relationship with the legendary Cléo.

It was clear that Jardin was bluffing. He wouldn't dare go to court with his flimsy story about Evan's *grande passion* with a society woman. He must have hoped to get an out-of-court settlement from Elizabeth for Aurélie and marry her. Alex now had the means to demolish the conspirators' scheme, but ironically he didn't want to use it. He didn't want Aurélie hurt. Yet she must be told, if only to prove to her that Jardin was using her.

He believed her need to know her mother's family was genuine and deep—but would she accept the truth if it turned out this daughter of an "ugly" Baratarian was her mother?

Wouldn't she hate him for spoiling her illusions? Would he lose her? The thought brought an actual pain to his chest.

As his horse trotted along under the wide-spreading oaks grayed by beards of moss, he noticed tiny splashes on the unruffled surface of the bayou, indicating a sprinkle of rain. He turned his mount off the road to stand under the shelter of oak branches and hung the reins on the horse's neck while he unrolled the lightweight cape tied behind his saddle. In a few minutes he was hunched under it to wait out the heaviest of the rainfall.

While he sat there, only partially protected, with an occasional trickle of rain running down his face, he was strongly tempted to say nothing of what he had learned to Aurélie. Wasn't it better to let her go on dreaming about a genteel lady than to present her with a mother she could not respect?

But what about his obligation to Elizabeth Crowley and Nanette? Even though he had been freed from their case—and would never change his mind about marrying Nanette—didn't he have a moral duty to present them with this evidence that Michel Jardin was lying about the woman with whom Evan had betrayed them?

When the rattle of raindrops on the tropical foliage along the bayou ceased, he had reached a decision. He would propose marriage to Aurélie first—and only after she had accepted him would he gently prick her illusions about her mother and ask her to go with him to talk with Jacques-le-grand's wife, who had known the Baratarian's daughter he suspected was her true mother.

He reached his office at last and, when he found no one waiting there to see him, rode on to the pension where Lafitte helped him out of his wet clothes and into a warm tub.

Cléo, accompanied by her maid, Esther, was leaving New Orleans for the first time since her arrival eighteen years ago, when Evan had left her to find her own way off the steamboat and through the bewildering city streets. As she stood with Esther on deck as the luxurious riverboat backed away from its loading dock and out into the stream, where its turning paddles began to work against the current of the Mississippi, she recalled keenly that day of her arrival and how she had trembled with excitement and terror.

A new railroad had been built, and begun its run into the interior parishes only that spring, but she had elected to travel by steamboat. As on that earlier journey, she was confined to the lower deck where the *gens de couleur libres* were allowed to reserve cabins, but this time she was not alone. From the time Evan had brought the small dark woman to her just before he left Cléo alone to return to his wife during the summer growing season, Esther had been her closest confidante. Through the years, and especially since Cléo had discovered that her daughter was at the convent and had made the supreme sacrifice of staying out of Aurélie's life, the two women had become close friends.

They stood at the rail as the city in its crescent disappeared behind the riverbanks, and marveled at the lavish mansions that had gone up on both banks of the river.

"So many more than when I came down the river," Cléo observed, reliving that fateful trip and remembering her adolescent emotions.

"I was so happy," she told Esther. *So deeply in love.* "I was carrying his child, and he loved me. But what did I know? I expected so much of him, Esther. I didn't see his feet of clay."

"He was a handsome man, *madame.*"

"He was, wasn't he? With that pale silky hair and those blue, blue eyes. I had never seen any man like him. And he did love me, Esther."

"But not enough," Esther said softly.

"No, not enough."

It was still necessary to stay overnight at Donaldsonville and await the daily steamboat which would carry them down the Bayou Lafourche. Cléo, who did not want to be recognized by anyone who might have been brought to her casinos, let Esther arrange with their coachman to be taken to a boardinghouse for the *gens de couleur*, where they spent the night in much less luxurious surroundings than those to which Cléo had become accustomed.

After they boarded the Lafourche steamboat the next morning, she exclaimed to Esther continually about how many more Acadian farmhouses there were along the bayous, and how much closer together. But the other memories that surfaced she no longer talked about.

Memories of Evan Crowley had traveled with her all the way. How blindly she had loved him, and how passionate had been her awakening! It was something not every woman experienced. Now that Evan was gone she could at last be grateful he had taught her what love could be, even though their affair had ended in so much pain.

In early afternoon they left the bayou steamboat and hired a carriage driven by an elderly black man.

"Can you take us to le Terrebonne?" Cléo asked him.

He broke into a smile. *"Mai, oui. Madame* is from *ce bayou, non?"*

She returned his smile. "How did you guess? I've been away for many years."

"It is the way you say 'le Terrebonne,' *madame.* Where do you wish to go?"

"Do you know of a respectable hostelry where I might get rooms and meals for myself and my maid?"

"Oui, la Pension des Avignons. A plantation house owned by two maiden ladies. I'm told it's a comfortable place."

"I am Houma. Will they give me rooms?"

"We will ask them, no?"

She agreed, and let him hand her into the carriage. Esther followed her. Cléo leaned out to ask, "Do you know of a plantation called Les Chênes?"

"Oui. We pass by. Do you wish to stop?"

"No, but point it out to me." Les Chênes was the plantation, owned by friends of his, where Michel visited nearly every summer. She had no doubt that was where he was staying now. Was Aurélie with him?

She had transferred all her joyous, innocent, and unselfish love from Evan Crowley to the daughter he had given her—and then taken away. Since discovering her at the convent, Cléo had subsisted on a daily glimpse of her daughter, watching her grow in stature and beauty in the nuns' care, and she prayed now that Aurélie was still in good hands, happy and well cared for.

It was just a notion, and probably only a mother's foolish fears, but she would not feel at ease until she was sure that Michel was not connected in any way with Aurélie's disappearance from the convent.

Chapter Twenty

There was an unusual running-about down in the courtyard and on the lower floor as another tenant arrived at the pension. Aurélie watched from the rear window in Madame Duclos's room where they were having tea. The window provided a view of the courtyard, and Aurélie saw the groom run out to hold the horses of the hired carriage while the coachman climbed down and handed out the new arrival.

She was a handsome woman in a fine traveling costume, wearing a fashionable hat on her shining black hair, but she brought only a small trunk, which the groom carried into the house, and a carpetbag, which her maid carried.

Alex did not come to the dining room that evening, and when the new guest did not appear, either, Aurélie asked Mademoiselle Claudette about her.

Their shy proprietress murmured that the new arrival was obviously a free woman of color whom she had turned away but that her servants had persuaded her to give the woman and her maid temporary shelter.

"She has been given a room in the servants' quarters in the kitchen annex, which my sister and I are persuaded is not illegal. It is difficult for these people when they attempt to travel, *non*?" Mademoiselle added apologetically, "I hope you will not take offense. She is quite refined and offered to pay well, and since she is not staying long . . ." Her voice trailed away uncertainly.

"Of course we won't take offense," Aurélie assured her, at the same time as Madame Duclos said kindly, "One does what one has to do," with a significant look at Aurélie. She added firmly, "I'm sure we will not encounter her in the course of our daily routine."

"No, indeed. She will take her meals in private," Mademoiselle said hastily, and rang for the soup to be brought in.

Later, in their rooms, Aurélie observed, "The new tenant was very well got up, and she travels with a maid. It would be most agreeable to have an opportunity to converse with her."

"No doubt," Madame said dryly, "but in your position you can't risk any unseemliness. It must be extreme poverty that brought Mademoiselle Claudette and her sister to allow the woman in as a paying guest, even if they have put her with the servants. It's a pity M'sieu' Jardin could not have persuaded his friends to put us up."

They gossiped for a while, Madame telling Aurélie much that she had not known about the "arrangements" white men made for octoroon mistresses, and predicting that the pension would quickly do downhill if word got around that the *mademoiselles* had taken an octoroon as a paying guest.

"If she had wanted to be charitable, she would have offered her a servant's room and said nothing. But to take pay from those women! Respectable ladies resent them, *chère*! Perhaps because they are often so beautiful. Was she wearing a *tignon* when she arrived?"

"No, *madame*, a hat. Very fashionable."

"You must be very discreet, *chère*, in everything you do. We have not heard from Madame Poitevin since young Charles left for Paris. I'm persuaded he was sent to France to remove him from your charms."

"Surely not, *madame*!" Aurélie said, somewhat deceitfully, and blushed. But not from thoughts of Charles. She was remembering Alex Archer's kiss and reflecting—with a delicious chill—how far from the mark Madame Poitevin was!

Cléo wryly adjusted herself to the meager comforts of the room she had been given in the pension, telling herself she was lucky to have it. There were few hostelries in the interior and probably none that would take her in. Her denial that she was African had not been believed, except by the Mademoiselles d'Avignon's servants, who saw her Indian blood as different from their own.

The room was clean. The whitewashed walls were obviously built of cypress logs caulked with moss and mud, the construction used on many of the older houses on the bayou. It was an effective barrier to the heat of the adjacent kitchen. There was a single bed with a moss mattress over crossed ropes, a type familiar to her from her childhood, a table and two chairs. On the wall were pegs on which to hang clothing.

It would do. After all, she reminded herself, it was as good as the home her father had provided for her and her mother on the Isle de Navarre. She could make her inquiries about Michel Jardin through the servants. They always knew who had guests and what they were doing, and she had money to pay for information.

Later she planned to visit the Indian village to see if anyone there still remembered her mother. She wondered if M'sieu' Weill, with whom she had left Evan Crowley's gold pieces, and the tavern keeper whose wife had befriended her eighteen years ago, would recognize the smartly dressed woman from New Orleans, who traveled with a maid, as the girl who had fished and trapped the marshes, poling her own pirogue.

She shrugged. It was a strange, nostalgic mood her two-day journey had produced. No, the nostalgia had begun before that, when she had missed Aurélie among the orphans at the convent.

Esther went to the kitchen for their trays and came back with the news that there were other guests in the pension from New Orleans, including a young man.

"But he's not M'sieu' Jardin. He's a lawyer with an office here."

"Who are the other two guests?"

"Two women; one young. They go to balls, and sometimes young men call."

"A mother and her daughter?"

"I don't know. Their maid—she call herself Julienne —she's not friendly like the other servants. She got little to say. The others say the old woman very strict."

"I'd like to see the girl," Cléo said.

After a moment Esther said, "I'll tell Julienne 'bout the hummingbird's nest out behind the kitchen. It's in a jasmine vine, so low I wonder the ma'm'selles' cat hasn't found the babies in it."

Cléo smiled at her.

She thought little of Esther's words and so when she looked out of her window after a late breakfast the next morning, she turned so weak that she grasped the back of the chair nearest her to steady herself, and had to assure herself she was not dreaming. She was looking at the tall, auburn-haired girl who had supervised the little orphans at the convent, the girl Cléo had convinced herself was her Aurélie!

She wore a simple white gown with her rich auburn hair pulled back from her lovely face by a ribbon and falling down her back. She was bending over the tiny gray nest with a rapt look, her hands clasped behind her back as if to prevent herself from moving closer and startling the tiny birds.

For a moment Cléo could not move. Then she seized the moment, telling herself there might never be another opportunity like this. Her heart was beating so furiously she thought it would escape her body, and she had no idea what she was going to say to her daughter when she left her room.

But she needn't have worried. As she approached, Aurélie looked up with a glance at once bright and tender and whispered, "Aren't they perfect darlings?"

With a whirring of tiny wings the mother hummingbird darted straight at Aurélie's face. Cléo instinctively grasped her daughter and pulled her to one side.

Aurélie's startled cry was choked off as the bird hovered for half a second just beyond her nose, then disappeared into the gray nest, which looked not much bigger than a caterpillar's cocoon.

Cléo let out her breath in relief. "I'm sorry," she said,

reluctantly relaxing her hold. "I was afraid she was going to pierce your eye." Her arms ached with the remembered feel of her daughter's slim body. They had yearned to hold her ever since her babyhood, and the touch of her flesh had sent an almost insupportable emotion coursing through Cléo. It was with difficulty that she kept her arms at her side.

She stepped back, afraid she could not control her emotion and aware that it could frighten the girl.

But Aurélie did not seem to notice. "That mother was protecting her babies," she said softly.

Cléo was startled to see tears in her daughter's eyes. "Did she wound you?" she exclaimed.

"Oh, no! I hope we haven't frightened her into leaving them. I should hate that!"

"She won't leave her nestlings," Cléo said. "Most wild creatures have a strong maternal instinct."

"Stronger than exists in some human beings," Aurélie agreed. Her young voice sounded bitter.

Cléo looked at her in dismay. "Why do you say that?"

They had walked a little away from the jasmine bush. Aurélie hesitated, looking at the woman with the pale gold skin and the almond-shaped eyes, so different from those of a Creole woman. There was something about her that drew Aurélie to her. Somewhat to her surprise she heard herself explain, "My mother abandoned me."

Cléo stifled a cry of anguished protest.

But Aurélie heard it, and she said cheerfully, "My father didn't—not quite. He pretended someone else was my father, but I knew him. He came to see me regularly at the convent, and supervised my education."

"That's something," Cléo said, out of her pain. "But why did your mother abandon you?"

"Because I'm illegitimate." There was an edge of defiance to the words. "My mother was a lady of quality, you see, and could not acknowledge a bastard."

"Your father told you that?" Cléo asked, the old anger and grief sending bile up to her throat.

"No, he never spoke of her. No one knows who she is and everyone is curious."

"But you are going to balls, the servants say, and you have young gentlemen callers." Her smile was gently teasing. "They gossip in the kitchen, you know."

"They gossip at the balls," Aurélie retorted. "I am invited, yes, but I am not really accepted." She explained, "It was my father's friend who told me what little I know about my mother. He said that my father had promised to give me a dowry."

What friend? Cléo wondered. *Michel?*

"Are you planning to be married, then?" she asked with apprehension.

A soft peach glow of happiness appeared on Aurélie's cheeks. Why, the child was in love! A spasm of fear was mixed with the deep tenderness Cléo felt.

"He has not offered for me," Aurélie confessed. "And of course I can't accept a proposal until I'm assured that my father did leave a provision for a dowry for me in his estate."

So that was Michel's game. Cléo asked carefully, "Is it the friend of your father who offers marriage?"

"Oh, he talks of marriage but I don't believe he loves me," Aurélie said, her blush deepening. "No, it is a young man I have met since we came here to see about my father's estate."

The young lawyer? Cléo's thoughts reached frantically for what Esther had told her about him. She must certainly contrive to make his acquaintance.

"And would your father consider him suitable?" Cléo asked lightly, reaching up to break off a magnolia blossom from a low-sweeping branch just above her head and handing it to Aurélie.

Aurélie took the bloom with a smile that illuminated her face with such yearning that Cléo caught her breath. "Most suitable," she said. "In every way."

Cléo returned her smile, believing that her daughter was truly in love. But was Aurélie mature enough to make her own decision about marriage? And what was Michel about, anyway? Cléo resolved to make careful inquires about the young lawyer. If he proved eligible, she thought sadly, her daughter would not need her; in fact, the best thing her mother could do to assure her happiness was to stay hidden.

But if he were not suitable—what could she do?

Aurélie smiled at her new friend, amazed that she had told her so much that was both personally and privately important to her. *It is because we are both outcasts,* she thought, *that we have so quickly become friends.*

"Do you know," she confessed, "I was hoping to converse with you when I saw you arrive last evening. You look so Parisian! What brings you to Bayou Terrebonne?"

"Old friends and old memories. I was tired of gambling men."

Aurélie's eyes opened wide at this frankness, and a faint question appeared in them. They were so like her own eyes that Cléo was reminded that her daughter might see the likeness between them at any moment. With an ache in her breast, she said quickly, "I own two gambling casinos in New Orleans. It's night work, you know, and it's been years since I've seen gardens and birds like this in the morning light."

"Gambling?" Aurélie said uncertainly.

"You're thinking it's not an occupation for a woman," Cléo said, "and the nuns would no doubt tell you that you're right. I'm probably the only female casino owner you'll ever meet!" she said, and laughed. "I'll say *au revoir* now, *chère,* because your duenna will not approve of our conversing. I hope you find happiness with your young man."

She walked quickly away from Aurélie, who watched her go with mixed emotions. She had felt a strong rapport with the woman when they were inspecting the hummingbird's nest, and she had been unusually candid with her. Now she wondered at that rapport, because the woman was so different from anyone Aurélie had ever known—a woman who owned casinos where men gambled the night away! Strange how one could speak so easily to strangers about intimate feelings one did not discuss with one's familiars!

Aurélie wished she could have asked the woman whether she was an octoroon.

Cléo returned to her room in the kitchen annex with the old war battling within her. Aurélie had become the beautiful, gently reared all-white daughter Evan had wanted, and Cléo still both hated and loved the father who could do what Evan had done.

As for Michel Jardin, she intended to see that Creole gentleman and get answers to some stiff questions. At least she had assured herself that Aurélie was well and properly chaperoned.

Madame Duclos's habit of taking a little nap in the afternoon gave Alex the opportunity he was seeking to speak to Aurélie without that gentlewoman's daunting presence. In order not to risk waking her dragon Alex slipped a note under Aurélie's door, asking her to meet him in the library downstairs. There he paced back and forth before the bookshelves, rehearsing what he wanted to say to her.

When she opened the door, she looked so enchanting in a simple afternoon gown of creamy white that all his carefully rehearsed sentences fled his mind.

"Chère Aurélie!" he breathed. "You look so beautiful! I can't find words—"

A quick warmth flushed her cheeks. Madame had decreed that white mourning was more suitable for the summer. It made her feel light as a bird to be out of her black gowns. "Is that the important thing you have to tell me?" she teased.

"Only part of it."

He had extended his hands toward her in an involuntary gesture, and she obeyed an irresistible impulse to put her own hands in them. As they touched, she felt such a fizz of excitement that she instantly tried to withdraw them, but Alex held them tightly.

"Do you have news of my mother?"

He hesitated, and she cried, *"Do* you, Alex?"

Alex cursed himself for that revealing moment of indecision. "No, *chère,* but today I heard an interesting story that, if you wish, I will tell you later. What I want to tell you now is this: I love you, Aurélie. I want to marry you. Will you marry me, *chère?"*

She felt such a surge of emotion that she grew faint and tears misted her eyes. "Oh, Alex, I do believe I'm in love with you! I'm so happy I'm giddy!"

He would have drawn her into his arms, but this time

it was she who held tightly to his hands, preventing it. "But you know that I can't say yes. Not yet."

"Why not, love?"

"How can I marry until I have a family to—to be happy for me, and to welcome you?"

"I can assure you that my parents and my two sisters, my brother-in-law and my young nephew, will prove to be all the family you could wish."

She shook her head regretfully. "It wouldn't be fair to them to bring them a nameless adventuress with no dowry." She could not bear to think of Alex taking an illegitimate orphan with no right to call herself by her father's name home to the family he had described.

"My darling, you can forget your dowry. You will need none at Bellemont, believe me."

Her heart was overflowing with love but she thought it would break. "It isn't the money, but the right to use my father's name, an acknowledgment that I am my father's daughter. I must have it."

His heart plummeted. Elizabeth and Nancy Crowley would never voluntarily accept her. How could he tell her that even now Nanette's jealous spite was beginning to turn the community against her? And he was partly to blame for that jealousy!

"I must know who bore me," Aurélie said. "I do love you, Alex, but I must finish what I've begun before I can give you my promise."

He put his arms around her and kissed her tenderly and her soft lips trembled under his. "Let me take you home to Bellemont," he urged, sure that once she was installed in the bosom of his family she would lose some of her obsessive need for acceptance. It was a close and loving tribe in spite of what his mother had divulged on his last visit home, and he marveled at how his parents had kept the tragic event at the decaying mansion, La Sorcellerie, commemorated by its mysterious vine-covered tomb, from darkening his childhood.

It was the deep love between his mother and father that had enabled them to rise above grief and regrets. He was convinced that if only Aurélie could see and experience that love herself, she would understand—but he could not change her mind.

She refused to talk further about it. "Tell me the story you promised," she demanded.

What else could he do? Holding her loosely, he said, "It's about a young girl whose father was murdered about eighteen years ago, leaving her an orphan." He had kept his tone casual, but Aurélie immediately tensed. "Your father took an interest in her," he went on carefully. "You see, she was *enceinte*—"

"Not by my father!" Aurélie exclaimed, pulling away from him.

"No one says that, love. What I was told is that your father offered to find a good home for her and her baby." He paused, undecided whether or not to go on, but finally finished, "She was one of the swamp people, native Americans whom people cruelly call '*les sauvages.*'"

Aurélie blanched. "What a sad story! But I'm glad you told me. It shows what a kind and generous man my father was."

"Yes," Alex said unhappily.

Her mouth trembled. "Are you perhaps thinking that it was only kindness that made him look after me, another orphan?"

"No, *chère*, I believe Evan Crowley was your father."

"And my mother was a woman of quality."

"I'm sure of that, whoever she was," Alex said

gravely. He hesitated again, then plunged ahead. "There's something I should have told you before I asked you to become my wife, Aurélie, but I didn't have the courage."

His formal tone filled her with apprehension. "Yes, Alex?"

"It's a long story, *chère,* an old family scandal that was kept from me until very recently. My mother, a wonderful woman who will love you as I do, had a half brother who was passed for white as her cousin. He was actually the son of her father and a *métis* who was—"

Aurélie had stiffened. "Why are you telling me this now?" she interrupted him, her eyes suddenly blazing in her white face.

"It is something you must know before you join my family, *chère*—"

"You could have told me before now. Why didn't you? Surely you can't be thinking that poor savage orphan my father befriended was my mother!"

"Aurélie, *chère,* I didn't say that. But it's one clue to your father's past. I think we should follow it up. The tavern keeper suggested that you talk to his wife. Perhaps he thinks she will tell you something she would not mention to me."

"Are you still working for Madame Crowley and my half sister?" Aurélie asked hotly. "Or is this your way of trying to make me distrust Michel Jardin, who has been so kind to me?"

"Aurélie, my love! Do you think I would deceive you? Especially about something so important to you? Perhaps I'm trying in my awkward way to say that even if your mother is not what you have been led to believe, it will make no difference to me or my family. What my parents have been through accounts for much that is different in the way we look at things. They will love you for what you are."

He couldn't bear the look he had brought to her eyes. "As for Jardin," he said, in sudden anger, "don't force me to say what I think of him! He has built up your hopes until you are not willing to follow any path that won't lead to the fairy tale he told you!"

A fury shook her. "A *fairy tale!*"

"You have to face that possibility, *n'est-ce pas*? Jardin has no evidence to support his story, and it seems incredible that such an affair as he describes could have been carried on in absolute secrecy, in New Orleans or here. Servants always know more than we think—"

"I can't believe—I won't listen to you!" Aurélie clapped her hands over her ears.

"*Chère*, please! Let's not quarrel, my darling. Say you'll marry me!"

"How can you ask that, if you believe my mother was a savage woman?"

"Aurélie, it's you I love and not your mother. If she were an orangutan, I would still love you!"

"That isn't amusing, Alex!"

"No, I guess it wasn't. I apologize. Will you marry me?"

She shook her head, too near tears to utter another word. Her dearest wish just then was to escape before she let him see how he had hurt her. She had seen through his awkward attempt to spare her feelings by revealing that his was one of those New Orleans families with never-mentioned relatives of mixed blood. It told her that he really believed that pitiable savage from the swamps was her mother!

She turned and seized the doorknob, wrenched open the door, and fled up the stairway.

"It's all nonsense," Madame Duclos said, when Aurélie had confessed seeing Alex and describing the scene.
She did not seem greatly shocked, but she sat down at
her small desk and took up pen and ink. "Pay no attention to it," she advised.

"If you are writing to Michel," Aurélie said, having
dried her tears, "pray tell him that I don't believe a
word of Alex's story." She was just terribly disillusioned
that *he* could believe it.

"I will tell him," Madame Duclos promised her. But
she was writing Michel about an entirely different matter.

Mademoiselle Claudette, with much embarrassment,
had left her apartments to remind Madame that she had
not made the promised second payment for their rooms
and meals. Madame was writing to ask Michel for the
money he had promised to bring from New Orleans.
She had not disclosed the problem to Aurélie. If Michel
Jardin had gambled away the money he had promised
to provide, she must speak of it eventually, but now was
certainly not the time.

Aurélie pleaded a headache when Madame suggested a game of cards, and did not tell her about Alex
Archer's proposal of marriage. But when Madame's Julienne had helped her out of her gown and then gone to
her mistress, Aurélie robed herself in her cotton night
shift and got into her bed to lie awake reliving those
stolen moments with Alex in the library.

When she thought of his kiss she could still feel a
strange tremor in her lips where his had touched them.
She remembered the crisp feel of his light brown hair
where it curled slightly at the nape of his neck and
wished she had run her fingers through it. It was something she had long wanted to do. When she remem-

bered the tender look in his eyes when he said, "I want
to marry you," she felt the delicious weakness of surren-
der that had been her response all over again.

He was everything she had dreamed of in a man,
strong and capable, yet even-tempered—tenderly protective, as when her half sister had publicly attacked
her—passionately in love with her, yet constantly teasing her—and, she had thought, perceptive enough to
believe her when she said she had recognized Evan
Crowley as her father even though he had attempted to
keep his identity a secret.

That was why it hurt so much that Alex disbelieved
Michel's story of her mother. If Alex loved her, how
could he imagine that a tale of murder and sin in the
swamps had anything to do with her?

The house was dark and very still when she finally
heard his step ascending the stair, and wondered where
he had been. She waited for the sound of his door opening and the quiet voice of his manservant, who awaited
him in his bedchamber.

She heard neither.

Gradually she became aware that he was standing at
her door and she waited with pounding heart for his
whisper or his knock. She felt the strongest urge to get
out of bed and creep to the door.

She was certain Alex was there, just on the other side
of it. It was the knowledge that she could open it and be
in his arms that kept her immobile in her bed. With a
warm flush, she became aware of her nudity in the
cotton shift in which she slept, and the awareness held
her tense, frightened of her own desire.

Not even a bird's peep from the trees beyond the
galerie broke the heavy, languorous silence. Aurélie
shut her eyes tightly and began a prayer to the Virgin

Mary, her heart beating so loudly she thought it must be heard beyond her door.

At last the quiet steps crossed the hall and Alex's door creaked. Her taut muscles relaxed, and she began to cry.

Chapter Twenty-one

The next morning when she brought their morning tea to Madame Duclos's room, Julienne reported that the new tenant was leaving.

"So soon?" Aurélie cried.

"Mais oui, a carriage has arrived, and her baggage is being carried out at this very moment!"

Aurélie ran to the window in time to see the fashionable green traveling skirt disappear into the coach. Just before the coachman closed the door, the woman from New Orleans and her dark maid both looked up at the window, almost as if they could see Aurélie standing behind the yellowing lace curtain, and the look on the woman's face was so mysteriously sad that it tugged at Aurélie's heart.

The coachman climbed to his seat, the groom let go of the near horse's bridle, and the carriage rolled out of the courtyard.

In mid-morning, as Aurélie and Madame Duclos were occupied with some needlework, a note was delivered to Madame. As she read it, her face seemed to swell, and reddened unbecomingly. She stood up, letting her needlework drop to the floor, and cried, *"Le chien!* I should have known from the beginning that he was not to be trusted!"

"What is it, *madame*?" Aurélie cried, alarmed by the signs of choler in her chaperone's face. "Please do calm yourself!"

Madame crumpled the note in her hand. "M'sieu' Jardin," she said icily, "informs us that he has gambled away his money and is forced to abandon your cause."

"What?" Aurélie exclaimed.

"He doesn't even apologize, *le cochon!*" Madame stepped over her needlework and paced the floor. "I should have guessed!" she said angrily. "It should have become quite obvious in these last weeks. There's an important ball on Bayou Black this weekend to which Michel should have procured invitations for us, but he has not done so."

"But must he beg an invitation for us?" Aurélie protested. "Have we not made friends?"

Madame turned to face her. "Haven't you noticed, *chère*, that since your young admirer, Charles, has been sent to Paris, his mother no longer invites us?"

Her tone was so cold that Aurélie felt chilled by it. "What are you saying, *madame*?" Only a moment before, Aurélie had been reflecting on the curious rapport she had felt with the tenant who had been put in the servants' quarters, and she thought again that there was a reason for it. They were both outcasts from society through no fault of their own; that was why they had been drawn toward each other.

"M'sieu' Jardin is a gambling man, *oui*," Madame Duclos said, letting her fury show now, "but it is not because of his gambling debts he is abandoning us. It is plain to me that his gamble is on winning the real, the uncontested heiress, your half sister! That is why he is abandoning your cause."

"Nanette? But—"

"And he sends no money for our rooms," Madame said bitingly, "which Mademoiselle Claudette has already mentioned twice." She crossed the room to her bellpull, and rang for Julienne. Her face was still flushed with rage. "It demeans me to have to remind him that he promised to take care of my expenses. I have the family connections and the respectability he needed but I am not wealthy, *chère*. I thought Michel Jardin was a man of honor, but he has made a complete fool of me! I will not tolerate this humiliation," she finished bitterly.

"There is no money?" Aurélie, bewildered by this outburst, echoed in alarm. "What will we do?"

"I shall return to New Orleans as soon as I can engage passage."

While Aurélie stood mute with shock, Julienne entered, and Madame inquired about the laundering of their clothes and ordered the maid to begin packing their trunks as soon as it was possible.

Aurélie felt ice flow through her veins. She was helpless without funds of her own. What was she going to do?

"Don't look so stricken, *chère,*" Madame Duclos said. "*I* am not abandoning you! I will take you back to New Orleans with me, and deliver you safely to the Ursuline sisters. More, I regret I cannot do."

"But I can't leave," Aurélie stammered. *Leave Alex?* "I haven't found my mother—"

"*Chère,* haven't you realized yet that Michel was using you? He hoped to prove you an heiress and then marry you. The money was his only goal. This proves it!" She crackled the note in her hand, and added, "He promised to pay me well for my help."

Aurélie gasped, "But I would never have married Michel!"

"Wouldn't you? Your obligation would have been difficult to ignore, *chère,* especially as Michel claimed instructions from your father." Madame gave a bitter laugh. "But Elizabeth Crowley is not the fool he thinks her. She refused to be frightened into letting you share in your father's estate. Now Michel has persuaded himself that he can marry your half sister, and get his hands on your father's entire fortune. But he will fail in that too," she said contemptuously, "because he can't resist gambling. Oh, no, it isn't likely that Madame Crowley will accept him for a son-in-law!"

Aurélie was trembling with shock. Leave Terrebonne? "But I can't go back to the convent!" Never see Alex again?

"Aurélie, dear, you have no choice. What will you do here? I've paid Mademoiselle Claudette out of my own funds for the rest of this week. After that, I will be gone and you will have neither chaperone nor funds. I regret I do not have the fortune to enable you to continue your search. I would help if I could."

Aurélie saw the genuine fondness behind Madame's anger over Michel's defection, and felt a warm surge of gratitude for the older woman's friendship. "You've been more than kind, *madame,* and I regret the loss you've suffered on my account. Someday I'll repay you—"

"With what?" Madame Duclos asked pragmatically. "If you were not illegitimate, you might find work as a governess, but—"

"I would ask the help of M'sieu' Archer in finding a position," Aurélie said, "if he had not asked me to marry him. That makes it impossible."

Madame stared. "M'sieu' Archer has proposed marriage? Then your difficulties are over! His family is one of the wealthiest in New Orleans."

Aurélie was silent and looked so downcast that Madame exclaimed, "Surely you haven't refused him?"

"How could I accept, *madame*? How can I go to him with no family, no legal name? He"—the tears that unexpectedly flooded Aurélie's eyes slipped out to run silently down her cheeks—"he wants me to journey down the bayou to talk to some people there about a girl who they say left there with my father—he thinks Michel Jardin has lied to us—"

"I'm certain of it! Well, in that case, we can't leave for New Orleans before the weekend, can we?" Madame said ruefully. "Because you can't go with M'sieu' Archer unless I accompany you."

"The girl—she was *une sauvage*," Aurélie said, her lips trembling.

"A half-breed?"

Aurélie nodded.

Madame sat down heavily. *"Mon dieu!* In that case—"

"I would rather not know," Aurélie said unhappily.

"I wish you had not told me, *chère.*" Madame sighed. "But if your young man suspects this, we will have to go, *non*?"

They sat in silence. Finally Madame said, "Wondering is worse than knowing, *n'est-ce pas*? I say go and find out for yourself if you can believe this woman is your mother. It will make no difference to me, *chère*. Whatever she is, you've grown into a lovely young woman with the education of a fine lady. Any man who possesses you will be fortunate."

Aurélie rose from her chair and embraced the older women.

"I hope you don't find her!" Madame exclaimed feelingly. "What do you need from her?"

"Maybe just to tell her what I think of her for abandoning me," Aurélie said bitterly.

"Perhaps you should be glad she did! Let's go and see these people who think they know so much. You will tell your young man that we will accompany him to wherever it is."

"*Oui, madame.* But I fear Alex is angry about my refusal."

"Then I will do the talking," Madame said, in her best dragon tones. "It is not proper that he should have tried to arrange a betrothal himself, in any case. He should have come to me."

"*Oui, madame,*" Aurélie said, smiling at her fondly.

They set out the following morning, in a carriage that Alex provided.

It was a hot and sluggish day, for the summer had advanced into August. The air was unnaturally calm, with no breeze off the Gulf. The trees seemed to droop in the heat, their leaves listless, their mossy garlands looking dead. No birds sang. Even the turtles and the alligators remained underwater, with only an occasional bubble on the surface of the bayou to reveal their positions.

Aurélie took pleasure in the appearance of Alex, who sat on the narrow seat facing them, riding backward. He was wearing a fawn-colored suit with a bright red vest under his jacket that was most flattering to his fair coloring. She watched the play of expressions on his face, the engaging smile that came and went on his lips as he talked with Madame Duclos, who kept up a lively gossip about the people she had met at the balls they had attended. Occasionally Aurélie encountered his gaze on her and detected a tenderness in it that made her aching heart want to sing, so that her emotional state was volatile, shifting from apprehension to hope to despair.

"Who is this person we are going to visit?" Madame Duclos inquired, as they approached the end of the road and saw the fishing skiffs and shrimp boats waiting to be unloaded at the warehouse dock.

"The tavern keeper across the road from the warehouse suggested that we talk with his wife about a young woman who had an illegitimate child."

"This will be a new experience for me," Madame said dryly. "But I fail to see how it can possibly be of interest to Mademoiselle Aurélie!"

"It was good of you to come," Alex told her. He wished heartily there had been a way to bring Aurélie without her chaperone so this interview could be conducted in privacy. He was not sure whether Madame Duclos was a partner in Michel Jardin's assault on the Crowley estate, or whether she was an unwitting accomplice. He was not at all certain of what the interview would reveal, and he dreaded the possibility of humiliating Aurélie.

The coachman drew the carriage team up under the trees a little distance from the weathered building. Alex jumped out and handed the women down, then asking their coachman to wait, guided them to the rear where a black man was cleaning fish on the stoop. He eyed them curiously.

"Is Madame Jacques-le-grand within?" Alex asked him.

"Oui, michie."

Alex knocked on the door. They waited while the sound of heavy steps crossing a wooden floor came to their ears. A plump Cajun woman with iron-gray hair opened the door. A large fireplace obviously being used for cooking could be seen in the wall on the far side of the room.

"Oui, m'sieu'?" she asked, her dark eyes moving swiftly past him.

Aurélie saw recognition leap to them when they gazed on her. She grasped Madame Duclos's arm, feeling faint. This woman knew her mother. She had recognized a likeness, Aurélie was sure.

Alex was explaining, *"Madame,* your husband suggested that I bring Mademoiselle Crowley to talk to you about a certain Coco who had a child about eighteen years ago—"

There was a crash from inside the room and the sound of something rolling across the floor. Aurélie pushed her way past Alex and the tavern keeper's wife into the kitchen, and stopped. Standing beside her overturned chair was the dark-haired, golden-skinned woman in the fashionable green traveling costume.

"You?" Aurélie breathed. For the first time she realized that the woman's eyes were almond shaped like her own, and very near the same color.

A pulse in the woman's throat was beating fast. Aurélie saw her shoot a warning glance at her maid, who seemed frozen in the act of bending to pick up the fallen chair.

It was Aurélie who moved first. She had caught the flash of gold on the floor. She walked over and picked up the engraved bracelet lying on the worn cypress plank. "Yours?" she said coldly, holding it out to Cléo.

"Thank you," Cléo said, and slipped her hand through it. "It was given to me many years ago by—an admirer. Ever since that day it's been in Mr. Weill's safe over at the warehouse. I've never worn it."

Aurélie's slender figure was stiff, her eyes dark with emotion. This was her mother. From the first time she had seen her she had sensed a cord binding them in some mysterious way. She was sure of it now. She said, tensely, *"Why?"*

Aurélie was sure her mother understood that she was asking, *Why did you abandon me?* but Cléo answered, with a shrug, "Because my father would have taken it away from me."

Alex had picked up two gold coins from the floor and he took them to Cléo. The expression on her face as she looked at them was as mysteriously sad as the look she had turned up to Aurélie's window when she was leaving the pension.

Madame Jacques-le-grand chose that moment to say, "This is Coco, *m'sieu'*. It is strange you should ask for her today because she left here eighteen years ago, and today is the first time I see her. She was this minute telling me what she do in New Orleans this many years."

Cléo said, with a wry smile, "If Madame Jacques-le-grand will permit, I'll finish telling the remarkable story of my life. Perhaps it will amuse your visitors, *madame.*"

"Oui, oui!" Madame Jacques-le-grand said, flustered. "Please sit, *madame, ma'm'selle—*"

Aurélie looked at Alex, who nodded. They sat around the table on the kitchen chairs and Cléo began to talk.

* * *

Halfway through Cléo's story, Madame Jacques's servant brought in the redfish and the tavern keeper's wife got up from her chair and busied herself, readying them for the fishermen who could be heard laughing and discussing their catch in the common room of the tavern.

Aurélie was experiencing something between a dream and a nightmare. The room she was in, and the events she was hearing, revealed a world far removed from both the convent life she had known and the plantation balls and morning coffees that she had recently attended.

Cléo's story about the theft of her child and her unending search wrenched their emotions. Madame Jacques wiped tears from her eyes between dipping the fish filets into the cornmeal. Cléo told them about Lee Hing's tutelage, her warm affection for him, and the surprise of her inheritance, holding back nothing except her discovery of Aurélie in the convent and her misplaced trust in Michel Jardin.

Her words were spinning around in Aurélie's head, and she felt sick with confusion and uncertainty. Her resentment of her mother's abandonment was warring with her sympathy for the sufferings Cléo described.

She had dared to look at Alex only twice. His keenly observant eyes were fixed on Cléo's face. The expression on his face was serious. *What was he thinking?*

Aurélie turned to Madame Duclos, who for once had lost the power of speech. Her chaperone looked stunned.

Alex asked, "What brought you to Terrebonne, Madame Cléo?"

"A nostalgia for the scenes of my youth, *m'sieu',*" she said, smiling.

"And have you not found your daughter?"

With her eyes fastened on Aurélie, Cléo said, "No, *m'sieu'.* I have little hope that she still lives."

"This young woman believes she is an illegitimate daughter of Evan Crowley. Her name is Aurélie."

"Indeed?" Cléo's eyes narrowed until they almost disappeared, and her full lips twisted. "He was a busy lover, *non?*"

Tears started to Aurélie's eyes. She was not even being given the choice of acceptance. Her mother was rejecting her again.

"Mademoiselle Aurélie is not your daughter?" Alex persisted.

"No, *m'sieu',*" Cléo said firmly. "It is impossible."

Madame Duclos pulled a handkerchief out of her bosom and blew her nose.

"What do you do next?" Alex asked Cléo. "Are you staying in le Terrebonne for a while?"

"For a few days. This morning I have hired a boat, a large pirogue that I can take to the Indian village where my mother grew up and then to Isle de Navarre, the *chênière* where my father took her when they married."

"That sounds like an interesting trip," Alex said, and to Aurélie's dismay added, "If you are returning here this evening, I'd like to go with you."

Cléo smiled. "Yes, it's not far, and I'd be glad for your company. Perhaps Mademoiselle Aurélie would like to accompany us?"

Before Aurélie could speak, Madame Duclos said decisively, "Me, I have no wish to journey farther into the marsh."

"It won't be necessary, since Madame Coco will be along," Alex said. "I'll send you back in the carriage after we all sample some of Madame Jacques's redfish, yes?"

"*Bon!*" Cléo smiled at Aurélie, but spoke to her maid. "Esther, you will go with Madame to the pension, and return here with the carriage for us this evening."

"*Oui, madame,*" Esther said.

Aurélie was kept silent by the confusion of her emotions. Her mother still denied her, but she and Alex were arranging an opportunity for her to speak with her, an opportunity she both longed for and dreaded.

"I will still take you back to the convent, Aurélie, if that is what you wish," Madame Duclos said. "But it is your decision. . . .Well, *chère?*"

Alex was looking at her too. He was not smiling. "Will you go with us or with Madame Duclos?"

There was a challenge in the way his hazel eyes held her gaze with their intent, serious expression. She felt, abruptly, as if their future hung on her answer.

If was as if an earthquake had violently shaken her world to pieces and when the dust had settled they made an entirely different pattern. There was a dull ache in her chest as she stood between Alex and her mother, waiting to board the pirogue that Cléo had rented.

It was larger than the average pirogue, still flat-bottomed, but with a tall mast and a sharply angled yardarm to which a sail was attached. There was no boom; at the bottom the sail was fastened to the horizontal bow of the canoe. Rigging ran from the rudder to the ends of the yardarm. Lying in the boat was was a long pole shaped like an oar at one end.

Alex said he had handled a sail when fishing with his father on Lake Pontchartrain, and Cléo said, "I've poled these bayous in a pirogue not much smaller than this."

Alex, who had handled a sail when fishing with his father on Lake Pontchartrain, said, "With a north wind pushing us, it's unlikely we'll have to pole."

A breeze had indeed sprung up from the northeast to allay the August heat. Alex boarded the craft and Cléo handed him the picnic basket. He stowed it under a seat, then held out a hand first for Aurélie and then for Cléo.

Alex took the rudder where he could also control the lines running up to the yardarm. Cléo and Aurélie sat opposite him. As soon as Alex cast off from the dock, the sail billowed out. Soon they were gliding down the bayou with silent speed.

Cléo smiled at Aurélie. "We'll pass my mother's Indian village but we won't stop there. I want us to have plenty of time on Isle de Navarre."

Alex wondered if Aurélie realized why her mother would not take her to the Indian village, where Cléo's people would immediately recognize Aurélie as Coco's daughter.

"Is the island a sandbar?" Aurélie asked.

"*Non, chère*, it's not on the coast. It's a *chênière* in the marsh, named for my father, Plácido Navarre. At one time he was a pirate, one of Lafitte's band, and he liked the Isle's isolation."

Aurélie flinched. Her grandfather was a pirate. With *Lafitte*.

"M'sieu' Weill told me my father's house has been kept in repair by some men who use it as a fishing camp and as a base during the trapping season. We'll picnic there."

It was not the kind of picnic Aurélie had dreamed of back at the convent. But at least she was with Alex, who seemed to think it not at all strange that they were journeying into the marsh with the woman he himself had described as *une femme sauvage*.

Her whole world had changed since she had left the convent, the mother superior, and her friends among the nuns. Her new friend, Madame Duclos, was on her way to New Orleans because the deceitful Michel Jardin was no longer able to pay their bills. Her new-found half sister hated her.

Only Alex was left, Alex whom she yearned for with all the pent-up love of her lonely soul . . . and this strange woman who had marveled with her over the miracle of a tiny hummingbird's nest, and then said, "I'm tired of gambling men," and boasted of owning two casinos! And because of her, Alex was lost to her. For how could he marry the daughter of *une sauvage*?

Alex had removed his hat. The wind lifted his light brown hair and tossed a lock over his forehead. Aurélie looked at him and thought, *I'll never love anyone else.*

All along the quiet waterway the front yards of Cajun farmhouses sloped down to the bayou's edge. here was no levee road here where traffic was confined to the water, only crude cypress piers and landings. The weathered houses, built on foundations high enough to guard against floods, were all similar, with gable roofs sloping down over front *galeries.* Cisterns to catch and hold rain water stood nearby on high platforms, and some houses had outside wooden stairs running up to the attic.

"That's where the boys in the family sleep," Cléo told them.

Many front *galeries* were furnished as outdoor living rooms. Cléo pointed to one that had been daubed with mud and moss, then whitewashed, giving it the look of a parlor with its line of chairs for sitting and watching the passage of vessels on the bayou.

They passed the Indian village, which had a few similar wooden dwellings with fishing nets and racks of small fur pelts drying in the fenced yards, but most were curious thick-walled buildings with an outer layer of woven palmetto matting. Some were square, but most were round hogans.

"The walls are made of mud and moss," Cléo told Alex. "The palmetto mats protect the mud from the rains."

Aurélie looked at the curious houses with a churn of emotions, thinking how she had tried to recognize her mother among the ladies drinking coffee on the grand *galeries* of the Mississippi plantation houses.

The houses became fewer and then disappeared, leaving only a flat expanse of high marsh grass through which the bayou wandered sluggishly. Cléo began pointing out things Aurélie would not have seen but for her. She identified the large birds that flew up, brown pelicans with their incredible beaks, snowy egrets, and the enormous creatures she called "snake birds" because of their long, sinuous necks.

"They're water turkeys," Alex claimed.

Cléo pointed to the metallic snout of a huge alligator and they watched it swim swiftly away from the approaching boat, barely visible underwater. She told them how to recognize the mud domes of the muskrats in the reeds near the bank, and pointed out some of the sleek swimmers. Then she fell silent, but there was an aura of vitality about her that told Aurélie she was in a private place, enjoying this strange world that seemed so alien to Aurélie.

"Isle de Navarre!" she said, pointing. "Over there. Do you see it?"

"It's like a mirage!" Alex exclaimed. "See, *chère*?"

Aurélie could see only tiny blobs of blue above the grassy horizon.

"Those are the oaks of the *chênière,*" Cléo told her.

The boat rounded a bend in the waterway and the distant blue foliage disappeared. But a few moments later it reappeared, and soon they were tying up at a small rickety dock. The water was very shallow and Aurélie noticed a small bay enclosed with wooden pickets rising out of the water.

"An old turtle pen," her mother explained.

Alex stepped to the dock and held out his hand to Aurélie. She grasped it and climbed out of the pirogue to look around the isle that had been her mother's home, while Alex helped Cléo.

There were the promised oak trees, the *chênes,* that gave the islands their name, but they were scrubby and provided little shelter from the wind, which seemed stronger ashore. There was not much brush, only some tall wiry grass. The few scattered houses were built a full story above the ground on platforms supported by cypress poles, with ladderlike stairways ascending to them.

None of them were occupied.

"Few come here outside of trapping season," Cléo said. "They have other homes on Bayou Terrebonne or Lafourche. But my father preferred to stay here."

Her own house stood on a point of land, with a bent

and twisted oak shading the yard beside the entrance stair. A beehive oven made of moss-and-mud bricks stood in the yard. "I baked our bread in that," Cléo said proudly.

"An Indian pirogue!" Alex exclaimed, pointing to a burned-out cypress log canoe lying under the house.

"It's mine. I poled it for many miles." Cléo stood looking at it for a moment. "It was made by my mother's relatives."

Flat lengths of plank stood against a crude fence. "I dried my pelts on those boards," Cléo said.

Aurélie stared, trying to imagine her beautiful, worldly mother skinning small animals and nailing their skins to the planks. It was difficult. There were bloodstains on them, certainly more recent than Cléo's time.

"Someone is still using them," she said.

"Squatters," Alex said. "I can run them off for you."

"Why?" she asked. "I'll never use them again, and it's a hard life, trapping and skinning the little animals, making a living in the swamp."

But as they climbed the steps to the *galerie,* Cléo threw back her shoulders, lifted her head to scan the horizon, and took a deep breath of the faintly briny air, revealing her pleasure in her homecoming.

"It seems so lonely and hostile," Alex commented. "Why did you want to return?"

"I've wanted to come back ever since Lee Hing's death. This was a world I had conquered. I took pleasure in that." Cléo's strange eyes gleamed. "I liked sharpening my powers of observation, knowing when the tide would turn, reading the signs of the changing seasons, and knowing where to lay my traps and my nets. I was young and strong and I knew how to protect myself."

Except from love, she thought.

"My father built this house well," she added absently.

The pirate, Aurélie thought. The nuns had told them how the privateer, Lafitte, and his band of smugglers had brought their arms and ammunition and helped defend New Orleans from the British in the terrible battle across the river, when the wounded had been ferried over in the carriages of brave Creole women to the convent for the nuns to nurse.

"Did your father fight in the Battle of New Orleans?" she asked her mother.

"Yes."

"What was he like?"

"He loved his drink, and it made him crazy. He brawled in taverns and one night someone knifed him."

This was the family she had longed to find! At least her mother was honest. Aurélie glanced at Alex fearfully, trying to read his expression, but it reflected only the concern he felt about their situation.

"Did Evan Crowley tell you that he was your father?" Cléo asked.

"No."

"How did you discover it?" she asked gently.

"I just knew. I think I felt his love for me. But—he didn't acknowledge me, not even in death," she said sadly. "The mother superior told me he had promised a dowry, but he left me nothing. He—he loved my half sister more."

Cléo gave a sharp shake of her head, but a shadow crossed her beautiful face. "He loved you very much, *chère,* to do what he did for you. But in the end he was too weak to carry it through, wasn't he? To acknowledge you as his illegitimate child. A weak man, but with a great capacity for loving."

This couldn't be real, Aurélie thought, as they sat down on the *galerie* chairs to have their picnic of crusty bread and cheese and fresh-boiled shrimp packed between wet leaves. They had an unobstructed view of the waterways and the ever-changing patterns of the sky.

"It's raining on the Gulf," Alex said, indicating a towering black cloud building up in the south.

"The wind is changing," Cléo said. "We'll get wet going back."

The wind had veered from the northeast around to the southeast, coming off the Gulf. It had grown stronger, and it was blowing the rain clouds rapidly toward them. Before they had finished their lunch, large drops spattered the ground below them and soon the rain was heavy, driven before a wind that flattened the marsh grasses. Slanting in on them, it drove them into the house to keep from being drenched.

The room they entered was sparsely furnished, and they brought in the chairs from the *galerie.* There was a bed and a crude kitchen cabinet holding plates and some big pots. A second room contained another bed and a clutter of traps and fishing gear. The air was warm and heavy with moisture. The noise of the rain pounding on the roof and the roar of the rising wind made so much noise that it was difficult to talk.

Cléo was restless, walking to the door to listen to the wind and peer into the falling rain, and then returning to them. Outside, though it was early afternoon, it was soon as dark as if dusk had fallen.

"I think we must resign ourselves to staying the night," Alex said, looking worried. "We couldn't take the boat out in this."

Cléo listened to the wind. It was howling now. Both

Aurélie and Alex came to stand in the door beside her. The small pier was covered with an inch of water. Above the wind's steady roar they could hear their pirogue knocking against the dock.

Alex stood up. "I'm going down to beach the boat. It will be safer on land."

"I'll help," Aurélie said. Cléo went into the house, coming back with a coil of rope.

They went down the ladder, Alex first. Aurélie staggered as the force of the wind struck her, and Alex caught her hand and held it tightly as they ran to the landing. Water was already flowing over the pier.

Cléo was tying the Indian canoe to one of the tall posts that supported the house. Alex called to her to come and help. The boat was heavier than an ordinary pirogue, with its mast and the sail, which Alex had dropped from the yard and tied down. The wind was pushing it out to the end of the rope, which was taut with strain.

Suddenly they heard a creaking as the house rocked with a gust of wind so strong that Aurélie and Alex clung to each other on the wet and slippery dock. With a crashing sound the boat's cypress-log mast toppled toward them, missing the pier, but falling on the taut rope and splitting it.

Aurélie stared at the flat-bottomed vessel, which was whirling around and drifting away in the water, now deep enough to cover all but the highest marsh grasses. They were looking out at a sea of water with no landmarks under a darkening sky.

"I'll get it!" Alex shouted above the wind, taking off his coat and handing it to Aurélie. But Cléo came splashing up and grabbed him by the arm, shouting, "No! You can't swim for it, Alex. Look how fast the water is rising!"

Aurélie grabbed his other arm. "Alex, please! You'll be drowned!"

They were all drenched. "We still have the pirogue," Cléo shouted in Alex's ear. "Help me get Aurélie back to the house."

Reluctantly he agreed, keenly conscious of their danger, and frustrated by his inaction. But Cléo was right. With both women clinging to him, he waded through the flood back to the house.

He stopped to look at the burned-out log canoe that was now their only means of transportation, and examined Cléo's fastening.

"You've secured it with a noose?"

"Not a noose, a loop. It must be loose," Cléo said, "so the boat will float at high tide." She picked up a long pole lying in the water that was now under the house, and carried it with her as she followed Alex and Aurélie up the swaying ladder.

In the creaking house they huddled together. Through the open door, they watched the land beneath them disappear with astonishing rapidity. Soon all they could see was water. Only the houses on stilts and the top half of the large oak were visible, the latter's branches bowed down by the fierce wind. The roof of a house at the far end of the *chênière* suddenly sailed off and swirled by them on the flood.

"It must be a hurricane on the Gulf," Cléo said, in a voice deepened with awe. "It will bring very high water, but if my father built his house as well as he claimed, we'll be safe."

"I shall pray to the Virgin Mary to save our lives," Aurélie said through trembling lips, "because I can't bear to lose either of you." She had not even stopped to think before including her mother, but she knew it was true.

Alex embraced her tenderly. "My dearest love," he said, and kissed her. Then he extended his left arm to Cléo. She moved into his embrace and together the three of them watched in fearful fascination as the waters rose toward the *galerie.*

"What will we do if it comes into the house?" Aurélie asked.

"Take to the canoe," her mother said matter-of-factly.

And be carried out to the Gulf, Alex thought, with such despair in his heart that he did not speak.

He knew—and Cléo certainly must know—that when the storm had moved on, the tide would change. The high water would recede as rapidly as it had risen. Not all of them rowing together, if they had had the oars, could keep such a tide from carrying their pirogue out into the waters of the Gulf where their survival would depend on the small chance of being seen by one of the Gulf steamers moving between New Orleans and Galveston.

Chapter Twenty-two

For what seemed an interminable time they dared do nothing but wait while the water rose steadily under the house and the wind howled around it, expecting at any time to be forced to leave their shelter for the cypress pirogue, which, as Cléo had predicted, rose with the tide and now bobbed only a few feet below the level of the *galerie*.

What light there was in the day gradually disappeared. But just before deep darkness descended, the wind lessened and the rain almost ceased, so that for a few brief minutes a ray of scarlet shone through a rent in the clouds.

"Look!" Aurélie said. "The storm is over."

"Ah, no," Cléo warned. "To venture out now would be to risk our lives. It may be only the eye of the storm. Many have been fooled and have died. We must wait and see." She was proved right when after an hour the wind, which had been coming from the north, shifted to the east and then the southeast, once again driving a heavy rain before it. They huddled, feeling a need to remain close together, praying the roof would not go.

Sometime after midnight Alex detected another lessening in the violence of the storm, and it became evident that the water was no longer rising. He went out on the *galerie.* The cloud cover had thinned enough to let a diffused moonlight glimmer through, and he could see that the high tide was receding as rapidly as it had risen.

When he reported this, Cléo said confidently, "Then the storm has passed."

A thought flashed through her mind with pure joy: *I'll see Paul again!* and she knew that she had been given another chance for the happiness that brings content. She would go to Paris with him, and they would live out their days together.

In her sudden relief of tension Aurélie was aware of nothing but her exhaustion. She could have dropped to the floor and fallen asleep. But her mother insisted that they must remove their outer clothing. "Never sleep in wet clothing!" she admonished.

They had stood so long in darkness that their eyes had become accustomed to the gloom, and they could distinguish objects well enough to move about. Cléo ordered Alex into the other room, and said, "Take a chair to hang your wet shirt and trousers."

Then she told Aurélie, "Take off your dress and I'll spread it over a chair for you. Your undergarments are almost dry. You jump into that bed, and I'll join you when I've stripped off my wet dress." She ripped down the cotton curtain which was the only door between the two rooms. "We can dry ourselves with this. Alex, don't you dare peek!"

"An excellent idea," Alex said, the darkness hiding his grin as it did Aurélie's blush.

Aurélie kept casting looks at the darkened doorway while she hurriedly removed her drenched dress and petticoat and handed them to her mother, feeling a rush of heat to her skin in spite of the chill of the storm.

With the curtain Cléo tried to dry first her daughter's long hair and then her own.

From the other room Alex unashamedly watched the two shadowy figures only partly revealed in their simple shifts—their striking beauty of form, so alike except for the maturity of one and the youthful slenderness of the other, the round firm mounds of their breasts gleaming through tresses of tawny and black hair. His darling, he was convinced, was the most exquisitely formed creature God, man, and woman had ever made. He drew in a long breath to quiet his quickening heart.

Presently both Aurélie and Cléo were under their blankets, and the rooms were quiet except for the drumming of rain on the roof and the occasional bump of the pirogue against a support of the *galerie*.

"*Bonsoir.*" Aurélie heard Alex's voice in the darkness, sounding intimately near and tender.

"*Bonsoir,* Alex," the two women said together.

Aurélie could feel the warmth of her mother's body in the bed beside her, and took comfort in it.

"*Bonsoir, maman,*" she whispered.

Her mother said nothing, but laid a protective arm across her.

"I was that baby who was stolen from you," Aurélie murmured. "You are my mother. You can no longer deny it, when we may die here—"

"I must. We won't die. You will take your place in your father's world, just as he planned. It was very important to him. *Bonsoir, chère.*" Cléo smoothed the hair from her daughter's brow and kissed her, and Aurélie slept.

Alex was the first to waken. Wrapping his blanket around him, he walked through the room where the two women slept and out onto the *galerie.* He looked out on a scene little different from the one they had seen on their arrival.

The brief, violent storm had passed. The land on which the house stood, barely four feet in elevation, he judged, was visible again. Sunlight sparkled on the surrounding water and on the wet marsh grasses that protruded from it. He estimated that the water level was only a foot higher than before the storm, but that was enough to change the landscape. He could see no landmarks that he recognized.

Neither the damaged skiff, nor the roof that had floated by in the night, were visible, as far as he could see. He looked over the railing and was greatly relieved to see the Indian canoe resting on the ground, still attached to the house support. It was their only means of transportation back to civilization. He suspected that they were going to be very grateful for Cléo's experience with the Indian craft.

Hearing a murmur of voices from inside the house, he called, "I'm coming in for my clothes!" and heard a little shriek.

Laughing, he wrapped his blanket closely around him and went through the outer room, past the bed where the dark head and the beloved tawny one lay close together, and two pair of bright eyes, remarkably alike in shape, gazed at him.

"We're on land again," he told them, and went into his clutter of traps and nets and crab pots to put on his clothes. They were still damp but considerably drier than when he had removed them.

When he came out again, Cléo and Aurélie were dressed in their ravaged gowns. "We're a sad-looking lot," Aurélie said, laughing.

"But alive," Alex said, with feeling. *If he had lost her . . . !* The thought was enough, if he needed more proof, to show him just how much he loved her.

Cléo had bread and cheese and part of a bottle of wine still in her picnic hamper, and they made a breakfast of that. Alex tossed the pole Cléo had saved down to the ground. Then they closed the house, went down the ladder-stair, and worked together to drag the heavy cypress pirogue to the water's edge.

Aurélie was sensitive to an aura of kinship that sharing the dangers of the storm had brought to them. It was a feeling of *family,* she realized with a surge of emotion, and her hungry heart expanded.

Cléo directed where Aurélie and Alex should sit. Revealing a surprising skill she skidded the boat off the wet reeds, jumped into it, and shoved the pole against the shore to push it into deeper water. With sure balance she poled them away from Isle de Navarre and they began the return journey across the newly shaped lagoons to M'sieu' Weill's warehouse.

Alex was so lost in the changed landscape that he soon gave up trying to figure out where they were, and put his trust in the remarkable woman who was Aurélie's mother, standing with her legs braced in the bottom of her pirogue, her strong arms expertly working the pole as if it had not been over eighteen years since she had last held one in her hands.

"It's something one never forgets," she said, when he remarked on her skill.

"Madame Cléo, I want to marry Aurélie. Will you give your consent?"

"You do not need my consent," she reminded him, smiling at Aurélie.

"What do you suggest? Is there someone else I should ask for permission? The mother superior, perhaps?"

Cléo considered. "She should be consulted, certainly."

"What about Aurélie's foster mother, Madame Boudin, the woman who cared for her in her first six years?"

She looked at Aurélie. "You didn't tell me about her. Was she good to you?"

"I think so. I remember little about her, but the mother superior said I cried for her when I first came to the convent."

A shadow crossed Cléo's face and was gone. "Then she should certainly take part in your wedding."

"I agree," Alex said.

"M'sieu'!" Aurélie said, with exasperation. "Are you perhaps forgetting something? I believe I recall refusing you when you proposed marriage to me!"

"I'm getting to that," Alex said, his eyes ashine with laughter. "I think I'll make my offer to the mother superior—"

"You'll have to tell her that Aurélie's search for her parents failed—"

"—and say that she would like M'sieu' and Madame Boudin to give her away."

"Would you lie to the mother superior?" Aurélie exclaimed.

"Not if I can help it," Alex said candidly. "I hope it can be done by simply failing to mention what has occurred these past two days."

"Can you trust Madame Duclos?" Cléo asked him.

"I'm willing to risk it," Alex said, with a look at Aurélie that brought a furious rush of warmth to her face and
neck. "Can you trust your friends at the tavern?"

"You will have to risk that, too, won't you? Marry her,
Alex, and if you are not a good husband to her, I'll have
your head."

Alex laughed. "Never fear, *madame.* I'll treasure her
and so will my family. Aurélie, will you marry me?"

Aurélie looked at him with fear and longing. What
was she to do? This was a deception planned and begun
long ago by her father. But what would it do to Alex?
"What if your family should discover that I have Indian
blood in my veins—"

"—or maybe Chinese and French and Portuguese,"
Cléo said mockingly. "What does it matter when you
have your father's English blood?"

"—but the law says—oh, Alex, isn't it dangerous for
you to try to marry me?"

"Not as dangerous for me as for you, my darling," he
said soberly.

"You must use the name Boudin," Cléo said decisively, "and to anyone who has heard of your quest to be
acknowledged by the Crowley estate you must say that
you failed to find proof that Evan Crowley was not
acting for someone else."

"Can we do this?" Aurélie asked, with tremulous
hope.

"We must," Alex said. "I want you for my legal wife
and I want our children to be considered legitimate. If it
becomes necessary, I'll take you away to a place where
such racial laws don't exist. I'll protect you with my life.
I swear it. And all the power and wealth of my father
will be behind us, I know."

"Then I say yes," Aurélie whispered. "It's weak of me, but yes!"

Alex would have embraced her, but froze when Cléo cried, *"Mon dieu,* no! You'll overturn us!" Then she began to laugh, and Alex and Aurélie, not knowing why she laughed but needing no reason in their happiness, joined in. Their joyous laughter rang out over the marshes and lagoons as Cléo poled the pirogue on through the shallow waters.

They found Esther waiting with a hired carriage at the tavern. She greeted them with profound relief. "I was so worried, *madame!* The coachman is in the tavern—"

"I'll send him out," Cléo said. "We must part, and quickly. I'm going to return to the Indian village. I regret that I can't take you there with me," she told Aurélie, "but they must not see you with me." It was the closest she had come to acknowledging in words their relationship.

"I wish you would stay with us. Now that I have found you—"

Cléo's eyes mirrored sorrow. "You must forget me."

Aurélie could not hold back her tears. "I will never forget you, never! I can't forgive myself for thinking you had abandoned me. I want you at our wedding."

"That is impossible, *chère."*

"We'll find a way to have you at Bellemont," Alex promised Cléo, who shook her head, obviously moved. "And we'll stay close to you, if I have to take to gambling!"

"Now, that's a possibility," Cléo said, smiling through her tears. "But I won't witness your wedding. Your servants would gossip, and your family's friends would be shocked. Besides, I am going to Paris for a year—maybe longer."

"Paris!" Aurélie cried.

Cléo slipped the gold bracelet from her wrist. "I want you to have this, Aurélie. Your father gave it to me."

Tears clogged Aurélie's throat. She threw her arms around her mother and sobbed, "Don't leave me!"

Cléo embraced her fiercely. "I'll always be with you, my child. You'll know where I am, and I'll always be there for you. Always!"

"Madame Cléo, I shall bring Aurélie to Paris on our honeymoon," Alex said, his own voice thick.

"Ah, that would be such happiness! We could be together there." She kissed Aurélie, then motioned Esther away from the carriage and they went quickly into the tavern.

Alex handed Aurélie into the carriage, then climbed in beside her and held her, weeping, in his arms until their coachman came out.

At the pension Madame Duclos was still awaiting passage on the Lafourche steamboat to New Orleans, and she agreed readily to chaperone Aurélie to Bellemont and happily accepted an invitation to their wedding. A week later, Alex and Aurélie, accompanied by Madame Duclos, arrived at Alex's family home on Bayou St. John.

Aurélie's eyes widened when a bevy of black children ran up the drive to open the iron gates, screaming a welcome to Alex when they spied him in the carriage. As the pair of bays trotted up the drive, Aurélie looked at the sprawling white house with its dignified double *galeries* supported by gleaming pillars and its wings extending to each side and was awed, both by its magnificence and the beauty of its extensive gardens. She reached for Alex's hand, and was glad Madame Duclos had accompanied them, that redoubtable lady having insisted on carrying out her duties as chaperone until Aurélie was delivered to Madame Archer.

Leaving Lafitte to attend to their baggage, Alex took Aurélie and Madame Duclos up the steps to the wide fanlit doorway. It was opened by a black servant who greeted Alex and his guests with warm dignity. "Welcome home, *michie!* Madame and Ma'm'selle Thérèse are on the rear *galerie.* Will you wait in the drawing room while I tell them you have brought guests?"

"No, I will take Madame Duclos and Mademoiselle Aurélie to them," Alex said. "Bring us coffee. And some wine!" he added. "I've a surprise for them."

The servant's gaze flicked quickly over Aurélie, and brightened. *"Oui, michie!"*

Alex led the way. Aurélie and her chaperone followed him down a wide hall toward the floor-length windows standing open at its end. Her heart was beating high with excitement and a tiny apprehension that had remained with her in spite of Alex's assurances that his family would love her.

Alex's mother and his sister looked very much alike, with their dark hair and eyes and the creamy complexion typical of French Creole women. They looked up in delighted surprise, then both rose, both exclaiming, "Alex!" and Thérèse threw her arms around him.

"I've brought you a houseguest, *maman,*" Alex said, disengaging himself from his sister to embrace his mother. "This is Aurélie Boudin—I believe you know Madame Duclos, who has acted as her chaperone since she left the convent. Aurélie, *ma mère*—and Thérèse—"

Melodie Archer shot her son a questioning glance as

she extended her hand graciously to Madame Duclos and then to Aurélie, who murmured, *"Madame."* Was this the girl he'd told her about, the one who claimed to be an illegitimate daughter of Evan Crowley?

Thérèse's eyes brightened. "I know I've seen you at the convent, Aurélie!"

"I remember you," Aurélie said smiling, "but I was in a younger class, and then, you see, I lived in the orphans' house."

"Aurélie's story is a special one," Alex said easily, "and we'll tell it some evening when we're all together. I took the liberty of ordering coffee out here, *maman.*"

"Excellent," Melodie said. It was immediately clear to her that her son was deeply in love with this lovely girl who turned back to her and said, "I've heard so much about your family from Alex, *madame.*"

Melodie thought of Nanette with sadness, but put aside her questions. "Alex is very special to all of us, and so you are especially welcome, *mademoiselle.* And you, Madame Duclos."

"I remember you now!" Thérèse exclaimed. "Weren't you the one who was always climbing a pecan tree to see over the wall?"

Laughing, Aurélie owned that she was.

"Sister Josephine used to say she was at her wits' end to know what to do with you!"

"She put me in charge of the smallest orphans, and made me responsible for their behavior," Aurélie confessed. "It worked very well."

They chatted about the Sisters they both knew while Alex's mother visited with Madame Duclos, and soon Aurélie was feeling very much at ease.

"It's going to be such fun having you here," Thérèse said. "Do you ride?"

"I've never been nearer to a horse than following one in a carriage."

"Alex and I will have to do something about that."

After a pleasant hour over their coffee and cakes Madame Duclos left to be taken in the waiting carriage to the relatives with whom she lived, and Thérèse took Aurélie to the lovely blue bedroom that was to be hers, a spacious room, with a four-poster bed, the necessary mosquito barre, a dainty rosewood desk, and a large armoire. Wide French windows opened on the *galerie,* with blue velvet drapes and wooden shutters that could be closed at night. It was such a room as Aurélie had dreamed of in the convent dormitory.

When they were alone, Melodie said to her son, "You love her, don't you?"

"*Oui, maman.* You and Papa will love her, too."

"What about Nanette?"

"I hope to discuss that with Papa this evening," Alex said, after a pause. "There is no hope of a reconciliation. In fact, if Papa agrees, I will return to New Orleans to work with him."

"I'll be happy to have you near, my son." Melodie gave him a tremulous smile of happiness.

Alex resolved that he would never tell her why he had quarreled with Nanette, because it had pained her so to speak of her half brother. But he would tell his father the truth of why he was now willing to leave the parish of Terrebonne and join his father's law firm.

"Aurélie is charming," Melodie Archer said, and his heart brimmed with happiness.

All New Orleans still mourned the dreadful loss of life in the hurricane that had struck Isle Dernière, the resort island lying in the Gulf off the mouth of Bayou

Terrebonne, the previous month. The storm that Aurélie and Alex had survived with Cléo's help, the storm
that had raised the level of the marsh lagoons by nearly
ten feet in four hours, had first swept over Isle
Dernière, demolishing every building, including a popular resort hotel, on the low-lying Last Island, in fifteen
minutes. Word had been slow to reach the city because
there were so few survivors. At last count two hundred
vacationers had lost their lives. Everyone was shocked
and saddened by the stories of death and destruction
and fascinated by the bizarre tales of survival that trick-
led in after the monstrous storm.

For this reason the garden wedding at Bellemont was
a simple one with few guests outside the family. Nevertheless, the ceremony was a beautiful one, with Alex's
older sister, red-haired Antoinette, as Aurélie's matron
of honor, and Thérèse a very pretty maid of honor.
Antoinette's husband, Robert Robichaux, was Alex's
best man. Madame Duclos and the mother superior
were among the few guests. Monsieur Boudin of False
River gave Aurélie away while Madame Boudin wept
tears of happiness for her, and for their reunion.

Garlands of fall flowers had been strung from tree to
tree, setting off the rectangle of an outdoor chapel, and
blossoms in large vases stood before the altar. Music
came from the trio of black musicians with fiddles and
guitars on the rear *galerie* and from birds singing mer-
rily in the magnolia and pecan trees edging the garden.

Before the ceremony Melodie Archer had kissed Aurélie in her upstairs bedroom and welcomed her privately into the family. Jeff Archer, Alex's distinguished-
looking father, an older edition of Alex himself, presented her with a necklace of diamonds and told her
gravely that Alex had made a good choice.

As Aurélie stood beside Alex and said the words that promised him her devotion, her heart swelled with happiness. She was not only joined to the man she would love forever, but she had the close and loving family she had dreamed she would one day find. But as she murmured, "I will," and sealed her promise to Alex with a kiss, a part of her was with the woman she had sought so long and finally found, only to lose again, the mother she knew was even now praying for her happiness in the elegant casino on the Bayou St. John only a few miles away. If only Cléo could have been present on this very special day!

In a way she was present, for gossip at the reception following the wedding was about Madame Cléo's former special assistant and close friend, Michel Jardin. It was whispered that the handsome rake, an inveterate gambler, had given up his favored position in Madame's casino, to once again pay suit to the Crowley heiress, now that her father was dead, and that he had once again been humiliatingly rejected, this time by her mother. The tidbit was passed from guest to guest with the Creole relish in gossip.

"Didn't I tell you?" Madame Duclos gloated privately when she kissed the bride. "How Michel would squirm if he could hear their laughter! And there are those who will see that he hears it, never fear!"

But Aurélie could not take pleasure in the gossip, for they also gossiped about her mother, making it plain that she was notorious in New Orleans.

There was dancing in the big ballroom for the younger people after the wedding supper served in the dining room under the famous Bellemont crystal chandelier. Alex and Aurélie led off the waltz, joined after once around the floor by Alex's handsome father and the lovely Melodie, and then by Monsieur and Madame Boudin. After she had danced with his father and Monsieur Boudin, and Alex had danced with his mother and his sisters, he drew Aurélie into his arms again. She was tense, her back straight and her hands clenched.

"What is it, *chère?*"

"I hate it when they talk about my mother!" she whispered. "Everyone is talking about her and Michel."

"You see now why she insists on staying out of your life. It is because she loves you." Alex danced her out on the rear *galerie* and kissed her. "We'll find a way for you to see her and circumvent the gossipers, my darling wife, I promise you," he said. "I'm going to steal you away for a little while. I want to show you something."

He took her down the steps to where Lafitte stood waiting with a saddled horse. "We have to ride," Alex said.

Aurélie gasped. "But I've never been on a horse!"

"We'll remedy that, *chère*, but tonight you'll ride with me."

He stepped in the stirrup and put his leg over the saddle. Lafitte lifted her and swung her up into Alex's arms, then picked up her trailing veil and laid it gently over her lap. Alex clucked at the horse and they started off.

The moon was almost full and its radiance bathed the beautiful house and gardens in its pale light, so bright it almost extinguished the fireflies under the trees.

The horse walked leisurely down the drive and through the open gates to the bayou and along the bayou road while Alex held Aurélie close to his heart and now and again found her lips with his own in a kiss that each time was sweeter and more exciting.

"What are we going to see?"

"I can't describe it. You must see it for yourself. It isn't far."

He guided the horse away from the bayou on a path into the woods. The moon was hidden there and the night was black. "Where are we going?" Aurélie demanded, straining to see through the darkness.

"Trust me," Alex said.

In a few moments a low gasp of pleasure escaped her. She was looking at a house, smaller than Bellemont but of such exquisite proportions that one overlooked its air of decay. Indeed, the moonlight on its peeling paint made it look silvery and more precious than if its white paint were new. It had an air of having housed great doings in its youth, and of settling now into a gracious relaxation.

"How beautiful!" Aurélie breathed. "What is it?"

"La Sorcellerie. The plantation where my mother was raised. Someday it will be our home, darling."

"Why not now?"

"My mother has never allowed its restoration. It's a long, long story which I'll spend many hours telling you, and it will be a while before we can change *maman*'s mind. But we will. Someday we'll light its beautiful chandeliers again."

They gazed at it until the moon dropped behind some trees, then Alex turned the horse back toward Bellemont and the room that had been prepared for their wedding night.

Don't miss award-winning author Meagan McKinney's new historical romance, *My Wicked Enchantress*, available next month from Dell.

Louisiana, 1746

Kayleigh opened her eyes.

She was not back at Mhor, her beloved castle. Nor was she in the hut she'd shared in New Orleans. Her surroundings were completely foreign to her. There were white linen sheets about her that soothed her hot flesh, and a cool morning breeze drifted in from double doors that led out to a gallery. From the gallery doors she could see two rows of spindly pecan trees, but she hardly took note of them. Having learned to survive on instinct alone, she turned her head sharply to see if anyone kept her company.

She was alone. Weakly she sank back against the pillows. Suddenly remembering the snake, she looked down at her hand. There were two telltale marks on the palm of her hand, which looked a bit swollen. A frown marred her pretty brow. She recalled the viper and the swamp and . . . her cousin Straught, but after that there was nothing. No memories at all. Her eyes scanned the room once more. Where was she? Who had brought her here and cared for her? How long had she been here? No answers came. Between the night the snake had bitten her and the present, it seemed, there lurked a shadowy void. Kayleigh touched the soft cotton of the strange smock she was wearing, then threw back the light cover sheet and scanned the room for her clothes.

With her head reeling even the simplest tasks were not easy yet she was determined to leave the bed. The room held nothing familiar. There was a wild cherrywood press in the pier. Its doors stood open, revealing only a dusty, empty interior. There was a walnut chair near her bedside, but the rush seat and provincial rococo chairback held nothing but toweling.

Where are my clothes? she asked herself. She looked down at the night smock she was wearing. Though she reveled in the fine smell and texture of the fabric, she knew it was not substantial enough to run away in. But then she noticed that the garment wasn't a night smock at all; rather, it was a man's shirt. It was so large that it fell past her knees. The sleeves were rolled up neatly to her elbows, but the top ties remained undone. The neckline was indecently low.

She tied up the front as best she could with her shaky fingers. How she ached to return to the soft bed with its cool, rumpled sheets! But she knew she had to find out where she was and who had taken care of her. She couldn't afford to stay in one place if Straught might somehow be able to find out where she was.

Throwing open the doors, she looked around the salon, but no one was there. The room smelled of linseed oil and turpentine, and she wondered if the floors had been newly varnished. The boards felt silky smooth to her bare feet.

What was it like to have such luxuries again? She tried to recall as she wandered dizzily through the room. She looked around her and was reminded of the grandeur of a past life. There were gilt marble-topped pier tables so new that the horsehair packing was still scattered near their crates. Two matching red baywood armoires towered at each end of the room. Pie paterae edged their cornices, and each was speckled with dove-gray paint. One of the massive pieces even had its doors wide open, and copper pegs from the shadowed depths of the interior twinkled back at her like orange stars.

There in the closed armoire, she decided, she might find something to wear. Feeling unbelievably light-headed, she made her way to the armoire. The salon was quiet and breezy as the magnolia-scented wind wafted through the louvers of the attached loggia, but she spent no more time appreciating the serene room. She was too intent upon reaching the armoire.

At long last her hands slid up the doors, and she heard the creak of the long iron *fiches* hinges. But she could hardly hide her disappointment, for the armoire held only stacks of musty linens and several bolts of barzin—no clothing at all. In frustration she leaned on the door and simply stared into the cabinet's interior, all the while wondering where she was going to find clothes.

"Looking for something to steal?"

A man's voice shot out from behind her. It was a deep, rich voice that could only have belonged to a nobleman. In the back of her dizzy mind, Kayleigh knew that she'd heard it before. Suddenly a chill ran down her spine, and she stumbled back to the side of the armoire. Turning her head, she sought out the person who had spoken. Her heart seemed to freeze in her chest.

She'd encountered this man before. He'd been on the docks the other day, and his blood had spilled on her petticoat. It seemed too awful to be true, but standing in the entrance to the loggia was Erath Straught's friend and traveling companion, the man named St. Bride.

Kayleigh stared at him in mute horror. She wondered if she was mistaken, but there seemed to be no doubt about it. The man before her possessed the same rough turquoise gaze that demanded subservience. He had the same handsome face that would make even a dock whore pine for romance. His unusual silver-touched brown hair was neatly queued with a leather thong. And he stood before her, his face an unyielding mask of disapproval. She was terrified.

"You!" she whispered.

"Ah, you remember me," he uttered drily as he walked up to her. "I certainly remember you. In fact, everytime I look at my hand, the nostalgia almost makes me weep!" He smiled then.

"I—I'm sorry about your hand." She looked behind him, sure to find her cousin there. She was surprised that the loggia entrance remained empty.

"But why be sorry? I'm sure you've attacked people before." He closed the gap between them. "Haven't you?"

"M-my cousin . . . where is he?" she asked, unable to stand her dread any longer.

"Your cousin?" He seemed surprised at her question. "And who might that be?"

Kayleigh paused. This man didn't seem to know who her cousin was. With sudden clarity, she knew she had remained alive because the man before her didn't know that she was related to Erath Straught. The sense of relief made her even dizzier, and she had to hang onto the armoire's door for support.

As if for the first time noticing her weakened condition, St. Bride reached out to steady her. But she drew back.

"No! Stay away!" she gasped. She didn't want him to touch her. She didn't want anyone acquainted with her cousin to touch her.

"I suggest you go back to bed. I've work to do in here, and I cannot spend my time waiting for you to faint!" Crossing his strong arms against his massive chest, he waited for her to go.

"I just want my clothes—then I'll be off," she assured him.

"You needn't any clothes to go back to bed." He stepped closer.

"No, no! Please, I would like to leave now!" She tried to slide past him, but his hands caught her. Gently he forced her back against the armoire.

"Stop this foolishness! I have work to do. We can talk later. Go back to bed, Kayleigh."

"Kayleigh . . . ? Kayleigh . . . ?" she whispered incredulously. With dark, frightened eyes she looked up at the man and was suddenly sure he had lied to her. The only way he could have found out her name was from Straught or from Bardolph. And Bardolph was dead, so that left only one possibility.

She'd planned to bolt. Had she been stronger, she was almost sure she could have made it. But as it was, she hardly took more than two wobbly steps before St. Bride pulled her up short. The force of his arm against her chest sent her backward, and then her head exploded with pain. As she grabbed her throbbing temples between her palms, she saw the sharp edges of a table come rushing up to her.

But the crack to her head never came. Instead she felt two strong hands save her from falling. From behind she heard a low, muttered curse: "You damned little fool!" Then two strong arms lifted her up and carried her back to her room.

"Please let me go . . ." She felt him place her back on her mattress, but the comfort of the bed couldn't calm the terror in her heart.

"Ah, there's that word again, 'please.'" He looked down at her. He shook her as if that would bring forth the truth. "Where did you learn such manners, Kayleigh?"

"My name is Kestrel!" she cried, unsuccessfully trying to pull away from his grasp. In the end, weak and breathless, all she could do was stare up at him. Meeting his hard, unflinching gaze, she finally summoned the courage to ask, "Who told you I'm Kayleigh?"

"You told me your name is Kayleigh. You were delirious from the snakebite, and I've come to the conclusion you must be delirious still." He let go of her arms. "Stay in your bed until you have permission to leave it."

"I just want to go. Please let me go!"

"You've no place to go now. You're out at Belle Chasse plantation, and there's nothing but swampland between here and civilization." As if that argument would finally convince her, he made ready to leave.

"Please let me go anyway!" She stopped him by grabbing the linen of his shirt. There was a long pause while he studied her face; then eventually his gaze drifted downward to rest where her shirt had come undone from her struggles. The pale rose half-moon of her nipple showed through the filmy batiste. She stared at it horrified; he stared at it thoughtfully. Mortified, she held on to him, afraid that any further movement would only decrease her modesty. His eyes met hers and they softened for a moment.

"You, of all people, should know that won't coax me into letting you go." He smiled, his teeth gleaming like stolen pearls. Then he refused to hear her pleas any longer. Reluctantly he pried her small hands from his massive chest; he stepped from the bed and wasted no more time in her room. The last thing she heard before he walked away was the bolt shooting home in the lock on her door.

What was to become of her? she thought wretchedly when he had gone. She was out in the middle of nowhere, confined by a man who was her cousin's comrade. How much time did she have before Erath would find her here? Who was this man St. Bride, anyway? She moaned. But how on earth could she *think*, with the clamor of a smithy's hammer echoing through her head? Grimacing in pain, she gave in to her fears. She would die if she remained at this man's wretched plantation. She knew without a doubt that Straught would find her eventually, and all the agony she'd been suffering would then be for naught.

Looking up at the locked door, she knew she needn't even try to get up out of bed again. She sighed heavily. In exhaustion, she let her head fall back against the pillows. How could it have happened? Bardolph was dead for only a few days, and already another man was controlling her . . .

"Do we let her go today?" Laban entered the salon the next day, tossing his cocked hat onto the settee. Outside the sun blazed.

"I've been thinking about those jewels," St. Bride said as if he hadn't heard Laban. He leaned against the railing of the gallery and stared speculatively into the cool depths of the salon.

"Does the girl go back to the quay today? The slave, Colette, needs supplies, and I told her she could accompany me to town. I can always take the black-haired wench too. Get her off our backs."

"Laban, do you believe in an eye for an eye, a tooth for a tooth?"

"In some cases, my friend. What are you thinking of?"

St. Bride traced the thin red scar that ran between his thumb and forefinger. His eyes then moved to the bedchamber door where his assailant was confined. "I think I've a use for Kayleigh. I'd like her to do something for me before we let her go."

"And what is that?"

"It's those jewels. Straught came so close to unloading them on the *Bonaventure*. Remember that wealthy American who disembarked at Bermuda? He was willing to pay a pretty penny for them, if I heard correctly. I want to make sure Straught still has them before we go any further."

"That would be ideal—but what does the wench have to do with that? You can't possibly want her to spy for you. She's not that trustworthy."

"Not spy, exactly. I'm thinking of just one evening. Give Straught a few drinks, a beautiful woman, the right questions . . . and I think we could get the answers we need. Then we could proceed without any worries."

"And what makes you think Kayleigh's the one to do that for us?"

"Because Straught is ripe for a really beautiful woman," St. Bride answered thoughtfully. "That's all he talked about on the *Bonaventure*. He said, rather enigmatically one time, that he wanted the most bewitching female in New Orleans. And if I know only one thing about that young woman in yonder bedchamber it is that she is truly bewitching." His eyes darkened as if he were thinking of the encounter of the day before. "I'm sure I've never seen a woman so utterly exquisite. The wench we've been saddled with is perfect for the task. She owes me for not taking her to the magistrate, and better than that, she owes me her very life."

"Her station, though—won't that be a problem?" Laban suddenly shook his head. "After all, from what I gather, Straught is rather particular. I don't see him cavorting with just any whore—"

"The girl is oddly well spoken. If we're explicit when we give her instructions, I think she can fool Straught well enough. Besides, I think Straught may be a bit homesick after all this time away from Mhor. And Kayleigh is, after all, Scottish. That's obvious enough from her slight brogue. No, she's just what Straught was hankering for on the *Bonaventure*. The more I think about it, the more I'm convinced."

"If that's what you want, my friend, shall I go get the wench?"

"Yes, that's what I want. Go get her." St. Bride rubbed his jaw, deep in thought.

She was caught between Scylla and Charybdis. If she made one foolish move, she would be devoured either by her cousin or by the enigmatic man before her now.

Kayleigh stood in the salon, squarely facing St. Bride. She'd been given an indigo-dyed osnaburg dress to wear, and her hair had been washed. It was now clean and silky. After waiting a full day to be let out of the prison of her room, she had been abruptly summoned. And she found the circumstances all very strange. There was only one thing of which she was sure. She was as frightened as she'd been the day she and Black Bardolph had fled Mhor Castle.

"Are you feeling better, then?" St. Bride asked her.

Kayleigh nodded her head. "I . . . I should like to leave—" she began.

"And you shall! But first, I would like some restitution for the damage you've wrought." He waved his scarred hand before her. Then he rose from his seat, leaned against the pier table, and surveyed her. "Kayleigh, what would you say if I told you I have decided not to take you to the magistrate? What would you say if I told you that I want to give you a sweet bag of gold and let you go free as a bird?"

"I would wonder if you were crazed," she replied.

"Crazed? Do I look it?" His eyes seemed to smile, but his mouth didn't.

"I think you do by half." She averted her eyes. He was making her uncomfortable, and she felt that he knew it. What did he have planned for her? "What do you want of me?"

"I want you to give company to a friend of mine."

"Give company—" Suddenly she stopped. She could feel the color rising in her cheeks. *Dhe!* Did he mean what she thought he meant?

"I'm sure a woman like you would find him quite attractive. He bathes regularly—"

"I don't care if you bathe regularly or not!" she cried out.

"No, no! Not me!" He seemed to be laughing at her, and his ridicule stung her to the quick.

"Not you?" How could this be happening? The man was actually asking her to bed down with one of his cronies!

"Come now! You see, this friend of mine is a rather closed-mouth sort," he explained. "And what I want is to find out some information he has. These things are delicate, you understand. I think he would tell a tempting little wench like yourself certain things that he would never tell me."

"I am not . . . what you're thinking I am!"

"You needn't let him bed you." He was nonchalant. "All I really want to know is if he has some jewels he has promised me. You can understand my predicament now, can't you? I really can't ask the fellow myself without implying that he's been lying to me. So that's where you come in, Kayleigh. We'll simply give you a go at him for an evening, and after that, you'll be free and clear of any reprisals from me."

"If I say no, what are those reprisals you speak of?" She looked into those damnable eyes.

"Far worse than what I'm offering you." He frowned and brushed her creamy cheek with his thumb. "Come now, love! You've surely done viler things for a bit of gold!"

"I can't think of any at the moment!" Indignant, she swatted at his hand. Her anger and frustration were peaking. She had no idea what she was going to do to get out of this impossible situation, but she was going to have to think quickly in order to flee Belle Chasse before she fell into bigger trouble.

"You'll like this gent, Kayleigh. He's a Scot like yourself. Has a castle near Inverness—you're familiar with Inverness, no?"

The blood suddenly drained from her face. "I am very familiar with Inverness." She stared at St. Bride in disbelief. He couldn't mean her cousin! What cruel irony was this?

"Good!" he exclaimed. "That will give you both something to converse about. I know you'll like Erath Straught, Kayleigh. I hear the women find him quite appealing. And I promise you a healthy reward if you discreetly obtain the information I desire."

If he'd brushed her with a feather, she would have fallen to the floor, her shock was so great. How could this be happening? How could she have ended up in such a situation? She stared at St. Bride in horror. Did he have any idea what he was asking her to do? She would prefer to return to New Orleans

—where she no doubt was wanted for the murder of Bardolph —than do what St. Bride was asking of her!

"I said I would give you a reward, Kayleigh," he prompted her. "What say you now?"

"No reward is necessary," she stated huskily.

"What?"

"I'll not need a reward, for I won't be getting that information for you."

St. Bride's head tilted back. His eyes narrowed. "Are you attempting to refuse?"

"I will not do your bidding!"

As if her refusal were as unexpected as snow in July, St. Bride appeared not to know what to make of it. He began to pace, circling her and studying her. "Come now," he began calmly, "I promise you a pretty new gown for the occasion and as much gold as you've probably seen in a year. Can you refuse that, little cutpurse?"

"I can," she answered nervously. She couldn't keep her eyes on him while he walked around her. Any minute she expected him to pounce.

"How about if I promise you a cottage—or, better yet, a shop—in that rubble and ruin you call New Orleans? Wouldn't you like that? Wouldn't that be just what you've always dreamed about?"

She closed her eyes to gather the courage to speak. "I will not do what you are asking—not at any price."

"No one defies me, you little Highland baggage! Don't you know that?"

Her eyes flew open. Suddenly St. Bride had the imperious air of a man far more important than a colonial planter. He appeared to be someone, as he'd said, who was definitely not used to being defied.

"But I will defy you! For I'm not a doxy for you to be casting upon your friends! I will not be used like that!"

"How proud you are, my beauty! But I wonder if you will be quite so haughty when the magistrate has you upon the whipping post!"

"I'll take the magistrate's hand over yours!"

There was a pause while St. Bride seemed to search for a new tack. "How did you end up in the swamps?" he pressed her. "Were you running from someone? Was someone after you, someone you'd stolen from? Were they about to catch you, and did you run into the swamps to hide? Would you like me to take you back to New Orleans?"

"I don't know."

"You don't know . . . like the night won't fall!" he said tersely. Then he softened. "You needn't be frightened of me, you know. You can stay here and rest as long as you need. I'll give you clothing and decent food."

Her eyes clouded a bit as she thought of those simple comforts that she had done without for months. How she wanted to accept! If only his offer did not involve Straught!

"And what else would you give me?" she finally murmured.

"You needn't fear getting with child. I don't ask that you bed the man. I'll let that be your choice." He extended his fingers to lift her chin, forcing her to meet his eye. "I'll let you take your pleasure where you find it."

"My pleasure will be found when I'm set free." She stared at him balefully.

"Then you'll do it?"

She shook her head and tightened her lips.

"Shall I take measures to convince you?" St. Bride's voice was low and ominous.

"Nay, for I shall never be convinced."

It was obvious that the man had rarely been crossed. Fury shot from his gaze, and he suddenly began shouting for his man. "Laban! Laban!"

Soon a big black man appeared in the loggia.

"Laban," St. Bride said, this time uttering words that drove terror into Kayleigh's soul, "take this bloodthirsty wench to town and deliver her personally to the magistrate."

The man came forward. She retreated several steps. "Wait!" She beat away Laban's hold, suddenly regretting her decision. "Is there not another alternative?"

"Laban, take her." St. Bride calmly motioned to his man.

"No! No!" she pleaded. "Don't take me there! Why did you save my life if you meant me to end up in jail?"

"Laban, take her," St. Bride repeated, watching her face closely.

"*No!*" She pushed away the black man's hands; then she turned and made for the loggia. She had gotten down the steps and through the courtyard, but even so, Laban was striding easily behind her, almost as if he was letting her wear herself out. And wear her out he did, for when she was just past the stables, the game ended. Releasing a cry, she felt her captor catch her by the arm and force her about.

But it wasn't Laban who had caught her: it was St. Bride. She fought to be free. Yet so soon after her illness, it didn't take much before she went limp like a tired kitten in his arms, all the fight temporarily sapped from her body.

St. Bride tilted her chin up, and her glaring eyes met with his amused ones. "Come along. I hear the magistrate's got a particular appetite for cutpurses."

"Don't wreak your vengeance through the magistrate," she panted. She struggled against his chest, but it was no use. She was too weak and he was too strong.

"I don't want to take you there. Don't make me do it." St. Bride's breath was warm on her cheek.

"I will not do what you ask!"

"Do you think I want to send you to jail? Do you think I want vengeance for this?" His cut hand brushed along her creamy throat. "You asked me why I saved your life. Well, it definitely wasn't so that I could see you hanged by that slender neck of yours. But if you refuse—"

"Oh, please just let me go! Let me go, and I shall never bother you again!" She struggled in vain against the forged muscle of his arms.

"Let you go? You spurn my offers of a better life in exchange for one evening's work! And all the while you cry to be set free, to go back to that damned wharf where I found you! Tell me this, little thief, is stealing and whoring there so much preferable?"

Stunned by his aspersion, Kayleigh could only look up with horror in her eyes. Embarrassment and anger flamed in her cheeks. She tried very hard to remain undaunted, but finally she could stand it no longer. Imperiously she said, "You ignoble wretch! I am no whore! And I curse you for saying that I am!"

"Ah, forgive me, my snow queen!" He shook her. "Of course your virtue is unquestionable!"

"It *is* unquestionable, and don't ever forget that!" She pulled her arm free of his grasp.

"Yes, yes! The quintessential virgin! You were out on the docks just to take the air!" His gaze lit upon the vulnerable pink of her lips. His eyes studied every generous curve of her mouth, until finally they lingered at the moist parting.

Suddenly she found his lips upon her own. But his was a

swift and angry kiss, for afterward she was quickly shoved aside. "Yes, you taste just like a virgin!" St. Bride spoke softly, but the sarcasm of his words dug into her heart.

"You vile oaf!" She tried to run from him one last time, but he seemed prepared for this. He let out a laugh and easily captured her, lifting her clear off the ground.

"I see our little Gaelic witch has a sore spot." His face drew closer, and she noted the angry spark in St. Bride's blue-green eyes.

"Put me down!" she commanded. With her feet swinging free and ungrounded, and her body pressed hard against the length of his, she was becoming increasingly aware of their differences. Her soft chest was jammed against the hardness of his, and she truly believed his arm would have been much more suitably placed around her waist than wrapped intimately around her buttocks.

"No kicking!" he warned, apparently amused by her discomfort. "I won't have a chit like you rendering me useless."

"Let me down!" She caught her breath and swallowed her hysteria. She didn't want to be held; she didn't want to be touched. Not by this man. He had already gone too far.

Noting her disdain, St. Bride slid her to the ground. But the trip was slow. She was sure it not only allowed him a growing knowledge of her body but she, in turn, felt the intimate geography of his also. When her feet touched the soft soil once more, she was more than ready to end their contact. But he seemed unwilling. He continued to hold her within his arms, his eyes sparkling with amusement. And something else, too, something she couldn't quite define, yet knew she didn't like.

"What a prize you are, Kayleigh," he said for no apparent reason.

She instinctively shoved at his chest. "Don't you be touching me like that again!"

Laban walked up just then and said, "The carriage is ready, St. Bride."

"No!" he snapped. "Let this bloodthirsty little wench cool her heels in the wine cellar for a while. Then we'll put the proposition to her again."

Laban came up and took her by the arm. He pulled her across the brick courtyard, ignoring her protests the entire way. Before she disappeared through the arched doors to the basement, she turned to level St. Bride with her stare. But he seemed only to be laughing at her. His eyes sparkled like the

Atlantic as he called out, "You owe me, Kayleigh! So think hard on what your life is worth. Think hard on the small cost of compliance."

The wine cellar was really the plantation's equivalent of a jail. It was certainly as dark, but once Kayleigh had adjusted her eyes, she was able to make out what was around her. Mounted on one wall were eight barrels containing a sweet-smelling port. Along the opposite wall, rack after rack of empty bottles waited to be filled. The third wall was taken up by a large table where the wine was bottled. The fourth wall, however, was nothing but a set of wrought iron bars. This, and an iron door kept the servants well locked out of the master's store of spirits. And kept Kayleigh well locked in.

It was cool on the bricked first floor of the plantation, but that was the only thing she found good about it. She spent several hours pacing the room, pausing now and then to shake the iron door, as if to make sure it was truly locked tight. It was. In the end, spent and exhausted, she slid down to the floor and put her head on her knees. *Dhe!* She was tired. How much fight did she have left?

A noise made her lift her head. The battened shutters of the door nearest the wine cellar were being opened. Light cascaded into the room beyond, and the dust motes flew like clouds of silver.

St. Bride walked in and stood in front of the wine cellar, casting a shadow where she sat. He paused and his stare became thoughtful as he pulled up a stool from a far corner. He sat down and easily placed his long jackbooted legs on the crosspiece between the bars.

"Have you thought on my offer? Or would spending the night here encourage you to make a decision?"

"I've come to a decision already," she countered warily.

"Ah, but not the right one."

"It's the right one for me." She rose from the floor and stood in the shadows of the wine racks.

"But what's a little seduction, Kayleigh? Seduction is easy. Surely you know that, for look how artlessly you do it." He grinned and lifted something to his lips. In the half darkness of the basement, she could barely make it out to be a small piece of sassafras root.

She studied him, desperate to figure him out. She noted he hadn't bothered to shave that evening, but the dark growth on his face only accentuated the brilliance of his teeth when he smiled. And he nonchalantly stared back at her, all the while chewing on the small piece of sassafras root. It was a provincial habit, yet this man seemed hardly of the lower classes. His soft batiste shirts were so fine that they possessed a better hand than silk. His shiny black jackboots were obviously of German design and custom-made just for him. Clearly, St. Bride was no peasant.

But he was definitely a heathen. Her thoughts grew darker as she watched him take great pleasure in biting the root and rotating it in his mouth. There was the tiniest smile on his lips while his tongue licked the root's edges. Quickly, before she could even formulate the reasons, she found the entire display abhorent. Abhorent . . . and yet fascinating. St. Bride's hard mouth was beginning to mesmerize her beyond explanation.

She caught her lower lip with her teeth and turned her head. "I've made my decision, so take your wretched self and begone from here."

"But I'm here to make you understand, love. What I'm asking you to do is so terribly easy."

"No, not easy!" she exclaimed while walking to the bars. She then put both hands on them and added, "What you ask is impossible!"

St. Bride's gaze never left hers as he stood and threw the sassafras root to the bricks. He then walked over to her. All he uttered was "Impossible?" before his hands covered hers, still clasped to the bars. She wanted to pull back, but she told herself there was no need to fear. What could the man do with several iron rails between them?

She couldn't have been more wrong.

The briefest of seconds passed as her gaze locked with his. Under his scrutiny, all her senses seemed to blossom until she was nearly overwhelmed with sensation. The iron between her palms turned to ice; the hands covering hers turned to fire. The pungent scents of steel, wine, and dirt assaulted her nostrils. The cries of the jays outside in the pecans became deafening, surpassed only by the resounding thump of her heart.

Quietly he came closer. As if by magic, she felt herself drawn to him. Her lips seemed attracted against her will to those harder, more forceful ones above her. She didn't want him to kiss her. In fact, she couldn't think of anything she wanted less. But as he lowered his head ever so slowly, she found herself accommodating by tilting her head back, presenting her lips to his.

Their mouths touched. The contact was shocking, exhilarating, dangerous. With a flutter of lashes, her eyes closed, and deep within her she released a moan. His lips tasted bittersweet with sassafras, and they moved with the utmost gentle persuasion. They possessed her until her feelings rioted in tumultuous anarchy. Summoning the will to free herself became a monumental task. Though fear made her want to draw back, something else made her pause. Something that tingled in her very center and made her legs grow weak whenever she felt the rough velvet of St. Bride's tongue run along her lips. Was the man some kind of a warlock? What was this power he was wielding? He was making her do things she had never even dreamed of doing before.

She wanted to pull away, and she did make one weak move. But before she could break away entirely, his hand left hers and ran up the back of her neck, forcing her to stay right where she was, forcing her to take and return his kiss like a wanton. The bars pressed against her cheeks, and soon she was cursing them for being in the way. By some strange magic she wanted to feel the scratchiness of his jaw and the breadth of his chest, not the unyielding iron that was between them.

"You see how easy it is?"

Her eyes flew open. Was St. Bride speaking? Had the kiss ended? Her free hand went to her lips as if she needed proof that it had. Her lips felt tender yet deliciously sated. Confused, her eyes met his and she stuttered, "Wh-what is s-so easy?"

"Seduction," he answered darkly. "Many fall prey to it. You should see to it that you don't."

"It has no effect on me!" she retorted.

He just smiled. "Well, then, that's good, is it not? It makes me think you're the perfect companion for my friend Straught. You can get the better of him without letting him get the better of you." Then he added slowly, "The way I just did."

"What makes you think it wasn't I who got the better of you?" she asked defiantly.

"Perhaps I'm not so sure." As if he spoke the truth, his face sobered. But in their embrace she was close enough to see the twinkle in his eye as he asked, "Shall we try it again so that we can make up our minds?" His hand tightened at the nape of her neck.

"Nay, that's not necessary at all!" She hastily shrugged off his hold and backed away from the bars. She wanted no more of his spells, for he was a canny sort, if she'd ever seen one. He was the only man who had gotten a kiss from the Kestrel. And if she didn't watch him, she might find herself in the same situation again.

"I can see you're going to be a rather obstinate young woman, Kayleigh. What more shall I do to convince you? It's such a simple task I'm asking you to do." He frowned and watched her retreat.

"Who are you that you think you can be so devious and controlling? I won't do your bidding, I tell you; and I shall not tell you again!" After her final refusal, she watched the anger flare in his eyes.

"We'll see if you're so inflexible in the morning. I daresay a night spent down here should make you sing a different tune . . ."

"I daresay it will not." She crossed her arms over her bosom.

"Fine. Have it your way," he said sternly. "I will play jailer for a few days . . . until you come to your senses and realize what's good for you."